THE SMUGGLERS

"Heart Attack," so-named because he had a heart attack while off-loading a boat filled with dope and would not go to a doctor until the job was done; his daughters, May and July, who haul marijuana and cocaine in dump trucks to Miami; their sister, December, who has earned the nickname "Dismember" for her bedroom antics while co-opting U.S. attorneys, DEA agents, and National Park Service Rangers with sex; and the enforcer, a giant named "Big Knocker."

THE TEAM

Nick Brown, the crafty agent, fighting smugglers on his home turf; Lance Cunningham, who plays it fast and loose while pursuing shifty drug-runners; Kimberly McBride, the brainy intelligence analyst who devises an electronic toy that puts the big hurt on the dopers; and Mike Love, the relentless Customs pilot tracking smugglers from above.

The sides are drawn . . . the war has begun!

NARCS III
AMERICA'S HEROES

AMERICA'S HEROES

ROBERT CORAM

A SIGNET BOOK

NEW AMERICAN LIBRARY

A DIVISION OF PENGUIN BOOKS USA INC.

PUBLISHER'S NOTE

This book is a work of fiction. Names, characters, places, and incidents either are the product of the author's imagination or are used fictitiously, and any resemblance to actual persons, living or dead, events, or locales is entirely coincidental.

SIGNET, SIGNET CLASSIC, MENTOR, ONYX, PLUME, MERIDIAN and NAL BOOKS are published by New American Library, a division of Penguin Books USA Inc., 1633 Broadway, New York, New York 10019

First Printing, February, 1990

1 2 3 4 5 6 7 8 9

PRINTED IN THE UNITED STATES OF AMERICA

To Ralph Cunningham,
a great cop

ACKNOWLEDGMENTS

I owe many people; especially the men and women who work for State Attorney Joe D'Alessandro in Florida's Twentieth Judicial Circuit. These talented and dedicated staff members, investigators, and lawyers were more than generous in sharing their knowledge, their experience, and their companionship.

Paul Winegar of the National Park Service provided numerous records of NPS affairs in Everglades National Park.

Sue Rusche of Families in Action, whose work, at long last, is receiving the recognition it so richly deserves, opened her extensive library.

Don Smith's assistance, editorial and otherwise, helped make this book possible.

And, as always, Jeannine was there.

AMERICA'S HEROES

Prologue

At 1:12 A.M. the tide was high and full in the Ten Thousand Islands of southwest Florida; it was "slack water," the time at the end of each tidal cycle when the great ebb and flow ceases and the world rests for a few moments before the moving of the waters begins again.

As is often the case at slack water, it seemed as if the very earth stood still. A gentle northeast wind sighed into nothingness. The cacophony of night noise from frogs and birds ceased. A high thin overcast blotted out the sliver of moon. Even the squadrons of voracious mosquitoes were grounded.

The water-wise people of the Ten Thousand Islands know that the most violent forces of nature sometimes rush into the vacuum formed at the time of slack water. Hurricanes come ashore at slack water; thunderstorms, with their attendant tornadoes and lightning strikes, attack at slack water.

At the mouth of Indian Key Pass, about a hundred yards north of channel marker number four, a woman in the bow of a small boat warily looked about. She listened with her head cocked. The boat was rock-steady on the black steel surface of the water. In the soft penumbra cast by the stern light, the boat's distinctive broad beam and a one-hundred-horsepower outboard engine in a well near the bow marked it as a mullet skiff. The rear of the boat was filled with hundreds of pounds of mullet; shovel-nosed fish that, until a moment ago, had been wiggling and squirming and flopping about. At slack water, even fish in the bottom of a boat sometimes are still.

The woman in the mullet skiff was known as December, and to her the sudden quiet that came upon the Ten Thousand Islands was filled with a latent malevolence.

December reached for a shotgun when she heard the putt-putt-putt of a throttled-back outboard engine. Her eyes, dark as the night around her, narrowed as she tried to see into the blackness. But Indian Key Pass, which links Everglades City to the Gulf of Mexico, was wrapped in the same empty darkness present before the creation of the world.

The noise of the outboard grew. The sound bounced off the mangrove thickets and ratcheted across the water until it was impossible to tell where the boat was located. December wiped the perspiration from her upper lip, reached under the control panel of the boat, and flipped a switch that activated the hidden tape recorder. She curled her tanned hands around the automatic twelve-gauge shotgun and turned until the long barrel was pointed east, up Indian Key Pass; the most likely location for the boat. She waited. And she wondered if, several miles out in the Gulf of Mexico, the men aboard the crab boat were watching on radar.

Then she saw the outboard poke its bow from the darkness and slide across the dark surface toward her. The boat was tan with a dark arrowhead insignia on the bow and the words "National Park Service" written on the side. The man at the wheel wore a gray shirt upon which a gold badge gleamed, green trousers, and carried a .357 Magnum in a shoulder holster of polished brown leather. The ranger eased back on the throttle and then, after a moment, cut the power and drifted toward December. He did not speak.

December leaned the shotgun against the bench seat behind the engine. She ignored the man as he tied the bow of his boat to her mullet skiff. She turned and threw a thin white tarpaulin over the mullet on the bottom of the boat. The ropy muscles in her legs were visible in the stern light, and her body glistened under a fine film of perspiration.

The heat was oppressive; one of those nights when even a serious thought makes one perspire.

December turned toward the ranger. With the thumb

and forefinger of each hand she pulled the thin sleeveless cotton blouse, damp with perspiration, away from
her body, flapped her elbows several times in a frustrated atavistic attempt to cool off. She and the ranger
stared at each other.

"They're out there," she said. Her voice was the
voice of rural southwest Florida; the flat twang one
hears from the natives of Everglades city, Chokoloskee, Ochopee, Copeland, and Goodland.

The ranger's lips tightened. His head drooped between his shoulders and he looked down at his boots
for a long moment. When he lifted his head, it seemed
as if he were unable to speak.

December sensed the ranger's turmoil. She smiled,
and the flash of her perfect white teeth against her
tanned skin was startling. She unbuttoned the light
cotton blouse, opened it, and flapped the edges to cool
her body. She stood, feet planted firmly on the deck,
head up, and pulled her arms wide and to the rear as
she looked south toward the Gulf, out where the crab
boat was waiting. Her shoulders were back and her
bare breasts thrust forward. For a frozen, heart-
stopping moment she did not move. And in that moment she appeared to be a goddess; a sea-drenched
bowsprit. Then, with a single swift movement she
shucked the blouse from her shoulders and dropped it
to the deck. Her right hand pulled at the zipper on her
jeans. She hooked her thumbs in the waistband and,
wiggling her hips, peeled them down the long tanned
columns of her legs. Her white briefs formed a narrow
ribbon, emphasizing the broadness of her hips and the
flatness of her stomach. She stared mockingly at the
ranger.

"You gonna be there?" she demanded. "You gonna
do it?"

The ranger did not answer. He was transfixed by the
sight of December. She was twenty-six and breaking
into the full bloom of womanhood; confident, aware
that she possessed a rare feral beauty. Her hair was
black and tousled. Her body was tanned evenly. There
was no bathing-suit line. The ranger idly wondered

where she sunbathed and he made a mental note to check a few isolated islands where he had seen her boat tucked into the mangroves.

"You gonna do it?" she repeated.

The ranger sighed. He was defeated and he knew it. His mouth twitched once in something approaching self-disgust. He stepped toward the gunwale and was about to move into her boat when she picked up the shotgun and pointed it at his heart. They were no more than five feet apart. She could not miss.

"Don't get in my boat unless you tell me you're gonna do it."

"You wouldn't shoot a cop." There was a distant question in his voice.

She laughed; a free and boisterous laugh that bounced across the blackness of the night. "Cop? I'm out here mullet fishing in the dark, and some guy tries to get in my boat. You could be a rapist."

"You're a hard woman."

Her lips twisted in a rueful half-smile. "About as hard as you are." She paused. "I'm asking you one more time. You gonna do it?"

The ranger looked over her shoulder into the impenetrable darkness; the darkness that stretched away forever.

"Yeah." His voice was soft.

"Yeah, what?"

"I'll do it."

"Do what?" The ranger had to be specific. December wanted details; she wanted him to acknowledge what he was about to do. She wanted it all on the tape recorder.

The ranger turned and looked toward the south as if he could see through the pass and into the blackness of the Gulf of Mexico. He knew the crab boat was out there. All he had to do was pick up his radio, make one brief transmission, and he could have a dozen local, state, and federal agents on the scene in less than an hour. They would swarm about in helicopters, fixed-wing aircraft, and go-fast boats. The heavily loaded crab boat could not escape. But he knew he would not make the call.

The ranger looked at December. She leaned the shotgun against the seat, then slid the white panties down her legs, her eyes never leaving his.

"Bring in the boat," he said.

She tossed the panties atop the seat, smiled, and then, as if talking to a recalcitrant child, said, "You're gonna escort it to the hill; not call anybody; and if another cop comes up on us, you're gonna tell him to back off, that this is your deal and you don't need help."

The ranger laughed, a hard bitter laugh. "The sheriff's son is working the radio and will know if the state attorney or the marine patrol are anywhere nearby; the state patrol has the road up at Forty-one blocked so no one can come into town; I'm the only federal law-enforcement officer in the park tonight, and I'm escorting your load to the dock. You're worried about cops?" His voice was disbelieving.

December was not deterred. Her people, the people of Everglades City, had survived for generations in this remote hardscrabble corner of Florida by not trusting outsiders. She nodded. "If one shows up, that's what you'll say."

"Yes."

"You know what's on the crab boat?"

"Yes."

"What?"

"About fifteen tons of grass." He paused. "Maybe a couple hundred keys of coke."

December's eyes widened in indignation. "We don't haul cocaine. That's bad stuff. All we do is move some weed." She paused. "And it's twenty tons."

"Okay. Twenty tons of grass and I'm escorting it to the hill."

December smiled. "Come aboard."

The ranger could have sworn her smile turned the night to day. He still was mesmerized by that brilliant flash of white. It seemed when she smiled that the temperature rose twenty degrees. The ranger slid the

shoulder holster off and draped it across the seat of his
boat. He stepped across the gunwale into the mullet
skiff. His gold badge glistened as he took off his shirt.
Quickly he took off his boots and pants.

She smiled, reached for his hand, and pulled him
toward the broad open stern of the mullet skiff. She
sank to the tarpaulin and pulled the ranger with her.

And then, before he lost the ability to think of anything save the pleasure of the moment, the ranger realized why he was escorting another load of marijuana
to the dock in Everglades City; the fourteenth load in
the past month. He knew the risk. But December made
the risk worthwhile; more than worthwhile.

December was one of four daughters spawned by an
Everglades City fisherman with the unlikely name of
"Heart Attack." He was given the name after he suffered a heart attack during an off-loading and would
not allow his crew to take him to a doctor until the
cargo was loaded aboard trucks and on the way to
Miami. Through some genetic joke, some anomaly in
the gene pool, Heart Attack, a semiliterate giant with
the face of a frog and the disposition of an alligator,
had fathered four of the most beautiful daughters ever
to walk the face of the earth. Their names were April,
May, July, and December. December was out of cycle
from her three sisters. She had been conceived in
March, a raw and blustery time in the Ten Thousand
Islands; a time when strong cold northeast winds hold
back the tides; when the water is churned and frothy
and when mud flats remain exposed for days; a time
when migratory birds, realizing they stopped too soon,
take off for warmer climes. Somehow December absorbed the strength of the Florida spring, the short
tempestuous cusp of a season between a mild winter
and a hot summer, into the very marrow of her bones.
She was a child of the water, of the mangroves, and
her heart pounded to a primitive beat.

As December pulled the ranger to the tarpaulin, the
tide began ebbing. The moving of the waters began.
Slowly, almost imperceptibly at first, the dark surface
swirled in a slow languid fashion. It was as if the gen-

tle northeast breeze, which had picked up again, was simply ruffling the surface. The overcast slid from the face of the moon and bathed the broad surface of Indian Key Pass, turning it into an endless sheet of molten gold. Night noises resumed. In the rear of the mullet skiff, hundreds of fish, slimy with fear and redolent with the briny seminal smell of the mangroves, began squirming and wiggling and flapping under the tarpaulin; under the entwined, writhing bodies of December and the ranger. The mullet skiff and the ranger's boat, tied tightly together, began a slow twirling minuet toward the yawning reaches of the Gulf of Mexico. The ebbing tide grew stronger and faster by the minute. The waters rushing through Rabbit Key Pass, Chokoloskee Pass, Indian Key Pass, and West Pass were white where they swirled around the mangrove roots in their pell-mell rush toward mid-ocean oblivion.

The mullet skiff and the ranger's boat twirled faster and faster, and the cries of December were like the moaning of the lusty spring winds that pound the mangrove thickets, blow unhindered across the Ten Thousand Islands, and hint at summer and the unrelenting heat that is on the way.

1

"The shit maggots are winning," Lance Cunningham said.

Nick Brown nodded, shoved his chair away from the desk, and stood up. "You got that right," he said. "Most of the dope in America is coming in the back door and nobody but us knows it. U.S. Customs is over in Miami talking about their airplanes and radar balloons, the Coast Guard says their cutters have the east coast blockaded, DEA says its task forces are a bunch of supermen; even the national guard is out there doing whatever the hell they are doing. They're all patting themselves on the back for keeping dope out of Miami." Nick snorted. "That's like protecting the virginity of a sixty-year-old prostitute."

Nick looked over the top of his reading glasses at the map on the wall to the left; the map of southwest Florida from Fort Myers through Naples and the Ten Thousand Islands and on to Cape Sable and the Florida keys—one of the wildest and most remote corners of America.

He took two steps and pointed at the Ten Thousand Islands. His stubby forefinger pounded repeatedly on the map. "Nobody is paying attention to the back door. The back door to America is wide open."

Nick rocked on the heels of his highly polished brown cowboy boots. "All you see on television or in the newspapers is Miami. Miami." He waved a hand in the air. "They got nine hundred federal task forces over there." He jabbed a forefinger at the map. "Look at that. The rednecks and the Cubans are coming in the back door and causing the biggest epidemic of drugs I've seen in twenty years as a cop; the greatest

domestic problem America has ever faced. The whole
country is going up in smoke.''

Nick stared at the map and slowly shook his head.
''There's not another place in the country like it; the
place is custom-made for dopers.''

He turned to face the two people sitting in big leather
chairs in front of his desk. ''And I'm telling you it's
gotta stop. Now. We got a job to do. We been on this
case a year and we got zip. I want some solutions from
you people.''

Lance Cunningham cleared his throat. His eyes were
dancing and a devilish smile played around the corners
of his mouth.

''Hasn't it always been that way?'' he asked.

Nick did not answer. He wrinkled his brow as he
looked at Lance. The guy was the best undercover
narc ever to strap on a badge, but everything was a
joke to him.

Lance, as usual, was not deterred by silence. ''Don't
the bubbas and the julios always come in the back way?
Hey, I used to work vice. I know. Besides, a book has
been written about those guys. A war story. Name of
it was *Don't Leave Your Buddies Behind*. Or was it
Behinds?''

Lance laughed. Kimberly McBride, the blonde and
very patrician intelligence analyst sitting next to
Lance, shook her head in displeasure.

Nick pulled his reading glasses from their perch atop
his nose and stared at Lance. His brow wrinkled. One
of the wrinkles plunged along his nose and curved under his left eye. A vein alongside the wrinkle throbbed.
The vein outlined the eye and gave it a three-
dimensional appearance. It was most intimidating. ''I
said I want solutions from you. Not more problems.''

Lance wiped the smile from his face and pretended
to study the map. He knew not to tangle with Nick
when what he called ''the bad eye'' was operating. His
boss, the chief investigator for the state attorney in
Florida's Twentieth Judicial Circuit, had very little
sense of humor these days. It had been a year since
the three of them, Nick, Lance, and Kimberly, had

resigned from the Broward Sheriff's Office and moved across the state to Naples. For a while Nick had loosened up. He joked, even used profanity from time to time; something he rarely had done when they worked in Fort Lauderdale. But Nick's first assignment, in fact, the reason he had been hired by state attorney Joe D'Alessandro, was to clean up Everglades City. And virtually no progress had been made. Even Nick's well-known religious nature had not helped his disposition. His fuse had gotten shorter and shorter.

Nick sat in one of the chairs in front of his desk and faced his two officers. Nick was an old-fashioned, plain-vanilla sort of man; rectitude personified. He was neither a scholar nor a profound thinker; his extraordinary success as a cop grew from his religious convictions; from the unshakable belief that he represented the forces of good and that it was his job to catch crooks and put them in jail. There was nothing at all sanctimonious about this; he simply had a job to do. His perseverance and tenacity had enabled him to solve cases that the fast-burners, the educated young cops, gave up on after a few months.

Nick was five feet, six inches tall and weighed a hundred and seventy pounds. When he sat down, his stomach reached out and tried to surround the gold belt buckle that was shaped like a curved alligator. Nick was forty, and his once-blond hair was turning gray. He pulled at his mustache that also was streaked with gray. He sighed. "The only arrest we've made in Everglades City was the sheriff's son. And the only reason we got that little slime ball was because he thought he was King Kong and could do and say whatever he wanted. His mouth got him caught. Little scuzz ball admitted"—Nick's voice rose and he repeated "admitted"—"that he personally brought in forty-seven boats loaded with dope." Nick paused. "One guy brought in forty-seven loads."

Nick shook his head and slouched deeper in the chair. "The sheriff found out I was about to arrest his son and called the DEA in Miami. The U.S. attorney comes over and they cut that kid a deal like I never heard of. He tells them of loads he's been involved in and they don't press any charges. He serves no time. What could the U.S. attorney have been thinking about? Even Valachi wasn't offered a deal like that. Forty-seven loads and the U.S. attorney lets him walk.''

''That person has generated some very bad karma,'' Kimberly said. She fingered the crystal necklaces that ranged down the front of her silk blouse; the black coral, the smoky quartz, the brown topaz, the garnet, and the rose quartz. And they were only part of her collection. She had every crystal in the book. Each had a specific function. Lance made a mental note to buy a book on crystals. He had a feeling that recognizing the crystals and the properties thought to be associated with each would tell him a great deal about Kimberly McBride, the hotshot former DEA analyst who Nick thought was the smartest person in his office.

Before Kimberly went to work for Nick, she had been a DEA agent. After she divorced her husband, also a Miami DEA agent, she joined the Forum and dabbled in a half-dozen other touchy-feely pop-psychology institutes; businesses that preyed on the emotionally crippled. Lance thought she had spiders in her head. Trouble with her was, she was too smart; she made things too complicated. Her emotions waved around in the breeze like exposed ganglia. Her ex-husband had waged such brutal psychological warfare on her that she had a permanent insecurity problem. She was a quivering bundle of insecurity; the first one present at every meeting and always carrying a thick stack of files and her lap-top computer. The files and the computer were her security blankets. Once, when Lance was driving out of a parking lot in Naples, he saw Kimberly get out of her car and carry her computer into a grocery store. She didn't need the computer to buy groceries, but it gave her a legitimacy she did not believe she otherwise had. The odd thing about all this was that she was very creative; very efficient. In the last big case in Broward County, the Turks and

Caicos investigation involving Doctor Death, she had proved she was a lot tougher than she thought she was; she could do what she had to do.

Kimberly continued. "I have information that the U.S. attorney might have been influenced by someone in Everglades City." She reached for one of the thick folders.

Lance shook his head. Kimberly was an unusual cop. Unlike most female cops, she never wore trousers; always a dress or suit. She was very organized. And he had seen the efficacy of her intelligence analyses. She was good. Spiders in her head, but good.

"Influenced in what way?" Nick asked.

"This is raw data. I've not verified it," she said reluctantly.

"So, what is it?" Nick insisted. "Who influenced him?"

She opened the file, thumbed through the papers, and found the one she wanted. A long finger with a manicured and elegantly polished nail moved down the page. She paused. She bit her lip.

Lance smiled. Whenever Kimberly paused like that, it usually had something to do with sex; even though she was a thirty-four-year-old divorcée, she still was not at ease with much of the information she analyzed, particularly if it involved the loose and lively sexual activities of drug smugglers.

"My information—this comes from a C.I. whom I was working and whom I believe to be reliable—"

Nick interrupted. "Was working? What happened?"

Kimberly paused a moment as she studied the file. Two of her informants had come to a particularly brutal end during the case involving Doctor Death. The disappearance of an informant was a sensitive issue with her.

"I don't know. He disappeared. I'm trying to find him." She slowly pulled a long forefinger down the page, refreshing her memory as she talked. "The C.I. said the U.S. attorney came to Everglades City and while there was introduced to a woman named December Wells. December is the daughter of Thorn Wells, who is one of our targets in Everglades City. Mr. Wells is a fisherman known as Heart Attack. The U.S. attorney stayed at the Rod and Gun Club in Everglades City, and December's car was parked outside his room every night.''

"Heart Attack," Lance said. "I love the names these people have. One guy down there is named Big Knocker because he's always beating up people.''

"That all?" Nick asked Kimberly.

Kimberly cleared her throat and did not look up from the report. "No. My C.I. further stated that one night he and several friends went to the bar at the Rod and Gun Club to meet someone. When they were leaving, they heard, uh, and I'm quoting here, 'groans, screams, and the sound of moving furniture' inside the U.S. attorney's room. December was seen coming from the room the next morning about daylight.''

Lance laughed. "Sounds like a good time was had by all.''

Kimberly cleared her throat. "One more thing about December," she said. "Among the young men in Everglades City, she is known by the nickname Dismember. Her sexual, uh, talents are a matter of considerable discussion down there.''

She closed the folder. Her mouth was tight.

Lance laughed. "Sounds like you need to send the world's great narcotics officer down there," he said. "Undercover.''

Nick ignored Lance and looked over his glasses at Kimberly. "I met the U.S. attorney. He's such a straight arrow. Married. Three kids. But that would explain it. It's the only thing that would explain it.'' Nick shook his head in bewilderment. "What is it about that town that corrupts everyone who goes there?'' He pointed toward the report clasped in Kimberly's hands. "See if you can get back to your snitch and verify that.''

Kimberly nodded. "I'll do a computer check with other agencies," she said.

"You know what's going on down in Everglades City this week? I just thought of this," Nick said.

Kimberly and Lance looked at him.

"They're lining up people for a network TV show. After we arrested the sheriff's son, some guy from, I think he said *Nightline*, it's the show with that Howdy Doody guy, called me. Said he was a producer. I told him about Everglades City and he went down there to tape some interviews. They're putting in a satellite dish, and will have live interviews mixed with the interviews they've already done. The TV guy called me about noon and said they interviewed the sheriff's son and he told them all about dope smuggling down there. This fisherman Thorn Wells that you mentioned, guy whose nickname is Heart Attack, was interviewed and is also supposed to be on live. Producer says they're going to show it next week."

Lance shook his head. "Dopers on network TV?"

"I couldn't believe it. You guys watch it. I don't stay up that late."

"Oh, so you're a cop, a drug warrior, one of America's new cult heroes," Lance intoned, his head turned to the left. "And what do you do?" He turned to the right, and, as if answering his own question, said, "What do I do? Why, I watch television." He turned back to the left, squeezed his hands together, and in a falsetto said, "Ooooohh. The danger. The excitement."

Nick and Kimberly ignored Lance. It was best to let him soar off into the ozone alone on his flights of fancy. He would return to earth. The guy's zany nature never abated; it just changed from one thing to another. At least he no longer documented his bowel movements in his "dump book." And he no longer went around asking what he called "the question of the week." But who knew what he would come up with next?

"Okay, let's get back to business," Nick said. Again he pointed toward the map. "This is a tough one. We got big-time problems on this case. The entire town is corrupted. Everybody in Everglades City knows everybody else. Only seven hundred and fifty people down there, and about eighty percent of them were born there. That's unusual for Florida. Usually half of every town is hemorrhoids.''

Kimberly's eyes widened.

"Tourists," Lance explained. "Tourists are hemorrhoids."

Nick continued. "Their families have been there forever. Impossible to get someone in undercover. And they're so clannish, that—with the exception of the person McBride talked to—we've been unable to flip anybody. Only one road goes into town, and the minute a stranger drives in, the whole town knows it. Surveillance is impossible. They grew up on the water. Nobody can track them or chase them through the Ten Thousand Islands. They know every sandbar and every oyster bar.''

Nick sighed. "Rednecks and Cubans. Bubbas and julios. Patriots and Communists. What a combination. But that's why the Cubans hire the Everglades City fishermen as off-loaders. Nobody can catch them in the mangroves. Their mullet skiffs and creek boats will travel on a heavy dew. They can haul seven or eight thousand pounds on a skiff, take it back up those creeks to roads we don't even know exist, and move it to Miami.''

Lance coughed. Nick turned to him. Lance's face was serious but his eyes were dancing. "Since the Cubans are involved in this, is there a possibility this investigation will finally reveal the location of Central Cuban Dispatch? Maybe it's somewhere in the Everglades. Maybe that's why I never found it in Lauderdale.''

Lance, who many times in Fort Lauderdale had enlisted the help of the uniform division to search for what he called "Central Cuban Dispatch," could cite numbers showing that ninety-eight percent of the stalled vehicles on the streets and highways of south Florida were driven by Cubans. Usually these were sun-faded old cars with ripped upholstery and trunks with a dark hole where the lock once had been; or else they were ancient and trembling pickup trucks with bald tires and smoky exhausts. Lance thought Fidel Castro was behind a plot to bring America to a nationwide gridlock; that all of these decrepit cars and trucks were dispatched each morning from a single location—Central Cuban Dispatch. He searched constantly for the location of CCD. It was difficult to know if he were serious or if this were another of his endless pranks.

Nick ignored Lance. His finger stabbed toward the map of Everglades City. "I was raised here in Collier County," he said. "I know these people." He shook his head in bewilderment. "They are very religious."

"Yeah," Lance said wryly. "They keep the Sabbath and whatever else they can put their hands on."

When Nick reluctantly nodded in agreement, Lance pressed on. "You know about the bubbas and I know about the julios."

"What do you know about julios?" Kimberly asked.

"They're confused. They think they're Latin lovers when they're nothing but fucking Cubans."

"Awright, that's enough," Nick said. He frowned on profanity around women. Usually Nick thought of female cops as cops first and women second; but not Kimberly McBride. "Don't underestimate these people. The julios or the bubbas. They're dopers and they'll kill you in a heartbeat." He looked at the two officers. "And they're smarter than we are. They're still out there smuggling even though you two brains have been after them for more than a year."

"Jefe, we can do this," Lance said. "You can put your Jesus brain to work and pray for us, McBride here can tune up her crystals and play with her computer, and I can be a cop; I'll turn on my devil brain and get out there and kick some ass. It's a great combination."

He settled back in his chair and added under his breath, "Of course, we could bring in the feds and have a real cluster fuck."

Nick's brow wrinkled.

"Look at the Bush League," Lance said. "They're the best the feds have and they couldn't find their rear ends with flashlights and search warrants. Only people worse are the Coasties.''

''The Bush League'' was how local law-enforcement officers in south Florida referred to President George Bush's highly publicized task force on narcotics; the federal government's front-line troops in the war on drugs; the agents known more for seizing credit from local agencies than for seizing drugs.

Nick swung his head from side to side. ''Well, if we don't do the job, the feds will come in and take over. They have the money and the resources to shake things loose.''

''Jefe, every time we work with DEA, you end up with the short end of the stick. Look what happened when the feds took a look at Everglades City. The sheriff found out about it and cut that deal with the U.S. attorney for his son. Remember when we were in Lauderdale? Remember the Turks and Caicos investigation? The Bimini investigation? Every time we work with the feds we get a royal reaming. Especially from DEA. Sometimes I think DEA stands for 'Don't Expect Anything.' ''

Nick pulled at his mustache. He could not disagree. But to him, the most important thing was to get the job done. He didn't care who got the credit. He looked at Kimberly. ''You having any luck with those history cases?''

Working history cases meant trying to pin down details of loads of dope that might have landed several years earlier, identifying possible informants, digging up details, more names, and then trying to move in and arrest someone before the four-year statute of limitations on smuggling expired. It was a paper chase; a long, laborious process that no federal agency would undertake and one that a local agency would undertake only as a last-ditch effort. The process was enormously time-consuming, and chances for success were slim.

Kimberly shook her head. ''Not much. The computer program is finished and I'm working on names and cases, but it takes a long time.''

"The way to bust up that bunch is for me to get in a boat and go offshore and wait," Lance said. "As much dope as they're bringing in, I could go trolling, and two nights out of three, I bet I make some cold hits. Then I could radio you guys on the hill and you could bust them when they got in close. We could kick some ass. We could crank up the jailhouse train."

"You can't take on that crowd by yourself," Nick said. "They're gators that walk upright. They're a pretty bad bunch."

Lance snorted. "Bad? Bad? Let me tell you about bad. My old man was a bear, my mother was a panther, and I was weaned on alligator piss. My baby-sitter was a snapping turtle, and, hey, I put on a rubber with a tire tool. I invented bad."

"You probably think you could win the Irish Sweepstakes by buying one ticket," Kimberly said.

Lance, puzzled, looked at her. "What does that mean?"

Kimberly shrugged. "Your philosophy of law enforcement is outmoded. What you propose simply is not efficient. It's not cost-productive. It's old-fashioned. Narcotics cases are not won by police officers playing around with boats or airplanes." She lifted the folder. "They are won here; on paper, by pursuing a paper chase, by knowing the law, by using intelligence, by utilizing the capabilities of computers. That's the only way we will break the Everglades City case."

A flash of annoyance crossed Lance's face. But before he could speak, Nick interrupted. "That's enough, you two. Stop squabbling. We're all on the same side." He looked from one to the other and he made a decision. "We'll do it both ways," he said. He tilted his head and looked through his glasses at the small dot on the edge of the Ten Thousand Islands; the dot representing Everglades City. "McBride, you continue with the paper chase. Keep climbing the ladder. Whatever you need, you got it." He turned to Lance. "You want to go offshore in the Whaler?"

The only boat available to the chief investigator's

staff was a thirteen-foot outboard-powered Boston Whaler; a boat meant for inshore waters.

"Hey, coach, send me in. I'm fresh. I ain't got no headgear, but I'm ready. I'm the narc from hell."

Nick smiled. "You might get a hit. And if we have a couple of arrests, we could find a hammer big enough to make some guy flip. Then we could bust this deal wide open."

Nick paused and stared at Lance. Among law-enforcement officials there is unanimity on the single most important ingredient of a great narcotics U/C guy—he has to be half-crazy; willing to hang his ass way out on a line. Lance was willing, even anxious. He was fearless. He thrived on danger. He had the gift of gab. And there was nothing he loved more than getting cozy with drug smugglers, men who—if they knew he was a cop—would kill him without a second thought.

Nick nodded. He would attack the Everglades City case the same way a cat would eat a grindstone—one lick at a time. McBride would be on her computer, Lance on the water, and he would be on the telephone.

"Do it," Nick said. "Take plenty of firepower and a couple of backup radios."

Lance's smile stretched until it covered half his face. His eyes widened. He leaned forward in the chair like a Doberman about to lunge for a piece of red meat. His eyebrows arched and his eyes danced when he looked at Kimberly, then at Nick. "My swash is buckled. I'll get you a dozen felony cases while Miss Computer Expert here is still shuffling folders."

"Well, if one of you geniuses doesn't come up with something, we're all going to have to go back to Broward County and see if we can get our old jobs back. You want to go back to work for the sheriff over there?"

"Ohhhhhhh, nooooo," Lance said in a falsetto. "A fate worse than death."

Nick shook his head. "I'll tell you what's a worse fate. Putting up with hemorrhoids."

Kimberly cleared her throat and looked at Lance.

Was Nick talking of tourists again or did he have a physical problem?

"They in your neighborhood?" Lance asked. He knew what Nick was talking about. He knew how Nick felt about the snowbirds who came down from New York and New Jersey and Pennsylvania; the men and women who lived in the expensive condominiums over on Marco Island; the brightly dressed people who wore lime-green slacks, madras coats, too much jewelry, and white shoes; always white shoes. The sans-a-belt crowd. The people who lived year-round in Naples thought the snowbirds fluttered about like exotic and brightly colored birds. Somewhat dotty birds. They spent their days roaming about in fluttering flocks; usually attending art shows, craft shows, or restaurants. One would hear of a local craft show and alert all the others. Their Mercedeses and Volvos and BMW's and Lincolns and Cadillacs would take to the roads like a cluster of armadillos. The tourists caused enormous traffic congestion. They filled local restaurants. They ambled about the malls. And much of their conversation was critical of the local people. Nick, like many people in southwest Florida, loathed the tourists. To him, a group of tourists was a hemorrhoid convention.

"Three dozen of them over near my house when I came to work," Nick growled. "Seven A.M. and the hemorrhoids are clustered by the road at some art show that doesn't open until midmorning. So many of them they had a portable outhouse set up."

Kimberly looked away.

"You know, jefe, dopers and tourists are a lot alike," Lance said.

"How's that?"

"They're both a pain in the ass."

2

Big Knocker was tall, six feet, six inches, and had to
bend over in order to see through the window of the
wheelhouse high over the bow of the forty-foot white
crab boat. He was thirty miles southwest of Everglades
City in the Gulf of Mexico. He had been traveling at
forty knots since the early-morning rendezvous at the
NOAH sea buoy called "the coke machine"; a favorite meeting and transshipment point for Cuban shrimp
boats and Everglades City crab boats. The shrimp
boats filled with contraband come out of Cuba, round
Key West, penetrate deep into the Gulf, then turn east
to the NOAH buoy. There the drugs are transferred
from Cuban shrimp boats to Everglades City crab
boats.

Big Knocker's crab boat was of a type known locally
as a Key West boat. It had the deep Gulfstream hull,
a hull that provides stability in heavy seas, and was
not one of the round-bottomed hulls known as a "wa-
termelon boat," a notoriously unstable vessel that will
turn turtle in any sort of weather.

The day was going to be calm; the first pale light of
dawn showed cloudless skies and unlimited visibility;
a six-knot breeze from the south was hardly enough to
ruffle the surface. The sun was not yet up, but already
the heat was oppressive. Big Knocker looked at his
watch. He looked ahead toward the rapidly growing
light in the east. In a few moments he would have the
light he needed. He picked up the microphone for the
two-meter radio, juggled it around in his big hand for
a moment, then replaced it. If there were problems,
December would have called. That young woman performed a valuable and expensive service for local dopers.

"Almost time," he said to the little Cuban standing beside him. "Stand off to the side with my brother. Don't let him get close. Anything happens to him and you're dead meat."

The little Cuban nodded. "This thing must be done?"

A snort was his answer. Big Knocker reached over and poked the Cuban in the chest. The Cuban winced and backed up a half-step. "You fucking aye better believe it. Ten tons of shit and two hundred keys of coke down below. If I don't make an example of this guy, I might as well get out of the business. Somebody will be ripping me off every day." Big Knocker looked through the window and said, almost to himself, "He ripped off two bales last trip. Didn't think I would know."

Big Knocker smiled. His mouth was a straight line of chiseled hardness. And his eyes were blank and impassive and empty.

The Cuban had been aboard the crab boat since the marijuana and cocaine were loaded from a Cuban shrimp boat hours earlier. He would ride with the load until it was loaded onto two garbage trucks. And he would follow the trucks into Miami. He had dealt with many gringos and knew most of them were more talk than action; blustery but soft men; *camarones*. This big gringo was different, he was to be respected. He loved to kill. He had more machismo than a dozen *cubanos*.

Big Knocker again scanned the gray horizon. Nothing. He adjusted the dials of his radar detector; a sophisticated fuzz buster that could detect radar emissions from a great distance; long before the radar operator was receiving a primary return from his vessel. Nothing.

Big Knocker knew how the marine side of narcotics interdiction worked. The cops liked to "cone" an area. The Coast Guard patrolled the high seas and in as close as seven miles from shore. Big Knocker was out in Coast Guard territory. Inside the seven-mile mark, he would be in U.S. Customs territory. Then, about two or three miles offshore, he entered the jurisdiction of the Florida Marine Patrol. But a coded radio transmission thirty minutes earlier had told Big Knocker the Customs boat out of Naples was tied to the dock. And the Florida Marine Patrol would not leave the dock for another two hours. All he had to worry about was the next few miles, until he had transited the Coast Guard zone. Then another load would be safe in the labyrinthine reaches of the Ten Thousand Islands.

Big Knocker's face was cut in stone and his eyes were fathomless. Most men, no matter how big they are or how tough they talk, will not kill another human being. They might be mean enough to beat up women and old men, or even men smaller than they, but there are few circumstances, outside of combat situations, when even the meanest of these men would kill someone. Big Knocker was different. Somewhere in his psyche, his DNA blueprint had been transmogrified into a DNA misprint. He exuded an aura of meanness that could be felt across a room. He could walk into a restaurant in Everglades City and, simply by being there, disturb the patrons so much that many would stop eating. One knew, simply by looking at this enormous man's empty eyes, that he would delight in taking a person's head between his hands and squeezing until it popped.

Big Knocker had begun his career as a doper by working for Heart Attack, who was his uncle, as an enforcer; and he did his work so well that he earned enough money to buy a crab boat and bring in his own loads. Now he and Heart Attack were equals. The difference was that Heart Attack preferred to hire other people to bring in his loads, while Big Knocker liked to run his own. Big Knocker was a legend in Everglades City. He raced airboats with such reckless abandon—he had caused four men to be sent to the hospital with broken limbs—that for the last six years he had won the world championship. And he was the only man in Everglades City who would entice a ten-foot alligator onto shore, wrestle it until the animal was exhausted, then kill it with a knife. At some tourist attractions, men wrestle tame, fat, overfed, even sedated alligators. But Big Knocker liked what he called "fresh gators" to wrestle.

It was as an enforcer for Heart Attack that Big Knocker came into his own. Drug smugglers are paranoid about fellow smugglers talking to the police. And sometimes smugglers become greedy; they hold out a few bales of marijuana or a few keys of cocaine to sell on their own, thinking the person who owns the load will never know. But the owner, if he is to survive in the business, does know. And, to keep down such displays of initiative, or to show what happens when a smuggler becomes a police informant, it is necessary to make an example out of malefactors. Big Knocker was good at that. He had taken care of a man a month earlier who he thought might be talking to the police. And now it was time to take care of one who was displaying too much initiative.

"Time to do it," Big Knocker said. "Look after Robert."

Big Knocker was amoral in all areas save one, and that was where his younger brother was concerned. His one weak point was his brother. He felt compelled to protect and shield his younger brother.

"Sí."

Big Knocker turned a switch that would throw the sound of the fuzz buster to a speaker on the mast. He pulled the throttles and waited as the heavily loaded boat drifted to a stop. Then he turned and dropped swiftly down the ladder to the deck below. From a freezer alongside the wheelhouse he took two five-gallon buckets of frozen blood and fish entrails; tied them to stout ropes and lowered them, one at the time, off the stern. He tied the lines to a cleat. Then he opened another locker, popped off the lid from a large plastic container, grimaced at the odor, and quickly poured the chopped-up fish overboard. Within seconds a greasy slick spread around the stern.

One crew member blanched. He had seen this before and knew what was to come. He looked at the

two humpers, the men who had been hired to off-load
the load from the shrimp boat to the crab boat, and
wondered which one it would be.

Three minutes later, even before the frozen chum
had begun melting, the first shark arrived; a fourteen-
foot hammerhead, lean and hard as it sliced through
the small pieces of chopped-up fish. On its third pass
through the fish, the big hammer rolled slightly to the
side and the two claspers on the aft portion of his
white belly were visible—a big male hammer; one of
the most aggressive of the man-eaters. Big Knocker
smiled. Sometimes it took ten or fifteen minutes to
attract the sharks. He would be finished here in short
order. He ignored the three men standing up forward
and watching him. Occasionally he glanced at his
brother Robert, a slender young man dressed far too
well to be aboard a shrimp boat.

Five minutes later two dozen sharks were churning
and roiling the water as they sliced into the frozen
chum and the fish blood that had been poured over the
side. The sharks quickly grew frustrated, because,
while the odor of blood was strong in the water, there
was very little to eat. Big Knocker opened the locker,
pulled out another container, and tossed forty pounds
of chopped-up bonito, a particularly oily fish, overboard. The calm surface of the Gulf churned to froth
for fifty yards off the stern of the crab boat as the fins
of the sharks sliced back and forth like blades in a
food processor.

Big Knocker stripped off his shirt and hung it over
a cleat. His chest, slabbed with muscle, was like the
bole of an oak. His white gum boots were planted on
the deck. His stout legs stretched and strained the fab-
ric of his faded jeans. He turned to the three men
standing at the foot of the ladder that led up to the
wheelhouse. His eyes swept the deck. His brother was
safe against the rail on the port side.

"It's time," he shouted. "Now. It's time."

He pointed toward one of the three deckhands; a
man who stood slightly apart from the others, and a

man almost as big as he, a fisherman whose family had lived in Everglades City for seven generations.

"Wendell, get your thieving ass over here," he shouted.

Wendell paused, then exhaled almost in relief. Big Knocker knew. Wendell stepped forward. The people of Everglades City step forward into whatever life has for them—be it good or be it bad. They walk with heads up and eyes forward. If good fortune comes their way, which is not often, so be it. If bad fortune, then they are used to it.

Wendell walked across the wide stern of the crab boat toward Big Knocker.

"You know what you did, Wendell." It was a statement.

"I do."

"You shouldn't oughta have done that, Wendell."

"Had my reasons."

"Don't matter, Wendell. You took what was mine."

Wendell stared at Big Knocker.

Big Knocker reached for the filet knife strapped on his hip. Every fisherman carries such a knife; usually a Rapalla; a thin-bladed knife that slices like a laser beam. Big Knocker pulled the seven-inch blade from the scabbard.

Wendell pulled a similar knife from the holster on his hip, balanced it in the palm of his right hand, sharp side up, and leaned forward.

"Wendell, ain't but one of us going to the hill today."

"How long you gonna talk?"

Big Knocker smiled again. As he moved forward, a new member was added to the pack of feeding sharks; a sixteen-foot tiger, a pelagic shark so big it had no natural enemies, a shark that moved through the pack in an almost leisurely fashion. Even the big hammer moved out of the path of the tiger. The shark, much fuller in body than the lean hammer and probably five hundred pounds heavier, cruised up to one of the blobs of chum, pulled back the skin around his mouth until his teeth protruded like serrated triangles, bit into the frozen chum, and shook his head with such force that a shudder ran through the length of the crab boat. Then he released it and slowly cruised in a wide circle, the dark spots on his back occasionally visible in the clear offshore waters.

"Somebody's calling you, Wendell," Big Knocker said.

"Your friend. And you're gonna join him."

The two men moved toward each other. It could have been a good fight, but Wendell never got a chance to acquit himself. The big tiger, frustrated by the blood smell coming from the chum, again locked his curved triangular teeth into the large frozen blob, held on, and shook his fifteen-hundred-pound body with every ounce of strength he possessed. The boat lurched.

For a half-second Wendell was thrown off-balance. And in that moment Big Knocker, in a sweeping overhead gesture, raked the Rapalla down Wendell's chest. The blade sliced hard across the sternum, then sank into Wendell's stomach and opened him to the crotch.

Robert drew in his breath in horror and turned away. But Big Knocker didn't notice.

A gray glaze slid across Wendell's eyes. The knife fell to the deck. Big Knocker quickly moved forward.

"Don't die yet, Wendell," he said.

As Wendell slumped, Big Knocker caught him, turned, and easily carried him ten feet and set him on the stern rail. He grabbed Wendell by the hair. "You still alive? Don't die yet, Wendell," he said.

Wendell's eyes rolled. "Fuck you," he mumbled.

Big Knocker smiled. "You a good man." He pushed Wendell off the stern.

Robert twisted and vomited over the side of the rail, then sank to his knees, rubbing his perspiring forehead against a cool steel stanchion. The Cuban watched, knowing that if he showed the derision he felt, Big Knocker would not hesitate to toss him overboard.

Big Knocker leaned over the rail and watched as the tiger smelled the fresh blood and came boring in like a freight train; a juggernaut of destruction. The shark rose to the surface a few feet before he struck; a froth-

ing bow wave surging from his body. The gigantic
mouth opened and the tiger's jaws locked around Wendell's bleeding midsection. The tiger, his tiny brain
remembering at some atavistic level the failure to bite
into the frozen chum, chomped down on Wendell with
such strength that the muscles of the shark's torso were
visible. Wendell's body was sliced in half; the legs
drifting slowly, turning, windmilling toward the
depths, were seized and fought over by other sharks,
while the tiger, in a half-dozen gulping motions, dis-
posed of the upper body. In seconds, all that remained
of Wendell was a cloud of dissipating blood and drifting tendrils of flesh.

Big Knocker used his bloody Rapalla to slice the
two lines on the stern, freeing the blobs of chum. He
wiped the knife on his pants and turned to the two
crewmen.

"If somebody wants to join him, all he has to do is
mention this to anybody."

Both deckhands were quick to nod in understanding.

Big Knocker turned toward his brother and for a
moment his face almost softened. Robert was standing
up, holding on to the rail, and wiping his mouth.

"Well, Robert?"

The young man sniffed. He looked at the blood on
his brother's arm and on the front of his chest. "I'm
going to the cabin."

Big Knocker stepped closer to his brother. The two
did not resemble each other in size, features, or manner of speech.

"I had to do it," Big Knocker said. He paused.
Robert would not look at him. "You gotta learn. Last
night you saw how we took on a load. You saw this
business here on deck. Now we take it to the hill. It's
business."

The young man looked out to sea. "It's your business," he said. He wrapped his arms about himself
and shivered. After a moment he turned toward his
brother. "What about the police?"

Big Knocker was annoyed. He hated to hear a man

express fear of anything. Then he tilted his great head back toward the sky and laughed. "They think we work just at night. They'd never imagine a load coming in at daylight. Won't be any cops."

He thought of December, who had cleared the way with the park ranger. He turned his back on his little brother and looked at the crew. "Let's go to the hill," he said. "We got a load to deliver."

Robert turned and walked unsteadily toward the cabin.

3

"Poopsie. What are you watching?" Barbara Bush asked her husband.

"Television," said the President of the United States.

"Oh," said Barbara.

The First Couple were in the family quarters at the White House. It was almost one A.M., but the President showed no sign of fatigue. He sat in a big overstuffed armchair wearing white pajamas of very light wool and a navy-blue robe emblazoned with the Presidential Seal over the heart. Soft leather slippers were on his feet. His hair was neatly combed and the light from the television set glinted off the rims of his glasses. He was lean and alert; the very embodiment of the world's senior preppy.

"Bar, I find this difficult to believe," he said with a tone of astonishment in his clear and firm enunciation.

His wife raised her head from the pillow. The flickering shadows from the television set had been dancing across the ceiling for almost an hour. It was impossible to sleep. Even when she shut her eyes, she knew those dancing shadows were twisting and cavorting in the air over her head. And the choppy muttering sounds from the muted volume were worse than having the set turned up loud. She could have asked her husband to go into the Lincoln Bedroom to watch television, but she wanted him near; she wanted to know he was in the room. The leader of the free world needed his relaxation. The first year of his administration had not been a good one; particularly where the war on drugs was concerned. The press had discovered that in south Florida the presidential task force on narcotics, which her husband, as vice-president, had supervised for almost eight years, was referred to as "The Bush League," and was having a grand old time with that. In addition, it seemed at times as if half the people in America were putting drugs up their noses, down their lungs, or through their veins. Ambition and hope and pride had been replaced by the beatific befuddlement brought on by what seemed to be an almost universal psychotropic daze. America was not becoming kinder and gentler; America was becoming meaner and more violent. America was doped up. And it was getting worse. Something was wrong; there was some basic flaw in the American psyche that caused hundreds of thousands of people to seek better living through chemistry. One of the most devastating criticisms from regimes critical of America was coming true—America was destroying itself from within. The violence that was part and parcel of drug trafficking reached such levels that, had it been written about in novels or shown in movies, it would have been distasteful and would have strained credibility. Even so, Americans, not just in big cities but in rural hamlets across the land, were frightened; frightened for their lives.

The price of cocaine was at an all-time low. Methamphetamines were being manufactured, it seemed, in every garage in the country. Crack could be bought in the most remote village in America. Heroin, of all things, was the new drug of choice for jaded middle-class druggies who had tried everything else. But worst of all was marijuana; the drug that started it all was back in astonishing amounts. Marijuana, the drug everyone patronized because it was the drug of entry that led to other drugs, the drug that was so common it was hardly considered a drug, was choking the country in a haze of sweet blue smoke. The presidential task force had long ago delegated enforcement of marijuana laws to local cops. The thinking was that very little marijuana was smuggled anymore; it was all homegrown. New growing and harvesting methods had produced strains of marijuana with tetrahydrocannabinol levels as high as ten and twelve percent. So let the locals take care of it.

Now intelligence indicated that marijuana, in multiton loads not seen since the halcyon mothership days of the sixties and early seventies, was being smuggled into America. This was realized after the DEA had told everyone the war against marijuana was won and had turned its investigative thrust to other drugs. And here was a guy on television explaining how it was all done and why nobody, especially not the Bush League, could do anything about it.

"Would you please turn up the sound?" asked the First Lady of the land.

The President pushed a button on the remote-control unit. "By golly, Bar, I'm glad you're interested in this. I want you to listen to this fellow and tell me what you think. It's a satellite hookup. Koppel is interviewing this fellow down in Florida."

Barbara Bush sat up in bed and reached for her glasses. Ted Koppel, the imperturbable Ted Koppel, was plainly astonished at the way the interview was going.

"Poopsie, why does Ted Koppel call him Mr. Heart Attack?"

"Because that's his name, Bar."

"Oh." The First Lady pushed several pillows against the headboard and sat up straighter. Ted Koppel interviewing someone named Heart Attack? No wonder Poopsie was muttering to himself.

"Where is Millie?" asked the First Lady.

"She had an upset stomach. I sent her to the Lincoln Bedroom."

"Ummmmh." She turned her attention to the television.

"If I understand you, sir," Ted Koppel was saying, "the people of Everglades City have always been lawbreakers. Is that correct?"

Heart Attack nodded in agreement. "You got that right. I was born and raised right here in Everglades City. My great-granddaddy was a pirate. My granddaddy, on my mother's side, ran liquor out of Cuba and the Bahamas right into southwest Florida. My granddaddy, on my daddy's side, poached egret feathers. My daddy poached gators. My mama's family was moonshiners and they sold fuel to German submarines in World War Two."

"That's quite a work history."

"Our family done good."

"And you're a drug smuggler?"

"Well, I ain't saying that. I'm saying if somebody wanted to smuggle marijuana, it wouldn't hurt nobody."

"Does anyone in Everglades City have legitimate work?"

"Fishing is what we do. Stone crabs and mullet, mostly. Few pompano. Grouper. But then the government come in and—"

"Just a minute," Koppel interrupted. "The government . . . ?"

"The National Park Service. They come in and took two million acres of our fishing grounds. Seems like everything we want to fish is what they call endangered. They stopped commercial fishing in most of the park. They put bag limits on fish, limited the number of traps we could set for stone crabs. They arrest us for getting a few turtle eggs to cook with. They arrest us if we shoot an alligator. We run over a manatee and it's a federal case. And they got dozens of people down there who don't do anything but look after panthers. You imagine that? The U.S. government pays people to go out and just look for panthers. They arrest us if we even take an air plant off a tree and give it to our wives. All their rules and a few bad fishing years just about broke us.''

''Air plants?''

''Yeah, they grow up in trees. Green hanging leaves. Pretty flowers.''

''Could that be a bromeliad?''

''Air plant. I told you.''

Koppel decided not to pursue the horticultural line of questioning. ''So the people of Everglades City turned to drug smuggling?''

Heart Attack nodded. ''I ain't saying that. All I'm saying is it wouldn't be a big step for us. We've smuggled something or other ever since our ancestors settled here.''

''Assuming that drugs are coming into Everglades City, how would you quantify the amount?''

Heart Attack stared into the monitor.

Koppel clarified his question. ''How much is coming in?''

Heart Attack shrugged. ''How many boats are in Everglades City? How many crab boats? How many mullet skiffs? How many creek boats?''

Koppel was silent.

After a moment the lean man with the hard eyes continued. ''We got families,'' he said. ''We got to put food on the table. We all got kids in school; kids to educate. They need clothes. All we know is the water. All we know is fishing. The federal government tells us we can't fish, but we still got to take care of our families.''

Koppel remained silent, letting Heart Attack talk.

''We not like most folks. We got no health insurance. No unemployment. None of these backups you people got. Every regulation the government makes hurts us. The weather hurts us. A couple of bad fishing years hurt us.'' Heart Attack shrugged. ''Man's wife or son gets sick, and he's looking at a ten-thousand-dollar doctor bill. Only way he can make that kinda money is doping.''

''He has a point, you know,'' said the President.

"Ummmmm," Barbara Bush said. She had seen many fishermen up in Kennebunkport; but none like this fellow.

"Do you have children?" Koppel asked.

"Sure do. Four of the prettiest little girls you ever saw. Raised 'em myself. Their mama died giving birth to the last one."

"And to support your daughters, you smuggle cocaine?" Koppel continued.

Heart Attack shook his head. "Now, look, I told you that before. I told your producer fellow that. We don't smuggle no cocaine. Some people around here might bring in a little weed. Might. I ain't saying they do. But we don't believe in hauling cocaine. That's drugs."

"You expect me to believe that?"

Heart Attack paused. He stared into the monitor at Koppel. "Mister, I'm gonna overlook your tone because you're from New York and you just don't know no better. But I just told you we don't smuggle no cocaine."

Koppel took another tack. "If I understand you, sir, walking just over the edge of the law is a time-honored tradition in Everglades City. Have any of the descendants of some of those lawbreakers you earlier described—the grandchildren of, for instance, the whiskey smugglers—gone into legitimate work?"

"Sure have," Heart Attack agreed. "Up in Fort Myers is a slew of them. Place called Whiskey Creek. Got its name during Prohibition because it was a favorite place for the liquor runners out of Cuba to offload. Whiskey Creek today is one of the fanciest subdivisions in southwest Florida. Got its start when the kids and grandkids of some of the liquor runners bought land there and built big homes. They went off to school. Now they're the doctors and lawyers and business people; biggest families in town."

"And their families got their money from rumrunning?"

"Lots of 'em did, that's right."

"Poopsie, didn't we go to Whiskey Creek during

one of the campaign trips?'' Barbara Bush asked. ''To some sort of fund-raiser?''

''A party, I think it was. That fellow is one of the biggest corporate lawyers in the Southeast. Very prominent family. Very prominent corporate clients. I've know him since college. His grandfather couldn't have been a rumrunner.''

''Oh,'' said the First Lady.

''Mr. Heart Attack, your town came to our attention when the son of the local sheriff, who we understand was about to be arrested for drug smuggling, made a deal with the federal authorities in Miami; a most unusual deal. He admitted his complicity in some forty-seven marjiuana-smuggling ventures. That seems a rather incredible number. Could that number have perhaps been exaggerated?''

Heart Attack grinned. ''I heard tell of people who've done more than that.'' It was clear he was talking of himself.

''Then hundreds of tons of marijuana are coming into Everglades City?''

''Right smart amount. Could be.''

''Don't you worry about being caught?''

Heart Attack scratched the side of his nose. He grinned and shook his head. ''Tell you the truth, no.''

''Why not? Do you pay off police officers?''

A sly smile played around the corners of Heart Attack's mouth. ''I ain't talking about that. All I'm gonna say is, they can't catch us.''

''The federal authorities—that is, the Coast Guard, the Drug Enforcement Administration, U.S. Customs, elements of the military—plus all of the state and local police, can't catch you? You don't worry at all about them?''

''You got that right.''

''I don't like this,'' said the President. He picked up a telephone on a small table beside his chair. ''Get me the attorney general,'' he said.

''Did you look at the clock?'' asked the First Lady.

''The attorney general needs to see this,'' said the

President. "I don't think he'll mind a telephone call from the President."

"No one can catch you," Koppel said. "Why is that?"

"You got to understand. We know the water. The charts say you got to go through the passes to get from the Gulf into Chokoloskee Bay. Well, we know other ways to get there; ways not on the charts. Police don't know the water. They're afraid to run the water at night. We live on the water."

"Dick, this is the President. I know it's late, but I want you to turn on your television and watch Koppel. Call me when it's over." The President hung up the phone and turned back to the television.

"Chokoloskee Bay is what?" Koppel asked.

Heart Attack smiled a quick superior sort of smile. Like most outsiders, Koppel pronounced "Chokoloskee" phonetically rather than as the locals pronounced it: "Chuck-a-lusky." Then he answered. "It's what you got to cross when you come in out of the Gulf into the Ten Thousand Islands and you're going to the hill. It's about ten miles long; two miles wide. Shallow. Real shallow. Good strong northwest wind on an ebb tide will push all the water out of the bay; nothing but a mullet skiff will run across there. Cops don't have mullet skiffs."

"What's the hill?" Koppel, a studious and erudite man, was enthralled by Heart Attack's unique expressions; by his use of the language.

"The hill is high ground; where you land a boat."

"A dock?"

"Could be. Could be just where a creek brushes up against a piece of land where there is a dead-end road. Could be under a bridge on Highway Forty One. The hill is wherever you land a boat. The hill is the hill."

"And the hill is where people in Everglades City off-load the drugs onto trucks? From there the drugs go where? Into Miami?"

"That's right."

"I gather, from your emphasis on the nautical skills of you and your colleagues, that this is your milieu?"

Heart Attack stared at Koppel.

"Your abilities on the water, particularly in finding your way from the Gulf through the Ten Thousand Islands, is unequaled. That's why you are able to engage in smuggling without being detected?"

"That's why the Cubes hire us."

"The Cubes?"

"Yeah, they own all the loads. From what I hear, they bring the stuff up from the south in shrimp boats. We meet them offshore, transfer the load, and bring it in. Sometimes we bring the crab boat right here to the dock." Heart Attack waved over his shoulder at the dock. The Barron River wrapped around the east side of Everglades City. And it was from a dock on the river that the interview was being broadcast. "Sometimes we transfer it to mullet skiffs or creek boats and bring it to the hill." Heart Attack smiled. "Leastwise, I hear that's how it's done."

Koppel was reeling. As he was listening, he was thinking. Thinking about the rednecks of southwest Florida. Patriots. Conservative. Xenophobic. Yet they were in business with the flashy-dressing, hip young smugglers from Cuba. Drug smuggling, perhaps even more than politics, made for strange bedfellows. Except for a slight wrinkling of his brow, none of Koppel's astonishment was evident as he continued his questioning.

"So the Cubans, members of a communist nation, hire you simply to move the drugs from the high seas to the hill?"

"That's right?"

"Can't they do this themselves?"

Heart Attack smiled. "They tried."

"What happened?"

"Ran their boats aground trying to come through the islands. We called the police. They lost their loads."

"You called the police on your employers?"

"Weren't our employers. They were trying to do it on their own."

"So if a load comes through the Ten Thousand Islands, someone from Everglades City has to be at the wheel of the boat?''

Heart Attack nodded. ''Otherwise it don't get through. Least, that's what I hear.''

''How do the Cubans and the fishermen of Everglades City get along? These are two quite disparate cultures. I should think there would be friction.''

Heart Attack thought for a moment. ''It's business. We don't let Cubes in our homes. Anytime we see a Cube in town, he's there to set up an off-loading. If somebody doesn't know about the load, there could be trouble. Like I said, it's just business.''

''But you must have differences.''

Heart Attack looked up with a quizzical expression, as if the answer might be written across the sky, then said, ''One big difference is that we always believed if a man loses a load, that load belongs to whoever picks it up. Reason for losing the load don't matter. He can't find his off-load boat, he sees a blue light and tosses it overboard, he just gets scared and dumps it, whatever; doesn't matter. He loses a load, it belongs to whoever picks it up.'' Heart Attack shrugged. ''We got people in Everglades City, bale hunters, they know when a load's going down; everybody in town knows. They know how to listen to a radio. If a load is lost, they scoot out there and start grabbing bales. They can sell them. They belong to whoever finds them. Cubes don't believe that. They say a load is theirs even if it's dumped. Sometimes they come looking for bale hunters.''

''Everyone in town knows when a load is coming through?'' Koppel was used to interviewing politicians and celebrities; people who were masters of equivocation and dissembling. To interview a rogue who casually admitted that everyone in town knew when a load of dope was arriving was beyond his experience.

''Sure do. When my oldest girls was in school, they knew when a load was coming in. Kids talk. Sometimes the kids act as humpers. Make a few bucks. That's how they get started in the business. They's lots of back-and-forth. One man might hire humpers from another; or he might lease his boats. In Everglades City, we all work together.''

Koppel paused and then, almost as if afraid of the answer, said, ''Humper?''

''Somebody what unloads a boat. Or loads the stuff on a truck.''

Koppel paused as he tried to digest this.

Barbara Bush was now wide-awake. ''They have schoolchildren involved in smuggling?''

The President shook his head. ''I never heard of Everglades City. Listen to this. By golly, it's astonishing that this sort of thing could happen in America.''

''Back to the bale hunters,'' Koppel said. ''What happens if a load is lost, then picked up by—what did you call them—bale hunters?''

''Well, there's a killing. Or the Cubes firebomb somebody's house.''

Koppel's eyebrows rose. ''The Cubans come ashore and kill someone who picks up bales floating in the ocean? Or they firebomb their homes?''

''If they lose a load, you can plan on it. It's not too easy for them anymore. Imagine how it would be if you tried to go ashore in Cuba and burn somebody's house. We wait for them. We know where they have to come ashore. And we watch the road.''

''So as long as business is good, you and the Cubans get along. Even though they are from a country that is less than friendly with the United States. How do you feel about doing business with the communists?''

Heart Attack leaned toward the monitor in anger. ''Mister, there's only so much slack I'm going to cut you. Even if you are from New York. I'm an American. I love this country. I voted for the President. What I do with the Cubes is business; just business. It puts food in my children's bellies and clothes on their backs.''

The President shook his head back and forth. ''Well, it's good to know this administration has the support of the drug smugglers.'' He continued shaking his head. ''Oh, my goodness.''

"Yes, I understand that," Koppel said, boring in, beginning to ask the hard questions. "But how can you profess to be a loyal American when every load of drugs you bring in—and, by the way, federal drug agents tell me that very rarely does a load of marijuana come in unless there are several hundred kilos of cocaine along with it. But every load you bring in, you are violating the borders of your own country. You are violating international agreements, federal, state, and local statutes. You, in a very real sense, along with the Cubans, have more or less declared war against this country. How does the rationale of feeding your children compare with your declaring war on America?"

"You New York son of a bitch. I see now why you wanted to stay up there rather than coming down here. You wouldn't say that if you were face-to-face with me. You—"

"Mr. Heart Attack," Koppel interrupted. "You will recall that you were invited to New York. We offered to pay your expenses. You chose to do this interview through a satellite feed there in Everglades City. Is that not correct?"

"That don't matter. I'm—"

"Mr. Heart Attack, just why did you agree to come on this program? You knew what we wanted to talk with you about and yet you agreed. Why?"

The abrupt shift in the conversation was disconcerting to Heart Attack. He grinned. "Well, I wanted to be on television. Something I always wanted to do. Guess I made a mistake."

"I guess you did," said the President of the United States. He reached for the telephone again. "If that fellow thinks he can pull on my wee-wee and get away with it, he has another think coming."

Barbara Bush took off her glasses and stared at her husband's silhouette. She could not believe what she had just heard.

"Who are you calling?" she asked.

"The attorney general. I'm going to order him to create a task force and send the DEA to Everglades

City. Those smugglers think they can't be caught. I'll show them. I'll make them see a thousand points of light.'' He nodded and half-turned to his wife. "It'll give me a chance to work on this assertiveness thing.''

Barbara Bush placed her glasses on the bedside table, moved the pillows from the headboard, and slid under the covers. At times her Poopsie was very presidential.

4

Andrea Dolan, secretary to Raymond Dumnik, the special agent in charge of the Miami office of the Drug Enforcement Administration, looked at her desk calendar and sighed. It was Friday. Shirley, who had brought a stack of papers to Andrea, heard the sigh and paused. When Andrea sighed, people listened. After all, she supervised the administrative staff of the largest DEA office in the world and could speed up or slow down everything from expense-account money to annual leave. Most of the DEA agents, people who, on the street, were larger than life, showed her a lot of deference. In addition to the power she wielded as Dumnik's secretary, she was one of the most attractive women in the DEA building. A full mane of tawny red hair surrounded a sharp-featured and lovely face. She was thirty-five but dressed as if she were twenty, oftentimes in tight or low-cut blouses and in miniskirts that showed her legs to great advantage. She was tall and slender with a drop-dead body. Andrea had a what-the-hell air about her—the desperation many women have when they see the first faint but unmistakable trace of cellulite, the first microscopic wrinkles about the eyes, the first shadow of a sagging breast; when they realize that they, too, are mortal, that they are no longer young and the clock is ticking. Andrea liked to

laugh and party. More often than not, she came to
office parties alone even though she was married to a
Coast Guard officer, a somewhat stodgy and inflexible
man who had a desk job at Seventh District headquarters.

"What's the matter?" Shirley asked.

"It's Friday," Andrea said. "Not a good day." She
twirled a lock of her long red hair through her fingers
and stared at the desk calendar.

"Why? It's the day we always go to Ma Grundy's
and have a few drinks."

"Then I have to go home," Andrea said in a resigned voice.

Shirley smiled and her eyebrows arched. "Trouble
with the hubby?"

"It's car-payment day and I'm not in the mood."
Andrea laughed. "At least not with him."

Shirley was puzzled. "What?"

Andrea smiled. "I didn't tell you about the deal I
made with Andy?"

"No."

Andrea pointed at a chair against the wall. "Slide
that chair over here."

Shirley pulled the chair close to Andrea's desk and
sat down. Her eyes were bright. "So tell me."

"Remember when I got these a few months ago?"
Andrea smiled widely so Shirley could see her braces.

Shirley nodded.

Andrea smiled and rolled her eyes. "Well, I used
that as an excuse not to do some things with Andy that
he liked."

"You mean . . . ?" Shirley giggled.

"Yeah." Simultaneously the two women uttered the
old line, "Under the circumstances, a blow-job is out
of the question."

"What did he say?"

Andrea shrugged. "He didn't like it. That's the only
way he wants to have sex. He likes his little visits to
the head shop."

"You cut him off?"

Andrea smiled an arch smile. "I told him I couldn't

do it anymore; that the braces hurt my lips.'' She opened her mouth and stretched her lips over her teeth. ''Told him I had to do this to keep the braces from cutting my mouth.'' She paused. ''I really didn't. But it was a good way to get out of it. That's all he ever wants to do.''

Shirley, eyes wide, leaned closer. ''So what happened?''

''Well, right after that, I got that new car. The Pontiac Formula car. Red.''

Shirley nodded. She knew the car. It was Andrea's pride and joy. She never put the T-roof up unless it was raining. She rode to work with her red hair blowing and her radio blaring and her skirt pulled high on her legs. She enjoyed the way men blew their horns and waved. Driving that car made her young again.

''The payments were eating me alive.'' She giggled. ''No pun intended. So I went to Andy and asked him if he would help me. He's got the first dime he ever made. Plus his mother left him some money. He didn't want to do it.'' She made a grimace. ''Said I had to be financially responsible. Then I hinted that if he made the car payments I might make some sacrifices for him.''

''You mean . . . ?''

Andrea giggled. ''Yeah, he gets a blow-job once a week if he makes my car payments. He likes Friday night. Always Friday night. That's his big night.''

''So you got a new Pontiac Formula car and all you have to do is do that for your husband once a week?''

Andrea shrugged her shoulders and rolled her eyes.

Shirley laughed. ''That's fantastic.'' She leaned closer to Andrea. ''Okay if I tell Alice?''

Andrea looked around Shirley's shoulder toward Alice, the secretary to the assistant special agent in charge. ''I don't care.''

As Shirley, trying hard to suppress her laugher, stood up and walked across the carpeted floor, Andrea's phone buzzed.

''Yes, sir,'' she said.

''Has the typist finished?'' came the voice of Ray-

mond Dumnik, her boss. He had been the narcotics
attaché in the Bahamas but had been sent back to Miami after only six months. There was a lot of talk
about a controlled delivery of nine hundred kilos of
cocaine that he let get loose in the Bahamas. No one
knew exactly what had happened. Dumnik knew of the
talk; of the speculation that either he was terminally
dumb or that he had been paid to let a load get through.
Now he was back, trying harder than ever to prove
himself.

The best way to describe Dumnik was to say that if
he stepped in a pile of horse manure, people would
think he was melting. He was living proof of the adage
that, in DEA, when you fuck up, you are promoted.
Just two days earlier Dumnik had decided he wanted
to supervise a surveillance at the Miami airport. He
had a hand-held radio in his briefcase and was following the bad guy through the terminal. At one of the
gates, the bad guy stopped. Dumnik opened his briefcase and was talking into the radio. He backed up,
knocked over a huge standing ashtray, and caused
enough noise for everyone in the terminal to stare at
him. The bad guy saw the radio and split before a
backup arrived.

Dumnik was a chronic boozer. Even in an agency
with more alcoholics than any other agency in the federal government, he was outstanding. Even in an
agency where two- and three-hour lunches were common, he was a legend: he often went to lunch at eleven
A.M. and didn't come back until midmorning the next
day. His alcoholism was at the point where he wore
heavy Pan-Cake makeup to hide the blue highways in
his nose; and he bought Listerine, which he used to
cover the scent of booze on his breath, by the gallon.
An invisible cloud of Listerine billowed out before him
wherever he went.

"No, sir. It will be about another ten minutes."

"Tell Pete and Melvin to come to my office."

"Yes, sir." Pete McBride, who was divorced from
a former DEA agent named Kimberly, was one of several supervisors under Dumnik; men with the title of

assistant special agent in charge. His responsibilities included supervising all DEA offices in Florida other than the one in Miami. Melvin Foster was a lower-level supervisor who was hustling hard for a promotion to GS-14. Andrea thought both men were a bit full of themselves. "King shits," as she privately referred to them. She thought Pete had been particularly cruel to his ex-wife, a woman Andrea had liked and who now worked for the state attorney somewhere over in southwest Florida.

Andrea wondered what was going on. Dumnik had been in his office when she arrived at eight A.M. Usually he arrived about ten and went to the cafeteria and drank coffee for a half-hour before coming to his office. This morning, as soon as she arrived, he called her in and told her with considerable pride that the attorney general himself had called in the middle of the night.

"For what?" was her skeptical response.

"A special enforcement activity. It's being done at the personal request of the President." Dumnik shrugged. "Actually, it's a bullshit deal. Small-time stuff. But we'll do it, get some good stats, get the attention of the President, increase our budget." Dumnik nodded in approval. His star was about to begin rising again.

He gave her a stack of paperwork on what he was calling "Operation Everglades" and told her to have it typed as soon as possible.

Her telephone buzzed again.

"Andrea, just occurred to me, Pete and Melvin said they want to bring in a few of their people. We're going to be working late tonight and we'll need some staff support. Get one of your people to work late. I'll approve the overtime."

"I'll do it," she said quickly.

"Don't you want to go home?"

"I know how you work. I know where all the files are. Things will go quicker if I'm here. I'll stay. I want to work on this thing if the attorney general is involved."

"Okay. Fine."

Andrea hung up the phone and smiled. She was pleased with herself. This was one Friday night she would not have to make a car payment. She reached for the phone again. She had to call her husband and give him the bad news.

5

Lance Cunningham was exhausted. He had been bailing water from the Whaler since before dawn. It was now nine P.M. and the nor'easter showed no signs of abating. Seas were running at least six feet; great rollers that swept in from the northeast with metronomic regularity. He was far enough offshore, at least eight or nine miles, that the Florida landmass offered no protection from the wind and waves. Twenty-knot winds, given eight or nine miles of fetch, can build powerful waves.

The water was slate gray, not the usual clear green found this far offshore, and the sea was filled with what Yeats called "murderous innocence"—angry vertical waves with sharp edges and with windblown crests that caused the Whaler to snap and twist as it rose high in the air. Then the small boat plunged down the backside of the waves, paused in the trough for a few seconds until the next wave lifted it high.

Lance had been exhilarated when the clouds first lowered; when visibility dropped and the nor'easter first began blowing. It was the sort of weather dopers liked. He was certain that patrolling in a ten-mile racetrack pattern—trolling, he called it—about six miles offshore would result in his finding a smuggler. Sometimes trolling was the only way to generate any action. He would pop a doper, put his devil brain to work and flip him, then start trading up. It was as scientific as McBride's computer.

The clouds lowered even more; the winds continued to rise, and the rain fell almost horizontally. The VHF scanner was empty of all but chitchat about the weather; no coded doper talk. Lance wasn't worried. He was out here on behalf of Nick Brown, the best boss anybody ever had. He was working on the Everglades City case, an investigation that had to be solved. Nick needed this one, and Lance was going to give it to him.

Anyone else in Lance's position would have been miserable. Miserable and frightened. Anyone else would have realized the extraordinary danger he faced. Being far offshore in a thirteen-foot open boat during a howling nor'easter was something that not even skilled seamen wanted to endure.

Lance was not concerned when the waves began breaking over the Whaler. It was lined with flotation equipment and said to be unsinkable. But if the boat filled with water, the engines would be inoperative. Lance began bailing. His yellow slicker hindered the bailing so he took it off. He was soaked. He wore boat shoes, jeans, and a T-shirt that said "HUMPTY DUMPTY WAS PUSHED."

About noon he turned on the loran to get a quick fix on his position. He knew he was being pushed further seaward, but he didn't know at what rate. The loran was inoperative; its circuits fried by pounding seawater. At three P.M. he reluctantly picked up a microphone and prepared to ask the Marine Patrol to come find him. He knew their boats would be tied up in this weather and that they would have to ask the Coast Guard to find him. He would not ask the Coasties for help. They were assholes. They would trade a simple rescue, which was their job, into a big-time debt.

Now both VHF radios were inop. Their circuits probably had been soaked by seawater. Lance reached inside the little equipment bag every cop carries on an operation and pulled out his hand-held radio. Just as he started to broadcast, another wave broke over the boat, soaking him and the radio. He keyed the radio. Zip.

The navigation lights and clearance lights didn't work. He raised the blue light on its pedestal and flipped the switch. Zip again. He was out of food, his last Snickers bar had been eaten, and there was only one bottle of water aboard.

Lance's boat was a derelict; drifting southwest into the yawning expanse of the Gulf of Mexico without radio, without navigation equipment, without a food supply. Any other cop would have considered himself, as Lance would say, in mega shit.

But Lance was not worried. He was the narc from hell; the man who had sauntered into the roughest waterfront bar in Naples and made friends with the toughest woman in southwest Florida; an irascible mean-spirited barmaid named Tequila Sheila. Tequila Sheila was a hundred and ninety pounds on the hoof. She had tossed many a fisherman out of the bar. It was said that if you ordered an entire freight train filled with the meanest women in the world, and, when the train arrived, Tequila Sheila was the only one aboard, you would have gotten your money's worth. One night, after far too much to drink, Lance had sneaked up behind her, seized her hips with his hands, and bitten her hard on the ass. She spun in surprise and anger, her fist drawn back. She was going to deck someone. Lance was sitting on the floor laughing. He rocked back and forth, holding his ribs, tears pouring down his face. Biting Tequila Sheila on the ass was like trying to bite Rhode Island. Tequila Sheila stared at him. After a moment, a smile tugged at the corners of her mouth. Then she leaned over, hands on her knees, and laughed. Soon the two of them, nose to nose, were howling. Then she picked him up, bought him a drink, and they became fast friends. He was the only man in Florida who could pat Tequila Sheila on the behind and not get put into orbit by a fist only slightly smaller than a Toyota.

For the man who tamed Tequila Sheila, a force-7 gale was nothing. Lance paused and assessed his sit-

uation. He had plenty of gas. His boat was still floating. And he worked for Nick Brown. He looked at the
rain-filled sky and muttered, "And I'm highly dedicated and highly motivated—a nineties kinda guy."

The storm could not last forever. Lance returned to
his bailing. He tried to whistle, but the wind was so
high and the rain so heavy, all he could do was blow
bubbles. He grinned. He was going to tell Nick he had
been kidnapped by a UFO.

6

Derek Tutwiler was the son of a Fort Myers fisherman,
who, because of his outstanding high-school academic
record, was offered a scholarship at Harvard, and
then, on the recommendation of State Attorney Joseph
D'Alessandro, at Harvard Law. Derek asked D'Alessandro for a job when he was graduated magna cum
laude from Harvard Law. He had planned his career
in some detail. In two more years, when he was thirty,
he would resign from the state attorney's office and
open his own practice.

Derek was inordinately proud of being a Harvard
graduate. His big ring with the dark crimson stone was
one of his proudest possessions. He polished the ring
several times each month and occasionally would be
seen staring at it with something that approached awe.
Were it someone else, his affection for Harvard might
have made the other lawyers and the investigators on
Nick's staff think him a stuffed shirt. Cops don't have
much respect for college boys, Harvard or otherwise.
But everyone in the office was fond of Derek. Nick,
who liked nothing better than chiding lawyers on the
staff, had virtually adopted Derek. He was the living
embodiment of the American Dream; proof that the
son of a fisherman in a remote Florida town could

graduate with the highest honors from one of the most prestigious universities in the world. Derek's stature in Nick's eyes was increased when the young man turned down job offers with law firms in New York and Washington to come home and work as a prosecutor in the state attorney's office. "He wants to put bad people in jail, not go with a bunch of fat-cat big-city lawyers," Nick said.

Derek was of medium height and had been a bit on the slender side until Nick and several investigators talked him into regular workouts at a nearby exercise club. Now his shoulders were wider and his chest was deeper.

Derek was the state attorney's representative on the task force formed by DEA, at the order of the President, to clean up Everglades City. In addition to U.S. Customs, the Coast Guard, and a U.S. Navy representative, numerous state and local law-enforcement agencies also were on the task force. The state attorney's office in the Twentieth Judicial Circuit, sheriffs from the five counties in the circuit, the Florida Highway Patrol, Florida Department of Law Enforcement, and the Florida Marine Patrol were members. More than two dozen people were part of Operation Everglades and they all reported to Melvin Foster, who reported to Pete McBride, who reported to Raymond Dumnik. Dumnik was task-force director. The cooperation was something of a one-way street in that all information gathered by all the agencies flowed up to Dumnik, but nothing flowed back downhill. Kimberly McBride was wide-eyed at the amount of raw intelligence data flowing to the DEA; dozens of investigative files, intel reports, backgrounders, and computer printouts.

Nick had worked with DEA often enough when he was in Fort Lauderdale to know that DEA was interested in three things: interdiction, arrests, and seizures. It would be a quick in-and-out to make a few stats, a few high-profile arrests, seize a few loads, and then they would pack up and leave. Everyone in DEA who was involved would get some sort of commendation. The President would express his gratitude to the attorney general. At top levels of the Justice Department, it would all be considered a major success. Meanwhile, the dope would still be flooding through Everglades City into America. Nick would continue to face the same problem he faced before the task force was formed.

This was Derek Tutwiler's first major involvement with DEA and he thought Nick's assessment unduly harsh. But Nick was right. Only three months after Operation Everglades began, Dumnik threatened to revoke the immunity given the sheriff's son unless the young man gave up a couple of loads. A week later the DEA busted two crab boats, eight mullet skiffs, and seized thirty tons of marijuana. Sixteen fishermen, including Big Knocker and Heart Attack, were arrested. Raymond Dumnik, who had come over from Miami to supervise the arrests, then held a press conference to announce that the President's mandate had been carried out; that Everglades City was clean.

Dumnik knew the cases were weak. But in one of DEA's periodic efforts at pretending it was cooperating with local authorities, he asked the state attorney's office to prosecute the cases. The good old boys in Everglades City figured they had been caught fair and square and pleaded guilty.

Derek Tutwiler made an impassioned plea for maximum sentences. He stood up in the courtroom and talked of the danger of corruption in the legal system, of the violence, of the amount of dope Everglades City smugglers had brought into America, and why it was crucial for the judge to keep the fishermen out of society for as long as possible.

Before sentencing, the judge, who was from a family that had lived in Whiskey Creek for three generations, called Derek into his chambers to let him know the court's intentions. "I'm thinking of one-year sentences," he said.

Derek was astonished. "Your honor, they'll be out in six months," he protested. "The state doesn't feel that is sufficient time, considering the magnitude of the offenses.''

"Boy, I appreciate your position,'' the judge said. "But—''

Derek was so agitated that he interrupted the judge. "Your honor, we are talking about thirty tons of illegal substances here.''

The judge waved his hand in dismissal. "First offenders. I'm not sure they realize the gravity of what they were doing. Those people are in deep financial trouble down there. Government has deprived them of virtually everything they have.''

The judge paused. "Besides, some of these folk are kin to me. I've known their families since I was a kid. I just can't come down on my kinfolk; not the first time they are caught, and not when the law provides for such sentences.''

Derek nodded. He stood, his hands over the back of a chair, fingers nervously drumming. The big gold ring with the crimson stone pounded out a heavy repetitive note.

The judge shook his head. "I just don't see how Nick Brown can take part in all this. He grew up in Collier County. Some of these people are his cousins. Sometimes I'm sorry the state attorney hired him. He'd arrest his mother.'' The judge stared at Derek. "You people in the state attorney's office are possessed of more than your share of zealotry.''

Derek was furious. "If that will be all, judge . . .'' He turned to leave.

"No, it's not all.''

Derek turned.

The judge continued. "Before we go back out in the courtroom, I want you to know the one-year sentences will be on a work-release program at the Deep Lake Prison at Copeland. It's only a few miles from Everglades City and they can all be with their families at night. They have not demonstrated any propensity for violence that—'' The judge held up his hand as Derek tried to interrupt again. "I know. I heard the testimony about one or two of those men, the one called

Big Knocker in particular. But there was no proof. It's hearsay and speculation.''

The judge paused. ''They can serve their time during the day; at night they can be home with their families.'' He looked out the window.

''Judge, some of those men will go back to smuggling tomorrow night.'' Derek could barely control his anger. ''They'll be doing time during the day and doing dope at night.''

''Conjecture, son, sheer conjecture.''

''Like you, your honor, I grew up here.'' He did not add that he had long known the judge's unofficial nickname in the state attorney's office was ''The Great Emancipator''—the man who had freed more people than anyone since Abe Lincoln.

''I know, son. I used to buy fish from your daddy.'' The judge paused and weighed Derek with a speculative eye. ''Since you grew up here, you should agree with me there's no sense in further overcrowding our prisons with good people; with people who can serve their time and still help out their families.'' The judge leaned closer to Derek. ''Good God, son. Thorn Wells is a widower with four girls to raise. I'm not going to put him in jail on his first marijuana offense.''

Derek knew when he was defeated. He nodded tightly, turned, and left the judge's chambers. After the sentencing, Big Knocker and Heart Attack casually sauntered from the defendants' table toward the center aisle of the courtroom. The two were talking quietly when Big Knocker turned and glanced at the prosecutor's table, where Lance and Derek sat. Big Knocker knew Lance was a cop—the guy just had the look— but Big Knocker didn't know for whom. He would remember the face. His gaze lingered on Derek. He stepped closer to the table and said, ''That was some speech you gave earlier about us going to jail.''

Derek was angrily pushing papers into his briefcase. He paused, looked up for a moment, then continued.

''What you got against me, college boy?'' Big Knocker asked. His impassive eyes held Derek.

The young lawyer angrily clamped his mouth shut.

He was not old enough to be philosophical about guilty people walking away from justice. He was not experienced enough to know not to become involved; to accept a judge's verdict, to wait for another day. His hand angrily drummed on the table. He did not answer. The big gold ring emitted a solid repetitive thunking sound. He had heard Nick say many times, "Sometimes you eat the bear; sometimes the bear eats you." This time the bear had eaten him, and he didn't like it.

"I asked you a question, boy."

Derek stood up and stepped toward Big Knocker. He looked up. The smuggler towered over him. But Derek had grown up on the docks of Fort Myers. He knew many men like Big Knocker and he was not afraid. For a moment the Harvard veneer disappeared and the language of the docks returned. "You're going to fuck up again," he said softly. "You're going to smuggle and you're going to get caught. And when you do, I'll put together a case that will stick. You won't walk again. You're a fucking asshole and I'm going to put you in jail."

"You know, boy, I believe you mean that," Big Knocker said. He stared at the young lawyer for a long moment. Then he nodded at Heart Attack and the two men sauntered down the aisle of the courtroom.

Lance looked at Derek and nodded in approval. This boy had potential; even if he was a lawyer.

"Mr. Dumnik, would you let me see all the intelligence data gathered on this case?" Kimberly said. She pulled nervously at her crystal necklaces and tried not to look at her former husband, who stood beside Dumnik.

Dumnik stopped in the hall of the courthouse, took a puff off his cigarette, and looked at Kimberly. "You used to work for me, didn't you?" Asshole. He knew who she was.

"Yes, sir, I did." God, the cigarette smoke, even mixed with a cloud of Listerine, smelled wonderful. A year ago she had quit smoking. She liked to think she was over the hump; that she had defeated the habit. But occasionally, and there was no predicting when it would happen, she would catch a stray whiff of cigarette smoke and it would smell so good that she instinctively took a deep breath, trying to draw the smoke into her lungs.

"How you like working over here in the sticks?" He laughed. Pete McBride and Melvin Foster laughed. They hung close to Dumnik, like a couple of remoras under the belly of a shark. A retinue of a half-dozen DEA agents, a school of lesser fish, followed at a discreet distance. She knew one or two of them, men who had been there when she worked as a DEA analyst for several years. She stared at Dumnik, not wanting to look at her former husband. But she could sense his mocking presence; see him rocking back and forth on his heels in that cocky macho way he had.

Kimberly forced a smile. It was very painful for her to allow Dumnik and his troops to have a laugh at her expense. But Dumnik could, with a word, prevent her seeing the task-force records; records she believed were a gold mine of intelligence; records that would be invaluable if she was going to put together the history cases Nick wanted.

"I enjoy it. Nick Brown is a fine law-enforcement officer."

Dumnik waved toward the courtroom he had just vacated. "Yeah," he said sarcastically. "This case showed that."

"What do you mean?"

"You send in some green lawyer, a kid still wet behind the ears, to prosecute the cases we made. He blows a sure thing and the assholes walk. Yeah, you work for great cops over here."

The two men with Dumnik laughed indulgently.

Kimberly bit her lip. Dumnik knew his cases were weak; that was why he had turned them over to a local jurisdiction. And Derek had done a fine job of prosecuting; good enough that the defendants pleaded guilty. It was the judge who allowed the defendants to walk.

But she needed a favor from Dumnik and could not say this to him. She shrugged.

Dumnik puffed on his cigarette and laughed again. "You coming to our party tomorrow night? We're celebrating the end of this case. Victory party. Everyone on the task force is invited."

"I'm not sure. If I can get a baby-sitter, I may be there."

"How old's that boy now? Three?"

"Five," Kimberly said, her eyes softening at the mention of her son.

"He look like his old man?" Dumnik grinned at Pete.

"It's too early to tell. Some people say he does." She waited, and then, not able to resist, added, "Maybe he'll outgrow that." She smiled to take the sting from her words.

Dumnik laughed. She noticed the Pan-Cake makeup around his nose was cracked and a maze of blue veins was showing. He waved his hands. "Sure, you can have the files. The task force is still operational, but that's just on paper. The case is over. Bring a van over and we'll check the records out to you."

"Thanks, Mr. Dumnik."

"What the hell are you going to do with them? This place is history."

"Yes, sir, you're right. But I want to study them and see how I might improve my work on the next case; see what I did right; see what I might change." She shrugged. "You know how analysts are."

"You still playing with computers, huh? You even got computers over here?"

"Yes, sir. Small ones. Nothing like what I had at DEA." Kimberly was wringing her hands.

Dumnik shook his head. Kimberly McBride was a loser; another person who should never have gone to work for DEA. She had found her proper level in the world; in a small town in a remote corner of Florida.

"Call Pete here before you come over." He grinned. "You know Pete. He'll set it up for you. But what the hell you expect to find, I don't know. Waste of time, in my judgment.''

"It may be.''

Dumnik spun around and walked toward the door of the courthouse. One of the young agents tarried. He checked over his shoulder to make sure Dumnik didn't see him, and spoke quickly to Kimberly. "Two loads are coming in tomorrow. A Piper Apache is landing at Naples at six P.M. and a boat will be seven miles off the number-one marker at Indian Key Pass at two A.M. the next day.''

Kimberly cataloged the information. "The aircraft is landing at the city airport? In the middle of town?''

The agent was backing down the hall after Dumnik. "You know that Everglades City bunch. They're bold. The info is righteous.''

"Why aren't you working it?'' Kimberly was suspicious. It was not like the DEA to give away a couple of loads, especially to a local agency.

The agent looked toward Dumnik's disappearing back. "He says no.''

"Why?''

The agent shrugged. "Didn't you hear him? We're having a victory party tomorrow night. Everglades City is drug-free.''

7

Mike Love, six feet and two inches of probity and rectitude, stood on the ramp at NAS Jacksonville and pointed to the heavily modified Piper Cheyenne painted in the distinctive blue-and-white colors of U.S. Customs. "I know you heard all this when you were checked out in this aircraft, but listen up anyway. This aircraft will kill you. I don't care if you kill yourself, but you're not gonna kill me. So before we fly, I'm

gonna tell you some things about it you didn't learn at
school; things you have to know.''

The young pilot, Mike couldn't remember his name,
would fly left seat for the intercept. The weather was
perfect, not a cloud in the sky. Only one bad guy
aboard the inbound Apache; the one flying up from
Cuba with a load of marijuana. The dope had come to
Cuba from either Colombia or Belize aboard a boat
and then was broken down into smaller loads for airplanes. Mike's longtime friend Nick Brown had called
from down in Fort Myers last night and given him the
information. If Nick said the information was solid,
you could take it to the bank. Mike had no doubt in
his mind that a doper was inbound with maybe a thousand pounds of marijuana aboard an Apache. It would
be Mike's job, as a pilot with the Customs Air Support
Branch in Jacksonville, to intercept the doper offshore
and track him to his landing site. The Miami air branch
initially was upset about Jacksonville coming into their
territory, but they were appeased by positioning a
Blackhawk helicopter near the Naples airport. The
'Hawk would be the bust aircraft.

Nick and Mike had worked together many times in
the past. They trusted each other. Mike would pick up
Nick in Fort Myers and then go offshore to make the
intercept. The doper was smart; flying from Cuba
around Key West and then into the Gulf before swing-
ing north and coming in America's back door. Lance
would lead a team of locals, who would be on the
ground. Customs and Nick's men would make the bust
together.

''Customs has eight of these aircraft,'' Mike said to
the young pilot. ''We call it the CHET—the Customs
High Endurance Tracker. It's a piece of shit. We have
the aircraft because a few years back, Piper got in bad
financial trouble. Reagan decided to bail them out.
Part of the bailout plan was ordering Customs to buy
eight of these pigs. DEA had to buy some also.''

J.T., the air interdiction officer who had transferred
from Miami, walked up. J.T. smiled at Mike and nodded toward the new guy. J.T. was a former Marine

and the best backseater in the business. He could get more information from the electronic detection equipment aboard the aircraft than any other AIO in Customs.

Mike stood in front of the twin-engine aircraft. "The aircraft is so dangerous the British refused to certify it," he said in his soft intense voice. "It shouldn't have been certified here either. The basic problem is, it's underpowered. Especially with all the extra weight we have aboard—the FLIR, radar, and extra fuel. We regularly take off with the aircraft two thousand pounds over gross. Lose an engine on takeoff and you're dead. It's that simple."

The young pilot nodded. This had merely been hinted at when he was checked out on the CHET. But if Mike Love said it, consider it gospel. The tall bearded man was one of the most respected and aggressive pilots in the Customs Air Branch; an old-timer of only thirty-nine years. Mike took it personally when a doper tried to bring a load of dope into America. And he was offended at the Customs bureaucracy that had him filling out paperwork when he could have been in the air. As a result, he usually was angry. That was good, because he took his anger out on drug smugglers. Customs pilots said if Mike Love intercepted a smuggler, the doper should give his heart to God because his ass belonged to the U.S. Customs Service.

"We get inside, I'll show you how screwed-up the cockpit is," Mike said. "Like the light switches. Three switches on the Citation turn on every light on the aircraft. This piece of garbage has a dozen switches to do the same thing."

Mike nodded toward the FLIR pod, the forward-looking infrared detection equipment, mounted under the nose. "You know about the FLIR," Mike said. This little high-tech mother translated thermal images—the heat signature—into video pictures aboard the aircraft. J.T., who sat in the left rear of the aircraft, had a large radar screen and FLIR screen. Small repeater screens were mounted up front between the pilot and copilot.

Mike pointed to the extraordinarily long engines on each side of the fuselage. "See the position of the FLIR. If you're making turns around a point, the FLIR will pick up the engine nacelle, the tip tank, or start strobing off the prop. So when the bad guy lands and you're orbiting over him, maintain an altitude of at least thirty-five hundred feet. Four thousand is better."

J.T. interrupted. "Don't forget. Drop lower and you'll block out the FLIR pod. Then I lose the bad guy."

"I thought Customs had good FLIR equipment," said the young pilot. "What kind is this?"

Mike snorted. "The wrong kind. It's Hughes equipment that was designed for helicopters. Choppers fly low and over land. Flying over water screws this thing up big-time. Plus, at the altitude we have to fly to avoid blocking out the FLIR, the lens shows too much. Half the damn state shows up on there."

"So why do we have it? I thought the war on drugs had top priority."

Mike laughed; a short angry derisive sound. "Just when I thought you were smart. We can't even get the modification for the FLIR that would bring it up to standard. And all we need is a circuit board. We've waited years. We make do with what we have."

Mike looked at his watch. "Let's get airborne."

Two hours later the CHET, with Nick Brown aboard, was climbing out of Fort Myers. The CHET, for all its faults, was a good climber and reached ten thousand feet in six and a half minutes. But visibility from inside the aircraft left much to be desired. The cockpit windows were tiny and cut off much of the view. The large nacelles blocked downward vision on both sides. The aircraft, in spite of its size, was cramped and tight for the crew.

"I'll tell you something else about this aircraft," Mike said to the young pilot. "We don't have a crew hatch. If we have to ditch, don't worry about it. J.T.'s electronics package, the FLIR and radar panel mounted behind you, will break loose and jam you into the panel. You don't have to worry about getting out because you'll be dead.''

''Encouraging,'' said the new guy.

Mike looked at his watch, checked his coordinates, and pressed the intercom switch. ''Nick, you said he will break the coast just north of Fort Myers, then turn and fly south?''

Nick, sitting across from J.T. in the rear of the CHET, spoke into the microphone of the headset he was wearing. ''That's affirmative. That's so when guys pick him up on the balloons, he'll be flying south. He won't fit the profile, so you won't launch.''

Customs had radar balloons on Cudjoe Key in the Florida keys, at Patrick Air Force Base about halfway up the east side of the Florida coast, and two balloons in the Bahamas. Customs boasted that the balloons had shut down airborne smuggling. What Customs didn't anticipate was a doper who would enter Florida's west coast at low altitude, then climb and fly south. Radar operators would think he was on a local flight. Smugglers flew north, not south.

''He's right,'' Mike said. ''We would never have launched on him without prior information.''

Nick nodded in agreement. Kimberly had called the DEA agent in Miami, the one who passed the original information to her, and asked him to tell her everything he knew about the flight. The agent had known a lot. And he was glad to pass it along, strictly on an unofficial agent-to-agent basis. Dumnik would never know.

''We should be picking him up in about five minutes,'' Mike said.

J.T. carefully adjusted the ''foot'' of the radar—the radar coverage on the ground. The aircraft was at ten thousand feet. The radar foot began nine miles in front of the aircraft and extended, theoretically, to eighty miles. As a practical matter, it was much less. When looking for a smuggler, the length of the radar foot is crucial. For example, if the CHET is cruising at almost three hundred miles an hour and the target is at two hundred, that means a closure rate of five hundred miles an hour. If the foot is only five miles or so, the backseater might get only two sweeps with his radar before the target punched through. But J.T. knew his business. He adjusted the radar until he was putting out a foot bigger than Sasquatch's.

"If he's on schedule and on course, I'll get him," J.T. said. J.T. closed the sun screen to his left. He didn't care about what was outside. He was interested only in the space-age symbology in front of him. For him, an interdiction was simply a matter of electronics, of geometry. The doper was dog meat. It was that simple.

Mike scanned the horizon. "Weather couldn't be better."

"Yeah," Nick responded. "I'm glad I'm up here. This weather brings the hemorrhoids out by the dozens. Between them and the old people, Florida is really screwed up."

Mike laughed. "What you got against old people?"

"You ever get behind them in traffic? All you can see are two hands on the steering wheel; maybe the top of a head. Usually blue. And you might see the top of another head in the right seat. They poke along at twenty miles an hour, ignore lights, turn whenever they want to, and they die."

"They die?"

"Every day. You see these two hands on a steering wheel; all at once they're gone. The guy has a heart attack and dies at the wheel. He slumps down and jams the accelerator to the floor and the car takes off across traffic, banging fenders, running over pedestrians, and it's all being done by a dead person."

Mike was shaking with laughter.

"Not so funny if you live down here. I heard somebody on TV say Florida is God's waiting room. He's right. All those people come down here to die. But they're determined to take a few people with them when they go."

"You're gonna be old one day," Mike said.

"Not me. I'm gonna die while I still got my marbles. I don't want to be eighty years old and walking down the street in a topcoat when it's a hundred and ten outside.''

''Topcoats?''

''Yeah, they're cold all the time. I think they're hiding liquor under there.''

J.T. leaned forward. A dot had appeared in the upper left center of his radar screen. His right hand reached for the joystick. He slid the acquisition symbol over the dot and squeezed the trigger. The dot changed to a diamond. Three sets of numbers popped up on the lower part of the screen.

''We have a judy,'' he said. ''Target bears zero-seven-niner, speed one-five-zero, altitude three-point-five. He's two-eight miles away.''

A sober professional attitude instantly came over the men aboard the aircraft.

''If you maintain present heading, we'll have about a two-mile offset,'' J.T. said. ''He's down low, so he won't see us.''

''He's on fumes by now,'' Mike said. ''Even if he has aux tanks. We've got about seven hours remaining.''

''He should be coming up off the left side of the nose. Down low,'' J.T. said. He was bent forward, eyes intent on the high-stakes video game.

Mike stretched and tried to see to the left. But the nacelles limited his visibility. ''You got him?'' he asked the new guy.

The young pilot leaned his head against the perspex window and looked down through the narrow slot between the fuselage and the nacelle. ''Don't see him.''

J.T. looked at the screen, did some quick mental calculations, then pushed up the sunscreen and looked at his left. And there below, far below, was a moving white dot. It was the doper. Mike had been watching the FLIR and radar screens and seen the aircraft pass below. It was all he could do not to seize the wheel and fly the intercept himself. But the new guy had to learn.

Mike's thumb, pointed toward the left, stabbed the air. "Break left and get low. Let's I.D. this guy."

The CHET swung into a tight descending turn to the left. Moments later the white dot became an airplane shape; then Mike could see the colors: red fuselage, white wings. Just as Nick had said.

"Watch your airspeed," he cautioned. The radar screen showed the CHET was overtaking the Apache at more than one hundred miles an hour.

Suddenly the FLIR screen went blank.

J.T. cursed. A moment later he said, "FLIR is tango uniform."

Mike shook his head in disgust. The FLIR was inoperative as much as it was operative. It was okay today with clear weather. And he had an eyeball on the bad guy. But if the chase had been at night, the bad guy might have gotten away.

Two minutes later the CHET was snuggled up under the rear of the Apache, no more than twenty feet away. Mud was visible on the lower part of the tail surfaces. The horizontal stabilizer was nicked and pockmarked from rocks striking it during takeoff runs from dirt strips. Exhaust stains from the engines could be seen under the wings. Mike could count the rivets in the bottom of the aircraft.

"Okay, looking good," Mike said. "Slide out to the right and let me get his number."

The new guy was steady. With one hand on the throttles, one on the wheel, and eyes locked on the tail of the aircraft ahead, he gently maneuvered the CHET a few feet to the right. A mistake here and there would be a collision, then an explosion, then pieces of aircraft, hundreds of pounds of marijuana, and five bodies tumbling toward the ocean a half-mile below.

Mike stretched. "Little bit more," he said.

The CHET moved another three feet to the right. "Hold it right there." Mike read the numbers aloud, then wrote them on the edge of a map.

"Okay, back off a mile and get a few thousand feet above this guy. He's history." Mike reached for the microphone.

"I don't know if we can reach Slingshot from here. We might have to relay through Domino." Mike tapped his fingers on the microphone in his hands. "Slingshot, Omaha Five Niner."

Reception was good. All the way across the Florida peninsula, in a small concrete building on the old Navy dirigible base in southwest Miami, a Customs radar operator picked up a microphone.

"Omaha Five Niner. Slingshot. Go."

Mike gave his position off the coast of Fort Myers and then read the aircraft number.

"Negative radar contact," Slingshot said. "You're beyond radar coverage out there. Stand by while I run the number."

Slingshot was the code name for a command, control, communications, and intelligence center—called C3I—operated jointly by Customs and the Coast Guard. Its job is to detect inbound airborne smugglers, identify them, and provide real-time intelligence for interdiction.

The Customs radar operator turned away from the huge color radar screen and punched the aircraft numbers into a computer. TECS, the secret Customs computer system that stored information about aircraft and known or suspected drug traffickers, almost instantly spit out an answer. The radar operator picked up his microphone.

"Omaha Five Niner. Slingshot. We have a hit. That aircraft is positive in the system. Suspected of bringing in three loads. Ownership unclear. Looks like they're moving a lot of paper to disguise ownership. The aircraft is not on a flight plan."

"That's our boy," said the new guy.

"No shit. Didn't you see the dope when we pulled out to get the number?"

The pilot shook his head ruefully. "No, I was so busy flying, I forgot to look."

"It's jammed with dope," Mike said. "Piled to the top of the cabin. You can see it through the windows."

"I thought this Everglades City crowd used boats," the new guy said.

Mike snorted. "They do whatever works. Occasionally they bring in an aircraft load. They would pack it in on their mothers' backs if they thought that would work."

The doper, now down to about five hundred feet, crossed the coast at Charlotte Harbor, then turned south to fly over Cape Coral. The Apache punched through the northwestern side of the traffic area for the Fort Myers airport, then began a gradual climb to about a thousand feet.

"Real smart," Mike said in reluctant admiration. "Now he's on radar but everybody thinks he probably took off from Fort Myers. This guy is a righteous doper. He's done this before."

"Hawk in position?" Nick asked.

Mike picked up the microphone again. A moment later he glanced outside the window, then at his watch. His conversation was urgent. A moment later he looked over his shoulder into the cabin. "You guys armed?" he asked over the intercom.

Nick and J.T. looked at each other and then at Mike. Both nodded. Nick patted his nine-millimeter Smith & Wesson. It had fourteen in the clip and one in the pipe; plenty of firepower unless the doper had an Uzi.

"Hawk's out of position," Mike said. "Too far east. Can't get here in time. We're the bust aircraft."

"Take down one and two?" J.T. asked.

"Do it," Mike said.

J.T. quickly turned off the number-one and number-two inverters as he prepared for landing.

"Here's how we'll do this," Mike said. "We'll wait until the guy is committed to landing. We don't want him to see us and run. Then we'll drop in behind him. J.T., during the rollout, you open the door. We'll be taxiing fast, so be careful. We'll block his aircraft. When he sees us, he might try to rabbit. Or he might start shooting. Be ready."

Mike turned to the new guy. The pilot pointed at the radio. He had set it to the frequency of the Naples airport. They could monitor the doper's initial call-up. Mike nodded in approval.

The doper, who had been tracking down I-75, crossed Bonita Springs and swung a few degrees east. He was lined up for a straight-in approach at the Naples airport.

"Naples tower, this is Piper November-one-two-zero-six-Papa. Five north. Landing."

Nick looked at his watch. Six-forty. After flying around the Florida keys into the Gulf of Mexico and then back toward Florida, the guy was only forty minutes late. The DEA information was right on target. Sometimes those guys were truly good.

Nick scowled. He was angry that a doper felt so little fear of the cops that he would land at Naples airport in broad daylight. The Everglades City boys were getting a little overconfident.

Mike pressed the intercom transmit button and said, "He just gave the tower a number that's different from his real numbers. Must be planning to park some distance from the tower."

Nick picked up his hand-held radio and, when Lance responded to the call, said, "We're about three minutes out. You in position?"

Lance's voice boomed out so loud that Nick had to turn down the volume control. "Not to worry, jefe. All is under control. He's mine."

"Stay out of sight," Nick said.

"Have your people call my people," Lance said. "Maybe we can do lunch one day."

"Get off the air," Nick said.

"Well, don't get a stiffy over it."

Nick dropped the microphone.

"Hey, jefe, you upset?"

"You get off the air." Nick spoke slowly, enunciating each word clearly and distinctly.

"Inquiring minds want to know. You upset?"

The vein along Nick's nose began throbbing. He pulled the radio close to his mouth. But before he could speak, the Apache dropped its gear and lined up for the landing.

"Okay, guys, heads up," Mike said.

The CHET remained high, as if it were continuing

south, waiting, watching, timing it to the second. When the Apache was no more than a few hundred yards from touchdown, the new guy dropped his gear, flaps, and pulled power. The CHET descended like an elevator. The new guy added power to slow the descent, then touched down on the runway just as the smuggler, who was heavily overloaded and had rolled all the way to the distant end of the runway, turned around.

"Your aircraft," Mike said. He struggled from his seat and cursed as he went through the narrow cramped opening into the cabin. J.T., wearing a blue Customs raid jacket, had lowered the rear door. The wind whistled into the cabin during the high-speed taxi. The two turbine engines screamed like enraged banshees and the hot oily odor of the exhaust filled the cabin.

"He's turning off the runway onto the grass," the new guy shouted.

J.T. and Nick stood together on the steps, holding the thin cable that supported the steps. Mike crowded them from the rear, anxious to stop the doper. Then, as the CHET slowed, J.T. and Nick, followed closely by Mike, jumped from the steps and ran toward the Apache. The three men lurched and stumbled and almost lost their footing.

The doper pilot was standing on the wing. But rather than running, he was leaning over, tossing something into the cockpit.

J.T. ran around the nose of the Apache, careful to avoid the still-turning props, while Nick ran from the rear. Both had their weapons drawn.

"It's burning," Nick shouted. A flickering white flame was visible inside the cabin of the Apache. The flames turned red, and black smoke began billowing high into the air. The smuggler, a muscular middle-aged man with a heavy suntan, jumped from the wing and ran. Nick, huffing and puffing at full speed, changed direction by ten degrees and caught the man at the edge of the runway, the sheer force of his charge throwing the man to the surface. Nick jammed his pistol into the smuggler's ear and jerked the man's hands behind his back. He sensed J.T. standing beside him as backup. Mike was trying to pull charts and the doper's supplies from the burning Apache. He wanted all the evidence he could get.

Nick quickly cuffed the smuggler. Behind him the crackling of the flames was growing louder. Nick could feel the heat. The doper's gas tanks probably were filled with fumes and could explode any second in a blast like a small nuclear bomb. It would fry all of them and blow up the multimillion-dollar CHET. He jerked the smuggler's shirt from his back. No weapons under the shirt. Then he rolled the man over, unhooked the man's jeans, and jerked them down around his ankles. No weapons around his waist or crotch. The smuggler was bleeding from the face, chest, shoulders, hips, and arms. A runway may be smooth to the wheels of an aircraft, but it's extraordinarily rough to one who is being jerked about the surface. The smuggler hadn't resisted Nick, but neither had he cooperated. He went limp and made Nick work.

"Man, what the hell you doing to me?" the smuggler complained.

Lance, who had been running full tilt across the tarmac, skidded to a stop in front of Nick. He was wearing green fatigue pants, red tennis shoes, a red Rambo rag around his head, and a T-shirt that said "SAVE THE WHALES. HARPOON A FAT WOMAN"—his typical raid regalia. "I called the fire department," he said. "I got men out on the road moving traffic." He watched Nick trying to move the smuggler. He laughed and said, "You're pretty old, Nick. Need any help?"

"Dammit, I'm not old," Nick grunted.

"You read this guy his rights?"

Nick squinted from the heat of the burning aircraft and gritted his teeth as he tried to pick up the smuggler. "That thing's about to blow. None of us will have any rights if we don't get the hell out of the way." He tugged on the smuggler's arm.

"Jefe, you're getting old. You got white hair in your ears."

Nick dropped the smuggler's arm and reached for his ears. "I do not."

"Okay, guys," came J.T.'s calm voice. "Time to go to warp six and get outta here."

The crackling noise of the burning aircraft grew louder. The heat reached out with increasing intensity. Lance and Nick and the smuggler were bathed in perspiration. Black smoke billowed upward as the tires on the Apache exploded, then caught fire.

Nick jumped when the tire exploded. "Cunningham, grab this son of a bitch's other arm. He thinks he some kind of civil-rights hero. Limp as a dishrag."

Lance grinned, reached down, and pinched the lobe of the man's left ear between his thumb and forefinger. He squeezed hard, digging the fingernails into the soft skin.

The smuggler screamed and scrambled to his feet, head leaning toward Lance in an effort to lessen the pain.

"Repeat after me," Lance said as if talking to a child. "I am in the custody of the narc from hell. I will follow his every wish."

"Man, you hurting me."

Lance squeezed.

"I am in custody of narc from hell. I follow every wish."

"Close enough," Lance said. "Now, come along with us to the other side of the runway, where you will be safe."

"Man, you hurting my ear."

Lance marched the doper across the runway into the grass and sandspurs. He pulled downward and the man fell to his knees. He pulled again and the man sprawled on his face.

"Be a nice asshole and stay there," Lance said. He planted his foot on the back of the man's neck and held him on the ground.

Nick looked over his shoulder. Flames had enveloped the Apache. The marijuana, plainly visible through the windows, was sending up a thick black smoke. Mike, gingerly holding a stack of smoking

charts and a backpack, waved for the new guy to taxi
the CHET out of the way; he did not want it caught
in the explosion. J.T. was waving his arms, giving
landing directions to the Blackhawk that finally had
arrived.

At that moment the Apache exploded. The dull
"cruuump" echoed across the vast open expanse of
the airport and caused spectators along the road, who
had stopped and jumped from their cars when they saw
the flames, to fall to the ground. An orange ball of fire
rolled over and over on itself as it climbed skyward
atop a plume of black smoke. The lawmen ducked as
the heat rolled across them. Then they looked over
their shoulders at the Apache. The aircraft's two propellers had continued to turn when the smuggler hast-
ily jumped out; but now the engines sagged and the
props chewed the ground for a second before stopping.
The engines and the tail surfaces were all that identified it as an aircraft. All the rest was burning and
melting. In the middle of the burning aircraft was a
dark square shape: the load of marijuana; at least a
thousand pounds.

Nick bent down toward the doper. "You're a dumb
dirtbag," he said. "You can't burn grass. That stuff is
so tightly packed the fire won't burn ten pounds of it.
Now you have a federal charge of destroying an aircraft added to your smuggling charges."

Lance looked down at the bleeding, defeated smuggler. "Aw, jefe, don't be hard on him. He was engaged
in a humanitarian mission. He was hauling hay to the
Midwest."

"Sure he was. This asshole is from Everglades City.
I've seen his ugly face before."

As a fire track raced down the runway, Lance looked
at his watch. "We gotta wrap this thing up. I have to
get a boat in the water."

Nick nodded. "Hold on a few minutes and I'll turn
everything over to our guys."

Nick looked down at the doper. Lance had his foot
atop the doper's neck, holding him on the ground.

"I'll be with the Marine Patrol," Nick said. "We'll

be in the mangroves watching for you. Try to do it right this time. Don't break the boat again. I don't want to have to come out and tow you in again."

"You worried about the boat? What about me?"

Nick snorted. "You ever read this guy his rights?"

"You arrested him."

"Can't you even read some dirtbag his rights?"

Lance, his foot still on the doper's neck, adopted a jaunty pose. His hand was stuck into his shirt. His head high. A wide smile creased his face and his eyes sparkled and danced. "He will now have his rights read by America's cult hero, the new superman, the mega narc. Out here on the front lines of the drug war it is me versus bad guys. Good versus evil. Light versus darkness."

Nick shook his head. "Crazy versus asshole," he said.

8

At eleven P.M. Lance was seven miles off the dark unlighted coast of the Ten Thousand Islands. The deal wasn't supposed to go down for another three hours; but Lance knew, as does every narc with more than two weeks on The Job, that dope deals never go down on schedule. Something always happens. A mechanical problem on a boat, an argument with the shrimp-boat captain over the amount of dope, wind, weather, misjudging the tide, not enough food—a thousand things can foul up a dope deal. And the same forces that affect dopers affect cops. Lance knew that catching a doper was simply a matter of who screwed up least. Tonight the cops would not screw up. Maybe the off-loading had gone down early and the bad guys were running ahead of schedule. Maybe the dopers had built in a time cushion they had not used. Whatever hap-

pened, he would be ready. The Whaler, its loran and
radios repaired, was ready. The starboard engine was
running a little rough, but he wouldn't need a lot of
speed to catch a crab boat loaded with marijuana. Tonight the seas were calm, not at all like his last time
at sea. There was no moon. It was a smuggler's night;
perfect for bringing in a load.

He was drifting, lights off, but with the radios on,
listening and watching. His eyes were bright with anticipation, and a wide manic grin split his tanned face.
He was wearing jeans and a T-shirt that said "IF IT
SMELLS LIKE FISH, EAT IT." In a shoulder holster was
his chrome-plated .357 Magnum with the six-inch barrel. He wore a blue raid jacket.

Shortly before one A.M. the VHF radio broke
squelch and blared forth an emergency message. The
volume and clarity of the signal indicated that whoever
was transmitting was within three or four miles.

Lance didn't know it, but the Coast Guard cutter
Dauntless was about twenty miles south, steaming toward his position on a routine cruise. And Big
Knocker, aboard a crab boat loaded with marijuana,
had detected the cutter's radar signal with his fuzz
buster. Big Knocker had extra incentive for being careful tonight. He was completing the first week of his
jail sentence. After being checked into the prison, he
had settled into a routine of slopping white paint on
the rocks that lined the long driveway, cutting grass,
sweeping floors, and a dozen or so other light chores.
Each day at six P.M. he was released to go home and
did not have to report to the jail until seven A.M. He
could not afford to be caught tonight. Tied to the stern
by a long line was his insurance policy—a twenty-
eight-foot go-fast boat powered by three outboard engines; a speed machine. Most go-fast boats used by
smugglers have a deep V bottom and are designed for
high-speed blue-water cruising. But the bottom of Big
Knocker's boat was flat. He wanted a boat that would
get him up into the shallow streams feeding into Chokoloskee Bay and then into the narrow serpentine

creeks that led farther into the Everglades; into a sanctuary where cops could not follow.

He leaned over the radar detector. There it was again. A high-pitched warbling note. The signal was stronger. He adjusted the set, then turned to another instrument. The radar signal, not impeded by the horizon or surface clutter, came from west-southwest. A powerful radar set was up and operating, and he was at the outer edges of its coverage. The signal was not yet strong enough to send back a primary return. But soon the boat, almost certainly a Coast Guard vessel, would be close enough for the radar to lock onto his boat.

Big Knocker looked to his right as if trying to see through the darkness toward the unknown boat. It could cut him off before he reached Indian Key Pass.

Big Knocker picked up a loran chart, pulled it close, and studied it for a moment. Then he wrote down a set of coordinates for a position thirty miles south. He picked up the microphone for the VHF radio, turned it to channel sixteen, paused a moment, then began talking in an excited tone of voice. It was this broadcast that Lance, two miles to the north, heard.

"Mayday. Mayday. Mayday. Coast Guard, Coast Guard. This is the shrimp boat *Spring Tide*. How do you read me? Coast Guard, Coast Guard. Mayday. Mayday. Mayday. This is the *Spring Tide*."

A moment later the radio crackled and a calm voice pushed by a powerful transmitter filled the wheelhouse. "*Spring Tide*, Coast Guard cutter *Dauntless*. State your position, number of souls on board, and your condition."

Big Knocker smiled. He was right. It was the Coast Guard. Well, they wouldn't be around long. "Coast Guard, this is the *Spring Tide*. I have six souls on board. We have an electrical fire that's out of control." He looked at the loran chart, his finger on the coordinates he had written earlier. He read the coordinates, then said, "Abandoning ship. You guys hurry."

"*Spring Tide*, we copy. Be advised we're about thirty nautical northwest of your position."

"How long will it take you to get here? I'm abandoning ship."

"Our ETA your position is one hour plus one-zero minutes. Can you control the fire?"

"No way. My crew is in the lifeboat." Big Knocker took a deep breath. "Can you send a helicopter?"

"Negative. The closest is Key West. We will be there in only a few more minutes than it would take the helicopter. Hang on."

Big Knocker smiled in relief. He had won the gamble. The coordinates he had given were close enough that the cutter would rush in at flank speed; but not far enough away to justify sending a chopper. He pulled the microphone close to his mouth and tried to sound like a panicky skipper.

"Coast Guard, can you hurry? After an hour, I'll start shooting flares every fifteen minutes."

"*Spring Tide,* before you abandon ship, lock your microphone in the transmit position. We're setting up for a DF steer to your position."

Big Knocker paused. He watched the instrument beside the radar detector; the one that indicated the direction from which the signal was being transmitted. A moment later the Coast Guard vessel had moved enough to show on the instrument that it was steaming south. It was again reaching the limits of radar coverage. Now the radar-warning detector was warbling, in and out, weak and erratic.

The Coast Guard had been neutralized. He would make a dash for Everglades City. Once he was inside the Ten Thousand Islands, no one could find him. He pushed the throttles full forward.

Two miles away, Lance looked around. He was bewildered by the conversation. The burning vessel had to be close. Yet the loran coordinates indicated the boat was much farther south. What the hell was going on?

He reached into his little equipment pouch and pulled out a set of night-vision goggles. He knew, he just knew, that the boat that had sent the boat-on-fire message was close, very close.

Then he saw it, a darkened boat, a crab boat by the structure, coming toward him. His practiced eye saw that she was riding low in the water—which meant she was loaded—but making good speed; about forty knots. A four-foot bow wave of white water was rolling out to either side. Then he heard the sound, the low rumbling of powerful engines. The engines were straining hard.

Lance realized what had happened. He took the glasses from his eyes and smiled in admiration. A man after his own heart; broadcast a phony boat-burning message—the one transmission the Coasties will bust ass to answer—and send them on a wild-goose chase out in the Gulf while slicko here runs for home. And it would have worked except for one thing—Lance Cunningham, the narc from hell, was in the path of the load of dope.

Lance quickly turned on the engines and left the throttle in the idle position. He raised the radio antennas that had been lying along the gunwales, elevated the pedestal holding the blue light, then called Nick on the VHF radio.

The message was brief. "Coming your way."

"Roger. Don't let him see you. Wait until I give the signal."

A few minutes later Nick called. "Be advised, about eight mullet skiffs just passed our position, heading out to sea. They're going to make the transfer offshore. Let them load the skiffs. Repeat, let them load. Then we move in."

Lance immediately understood. The more boats caught loaded with dope, the more people who could be arrested. If he moved now, the drivers in the mullet skiffs would say they were doing nothing but fishing.

A half-hour later the mullet skiffs circled the crab boat. One was tied to each side. Each boat sent humpers aboard to help the crew. The first two were loaded and, gunwales almost awash, slowly made way toward the mouth of the pass. Once inside, they would be safe. Two more mullet skiffs pulled alongside the crab boat and the off-loading continued.

Up in the wheelhouse, Big Knocker stared into the darkness. His heavy brows lowered in concentration. Something was wrong tonight. The feral instinct for survival that had stood him in such good stead so many times was sending out disquieting alarms. Something was wrong. He was close enough to the beach that he felt safe in switching on his radar. The Coast Guard cutter, with its electronic detection equipment, was too far to the south to be a consideration. He looked at the radar and almost immediately saw two mullet skiffs, now a half-mile in front of the boat. He smiled in satisfaction. This would be one of his most successful loads. And he would not even be suspected because he was under a jail sentence. Then his smile turned to a frown. In the lower left corner of his radar screen was another target; a single target about a mile behind him. He studied the screen for a long moment. The single boat was slowly edging closer. Either the boat was making for Indian Key Pass or it was shadowing him. But one small boat—he knew it was small by the size of the radar return—could not harm him. Unless it was the cops. But the cops would have more than one boat. He bent closer to the screen. And then he saw them, almost masked by the mangrove thickets on the ocean side of Kingston Key. Three boats. What were they doing behind the mangroves?

At that moment Nick gave the signal to move in. The three boats jumped from the mangrove thicket, blue lights flashing as they fanned out to race toward the crab boat. Big Knocker knew one would stay behind to seize the two mullet skiffs. The other two would be coming for him. He looked over his left shoulder. Another blue light.

It was a bust.

Big Knocker slid down the ladder to the deck. "Throw it overboard! Overboard!" he shouted to the crew. He ran to the edge of the boat and told the skipper of the mullet skiff, "Throw it overboard. It's a bust."

The men on the rear of the crab boat and aboard the two mullet skiffs tied to the boat worked feverishly. They didn't need to be told what would happen if they were caught with dope aboard. The four mullet skiffs waiting to be loaded moved away from the crab boat.

No one noticed that Big Knocker had gone to the stern of the crab boat. He had pulled the go-fast boat closer so it wouldn't become entangled in the towline while the mullet skiffs were waiting to be loaded. He jumped aboard, fired up the engines, and almost immediately pushed the throttles full forward. He would head south for a half-mile or so, far enough to get around the blue lights; then he would swing into the Ten Thousand Islands.

Lance saw the quick surge of white water as the go-fast boat accelerated, and guessed what was happening. He changed course toward the mouth of Indian Key Pass. Maybe, just maybe, he could head the guy off. He knew it was the skipper of the crab boat; the man behind the load. And he wanted him. Whoever it was, they had to catch the main man.

The speed with which Lance dashed through the covey of mullet skiffs caused the skippers to instinctively retard the throttles. These cops were crazy. It was the same with the two loaded mullet skiffs making for the shore. One of the skippers looked over his shoulder, saw the blue light bearing down on him at high speed, and knew it was over. He stopped tossing bales overboard and sat down to wait for the inevitable.

Lance was zigging and zagging through the bales. The bale hunters of Everglades City would be out in force tonight. He continued toward the mouth of the pass. To the south, he could see the white froth behind the go-fast boat. It, too, had turned toward the islands and was racing flat out.

As the two boats, a half-mile or so apart, entered the islands, they were like two cars racing down parallel streets, visible to each other only at intersections. In this instance, the intersections were the open spaces between the small mangrove islands.

As Lance roared at full speed into the pass, he saw the go-fast boat sliding behind Kingston Key. He turned the corner by the number-four channel marker and raced up the channel. Between the small clumps of mangroves west of Jenkins Key he had another glimpse of the smuggler. How the hell could the guy run a boat back in there? Lance had studied the charts and knew the passage was little but shoals and mud and oyster bars. The doper was racing through there like it was blue water. If a doper could do it, America's hero could do it. Lance angled closer to the edge of the channel. As he rounded the eastern tip of Jenkins Key he looked at the doper's boat, read the vectors, and cut his boat hard to the right. He would intercept the doper in the big area of open water. The doper popped from behind the other side of Jenkins Key. Lance laughed. He was going to do it.

At that moment his boat hit a mud bank and decelerated so quickly that Lance was thrown forward against the wheel. He shook his head and looked up in time to seed the smuggler, who had cut across his bow and was now in the deep water of the channel, disappearing at high speed toward Everglades City.

Two hours later, guided by Lance's radio calls, Nick came slowly up the channel. He stopped at the edge of the mangroves and turned on a powerful searchlight. The beam picked out Lance, who was standing in water less than knee-deep, leaning on the side of his boat swatting at mosquitoes.

"Hey, jefe," Lance shouted in a jocular voice. "You glad DEA cleaned up Everglades City?"

Nick chuckled.

Lance slapped at the mosquitoes. "You took your sweet time getting here," he said.

"How old are you?"

Lance looked at Nick in bewilderment. "What do you mean, how old am I? I've spent half the night on a sandbar and you want to know how old I am."

"You must be a lot older than you look. You drive like old people do. I bet the last anybody saw of you was two hands on the steering wheel and the top of your pointed head sticking up from behind the seat.''

''I'm not old enough to have bales of white hair poking out of my nose and ears the way some people do.''

Nick touched his nose to see if hair was poking out. Then he shouted to Lance. ''We got a crab boat, two loaded mullet skiffs, and we arrested eight people. We got the names of another eight in the empty mullet skiffs. They're dirty but they didn't have any dope aboard so we had to let them go. By the time McBride gets through questioning everybody, we'll have enough information and enough intelligence to start our own task force.'' He paused. ''What'd you get?''

''Hey, jefe, get over here and pick me up.''

''What'd you get? I didn't send you out here just to ride around. What'd you get?''

''Well, I was chasing . . .'' Lance's voice trailed away in a mumble. Then he shouted, ''Pick me up.''

''Too shallow. Even hemorrhoids know not to go over there. You gotta swim.''

Five minutes later Lance, soaked and bedraggled, holding his pistol high out of the water, climbed aboard the boat.

''The narc from hell doesn't like to swim,'' he grumbled.

''What'd you get?'' Nick asked. He was grinning broadly.

Lance took off his shirt and jeans. He grinned. ''Maybe a park ranger.''

''Whatta you mean?''

''Hey, I wasn't sleeping out there. You think I was off the clock? I saw one of the park boats circling around in the pass. You got any extra clothes?''

''Look in the locker. The ranger didn't come up on the radio.''

''Maybe he didn't see all the boats. After all, there were only a dozen or so that went by him.'' Lance's voice was muffled as he dug through the locker. Nick believed in being prepared. There were two or three of everything inside the cavernous space.

"Get those blue coveralls. They're big enough for you. You think a ranger is working with these people?"

"What better escort through a national park can a bunch of dopers have than a park ranger?" Lance pulled on the coveralls. "And I don't think they bent him with money."

"What do you think it was?"

"Saw somebody else out here tonight."

"Don't drag it out."

"Remember McBride's intel report on December? One of Heart Attack's daughters?"

"So she's bent a ranger," Nick mused.

"Probably in more ways than one." Lance combed his hair with his fingers and moved to the left seat in the front of the boat. He looked at Nick. "We need a new boat."

"Why?"

"We need a blue-water boat. A faster boat. The Whaler won't cut it."

"That's a good boat," Nick said.

Lance snorted. "You can't have America's hero chasing dopers in a toy boat."

Nick grinned. "Only one thing wrong with the Whaler."

"Yeah?"

"It's got a loose screw on the steering wheel."

"Down, Boswell. Get down," Kimberly McBride ordered. Boswell, a great yellow cat, fat with age and arrogant simply because he was a cat, appeared astonished that she would raise her voice to him. He was standing atop the stove and he was nonplussed because each burner on the stove had a pan sitting on it. Boswell wended his way through the pots and sat down on the corner of the stove. He began licking his paws, then wiping his face. Kimberly stood up from the kitchen table and reached for Bos. She placed him on the floor. He looked over his shoulder at her in disdain, emitted an annoyed little squawk, flicked his tail once, and stalked off.

Bos was not happy with his new home. Ever since she had moved from Fort Lauderdale a year ago, Bos had made it abundantly clear that he did not approve. First, he began jumping atop her dresser in the middle of the night and, with a dainty paw, sweeping whatever was atop it onto the floor. Off went a perfume bottle, a small porcelain bowl, a picture of her son. More than once these middle-of-the-night crashes had caused her to sit bolt upright in bed. After she removed many of the items from the top of her dresser, Bos began jumping onto the bed and stalking about, purring with the volume of a John Deere tractor. If she ignored him, he began licking her eyelids with his raspy tongue. So she burrowed under the covers. That confused Bos for about two days. Then he discovered her alarm clock. A few minutes of swatting the buttons with his paw resulted in the alarm going off at three A.M. He squawked and ran away the first time, but then apparently decided he liked the middle-of-the-night furor this caused. Now, just infrequently enough to be unpredictable, he would set off the alarm in the middle of the night. Recently he had discovered still another way to show his displeasure—by urinating on one of the burners atop the electric stove. When Kimberly later used the stove, the most horrible odor imaginable permeated her house. After she cleaned the burner, Bos urinated on it again. Now she kept pots atop the stove.

In distress, she had called her veterinarian, a young woman who practiced holistic medicine and who used acupuncture with animals. The vet, although she was looked upon with benign skepticism by her professional colleagues, had cured animals with terminal disorders; animals other vets had given up on. After ten minutes of questions, the vet rendered her opinion: Bos was angry with Kimberly; he was disturbed about the new home, and he needed a lot of love and attention.

Kimberly understood. She felt as if she needed the same; that she was getting a bit waspish since her divorce three years earlier. The divorce had left her with deep scars that she was only beginning to be aware were there. Combined with the insecurity from her early years, the aftermath of the divorce sometimes left her feeling unable to open the door and go to work; that her life was out of control. She had been to therapy long enough to have an intellectual understanding of what was going on. Her father, a gruff career Army officer, had never once praised her. Not for anything. It might have come from his guilt over having an affair that had lasted for more than a decade. He died when she was eighteen and one of the last things he said to her was, "You'll never amount to anything." He never told her he loved her. He never held her the way most fathers hold their daughters. And her mother, who was dominated by Kimberly's father, did little but smile through it all. Life, for her mother, was one long silly smile. Kimberly, during her divorce from Pete, realized with fear how she had unconsciously replicated her childhood experience. Pete, after he became involved in an affair, became critical. Nothing pleased him. He never touched her. The two most important men in her life, her father and her husband, spurned her.

After she had divorced Pete, she left DEA and went to work for Nick as an intel analyst for the narcotics squad in the Broward County Sheriff's Office. The success of the Turks and Caicos operation, in which she played a pivotal role, proved she could do something well and enabled her to begin cutting the emotional ties to Pete. "The sperm donor" was how she sometimes referred to him now. He could no longer intimidate her or make her feel guilty. After all, he was the one who had had the affair; he was the one responsible for the dissolution of their marriage.

Nevertheless, being the sole parent of a five-year-old boy was difficult. Pete, the sperm donor, had visiting privileges but rarely spent time with his son. Nick had a son the same age as her son and occasionally took the two boys fishing. But her son needed a man in the house; some sort of role model, an example to live by.

She looked at her watch—five A.M. In two hours she would have to awaken her son. They would have breakfast. She would drop him off at the Montessori school and then go to work.

She sat at her kitchen table and caressed the crystals spread before her. She felt the warmth of the rose quartz, then fondled the green malachite, the blue tourmaline, and lingered for a while over the pyramid-shaped piece of lapis lazuli.

In the middle of the night Kimberly had been awakened by a nagging something in the back of her mind; something to do with the inventory of equipment found aboard the crab boats and mullet skiffs Nick had seized. Among the electronic equipment on each boat was a two-meter radio. She had never heard of a two-meter radio being used by smugglers. She wasn't quite sure what a two-meter radio was.

The Everglades City case was a hodgepodge of disparate elements. Even though a number of people had been arrested, it was difficult to tie them together. There was no sense of motion in the case. It was like trying to control a giant bowl of Jell-O. The case was extremely frustrating to everyone but Nick and Lance. Nick plodded along, absolutely unshakable in his belief that ultimately he would prevail. And to Lance it was all a game.

Impulsively Kimberly dug into her purse and found the list of home telephone numbers for Nick's investigators. She thumbed down the list until she came to the name M. Dickman. She dialed the number. Dickman and Bill Yaeger, whom, for some reason, everyone called Joe Willy, were the computer and electronics wizards of Nick's office. Both were former cops with the Fort Myers police department. Their innovations in electronic-surveillance techniques were legendary. They had used video cameras and thirty-five-millimeter cameras with night scopes before anyone else in Florida, including the feds, had discovered the technique. Because the Fort Myers police department, like most police departments, always was strapped for money, they became expert scroungers. As their equipment was not the best, the techniques and adaptations had to be good. When they put a body bug on someone, it worked. When they put a bug in a car, it worked. When they debriefed someone, the recording was loud and clear; they learned early never to make a tape recording in a room with an air conditioner. It causes a blur of white noise in the background. They learned to use the antenna for a car radio as the antenna for their police radios so there would be no telltale extra antenna to alert the crooks. Both were computer programmers who were working on a new program for investigators to use. All Kimberly knew about it was that it had something to do with tracking telephone calls.

"Hello," came Dickman's gruff voice. He was all business and had a very low tolerance for small talk. Maybe that was why everyone called him by his last name. He was a very macho guy who probably got into more fights than any other investigator. He was a tough, no-nonsense guy; a real pro. She heard a rustling noise in the background and knew he was reaching for a cigarette. The guy smoked constantly. He ignored No Smoking signs in the office.

"Dickman. McBride. Sorry to awaken you, but this is important."

"What do you want?"

"Have you ever heard of dopers using two-meter radios?"

Dickman took a puff from his cigarette. "Why?"

"I was looking at the inventory of the equipment on that crab boat, the one seized in the deal at Everglades City the other night, and it had a two-meter radio on board. Is that common?"

"Where are you?"

"At home. Why?"

"You're worrying about two-meter radios in the middle of the night?"

"Couldn't sleep."

She heard the sound of Dickman's raspy breath as he puffed hard on the cigarette. Then he said, "I heard you were pretty smart."

"What does that mean?"

"Don't get huffy. There have been two-meter radios on every dope boat boarded or seized during the past six months. Nobody's paid any attention. Joe Willy and I just snapped to it. Guess I was surprised by your question. You read the Coast Guard reports about vessels they've seized?"

"Yes, but—"

"Joe Willy noticed . . ." Dickman broke into a spell of coughing. "Goddamn cigarettes," he mumbled. "Joe Willy noticed that when the Coasties seize a vessel and inventory the contents, they never break out the types of radios. They just list 'radios' or 'electronic equipment.' Right?"

"Yes."

"Well, Joe Willy and I went to the yard where they keep seized boats and went through them. Every one of them had a two-meter radio. Dopers have been using them for God only knows how long. Nobody snapped to it."

"Why not? That's important, very important, for intelligence purposes."

Dickman took another puff on his cigarette. She could hear him. And for a moment she wanted a cigarette. "You're right. A two-meter radio is a ham radio. It requires a license to operate. You have certain operating procedures that have to be used; call signs and proper signing-off techniques."

"You think the dopers in Everglades City are using them? Is that why our scanners are not picking up radio traffic?"

"Looks that way. We need to get down there and check out some boats. Those people ain't exactly rocket scientists, but when it comes to getting around the law, they've had lots of experience. If they're using them, it explains why we never pick up smuggling talk on VHF.''

''Dickman, why didn't the Coast Guard tell us about this? It could have opened up the case months ago.''

''Lemme tell you about the Coasties, McBride. They're out there letting the world know they're the number-one drug busters, right? The guys doing more than anyone else.''

''They give that impression.''

''The Coasties are on the high seas; the ones who first intercept the big loads of dope. I'll tell you something about smuggling grass; it has an odor that cannot be hidden. No matter how you wrap it, the odor is there.''

''Okay.''

''You're talking about a shrimp boat with maybe twenty tons aboard. You come up on it from downwind and you know you've made a hit. From maybe a quarter-mile away you can smell it. I'll tell you something else. A trained dog cannot be tricked. No matter how the dope is wrapped or what substances are used to throw off the dog, if there's grass aboard a boat, he'll find it.''

''So?''

Dickman's voice grew angry. ''So the Coast Guard won't put dogs aboard their boats. They refuse to use one of the cheapest and best tools available.''

''Why?''

''Because they don't know how to teach a dog to shit in a sandbox. They don't want dog crap on their clean pretty boats. So they don't use dogs.''

''You're not serious?''

''It's too early in the morning to joke. Come by my office later and I'll give you some stuff on two-meter radios. Joe Willy and I were about to ask Nick to buy some equipment to monitor two-meter broadcasts. You back us up?''

''Dickman, I'll do more than that. Let's put together a list of everything we need; I've been thinking about this for a while, and this is the time to go to the state

attorney. I'm thinking perhaps of a van filled with everything electronic you can put in there. Video cameras. Still cameras. The works. Sort of a roving
miniature NSA. What do you think?''

"I think you're okay.''

"Thanks, Dickman.''

"For a woman.''

"Never mind, Dickman.''

She hung up and reached again for the piece of lapis
lazuli. And she wondered how many loads of marijuana had gotten through simply because the U.S.
Coast Guard could not train dogs to use a sandbox.

10

The most striking and remarkable thing about Everglades City is the buzzards; they're on the ground, on
pilings along the river, in the trees, and in the air.
They are everywhere; and in such great numbers that
someone should consider renaming the town Buzzard
City.

As one drives across the bridge over the Barron River
and enters town, a row of fish houses along the river
is visible to the right. A trash dump, placed between
an apartment building and the river, is near the fish
houses. It's understandable that the buzzards might
congregate atop the trash dump—they are there by the
dozens. But what surprises one is how they stand
around the grassy open area surrounding the dump.
They stand there calmly, like commuters awaiting a
bus. And they seem to have no fear of humans. You
can approach buzzards here at a very close range; so
close that their full ugliness can be appreciated. It's
easy to identify a buzzard. Whether in flight or on the
ground, they are distinctive. For instance, in flight,
pelicans are identified by their downward-pointing

wings; eagles and other raptors by flat horizontal wings; and buzzards by their distinctive upward-pointing V shape. In flight, buzzards have a certain lazy elegance, perhaps because their features are blurred by distance. Up close there is nothing at all elegant about them. The features of a buzzard, or—if one wishes to be precise—the turkey vulture, have very little sheen. They are a flat dull black. Other features one notices at close range are their mottled skinned heads, the wary eyes, and the long hooked beaks. The buzzard is said to be the only bird in Florida with a sense of smell, a fact that, combined with its obvious predilection for Everglades City, should cause city fathers to pause a moment. When the buzzards perch atop the trash dump or stand on the grass, their heads are not raised as is the eagle's, nor is there an air of pride about them. Instead they skulk; their heads sink low. Their bent wings are raised. And it looks for all the world as if they're wearing capes with high collars. Their wings are slightly spread in an effort to stay cool, and there is about them a certain repulsive malevolence. They are waiting; waiting for something to die and to rot.

More than one guest at the Rod and Gun Club, the faded but elegant caravansary on the Barron River, has been startled when leaving the hotel for an early-morning walk and coming upon two or three trees filled with roosting buzzards; dozens of buzzards. They even hunker atop the cross-members of light poles, lined up like black-suited deacons of doom.

In addition to the abundance of buzzards, another thing one notices upon entering Everglades City is that the town is sun-blasted and faded; there is an air of seediness to everything. And the road signs are riddled with bullets. The tight clusters of clean holes indicate it was not random shotgun blasts that ripped the signs, but rather half a clip from an automatic rifle.

To the discerning eye, crab boats along the docks are extraordinarily well-equipped with electronics. A veritable forest of antennae sprout from the wheel-houses. Many boats carry radar, loran, two or three radios, and several fly the skull and crossbones.

The Homes in Everglades City are small frame structures; mostly white and yellow. A few are neat and freshly painted, but most of them are tired and wan. Many are built on stilts. This does three things: raises the structure in case of a storm surge, provides a cooling breeze, and protects dwellers somewhat from hordes of carnivorous insects. The yards are clean, and a few are filled with the flowers that are the glory of subtropical Florida—bougainvillea, hibiscus, amaryllis, firecracker, oleander, orange trumpet vine, periwinkle, poinsettia, and lantana. Grapefruit trees afford local people the luxury of picking their own breakfast fruit, but for some inexplicable reason, most of the heavy-bearing trees remain unpicked.

While most of the houses are essentially the same, some stand out because of what one sees in the yards. There may be a screened-in swimming pool, an air boat, a swamp buggy, a shiny new car, a four-wheel-drive pickup, and even an ATV. All are toys bought by smugglers. A surprising number of the cars and four-wheel-drive vehicles are new. If you are driving through town and see the man of the house come out and he's carrying a new rifle and wearing a pair of six-hundred-dollar cowboy boots, you have found a player.

Everglades City has a tiny airstrip on a point between the Barron River and Chokoloskee Bay. The runway headings are one-five and three-three. The shortness of the strip dictates a precise approach. A pilot must be careful when landing on runway one-five or he might hit the channel marker in the Barron River. People in Everglades City laughingly tell visitors of their "international airport," a facility that occasionally has flights from Colombia, Jamaica, and the Bahamas.

For most of the year, Everglades City is home only to the locals. From April until December the blistering heat, humidity, frequent thunderstorms, and plagues of voracious mosquitoes keep tourists away. The tourists come when much of country is in the dead of win-

ter, usually by car, and they usually prefer the Rod
and Gun Club, the old hotel on the river where several
U.S. presidents have visited. Locals avoid the Rod and
Gun Club; they like the town's other hotel, the Captain's Table. Tourists are easy for locals to identify.
Their cars have out-of-state license plates; they dress
in what they imagine to be "Florida clothes," and
they wander about town snapping pictures, all the
while with the fixed stupid smiles of those who know
they are strangers in a strange land. In the Oyster
House, the best of the local restaurants and perhaps
the one spot where tourists and locals sit side by side,
the tourist invariably order stone crab, the local delicacy available in the winter and more than sufficient
reason to go to Everglades City. People from all over
America go to Everglades City in the late fall and winter solely to eat the legs of the stone crab—to many,
the grandest delicacy of the sea.

Most of the mullet caught locally, a fish that ac-
counts for ninety percent of the local fish harvest, is
shipped to Japan. The stone-crab harvest—depending
upon the vagaries of the season—range from a low of
about sixteen thousand pounds to upwards of a quarter
of a million pounds.

Everglades City is somewhere near the middle of the
forty-five-mile stretch of Ten Thousand Islands between Marco Island and Cape Sable. Much of the surrounding country is part of the Everglades National
Park, a refuge of almost one and a half million acres.
More than a million acres of the park are classified as
"wilderness" and are thus subject to all the restrictions
of any wilderness area. Six hundred and twenty-five
thousand acres of water are in the park. The endangered or threatened species around Everglades City in-
clude the Florida panther, West Indian manatee, brown
pelican, peregrine falcon, Florida Everglades kite,
southern bald eagle, Cape Sable seaside sparrow,
American alligator, American crocodile, and the
hawksbill, green, and loggerhead turtles. No one can
kill, wound, capture, molest, remove, or disturb a long

list of flora and fauna in the wilderness around Everglades City.

Everglades City was the county seat of Collier County until 1960, when Hurricane Donna skipped across the four-mile stretch of islands separating Everglades City from the Gulf of Mexico. Donna arrived at high tide, at slack water, and lingered for hours, brutally lashing the little town with winds of more than one hundred and fifty miles an hour. A fifteen-foot storm surge roared in from the Gulf, sliced Jewel Key into three pieces, demolished several islands, changed the shape of dozens of other islands, and, with virtually no loss of energy, rumbled on at freight-train speed for Everglades City. Everglades City is five feet above sea level, and when the wall of water struck, it swept away everything in its path. After the storm passed, a pile of dead animals ten feet high was collected and then tossed into the river. Even today, three decades later, the signs of Donna are clear throughout the Ten Thousand Islands.

After Donna virtually leveled Everglades City, the seat of government moved to Naples on the west coast. Naples is a half-hour in time but a hundred years in distance from Everglades City. It is a boom town; a city on the make; an overgrown fishing village that almost overnight has become synonymous with tourism and wealth. Marco Island, just below Naples, is one of the wealthiest communities in America; an island chockablock with high-rise condominiums; all built since Donna visited. Marco Island glitters and sparkles in the bright sunshine, and no one seems to care—surely they know—that the steel-and-glass-and-cement towers are temporary; that the next Donna, the next full-blown hurricane with winds of a hundred and fifty miles an hour and with a fifteen-foot storm surge, will level the island with a horrific loss of life. Such a storm is overdue.

When Naples became the county seat, most government officials were from Everglades City and began commuting down Highway 41, the road that links Homestead to Naples; the Tamiami Trail, or, as it is known locally, simply "The Trail." The good old boys who were government officials looked upon county government as pretty much a home-grown affair. Fathers, sons, cousins, in-laws, were all mixed together. And nowhere was the family connection stronger than in law enforcement. Almost everyone in the sheriff's department was related. In addition, the sheriff and his deputies knew all the families in Everglades City. If they were not related, they were good friends. The boys who were to become cops grew up side by side with the boys who were to become dope smugglers.

State Attorney Joe D'Alessandro in Fort Myers recognized the potential problem. After all, there was no federal law enforcement between Tampa and Miami. Southwest Florida was wide open. It was clear to D'Alessandro that a remote incestuous community with a long history of lawbreaking could have a corruptive influence on law enforcement. And he was right. It seemed that almost every law-enforcement officer sent to Everglades City became bent.

The Florida Highway Patrol and the Collier County sheriff at one time shared a substation on Highway 41 at the turnoff for Everglades City. A tall and very expensive radio tower was installed so they could be linked with the outside world. The station was closed after eleven troopers were fired for cheating on their travel vouchers. The greatest amount involved for a single trooper was about four thousand dollars; a relatively small amount of money to destroy one's career. Cops, perhaps more than most other people, have difficulty making transfers from law enforcement into the mainstream of business and commerce. Their training as cops gives them a certain mind-set that often does not adjust to other jobs; once a cop, always a cop. But there was something in Everglades City, something inherent in the remoteness, the wildness, the primitive nature, the sultry heat, that caused cops to think normal rules of conduct did not apply. Cops who might never have been bent in any other environment became bent in Everglades City. The careers of dozens of cops were ruined.

Men of integrity found it very difficult in Everglades City. The son of a cop would be classmates with the son of a drug smuggler. The cop was struggling to make a living and could not provide all he would like for his family. The son of the smuggler wore gold jewelry, a fancy watch, had a new car, a fast boat, and lots of spending money. The son of the cop might rarely eat dinner at even the Oyster House, but the sons of dope smugglers jumped into their boats and went down to Key West or across to Naples for dinner.

Cops from the outside were immediately recognized when they came to Everglades City. The sheriff's son, until he was allowed to make a deal with the feds about his smuggling activities, was radio operator in the state-patrol substation. In addition to the sheriff's radio, he had radios for the state patrol, the Florida Department of Law Enforcement, the Marine Patrol, and the state attorney's office. It was impossible for any local or state law-enforcement agency to work in the area without the sheriff knowing it. Federal agents tended to look upon Everglades City as a small insignificant anomaly—the way the Bahamian government has long looked upon the island of Bimini—sure there was some smuggling over there, but not enough to be significant. And since the sheriff made it clear he did not want any federal agents in his county, they generally stayed away.

Everglades City was long overlooked by law enforcement for another reason. It is a small remote part of the Twentieth Judicial Circuit, the largest judicial circuit in Florida, and perhaps the most diverse in America. Two of the richest and fastest-growing communities in America are near Fort Myers. Naples has rednecks and fishermen and multimillionaires. The inland counties are cattle country, where, until a few years ago, deputies wore blue jeans, cowboy boots, and six-shooters. South and west of Lake Okeechobee is sugarcane country; a flat sun-baked land of misery for thousands of West Indians imported each year to cut the cane. Other migrant workers move through by the thousands. Southwest Florida has large, generally impoverished, black communities, and a new community of Hispanics is making its voice heard. And off to the side, stuck in the mosquito-infested wilderness of the Ten Thousand Islands, is Everglades City.

When outside cops come to Everglades City, they usually broadcast their presence by having strategy meetings at Jane's Restaurant in Copeland, about five miles from Everglades City. Jane's also is a favorite restaurant for smugglers. If the locals see out-of-town cops—and cops are easy to recognize—the word immediately goes out. And whatever deal has been in the offing for that night is canceled.

Outside cops who naively believe they should display local courtesy and notify the sheriff before coming into Everglades City, are usually introduced to December. She, in turn, introduces a dozen or so cops to the realms of unearthly delight; and in the process co-opts them, sending them back home sore, filled with embarrassment and remorse, and, most important of all, with official reports minimizing the amount of smuggling in Everglades City.

So while the buzzards soar overhead, stand about the dock and the garbage dump, and roost in the trees and utility poles along the Barron River, the people of Everglades City go about their business. They are good, hardworking, family people who are only trying to make a living. If they occasionally smuggle in a little weed, so what? It puts food on their tables and clothes on their backs. No one is hurt. All the people of Everglades City want is to be left alone.

11

April and May, the two middle daughters of Heart Attack, looked at each other, smiled, and climbed into the cabs of the two enormous garbage trucks. April led the way out of Everglades City. About a mile away at Carnestown, the intersection of State Road 29 and U.S. 41, she turned right.

April and May moved easily up through the gears on the big trucks, double-clutching with practiced ease; as they held the RPM's high and smoothly accelerated the sound was like moaning, slowly awakening monsters of the macadam. Black diesel smoke poured from the twin chrome stacks behind the cab of each truck. Only the slightest puffs revealed when April and May changed gears as they moved eastbound and down along the Trail toward Miami.

As the sound of the two trucks faded, a woman in the A-frame store across the road from the service station in Carnestown smiled. The A-frame had been built as the headquarters for the Florida State Patrol and the Collier County sheriff's office. But then Nick Brown had discovered the sweetheart deal the cops had going and that the sheriff's son, who was the radio operator for all the law-enforcement agencies working there, was a doper.

The cop shop at Carnestown had been closed for several months. In its place was the Chamber of Commerce and all sorts of cheap and shabby knickknacks for tourists: plastic alligators, rubber snakes, toy wigwams; tawdry gewgaws that, so it would seem, not even a New York tourist would buy.

April and May barely slowed as they went through Ochopee. A cop there looked up at the sound of the two smoke-belching behemoths. April rolled down the

tinted window, then leaned out and waved, her blonde
hair streaming, her smile like a sunrise over the Everglades. She reached up and pulled the cord for the
air horn. With the touch of a maestro she played the
cord, causing the long mournful wail to rise high and
then fall away like the sound of a distant train whistle.

After April came May, equally beautiful, as she
waved at the cop.

The cop, mouth open, lifted his hand in an almost
diffident wave. "Great God Almighty," he sighed.

Five minutes later, the two-meter radio hidden under the panel in each truck, broke squelch. "Bears at
Forty Mile Bend," said a soft voice.

April smiled. She and May knew what to do. Simultaneously the two young women turned off the air
conditioners in the big trucks. They lowered the tinted
windows and let the hot humid midmorning air of the
Everglades blow through the cabs. Each unbuttoned
the top two buttons of her sleeveless cotton blouse.
The old ways worked best; that's how they became old
ways.

By the time the two trucks, running almost bumper
to bumper, reached Monroe Station, April and May
were perspiring. Their upper lips glistened with tiny
crystalline diamonds and their hairlines were moist.
Their thin blouses stuck to bare skin, outlining and
emphasizing the abundance of their blessings.

It is said that a man died for every mile of highway
when the Tamiami Trail was being constructed. The
two-lane road pierces the heart of the Big Cypress National Preserve and the Everglades before slicing into
the southwest corner of Miami. The dark artery called
the Tamiami Canal runs along the north side of the
road. Australian pines form a barrier of sorts along a
few miles of the Trail; but most of the road is through
a trackless swamp. The Trail is a long, lonesome, and
lightly traveled stretch of road.

As the trucks rounded Forty Mile Bend, April
looked in the mirror. Except for May's truck snuggled
up tightly behind, there was no other traffic in sight;
and that meant no other traffic for miles along the road

just traveled. April saw the state troopers ahead, stopping all eastbound vehicles, and she and May lightly applied the air brakes, causing much wheezing and sighing as the two trucks eased to a stop.

" 'Morning," said April to the grizzled state trooper who, along with a much younger partner, was working the roadblock.

" 'Morning, ma'am," said the unsmiling sergeant. "See your driver's license and proof of insurance, please?"

"Sure can," said April. She opened the door wide and swung her bare legs over the edge of the seat. She slid forward a few inches, causing her shorts to ride high on her legs; to push and bunch into her crotch. The sergeant looked away but the young trooper was in hypershock.

April slid forward, then dropped to the pavement. Her breasts bounced. She held one leg to the side and, with an embarrassed look, pulled at the bottom of her shorts.

"Didn't know I'd be talking to the law this morning," she said in half-apology. "Else I'd a dressed better." She wiped perspiration from her brow. "God, it's hot."

"Do you have your license and proof of insurance?" the trooper repeated.

April smiled and reached with her right hand into her rear pocket for her license. An expression of perplexity came over her face. She reached back with her left hand, apparently not aware of how the movement thrust her breasts forward until they seemed anxious to leap from her blouse and attack the trooper.

"Here they are," she said.

The sergeant examined the documents, then returned them to her. He wrinkled his nose at the smell arising from the truck. "What are you hauling, ma'am?"

April jabbed her left thumb over her shoulder. "Me and my sister back there, we're hauling garbage to a landfill in Miami. City garbage. We from Everglades City."

"No waste-disposal system over there?"

"Naw, we just a little town there in the edge of the national park. Trying to be good citizens by hauling our garbage away. Park Service is real concerned about the environment and about pollution."

The sergeant looked at the young trooper and motioned for him to check out the truck. The trooper would rather have checked out the two young women. But he grabbed the chrome handles along the front of the truck bed and muscled himself up the steps. He peered over the top, wrinkled his mouth, and made an exclamation of disgust at the odor rising from the garbage rotting under the hot morning sun.

"Sarge, it's garbage."

"Probe it," the sergeant said.

"Yes, sir." The young trooper climbed down as May sauntered up from the second truck.

"What you doing to our garbage?" she said with a laugh. She wiped the perspiration from her neck. Her hand slid across the top of her breast, loosening another button. She put her hands on her hips and turned to look up at the truck. When she turned, her blouse gaped open. Her left leg relaxed at the knee while her right leg remained straight, thrusting her hips to the side.

"Just checking you out . . . I mean, just checking the garbage . . . I mean putting in the probe . . . I mean . . ." The young trooper gave up and walked several steps to the patrol car, where he seized a long metal rod.

"You looking for drugs, ain't you?" May said as if the very idea were ridiculous.

In an effort to salvage himself, the trooper made a jabbing motion with the metal rod and said, "I have to stick this in and . . ." He blushed as May laughed.

The trooper climbed up the truck again. As he swung the probe around, May, legs spread and hands on hips, looked up at him and said, "You be careful up there."

"I will," he said, looking down. "I do this every day." He didn't want to stir up the garbage and cause it to stink any more than it already did. He slid the probe in at an angle. From the ground the sergeant couldn't see what he was doing.

"You do that every day, you must be pretty good at it," May said.

"Doesn't take much skill. Anybody can do it." He looked down, enjoying the view.

"Not anybody can do it right."

The odor from the garbage was overpowering. Rotted fish were across the top of the truck. The trooper wanted to climb down, but he also wanted to continue enjoying the view of May's sweat-covered breasts.

"Find anything?" the sergeant said.

"No, sir."

"How often you ladies haul these loads?" the sergeant asked.

"Couple times a week," April said.

"Lot of garbage for such a small town."

"You right about that. But it's all the stuff from the fish houses and crab houses," April said. "Being in the park, we're not supposed to dump that in the river. Park Service asked us to haul it away."

"The city got a federal grant," May interrupted. Her voice was proud.

"Me and my sister went to the SBA; got us a loan, then signed the contract with the city," said April. She laughed. "Beats working on a crab boat."

"You need to get a tarpaulin to cover those trucks," the sergeant said. "Some of that stuff might blow off on the road."

"Nobody ever told us that," April said in surprise.

The sergeant nodded. "The law says can't have open trucks hauling material on the public roads of this state. Trucks have to be covered. You get yourself a tarpaulin."

"Where we get those?" May asked.

"I don't know. Check with some other truckers. But you better have them when you come along next time. I catch you again, and I'll have to give you a ticket."

"We'll do it this week," April said.

"Awright, ladies, that's all. Won't hold you up any

longer.'' The sergeant nodded. The young trooper had a painted-on puppy-dog smile and his head was bobbing up and down like an out-of-control marionette.

The two young women smiled, nodded, and both said ''Thanks'' as they turned and sauntered back to their trucks, their hips rolling like well-oiled precision equipment. April gave the two cops a good look at her legs and the workings of her behind as she climbed into the cab.

Then the two women were gone. In a cloud of black diesel smoke mixed with the rhythmic rising song of powerful engines and the smooth meshing of gears, the trucks slowly disappeared into the haze far down the Trail.

A mile down the road, as her truck was rocking along at fifty-five miles an hour, windows up and air conditioner blasting away, April picked up the microphone of the two-meter radio.

''Wild Cherry to Proud Princess. How you hear me?''

''Proud Princess. Come on.''

April responded; her voice filled with disgust. ''Ugghhhh! Did you see how that slimy little bear was looking at you? Made me want to throw up on that monkey suit of his.''

May came back. ''And the other one; the old bear; God, he was horrible. I wanted to skin him. I wanted to take my knife and cut off his balls.''

April laughed, a high lilting sound like the soft tinkling of crystal bells. ''Main thing is, we're rolling. Free and clear. Wild Cherry signing off.''

''Proud Princess signing off.''

The state troopers manning the roadblock at Forty Mile Bend, particularly the young trooper, would have been astonished if someone had told them the two women in the big trucks were lesbians. They wouldn't have believed it. But it was true.

And that was not all. As the two beautiful young women motored on down the Trail toward Miami, their two trucks pouring out black diesel smoke from the high twin chrome stacks on each cab, an experienced ear might have thought the trucks were laboring. And they were; not so much from the garbage as from the ten tons of marijuana each truck hauled under the garbage.

12

Kimberly sat in the straight-backed chair at her kitchen table, feet planted firmly on the floor, back straight, and caressed the onyx necklace as she stared at the screen of the lap-top computer. It was 6:15 A.M. and two hours earlier Bos had awakened her when he punched the alarm. Unable to return to sleep, she dressed, placed her computer on the kitchen table, and went to work. Now, as she caressed the necklace, she closed her eyes and thought of grounding, focusing, and centering. After a moment her fingers dropped lower and found the violent tourmaline and she thought of calmness, regality, harmonizing, and increasing her mental powers. Then she touched the red coral, a stone with the qualities of heat and high action; a stone that enables one to break through long-established mental conditions and create rapid change.

Suddenly her eyes snapped open. Her mouth tightened. She almost flung her hand away from the necklace toward the papers on the table. She was an honor graduate of Penn State University and far too bright to give the business of crystals a second thought. Occasionally she realized that this interest in crystals was like the turbulence behind a fast-moving boat; it was part of the turmoil from the wake of her divorce. Women do odd things after a divorce. One of the female lawyers on the prosecutor's staff had recently divorced and announced to the staff she was buying a camera and a sports car and having a boob job. She already had the camera and sports car, and next week was taking a week's vacation to go to Jacksonville for the boob job. That others indulged in such behavior brought no consolation to Kimberly McBride.

She pushed back from the table in something approaching self-digust and said to the empty room, "The only thing that works is work." She shook her head as if to clear the mists of necromancy, picked up the sharp pencil, tapped it on the table a few times, and pulled the papers close.

A rueful smile crossed her lips as she studied the report she had prepared for Nick. Lance thought she was under some sort of spell because she studied crystals. But he, and almost every investigator on Nick's staff, was under an even more mesmeric spell; the thought that they were spinning their wheels investigating marijuana smugglers; that while marijuana was illegal, it was a relatively harmless weed and that the real crux of the Everglades City investigation was the cocaine smuggled in with the marijuana. The cops seemed to be embarrassed that they were investigating the most commonly used and heavily abused illegal substance in America. Next to alcohol, which was legal, more Americans regularly used marijuana than any other drug—somewhere around twenty-five million people—and their ages ran from eight or nine years old up to God knows where. Retired people in their seventies had been arrested for marijuana usage in Fort Myers. Nick knew how his investigators felt, so he directed Kimberly to go into the computer and prepare a report that, as he said, "will change their minds and charge their batteries."

He wanted his investigators to realize that the people of Everglades City were not simply harmless fishermen, but rather Americans who had declared war on their own country.

The pervasive feeling, among both the general population and—to a surprising degree—the law-enforcement community was, since marijuana was relatively harmless, why place undue emphasis on it? Why not go after the sexy stuff, the crack cocaine, methamphetamines, heroin, uppers, downers, prescriptions, acid, and all the rest of the pharmacological cornucopia of illegal substances that Americans were snorting, smoking, swallowing, drinking, and injecting? Why waste time with a few pounds of *Cannabis sativa;* the blessed hemp of the Rastas?

Kimberly tapped her pencil on the table. She ached for a cigarette. Her left hand unconsciously crept to the second necklace, the one of red coral, as she looked at the first page of the report. It was a summary; brief enough for the investigators to read without feelings as if she were subjecting them to a correspondence course on the evils of marijuana. It was a factual, straightforward listing.

She had considered America's drug problem far more than most people. And she had access to data most people didn't know existed. She thought she had a couple of answers; that she knew what should be done. But no one asked her. Policy, like snowballs, rolled only downhill. George Bush, the man who last fall had said what the drug problem needed was a few good volunteers, was the man in the catbird seat. Old George was going to solve the most wretched social problem in America with volunteers. If it weren't so sad, it would be humorous. If George would call her, she would give him other solutions. For instance, he could use the seized assets of drug smugglers to finance construction of new jails, additional cops, and treatment programs. Dope money also could be used to clean up drug-ravaged neighborhoods; to educate parents. Each family could reach out to another family until the number of drug-free families was greater and more powerful than the druggie families. Emphasis had to be placed on long-range-prevention goals even while law enforcement kept up the pressure. That would do for a start.

Kimberly glanced at her watch and decided to go over the report one more time. She was not worried about the accuracy of the report. Most of the information came from Sue Rusche at the National Drug Information Center in Atlanta. The center contained more than four hundred thousand documents and was probably the single greatest source of drug-abuse information in America. While Kimberly was not worried about the accuracy of her information, she was concerned about something most people would consider almost trivial—typos. The most brilliant person in the state attorney's office, and she was worried about typos. Her reports had gained so much weight that the investigators had begun going over them word by word, looking for a misspelled word or incorrect punctuation, anything they could find that would prove the infallible Kimberly McBride had made a boo-boo.

Kimberly scanned the first page.

In New Hampshire a bus driver lost control of his vehicle and seven children were killed in the wreck. Blood tests revealed the driver had measurable amounts of THC, the psychoactive ingredient of marijuana, in his blood.

In Washington, D.C., the driver of a double-decker tourist bus tried to go under a bridge that was far too low. Thirty-two people were injured. The driver had been smoking marijuana.

In Brownsville, Texas, a sixteen-year-old kid killed his mother because she nagged him about smoking marijuana.

A tourist jumped out of an Atlanta hotel window and killed himself. He had been smoking marijuana.

A man went berserk on Madison Avenue in New York, shooting at whatever struck his fancy. One person was killed. The shooter had been smoking marijuana.

During a hotel pot party, one of the participants pulled an automatic weapon and started shooting. Twelve people died.

A prison inmate killed a warden during an office interview. The inmate was high on marijuana.

A Brooklyn subway driver wrecked his train. One person was killed and one hundred and thirty-five persons injured. The driver was high.

A Conrail train crash resulted in the death of sixteen people and injuries to a hundred and seventy-eight people. The driver had been smoking marijuana.

A commuter airliner crashed in Colorado and nine people were killed. Blood tests revealed high amounts of THC in the pilot's body.

A New Jersey tour bus ran off the Garden State Parkway and forty-four people were injured. The driver was high.

A Department of Transportation study found that in the previous two years there had been sixty rail accidents in which thirty-three people died and three hundred and sixty people were injured—in all of these, one or more of the railroad employees involved were using marijuana.

Another study revealed that among murder victims in San Antonio, Texas, forty percent of those between the ages of twenty and thirty were using marijuana. And in traffic accidents in which there were fatalities, twenty percent of those judged to be at fault were using marijuana.

More than one-third of the patients at a Maryland shock-trauma center had used marijuana before they were injured.

A nationwide study of big-city emergency rooms revealed that among patients admitted for drug-abuse treatment, marijuana was second only to crack cocaine.

Kimberly flipped the page. The second part of the report dealt with the deleterious health effects of marijuana; memory loss, birth defects in the third generation of users, increased pulmonary diseases, infertility—it went on and on. It was incredible to Kimberly that a data base containing hundreds of irrefutable examples of marijuana's baneful effects could be ignored by so many; that the belief marijuana caused no harm was so pervasive.

The third part of her report documented the connection between marijuana and other drugs. Seventy-four percent of those who used marijuana on a regular basis also used cocaine. There no longer was any doubt that marijuana was what drug counselors call a gateway drug.

She made a noise of distaste and disgust; partly because she had been as guilty as anyone about overlooking the ubiquitous nature, the ramifications, and the seriousness of marijuana usage. She felt a brief flash of anger that she had not known all this. Maybe Pete and her father had been right; maybe she did not know how to do a good job. Maybe she should stay home and do a better job raising her son. But she had to work. She sighed, pulled the necklaces together in her hand, and continued reading.

The final page spoke of the amount of marijuana being smuggled through Everglades City. After the glory days of pot in the 1960's, the federal drug-interdiction effort swung to more glamorous and newsworthy drugs. The feds explained the ho-hum attitude toward marijuana by saying the prevalence of home-grown marijuana was far greater than imported marijuana. The official position of the feds was that so many tons of domestic marijuana of such superior quality were being grown, and the THC content was so inordinately high, that no longer was there any need to concentrate on interdicting those smuggling marijuana. The amount smuggled was insignificant. The need was to stop domestic growers, and that was the responsibility of the individual states. Thus the federal government, like Pontius Pilate, washed its hands of the whole unpleasant business and moved on to headlines about cocaine.

Kimberly's conclusion was that the government's conclusion was balderdash. The feds had been brainwashed by the ceaseless lobbying of such organizations as NORML, the National Organization to Reform Marijuana Laws, which said over and over that domestic marijuana was the biggest cash crop in America; that it contributed more to the American economy than corn, wheat, soy beans, or any other crop. NORML, however specious its logic, was a genius at getting good press. Virtually every newspaper in the country had run the NORML press releases about the pervasive nature of home-grown dope. No one stopped to think how this self-serving drivel contributed to NORML's agenda of legalizing marijuana.

All one had to do to show the fallacy of NORML's position, and the fallacy of the U.S. government's echo of that position, was to take a look at the amount of marijuana coming into America. God knows how much marijuana was being smuggled by boat or aircraft into other parts of the country; but the tonnage coming into Everglades City alone was enough to refute the positions of both NORML and the U.S. government. If pot was America's number-one cash crop, and if the THC was ten or twelve percent, and if domestic pot was the best in the world, then why in the hell were hundreds and hundreds of tons of what, by extension of the government's position, was low-THC inferior pot being smuggled?

The answer was as simple as it was inescapable. NORML's trumpet-blaring about domestic pot was the ultimate triumph of hope over reality; neither large amounts nor extraordinarily high-quality pot was being grown in America. Sure, some pot was grown in California and in the South; small amounts in national forests; but rarely were plots found any larger than a garden. Mostly it was a few dozen plants here and there under grow-lights in closets and barns and warehouses. Most pot smoked by Americans still was being smuggled into the country. And much if not most of it came into Everglades City. It then was trucked to Miami and stashed in warehouses before being broken down and shipped all over America. Some of it left Miami by air. But because of the bulk, most of it went by road. It traveled under piles of manure in horse trailers driven by young women with New England accents. It traveled in campers and recreational vehicles driven by old people. It traveled in trucks upon whose sides were the corporate imprimaturs of America's biggest and best-known companies. It traveled by bus. It traveled by car.

Kimberly sighed and shook her head. She saved the information on the screen, turned off the lap-top, and leaned back in the chair. She caressed the red coral necklace. As soon as she arrived at the office she would print a copy of the report. After Nick read and approved it, she would have copies distributed to the investigators. Then, to quote the President, perhaps they would see a thousand points of light.

13

Big Knocker picked up the telephone on the first ring. His eyes never left the television set. "Yeah," he growled.

"Señor, you are home. That is good."

Big Knocker paused. "Who is this?"

But there was no answer; only a click when the connection was broken.

Big Knocker slowly hung up the phone. His eyes narrowed as he leaned back in the chair, stared unseeing at the television set, and considered how he would prepare for what he knew was coming. First, he had to notify his younger brother; Robert lived two blocks away and had to be protected. He picked up the telephone.

"Robert, what are you doing?" he asked in his abrupt fashion.

"Watching TV. Why?"

"You by yourself?"

"No," Robert said, a defensive whine coming into his voice. "Bobby is here."

"Turn off all your lights and lock the doors. Now."

"Why?" The whine was more pronounced.

"Goddammit. Just do it." Big Knocker had no patience tonight.

He walked around the small house. It was built on stilts and stood about eight feet off the sandy soil. The house faced the Barron River and was between the fish houses and the Rod and Gun Club. No trees were in the yard, so he would have a clear field of fire. He wondered for a moment if the men would come up the river by boat or along the road by car. Probably by car. They would have called from nearby, perhaps the service station about three miles away up Highway 29 at the intersection of Highway 41. He looked at his watch. They would be arriving in minutes. It was okay. He had been expecting them.

He picked up the Ruger Mini-14 leaning against the wall near the front door. The clip was full. He turned on the light in the rear bedroom and in the kitchen, then shut the doors leading from those rooms into the living room. The light would be visible from outside. He turned up the volume on the television set until the sound easily could be heard in his front yard. He turned off the lights in the living room and looked out the window. No cars. Quickly he opened the front door, raced down the steps, and into the dark shadows under the house.

He had been expecting the call. Ever since the deal was botched a week earlier, he had been wondering when the Cubans would make their move. Much of the load tossed overboard that night had been seized by bale hunters; men who had gone out in darkened boats and, while the cops were just a few yards away, plucked bale after bale from the water.

The telephone call was a scare tactic. It was to send a message. Cubans were that way; all posturing and macho, always hustling their balls and standing around trying to be badasses. Cubans had to take lessons to be badasses. It came natural to Big Knocker.

He stood under the house, the Ruger at the ready. He was so big the rifle appeared to be almost a toy. He smiled his eager smile of anticipation. The Cubans were so full of themselves, so overflowing with macho bullshit, that they probably thought he was upstairs trembling in fright.

He saw the flash of car lights coming down the narrow twisting river road and moved deeper into the shadows. A hundred yards from his house, the lights flicked off. The car approached silently. Big Knocker knew the engine had been turned off and the car was coasting. He wondered if the Cubans were smart enough to open the doors before the car stopped.

They were. They had planned ahead. When the new Cadillac stopped at the edge of his yard, not only was there no sound; there were no lights. Push buttons that control the interior lights had been taped in the down position. The car doors were left open as two men walked across his yard. They were ready for a noisy shooting and a fast getaway.

He studied them as they crossed an area brightened by a nearby streetlight. Young guys. On the small side. Slender. He couldn't see their clothes well, but he knew they were wearing cheap brightly colored clothes, jewelry, and pointy-toed pimp shoes. They were also carrying automatic rifles. It looked as if both had MAC-10's with the noise suppressors attached. Mean little weapons. They could turn his living room into splinters in seconds.

The two Cubans held their MAC-10's at the ready as, with exaggerated stealth, they slowly crept up the stairs toward his front door.

Big Knockers slid the safety off his Mini-14 and moved toward the edge of the house where he would have a clear shot. Now the two Cubans were halfway up the steps.

He stepped from under the edge of the house, rifle at the ready. "Hey, pendejos," he said softly.

The two Cubans were standing close together; an easy target. As they whirled toward the sound of his voice, he pressed the trigger. The Mini-14 went into its death chatter and emptied half a clip. The two Cubans were knocked off the steps by the impact of the high-powered bullets. They never fired a shot. Their MAC-10's fell to the steps.

Big Knocker ran to the Cubans. Without pausing, he popped two rounds into the ear of each man. The bodies twitched.

Big Knocker leaned the Ruger against the steps, bent down, and turned the Cubans over so both were face-down. He grabbed a handful of belt and trousers from each man and stood up, a body in each hand, and walked stiff-legged across his yard, across the street, and then to the edge of the long docks that covered this side of the river. He dropped the bodies into the water. They had enough lead and enough holes in them to sink. But even if they surfaced, who would care?

He walked back across the road, picked up a hose coiled by the faucet at the bottom of the steps, and turned on the water. Quickly he hosed down the steps and the yard where the Cubans had fallen. He turned the hose on the road.

He was not worried about his neighbors. They would say nothing about the gunfire. They would not even mention it to him. It would be as if it never happened. People in Everglades City stuck together.

He wondered briefly about Robert. The one clear facet in Big Knocker's dark and murky personality was his unswerving concern for his brother; the only person in the world he felt protective toward. He would do whatever he had to do to protect his little brother.

Big Knocker picked up the two MAC-10's and his Ruger and went inside. He placed the weapons behind the sofa and called Robert.

"Pick me up in ten minutes at the Chokoloskee Bridge," he said.

There was a pause. Big Knocker, anticipating his brother's response, said, "Never mind why. Just be there." He hung up and strode out the front door toward the Cadillac. Killing the two men had roused his blood lust. He was angry about his load being seized a week earlier. Cops were beginning to put the squeeze on Everglades City. The DEA had packed up and left town. They were a joke. It was the locals he was worried about. He was smuggling as much now as he had done in the past, and he was worried about some of the men who had been arrested the night his load was popped. The police would try to flip them. And then that smart-assed little state's attorney, the college boy who wanted to send him to jail, would be on his case again. He could deal with cops, but he was a bit wary of what he did not understand. And he did not understand the law. He knew the young lawyer could hurt him. But before that happened, he would do some hurting himself.

Big Knocker drove slowly through the narrow streets of Everglades City, rounded the traffic circle, and slowly drove east toward Chokoloskee Island. He pulled into the parking lot at the National Park Service visitor center, waited until he was certain no one was following, then continued. He turned off the lights as he drove onto the causeway. At the bridge he pulled off the road and pointed the Cadillac toward the deep channel that crossed Chokoloskee Bay. He engaged the emergency brake and pressed the buttons that rolled all the windows down. Then he carefully wiped the steering wheel. He stepped outside and found a piece of coral weighing about five pounds, leaned through the open door, and—in a single motion—dropped the coral on the accelerator and released the emergency brake. The engine of the Cadillac surged and the car leapt over the crest of the causeway into the deep channel.

Big Knocker stared at the bubbles until they stopped. He dusted his hands together as he looked down the causeway at the approaching lights of a car. Probably Robert. He nodded. He knew how he would kill the lawyer.

14

It was ten P.M. when Derek Tutwiler strolled from the hotel bar three blocks from his courthouse office in Fort Myers. With him was Grace Ford, an assistant state attorney who was the office's tax expert. Grace was a sassy little blonde from Edison, Georgia. The state attorney's office was a closely knit group of investigators and lawyers, and several nights each week a dozen or so would gather after work at the bar of the waterfront hotel. Derek and Grace were the last to leave that night. They had been discussing ways to use tax laws in pursuing the Everglades City investigation. Even though downtown Fort Myers, particularly along the waterfront, is something of a combat zone at night, neither Derek nor Grace was particularly alert for danger. Both had been drinking, both were young and invincible, both were rising stars in the office of the state attorney.

"I'll give you a ride back to your car," Derek offered. "I'm parked across the street."

"Sure it's no problem?"

"None at all. Come on."

When Big Knocker stepped from behind Derek's Ford, the two lawyers at first assumed he was another person looking for his car. But then Big Knocker stepped toward them and pulled a small pistol from his pocket. Grace's first thought was that this was some sort of joke. The gun was wrapped in tape; it had to be a toy. Besides, who would be crazy enough to try to rob two members of the state attorney's office?

Then, at the moment Derek recognized the man with the gun, Big Knocker spun Grace around and stuck the pistol in her rib cage. "Get in the car. Both of you. Don't get cute, college boy, or your little friend will be dead."

Derek started to speak, but Big Knocker motioned his head toward the car. "Get in. Now. You drive."

Derek unlocked the car and slid under the steering wheel. He unlocked the door on the passenger side. Grace was pushed to the middle of the seat by Big Knocker. She was dazed by the speed of events. She didn't know what was going on.

"I told you in court you would screw up," Derek said angrily. "But I didn't realize how badly it would be. When this is over, you're going to jail for a long time."

"You know this person?" Grace asked in surprise. "Strange friends you have."

"He's a doper from Everglades City. He—"

"Shut up, college boy. Just drive. Go up Anderson

Avenue, then south on I-75. And don't get cute." The pistol was jammed into Grace's right breast.

"You know we are with the state attorney's office?" Grace said.

No answer.

"You sure you want to do this?" Grace asked. "You know the penalty for armed robbery?"

He jabbed hard with the pistol. She cried aloud.

"I'm trying to be calm," she said. "I don't know how to handle this situation. But if you prod me with that pistol again, you're going to have a hysterical woman on your hands."

Derek drove slowly from the parking lot, turned right, then at the underpass turned left, passed the courthouse, and drove east on Anderson Avenue.

"Please move the gun," Grace said.

He jabbed her again. Hard.

She whimpered in pain and in the first chilling onslaught of fear. The man was so implacable.

Derek leaned forward and looked at Big Knocker. "Why don't you let her drive? Let me sit in the middle. It's not necessary to hurt her. We'll give you our money."

"I know," Big Knocker said.

Derek's Harvard ring began a rhythmic patter on the steering wheel.

Grace wiggled. She tried to slide closer to Derek. But Big Knocker was so big and so tall that his legs were bent toward the center of the car, pinning her to the seat.

As the car turned south on I-75, Big Knocker said, "Okay, no speeding. Get off at the airport exit and go east."

Five minutes later, as the car passed the big regional airport and continued into an area where roads had been cut but where there was no development, Big Knocker suddenly asked, "How much money you got on you?"

Grace leaned forward to look in her purse. Big Knocker seized her hair and jerked her upright. "You got a gun in there?"

"No. We're not armed," she said. She was near tears. She had never experienced the absolute fear that comes with having no control over a situation.

"Turn off here." Big Knocker pointed toward a dirt road leading into a pine thicket.

As Derek turned the wheel, he slid the Harvard ring off his hand and dropped it on the floor. Big Knocker would not get his ring.

"I have about eighty dollars, I think," Grace said.

"About thirty," Derek said.

"Stop here," Big Knocker ordered. "Turn off the lights."

For a second, no one spoke. "Okay, give me your watches, rings, and money. And don't try anything. I'd hate to kill this college girl."

It was awkward, shifting about in the car digging into pockets for money, pulling off watches, and then carefully passing it all to Big Knocker. Without looking, he stuffed the booty into the pocket of his windbreaker. Still holding the gun in Grace's ribs, he reached across with his left hand and opened the door on his side. The overhead light came on. Big Knocker slowly stepped from the car, but his upper body was still inside. Derek saw Big Knocker's intentions in his ice-blue eyes.

"Look out," he said.

They were the last words he ever spoke. Big Knocker fired. The little twenty-two-caliber pistol didn't make much noise. It sounded like a cap pistol. The surprising thing to Grace was how far the flames leapt from the barrel—maybe two feet. The first shot hit her in the arm and burned across the front of Derek's chest. She screamed. Derek tried to throw himself in front of her. When he leaned forward, Big Knocker pulled the trigger.

Click.

A misfire.

Click.

Another misfire.

Then the pistol fired. The bullet hit Derek in the

temple. He collapsed across Grace's lap, his hands on the seat beside her.

The pistol fired again. The bullet hit Derek in the top of the head. She felt his body twitch.

Then the gun pointed toward her.

Click.

She screamed. That horrible click. The waiting for the pistol to fire; waiting for flames to spurt from the barrel, waiting for the impact of the bullet. Blood from her arm and from Derek's head was all over her clothes. The weight of his body held her to the seat. She had never felt so helpless. She threw her arms up in defense.

Then the little revolver fired again. The last thing Grace saw was the flame coming toward her head. She was knocked across Derek's body. Her right hand fell over his hands.

Dimly, from some far-distant place, she heard the car door shut. The overhead light went off. There was silence.

As she slipped farther and farther into the darkness, she heard a horrible rasping noise. Derek was going into Cheyne-Stokes breathing; what laymen call the death rattle. She wondered if she, too, were making the same sound.

She squeezed Derek's hand. Where was his Harvard ring? He was so proud of that ring. She thought he squeezed gently in return.

For a moment she was confused. The overhead light was off but she sensed the presence of a great white light; a warm, comforting light that beckoned her. She tried to smile. The light gave her a great sense of peace. It called to her. She could not refuse the summons.

15

The unthinkable, the unspeakable, had happened. Not one, but two law-enforcement personnel had been brutally murdered. It was a crime that shocked and galvanized the office of State Attorney Joe D'Alessandro.

A pall lay over the third floor of the courthouse in Fort Myers. The office had been in a bleak mood since Derek and Grace were murdered a week earlier. The bodies had been found, Grace slumped forward over Derek on the front seat. Either Grace had slid across the seat away from the robber or the robber had ridden with them to the murder scene. There were no leads; they had been robbed and killed. A cheap twenty-two-caliber pistol—a Saturday-night special—had been found tossed into the bushes. The serial number had been etched with acid, the weapon was wiped clean of prints, and it was impossible to trace. Nick's investigators were looking at the cases both lawyers were involved with; searching for a defendant who might have killed them. But Grace had been a tax lawyer. Derek was working the Everglades City case, but that was too obvious. The people in Everglades City had received such minimal sentences they had no motivation for murder. The prevailing theory was that these were random homicides, committed probably by some kid swacked out on crack cocaine. There was not much to go on.

Nick's face was permanently set in an angry basilisk stare. The vein along his nose and under his left eye seemed to throb constantly. The three-dimensional effect was such that most people in the office spoke to him softly, said what they had to say, and then got out of his way. He was taking the deaths of Derek and Grace very hard. And he was taking the matter personally. He felt a great deal of pride in Derek and did not realize, until Derek was dead, that he had looked upon him almost like a son, as something of a serious and studious version of Lance.

Nick took off the reading glasses, rubbed his eyes, then leaned forward in his chair. His voice was distant and distracted as he looked at Kimberly and Lance. Today he had little interest in the Everglades City case. Finding a murderer was far more important. Lance had no homicide experience; his ten years as a cop had been mostly in narcotics, so he would stay on the Everglades City case. And Nick had a gut feeling that the homicides were not the sort of case on which McBride's skills as an analyst could be best utilized; she, too, would stay on the drug case.

"McBride, how you doing with the information you getting from the dopers we've caught?" he asked.

"It's just beginning," she said. "Most of the people arrested are worker bees; they're so compartmentalized they don't seem to have the big picture. None are high enough in the organization to know much. The Great Emancipator showed them they don't have to be afraid of court, so it's slow going."

"Anything at all promising?"

"Not really." She glanced at Lance. "Lance may have been right about some aspects of this case. What we need is a good snitch; somebody who is on the inside and at a high level; somebody who can bring in a U/C person." She looked at the stack of files in her lap. "I'm working with the computer, trying to tie people together in the history cases. We're making a little headway—for instance, we know about a load coming in today. And every time we pop someone, we have a few more pieces of the puzzle. Unless we get a high-level informant, it will be months before we're ready to move on those people in any significant fashion."

Nick sighed. Again he rubbed his eyes. "Great," he mumbled.

One of the few things that made Lance uncomfortable was gloom and doom. It was time to lighten things up. Nick needed some good news. "Jefe, you hear what happened at Miami DEA over the weekend?"

"No telling," Nick said. He had worked with DEA often enough to have little use for them.

"They lost a couple of keys of coke from the evidence room."

Nick looked up in astonishment. "A couple of keys? What happened?"

"Some suspicion that a young agent might have taken it."

Nick shook his head. "They've gotten so much money for the war on drugs, they went on a big hiring spree. I bet ninety-five percent of their agents have less than five years' experience. Babies. And too many of the supervisors are alcoholics or eaten up with the dumb ass."

Kimberly tapped a forefinger against the files in her lap. "When I worked over there, the procedures for keeping track of seized property—not just narcotics—left a lot to be desired. They were always having trouble. Things disappeared constantly from the warehouse where they stored seized boats and vehicles."

"Boats?" Lance asked. "They got boats in that warehouse?"

Kimberly nodded. "Dozens."

Lance nodded. The beginnings of a marvelous idea were rolling around in his head.

Kimberly turned to Nick. "Speaking of DEA, Melvin Foster, one of Mr. Dumnik's assistants, called me this morning."

"What'd he want?" Nick said in a querulous tone.

Kimberly smoothed the skirt of her green linen suit, then unconsciously began rubbing the rose-quartz necklace that hung down the front of her white blouse. She was by far the best-dressed cop in the office. She dressed even better than the women lawyers. Kimberly cleared her throat. "He said he'd heard we were making some arrests in Everglades City; that we'd had some seizures. He reminded me that the Great Emancipator released the last group of defendants we took to trial, and that the task force, Operation Everglades,

still exists on paper. He said we should let him know
if we have an operation going.''

"What'd you tell him?" Lance asked.

Kimberly shrugged. "Told him the DEA had
cleaned up Everglades City; that we had a few arrests
fall into our laps.''

Lance laughed and clapped in approval.

Nick pulled at his mustache. "Those people are
afraid they might have to go back to the attorney general and say, 'Whoops, we were wrong. Everglades
City is still a sewer.' They would love to come in and
take over. You think he was suspicious?''

"I don't know. I think he bought it.''

"Did he know about the deal going down today?''

"If so, he didn't mention it. But he did say he would
be over in a few days to talk to you.''

Nick slowly turned his chair until he was facing the
wall map of the Ten Thousand Islands; a bewildering
maze of countless islands and mangrove thickets. He
shook his head. "Folks, we are not doing our jobs.
The dopers in Everglades City are running wild and
we don't have clue one about Derek and Grace.''

Lance looked at Nick. The double homicide, piled
atop the Everglades City case, was weighing heavily
on him. Nick was not nearly as rigid as he had once
been; he wasn't so much a by-the-book cop as he had
been in Fort Lauderdale. But two decades as a cop had
eroded many of his most cherished religious beliefs.
The things he held most dear were being boiled away
in the caldron of police work. That disturbed Nick;
disturbed and angered him.

Nick sighed and turned back to face Lance. "I can't
go on that bust with you and Mike. I've got to shake
something loose on the homicides. Go by yourself.''

Lance smiled. "I got it under control.''

"I'm glad somebody thinks something is under control," Nick mumbled. "Those maggots in Everglades
City are bringing in so many loads, they need to put
traffic lights up in the creeks. They're using airplanes.
Everybody is concerned about Miami, and God only
knows how much dope the rednecks are bringing in

the back door." He nodded toward Kimberly.
"McBride tells me they got this secret squirrel radio
system. You tell me we got a bent park ranger. I know
we can't trust the sheriff's department over there, and
they monitor every radio frequency we got. DEA wants
to blow into town, foul up my investigation, write a
press release, and move on. Hemorrhoids on every
street corner. Old people running off the road and dying."

He sat slumped over in his chair, head pulled down
into his shoulders. "I don't know what Florida is coming to. Maybe we should drop a couple of nukes up
around Gainesville and blow away the south end of the
state. Either that or make it a foreign country and declare war on it."

The gloom and doom were making Lance nervous.
He leaned over the desk in curiosity. Nick looked up
at him.

"You got white hair in your ears too," Lance said.

"What?"

"I thought it was just in your nose. It's in your ears
too. Big wads of it. Jefe, you are getting old fast. Is
your life insurance paid up?"

It took all of Kimberly's willpower not to sneak a
quick look at Nick's ears. But she managed. She stared
at Lance in astonishment. She had never gotten used
to the banter between the two men.

Nick brushed his right hand against his ear. "That's
awright. I'm not a psycho case. The only reason I hired
you is because you couldn't get a job anywhere else."

"Hey, I'm a mega narc. Just knowing I'm on the
street makes dopers tremble." Lance sliced his eyes
toward Kimberly, then rolled them. "Of course, I don't
know much about computers and data bases and strategic planning and all that fancy stuff. I'm just an
old-fashioned street cop."

Kimberly looked at him calmly. "And you're truthful."

"How does it feel to be a widget head?" Lance
asked.

"How does it feel to know you have one of the best minds of the eighth century?"

"Hummm, her hormones are sloshing around." Lance sighed.

Kimberly's level gaze never wavered. "The little man obviously has a case of emotional diaper rash. And speaking of hormones, perhaps he's afraid his testosterone level needs adjusting."

"Awright, that's enough, you two," Nick growled. "I've told you before, you're supposed to be on the same side. Every time I talk to you two, I feel like a baby-sitter." He looked at his watch, then pointed to Lance. "Get outta here. It's time for you to meet Mike. He's picking you up in the Blackhawk in a half-hour."

Kimberly looked at Lance. "You did read the file I gave you on this operation? You remember the details?"

Lance tapped his finger against his head. "Hey, I'm just a street cop, not a nuclear physicist. Tell me my name again."

"Get outta here," Nick said. "Or I'll put you in uniform and have you directing hemorrhoid traffic."

Lance stood up, slapped the heels of his boat shoes together, saluted, and said, "America's hero is outta here. He's gone. He's history."

16

Lance jumped into the open door of the Blackhawk helicopter and slipped on a headset.

"The sensor bird has him," Mike said over the intercom. "He's less than an hour out." He flicked his left thumb toward his copilot, signaling him to handle the radios and to watch the gauges that monitor the stabilator. He pulled collective slowly and the blades atop the Blackhawk bit deeper into the humid air. The banshee wail of the two turbines turned into an ear-splitting shriek. The chopper surged and vibrated, anxious to leap from the grass just off the short runway at Port of the Islands, a small resort west of Everglades City on the Tamiami Trail.

"You guys in the back ready?" Mike asked.

Big Ed, the leader of the four-man Customs apprehension team in the rear of the chopper, thumbed the switch on the cord leading to his headset and spoke into the microphone. "Do it."

Big Ed stood about six-feet-four, weighed about two hundred and fifty, and had a drooping pirate's mustache. He wore a red Rambo rag around his head. The name tag over the left breast of his flight suit said "Drug Warrior." He looked at the other three members of his team. They wore black military fatigues that were bloused into jungle boots. Automatic pistols were strapped on their hips and they carried CAR-15's. Their faces were serious as they checked their weapons and radios. These boys were predators; sharp, aggressive, and persistent. They were ready to rock and roll.

One other man sat in the rear of the Blackhawk; a man in his mid-forties, wearing glasses, average height, average build, rather bland and nondescript; an FBI agent from Miami who had wanted a courtesy flight aboard the Blackhawk. When Lance was introduced, he held out his hand toward the feeb and said, "Hi, I'm current occupant." The FBI agent was so nervous about the chopper flight he never noticed.

The Customs crew was glad to take the feeb along on what was almost certain to be a chase. They were proud of what they did. Using a 'Hawk to chase a doper to ground, arrest him, and seize his dope is the most dangerous job in aviation. There are many great pilots walking around who couldn't hack it with the Customs Air Wing; they are hot sticks, but they don't have the cojones to mix it up in midair with a doper. However, there had not been much mixing it up of late. During the past few months, most of the 'Hawk flights had been nothing but turning gasoline into noise; there wasn't that much action around Miami anymore.

Big Ed poked Lance with a finger the size of a banana and said, "Glad you called us. We haven't had a target in almost a month."

"You guys chased a lot of the dopers out of Miami. Now they're all over here," Lance said.

"Mike tell you he's down here TDY for several months?"

"No."

"Since you guys work with him so well, and since you're giving us a lot of work, the heavy breathers at Air Ops East sent him down for a while. They like for us to be in on the action."

Lance checked his seat belt. "We like working with Customs," he said. "You guys don't try to screw us the way DEA or the Coast Guard do."

"Name of the game is to catch bad guys."

"Wish all the feds believed that," Lance said.

The helicopter was painted a flat black with a gold stripe around the nose and down each side of the fuselage. "Coke Buster" was written on the nose. The Blackhawk looked like a malevolent oversize insect as it rose until it was only a few feet above the palm trees, then gently swung onto a southerly course that would take it southwest of Everglades City.

Lance keyed the intercom. "According to our info, the bad guys are landing at Everglades City. We have a crew hidden at the airport there to help with the bust. We don't need to get too far south."

"I'm just going about fifteen miles," Mike said. "We'll pick him up around Pavilion Key."

"Then we'll do the cha-cha-cha on his ass."

Mike chuckled. "You got it, guy." He paused. "Got any more intel on the pilot?"

Off to the left about three miles away was the airport at Everglades City. Looking down at the short runway with water at each end was almost like looking down at the deck of an aircraft carrier. The air around Everglades City, as usual, was filled with buzzards. Dozens of the dark graceful silhouettes, wings canted upward in the distinctive V shape, could be seen soaring in the thermals. Mike kept a wary eye on them. Bird strikes to an aircraft are not taken lightly; particularly if the bird is as big and heavy as a buzzard and filled with rot.

"No more than what Nick passed along," Lance said. "A julio. Says he won't be taken alive. There's a bubba from Everglades City aboard. He's riding shotgun."

A faint smile of anticipation pulled at the corner of Mike's mouth. "Another one of Fidel's boys, huh? Tough guy."

Big Ed snorted. "We'll see how tough that son of a bitch is when I make him eat a yard of runway. My guys will—"

The helicopter had crossed Chokoloskee Bay. Ahead were the Ten Thousand Islands. Suddenly Big Ed was interrupted by a blare from the radio. "Omaha Seven Six, Slingshot."

"Slingshot, Seven Six. Go."

"Omaha Seven Six, your target bears zero-zero-five for three-eight miles. Yellow-and-white Aztec. The sensor bird, Omaha Five Two, is behind him and advises he has you on radar."

"That's affirm, Slingshot. We're standing by." Mike switched to intercom. "Okay, guys, heads up. We got contact."

Lance bent over in an effort to look through the windshield. Then he looked out the open side door of the Blackhawk, searching to the south for a sight of the doper.

To the left, at about the ten-o'clock position, was a single bird soaring a few hundred feet above the chopper. The straight, pointed wings identified it as an American eagle. Mike watched in appreciation.

The chopper was low; pounding hard to the south to intercept the inbound smuggler. Air rushing through the open doors of the 'Hawk offered little relief from the heat. The air was hot and humid, a blast furnace laden with moisture and the salt and mud and oyster smell of the mangrove islands. The islands were a brilliant green against sediment-filled shallows. The mangrove thickets and the small cays were of every conceivable size and shape, and from the air they appeared as bright green blobs flung by a giant hand across the edge of the Gulf.

Mike angled south a few degrees, positioning himself with a skill born of long experience. With the afternoon sun behind him, he could hover low over a mangrove island and be virtually invisible to the inbound smuggler.

"Omaha Seven Six, Slingshot."

"Seven Six. Go."

"Omaha Seven Six, your target now bears one-seven-zero for one-three miles."

"Say altitude."

"Sensor bird reports he is at angels five and descending." The sensor bird was a heavily modified Cessna Citation, the elongated nose of which was packed with a model of the same radar found on an F-16, and with a state-of-the-art FLIR, much better than that aboard the CHET.

"Thank you. We should have a visual in a couple of minutes."

As the Blackhawk reached Rabbit Key, Mike slowed. Pavilion Key was ahead; across a three-mile stretch of open water. The inbound doper might see him silhouetted against the water if he tried to reach Pavilion Key. He decided to wait. The crew of the sensor bird had him on radar and would realize what he was doing. There would be no radio conversation. Ever since the Turks and Caicos investigation, when it was found that Dr. Goldstein's pilots were using the infamous Blue Box to monitor Customs radio transmissions, crews were squirrely about talking on the radio. And the secure frequencies, the ones where the conversation was scrambled, performed so poorly, it wasn't worth the effort

Lance looked below at the great expanse of water. "Hey, Sky King," he said over the intercom to Mike. "If we crash, how do we get out of this eggbeater?"

Big Ed laughed

"You don't," Mike said.

"Whatta you mean, I don't?"

"If this thing falls out of the air, the two seats up front can take about ten G's. You don't have any protection back there. When we impact, the rotors break off and the weight of the two engines rolls this bird over. Sinks like a rock. The pilots can get out. The procedure for you, once we know we're going in, is to put your hands on a known point of reference and hold on. Keep holding on during the impact, then wait until the blades break off and we turn turtle. At that moment, before we go down, try to get out."

"Try?"

"Yeah, but you won't make it. You'll be disabled in the impact and all you can do is sit there strapped to your seat while this bird goes to the bottom."

"How much of your flying is over water?" Lance asked.

"About ninety percent. Maybe more."

"Hmmmmm," Lance mused. "Hope you guys got good mechanics."

"Don't worry," Big Ed said. "Goes with the territory."

The helicopter dropped until it was only a few feet over a dark brown circle of trees; an area where there had been a lightning strike a year or so earlier. It was only moments later the headsets of those in the 'Hawk emitted two squawks. The sensor-bird crew had broken squelch; a signal that the bad guy was near.

Then Mike saw him. The yellow-and-white Aztec was low, no more than a thousand feet, as it came in from across the Gulf and reached the edge of the Ten Thousand Islands. As the Aztec crossed Crate Key, Mike slowly rotated the chopper in its hover, like a great bug keeping its eye on the prey, until the bad guy crossed the arm extending east from Lumber Key. Mike leaned forward, waiting, eyes locked on the Aztec. Then he pulled collective, causing the Hawk to leap in pursuit.

"Sun was on him when he passed. The guy is loaded," Mike said.

"Up above the seats?" Lance asked.

"To the top of the cabin. Must be at least a thousand pounds."

"Our snitch says there's two hundred keys of coke on board too."

Mike laughed as the chopper swung in under the doper; a quarter-mile in trail. "I thought these good ole boys down here didn't touch cocaine; that all they did was a little grass."

"Hey, lemme tell you about this bridge I know about." Lance laughed. "I can sell it to you cheap."

"He's dropping," Mike said. "Getting set up to land." His voice turned quizzical. "Why would he do that? He's still about six miles out."

Mike realized what the doper was doing in the split second before the wing of the Aztec dropped as it banked into a steep turn. "Hold on, guys, he's checking his six."

The helicopter dropped low over a mangrove island as the Aztec turned west for about a mile, then turned south.

"Where's the sensor bird?" Lance asked over the intercom.

"Once we swung in behind the bad guy, he climbed up high. He's watching on the FLIR," Mike said. His eyes were intense on the silhouette of the doper. "He's got the sun behind him now. He'll see us in another few seconds."

Mike paused. Then the Aztec twitched. Mike knew the sign. It came when the pilot saw him and, in an instinctive reaction of panic, locked his hands on the wheel and stiffened his feet on the rudder pedals. This caused the tail of the aircraft to twitch.

"Heads up, guys. He's seen us," Mike said. He cursed under his breath. "Lance, I'm alerting your guys at the airport."

"Tell 'em we got the load. They can take the rest of the day off."

Mike, knowing the doper pilot would tell the off-loading crew at the airport in Everglades City to bug out, called and alerted the hidden cops. The road would be blocked and the cops would move in on the ground crew.

There now was no need for the chopper to stay low. Mike initiated a rapid climb. Everything was all out in the open. The dopers knew the 'Hawk was there and that they could not outrun it. They also knew they were low on fuel, while the 'Hawk, famous for its long legs, probably was good for five or six hours. Now it was boiled down to the basic: good guys against bad guys, showdown time.

But how would they react? Would they try to jettison the cargo and come in clean? Unlikely. Too much grass packed too high. No way they could toss it out in flight. Would they go ahead and land and accept the inevitable? Some dopers did. The bubbas were unpredictable; sometimes, when a good old boy knew it was all over, he would simply give up. Sometimes he would shoot it out. The Cube had said he would never be taken alive. Julios were crazy. This guy might open the storm window and start shooting. Or, if he thought he was a hotshot pilot, he might get cute. Well, his options were limited. It was a bright, almost cloudless day. There was no place to hide.

A moment later, Mike had his answer. The Aztec continued on its turn until it was pointing directly toward the Blackhawk. The nose of the Aztec lowered. It was on a collision course with the Customs helicopter. Mike grinned in anticipation.

"Heads up," he said over the intercom. "This guy wants to play."

It was not uncommon for a doper who had been bounced by a Customs aircraft to take violent evasive maneuvers. Some dopers try to intimidate the Customs pilot, to make it a one-on-one test of pilot skill; others panic, dive for the deck, and try to flee; and still others, like this guy, want to ram the Customs aircraft. It is not an effort to frighten the government pilot so the doper can gain a few moments and break away. With the Cubans it is a macho attempt to die gloriously.

The feeb jerked his seat belt and shoulder straps until the harness was so tight he could hardly breathe.

"This happen often?" he asked. His voice was almost a squeak.

"Not often enough," Big Ed said. He wore a pirate's grin.

"Exciting, huh?" Lance said to the feeb. He leaned closer, eyes dancing, mouth in a wide maniacal grin, and said, "Makes you get a stiffy."

The feeb's eyes narrowed in confusion. Stiffy? That couldn't mean what he thought it meant.

Lance pressed the intercom switch. "When he passes us, can we hose him down?" Lance had a seat by the open door. He would borrow one of the CAR-15's and empty a couple of clips at the doper. They were over the unpopulated mangrove islands; no civilians were below. A little air-to-air combat would teach the doper the majesty of the law.

The feeb's eyes widened. Big Ed and the apprehension team laughed. Lance had worked with them on other cases and they knew he was crazy. They had so many restrictions placed on the use of weapons that sometimes they wondered why they carried them. Many times they had wished they were local cops. Locals had more leeway to practice street-level law enforcement; to administer a little home cooking.

"No," Mike said over the intercom. He laughed. "You crazy son of a bitch."

"Hey, this is a julio doper who busted our border." Lance paused. A sudden thrust struck him. "Wonder if he has anything to do with Central Cuban Dispatch."

The feeb looked at Lance in bewilderment. What the hell was Central Cuban Dispatch? Were the locals holding out on the bureau? The FBI was responsible for counterintelligence against foreign governments operating in America. He made a mental note to check the bureau's computer for any information on an organization known as Central Cuban Dispatch.

Mike slipped the chopper hard to the left and, at the same time, popped it upward a hundred feet. The doper roared by on the right, banking hard in a futile effort to ram the much more agile helicopter.

The feeb grunted.

Mike swung in tight behind the doper, staying on his tail; not giving him a chance to turn back toward the chopper. The Aztec pilot banked hard left, then hard right. Mike easily stayed with him.

"Let him play," Mike said. "I'll take his best shot."

The Aztec went vertical; the nose rose higher and higher until it pointed almost straight up. The aircraft slowed rapidly as it climbed.

The eyes of the FBI agent were so wide they appeared solid white.

Mike swung to the right.

"He's going to hammerhead back on top of us," Mike said.

A few seconds later the heavily loaded Aztec ran out of airspeed. In the moment before it either would have done a tail slide or flopped over into a whip stall, the pilot ruddered it hard left, pivoting on the left wing tip until the nose was pointing at the ground and the aircraft was rapidly gaining speed. Mike backed and turned the chopper, keeping his eye on the Aztec.

The FBI agent vomited. He was strapped in so tightly, he couldn't lean forward. Vomit stained the front of his fatigues.

Lance snapped a quick look at the agent. "You had oatmeal for breakfast," he said as if he had made a great discovery. He turned his attention out the open window as the Aztec screamed past, trying to bank into the chopper.

"How'd you know he would go left?" he asked Mike.

"Easiest way for a recip to go. He's too heavily loaded to pull it to the right."

For the next half-hour the airborne duel continued. The Cuban doper tried over and over to ram the Blackhawk. As the battle edged its way north over the Everglades, it also worked its way closer and closer to the ground. The feeb threw up again. His eyes were shut and his head lolled. Perspiration streamed down his face, but he made no move to wipe it away.

Then the doper, rather than trying to turn into the chopper as it made another futile pass, broke and ran, trying to use the few seconds' advantage he had gained to get down over the tops of the sawgrass; to merge with the vegetation and elude detection.

Mike was on his tail in seconds. The Customs men aboard the chopper knew its distinctive thumping resonance could be heard inside the cockpit of the Aztec; a continuous reminder to the Cuban pilot than he could run, but he couldn't hide.

The radio was a constant chatter of conversation. There was no need for security once the doper saw the Blackhawk. The Coast Guard, ever mindful of a chance to grab some glory, had overheard enough radio traffic from Slingshot to dispatch a helicopter to the scene. At the same time, Coast Guard officials called radio and TV stations in the Miami area to announce that, even as they spoke, a Coast Guard helicopter was engaged in a dangerous chase with an airborne drug smuggler.

The Coast Guard chopper was five miles away when the doper crashed. The Cuban had made a mistake. He was too low and clipped the top of a cypress tree, causing him to splat into a shallow pond and flip inverted.

Instantly Mike was down; landing on firm ground about a hundred yards from the crashed Aztec. Lance and Big Ed, followed by the apprehension team, were out and running before the chopper landed.

Lance saw Big Ed angling toward a figure trying to struggle out from under the wing. "I'll check inside for the other one," he shouted.

The two men splashed through the shallows and then into deeper water. Big Ed grabbed the arm of the man hanging on to the right wing. Lance surged ahead through the chest-deep water, then took a deep breath and disappeared under the surface. The door of the Aztec was open. The water was shallow enough that light from the surface filtered down, giving the interior of the aircraft a dim and murky appearance. The pilot, upside down and tangled in the seat belt, was not moving. Lance pulled hard. Then harder.

He surfaced, sputtering and wiping water from his eyes. "Lend me your knife. I've got to cut him out," he told Big Ed.

Big Ed passed him the knife he carried on his left hip. Lance took another deep breath and disappeared. Several minutes later he again sputtered to the surface, struggling to hold the doper's head above water.

"His neck's broken," Big Ed said.

He turned to the members of the apprehension team and motioned for two of them to take the pilot's body ashore. The third man he motioned forward to take the other doper.

"His arm is broken and he hit the glare shield on impact. Fucked up his face pretty bad. I don't think he'll give you any trouble. Search him and cuff him."

"Got it." The Customs officer turned toward the doper. "Let's go, asshole."

Lance and Big Ed, without speaking, slumped underwater. Lance first reached for the cargo. If there was cocaine aboard, it would be on the top, available for easy reach. Dopers usually tossed out the cocaine first to the ground crew, one member of which took the cocaine and split while the marijuana was being off-loaded. Lance groped and pulled until a bag was dislodged. He passed it to Big Ed. Then he scooped up everything he could grab that was loose in the cockpit—a flight bag, hefty with contents, and a rifle. Lance recognized the feel. It was an AK-47 with the short pistol-grip stock.

As the two men surfaced, a white Dauphin helicopter with an orange stripe across the nose hovered off to the side. The cargo door in the rear was open and a Coast Guard enlisted man was leaning out, watching.

"We can give those guys some business," Big Ed says. "They can run a SAR mission on this scumbag and haul off the pilot's body."

Search-and-rescue is the historic mission of the

Coast Guard; the role it has as its first priority and the role it best performs.

But the Coast Guard pilot radioed Mike that surface winds were too high; he couldn't land.

Big Ed's apprehension crew laughed. They were monitoring the conversation on the headsets that were attached by "pigtails" to radios on their belts.

"We did it. Why can't the Coasties land?" one said.

"They're pussies from hell," Lance said. He danced in a circle, arms over his head, shouting, "Pussies from hell. Pussies from hell."

"Heads up, guys," Mike suddenly shouted with alarm in his voice.

Lance and the Customs crew looked up. The white cargo door of the chopper had broken loose and was falling. They turned and ran as the door tumbled to earth a few yards away, bounced, then was still; a crumpled piece of metal.

The FBI agent, who had stumbled from the Blackhawk and was walking around trying to regain his strength, was closest. He shook his head in bewilderment and stared at the piece of metal.

Lance stopped leaping about, looked up, and said in amazement, "Their chopper is falling apart."

Then Lance and the members of the apprehension team began laughing. They became almost hysterical as they walked about, stooped over, holding their stomachs, and laughing until they were wiping tears from their eyes.

Lance turned to Big Ed in disbelief. "The Coasties want you to pick up their door and return it to them in Miami," he said. "Maybe we should Fed Ex it. They probably need it."

That set off more laughter.

Then Big Ed pressed the transmit button on his portable radio. "Mike, tell them we'll bring them their door and we'll run their SAR mission; but for them to get the fuck out of here. They're polluting the atmosphere."

A moment later all was quiet in that corner of the Everglades. The blades atop the Blackhawk had slowly wound to a halt. Mike and the Customs crew would wait until Lance's fellow agents arrived to take charge of the load of dope. Then they would take the injured doper to a local hospital.

"What are you going to do with the pilot's body?" Mike asked Lance.

"Use it for fertilizer, I guess. I don't know. What do you do with dead julios?"

Mike laughed. "Your problem, guy."

Neither man spoke for a moment. They watched the feeb, who was sitting on the grass near the bent door from the Coast Guard helicopter and looking at the body of the Cuban. His familiarization flight had given him far more than he'd anticipated; or wanted.

Mike nodded toward the feeb. "We took off in such a hurry, I didn't have a chance to tell you what he said."

Lance looked up at Mike. "The feeb?"

"Yeah. He works for some big FBI guy in Miami; the one who supervises DEA over there. Says DEA is planning to come over here. They're cranking up a task force for some big operation. Everglades City Two, he called it."

"Ohhhhh, shit," Lance groaned. "We got trouble with a capital T. Wait till Nick hears about this."

17

"Who's that?" Lance asked Nick's secretary. He watched two men enter Nick's office and shut the door.

Cheryl didn't look up from the computer. "DEA outta Miami."

"Hummmmm." Lance didn't like it when DEA agents visited the office. It was always bad news. He turned and began walking down the long hall toward the front door.

"Don't leave," Cheryl said, still not looking up from the computer. "Nick wants you in there in a few minutes."

"I'll be right back," Lance said. Had Cheryl looked up, she would have been warned. Lance was wearing his maniacal look. His grin was wide and his eyes sparkled and danced.

"Man, every muthafucker I ever killed had on a three-piece suit." The speaker, a tall, muscular black man, rolled his shoulders, bounced on the balls of his feet, and turned to his partner. "I mean, what is this shit?"

Nick tilted his head forward and looked over his reading glasses at the two men standing in front of his desk. The black guy, a DEA agent, was impeccably dressed: crisp white shirt, paisley tie, tan poplin suit. Nick couldn't see the agent's feet, but he knew the guy was wearing well-shined loafers. It was the way a certain type of ambitious DEA agent dressed; part of the package. Every time Nick saw a DEA agent with shined shoes, it made him wonder about his belief that a pair of well-kept shoes was the sure and certain mark of a good guy.

The second man in front of his desk, an apple-cheeked kid, also was dressed in a suit, white shirt, and expensive tie. These two looked like federal agents. They were bandbox crisp, hard-chargers, climbers, and probably very good investigators. They probably also never left their asses exposed to bureaucratic sniper fire.

"I said, man, what is this shit?" the black agent repeated.

"What?" Nick asked.

The black guy blew out his breath in an explosion of impatience. He shifted from one foot to the other, looked at his partner, and stared back down at Nick.

"Man, I'm Melvin Foster. DEA. Group soup on the task force. I'm from New Jersey. Exit six. I worked in the city, you know, New York, after I got outta Quantico. Class-one violators is what I worked. Nothing but the baddest of the bad. I had to kill a couple of guinea bastards up there. Both of 'em wore three-piece suits. Now they send me down here U/C to the asshole of America. Man, from what I hear, if you wanted to give the world an enema, Everglades City is where you would put the tube. They tell me I'm gonna be working with fucking rednecks; bunch of muthafucking fishermen. You believe that shit, man? You believe that?''

Nick took off his glasses and slowly placed them atop his desk. ''No, I don't believe that.'' He looked at the other agent; the young guy. ''Who are you?''

''Ben Blumen. DEA,'' said the apple-cheeked kid.

''Ben Blumen, huh? Where you from, Ben?''

''Kansas, sir.''

''Kansas?''

''Yessir. Kansas.''

''Umm-hmmm.'' Nick paused and rubbed his eyes. ''Ben, you ever been fishing?''

Ben looked at Melvin. Melvin shrugged and rolled his eyes.

''No, sir.''

''Never?''

''My family farmed. We never had time to fish.''

''Ben, you ever seen the ocean?''

Ben smiled and nodded. ''Yessir. When I passed through Miami, Mr. Dumnik—I think you know him— asked me the same question. I told him no, so he had one of his local agents take me over to Miami Beach. I saw the ocean.''

Nick stared.

''Big,'' Ben said.

Nick stared.

''The ocean. Big,'' Ben said.

''Yes.'' Nick nodded. ''Big.''

Nick stared at Ben. After a moment he said, ''Ben, you ever seen a cluster of hemorrhoids?''

Melvin snorted with impatience. ''Man, what is this? You supposed to brief us and show us around; we supposed to do some shit with a fish house or something, then we bust some honky ass down in that two-bit fishing village. That's it. Period. End of story.'' Melvin rolled his shoulders, shifted from one foot to the other, jabbed a finger toward Nick, and said, "So let's get on with it, huh?"

Nick put on his glasses, leaned back in his chair, and looked up at the two men. He could throw these assholes out of his office. Dumnik had heard he was arresting people in Everglades City and his bureaucratic survivor's instinct had come into full play. The DEA was moving back into the case; calling it Operation Everglades City II. The idea, judging by the appearance of Melvin and Ben, was to inject some new U/C blood into the case. Even if Dumnik ran in two U/C guys, Nick didn't have to talk to them. But on the other hand, this could be interesting. A street-wise smart-ass black guy from New Jersey and a corn-fed Jewish kid from Kansas were coming in to work with redneck fishermen. My God, what would DEA come up with next? The black guy had never had his feet off concrete and the Kansas kid wouldn't know a mullet from Moby Dick. And they were going to work undercover in a fishing town. Melvin would be one of the few black guys ever to come to Everglades City; that bunch of racist fishermen would have his ass for breakfast.

Oh, well, if Dumnik wanted him to brief these guys and show them around, he would do it. Nick looked over his glasses at the two men.

"You men have any other clothes with you?"

"Yeah, man, we got some cammies, some boots; we got all that good shit. We ready," Melvin said.

Nick reached for the telephone. "Gentlemen, I'm in the middle of a homicide investigation, so I can't go with you. But I'll have one of my men show you around; put you in a boat; take you down in the Ten Thousand Islands, let you see some of the creeks, the off-loading sites, give you an overall picture of what we're up against."

"Man, I'm ready to get down there and kick some honky ass," Melvin said. "Clean that place up. Get back to the world." He smoothed his tie.

"This *is* the world," Nick said. He pressed a button on the phone.

Melvin laughed. "What be the name of this dude you running in on us?"

"The dude's name be Lance Cunningham." He pulled the phone close to his mouth. "Cunningham out there?"

Cheryl looked up. Dickman and Joe Willy, the two electronics wizards, were standing a few feet away in front of the door to Nick's office. Their backs were to her. Behind them, she could see Lance's head. The three were shaking in silent laughter. Beyond them, Virginia, Nick's second secretary, looked over the divider and did a double-take. Her eyes widened. Lance put his finger over his lips, motioning her to silence. Virginia turned back to her computer but her soft giggle could be heard across the office.

Cheryl was bewildered. What was going on?

"He's here."

"Send him in."

Cheryl replaced the telephone. "Hey, you guys, knock off the horseplay. Lance, Nick wants you in his office."

"Okay," Lance said. She still couldn't see his face. Dickman and Joe Willy, both of whom were big guys, blocked her vision.

Joe Willy reached to his left, twisted the knob on Nick's office door, and pushed it open.

Cheryl had a brief glance at Lance's face as he entered and shut the door. "What is that on his face?"

Dickman and Joe Willy, giggling, crowded near the door. "Flour," Joe Willy said.

"Flour?"

Dickman shook his head in disbelief. "He got a cup of flour downstairs from the cafeteria and rubbed it all over his face and shirt. Said his devil brain had control." He waved for quiet. Cheryl leaned across her desk. From Nick's office came Lance's loud, anxious voice.

"Boss, it just blew up my nose. I swear it. I was in the evidence room and there was a draft and all at once cocaine was all over me. It just blew up my nose. It's only two or three keys.''

There was a moment of shocked silence. Then a strange voice said, ''Muthafucker. A cokehead.''

Then Lance's voice: ''Boss, I been hearing about DEA agents in Miami snorting coke from the evidence room and I want you to know I don't believe it. I bet it just blew up their noses like it did mine. I was in there working, and poof!—it just blew up my nose.''

18

Robert, Big Knocker's kid brother, smoked two joints, giggled, stretched languidly, and slowly rubbed his groin. Then from a glassine envelope he carefully poured a little pile of cocaine on the glass-topped table. He opened the single blade of a small knife, the sort of narrow lightweight pocketknife men carry to clean their fingernails, and, with the point of the blade, very slowly searched through the pile for small lumps of cocaine. These he gently pulled into a separate pile. He used the sharp edge of the knife to methodically chop and rechop the first mound of cocaine until the grains were almost powdery in their consistency. Then he reached for a small jar of Vaseline.

His lean tanned face was intense as he used his finger to scoop out a dollop of Vaseline and scrape it onto the table near the cocaine. Small beads of perspiration dotted his brow as he leaned over, brow wrinkled, and ever so gently mixed the Vaseline with the cocaine; first with the powdery cocaine until it formed a paste; and then, even more gently, with the small lumps.

With the skill born of long practice he folded and blended; careful not to break the lumps. Then, like a master chef staring at an esoteric blend that only had to be put into the oven before working its magic, he sat back and stared at the greasy paste. The corner of his mouth twitched into an anxious smile of anticipation.

Robert wished he were not alone; wished his friend Bobby were with him. Bobby could administer the cocaine for him. Then he could do it for Bobby. He stood up and walked across the room to make sure the door was locked. He turned off all the lights except a small lamp. Then he returned and stood over the glass table, its polished surface picking up the shadowy reflection of his face.

He kicked off his white loafers. His feet were bare of socks. Robert licked his lips. With both hands he slowly unbuckled his belt and pulled down the zipper of his pants. He pushed the loose-fitting black cotton trousers down his legs, stepped out of them, and tossed them over the back of a chair. There was a coquettish, almost womanish twist to his hips when he hooked his thumbs into the waistband of his silk boxer shorts and dragged them down his legs. When they reached his knees, he stopped and let them fall to his ankles.

He sighed, stepped from the circle of silk, and, his eyes staring at the mound of paste, slowly rubbed his hands across his stomach. Then his hands were lower and his shoulders slumped as he aroused himself; moaning softly as he fondled himself.

A moment later he stopped, and then, legs spread, leaned over the table and swiftly scooped a small amount of the paste onto a forefinger. He leaned over the table, moved the forefinger behind, reaching, exploring with a middle finger, then slowly moving the Vaseline-and-cocaine-coated forefinger into his anus. He groaned. A moment later he scooped up another finger covered with lumps of cocaine and Vaseline and gently pressed it into himself. He grunted as his sphincter muscle involuntarily contracted at the intrusion of the lumps. He dragged a straightened finger across the remaining paste and went through the routine a third time.

He had tried cocaine every way it could be used. Many people snorted it because it was so quickly ab-

sorbed by mucous membranes in the nose. Some
smoked it as crack cocaine. In fact, that was the quick-
est way to absorb it into the system. When one considered that a deep inhalation could scatter the powder
throughout one's lungs; and that a person's lungs had
about the same space as a football field, it was a won-
derfully quick way to ingest cocaine. Some shot it up,
like the euphoric rush that came when the cocaine wal-
loped the system. But Robert liked this way. Bobby
had showed him how to do it; had explained how the
cocaine would slowly be absorbed into the blood-
stream through the mucous membranes in the lower
colon. The powder was absorbed quickly; a burst of
nirvana. The lumps were like spansules, slow-release
capsules of bliss. Not only was there the long delight-
ful rush from cocaine; administering it this way was
so much more fun than the businesslike snorting, the
plebeian smoking, and the distasteful shooting up. This
was so much more pleasurable; the administration was
an ecstatic foretaste of what was to come.

Robert looked down at the reflection in the glass
table. He reached down, wiped the greasy remnants
of the cocaine paste across the end of his erect penis,
and began masturbating. He watched himself in the
reflection of the glass table. And again he wished
Bobby were with him. Bobby did this so much better.

19

"Okay, McBride, show me what you spent a hundred
thousand dollars of taxpayers' money on," Nick said.
He stepped out of Kimberly McBride's Mustang convertible, hitched up his creased jeans, and slowly
turned in a circle as he made sure no one was watching. He stood in a mini-park, a little picnic area, along
the causeway across the river from downtown Fort

Myers. A thick screen of oleander bushes prevented passersby from seeing most of the park. A marked police car blocked the entrance; no one would be allowed to enter for the next few minutes.

Kimberly stepped from the car, licked her lips, fondled the black coral necklace hanging over her white silk blouse, and thought for a quick moment how black coral calmed one's mind and helped one become centered. She turned and reached into the car for her laptop computer, paused, and reluctantly decided to leave it. She straightened and pointed toward the innocuous white van parked in front of her car. A plain garden-variety van of a model seen by the thousands every day on Florida roads. Nick looked at it carefully, searching out the telltale signs for what he knew was inside. The van had heavily tinted side windows. A short coiled antenna was on top, obviously for a cellular telephone. Darkened windows were common in Florida as a method of diffusing the brightness of the semitropical sun, and cellular telephones were in such widespread usage that no one would pay attention to the coiled antenna. There was nothing to reveal the contents, the purpose, or the capabilities of the van.

"You left it parked out here?" Nick asked.

Before Kimberly could answer, Nick walked toward the van, his highly polished brown cowboy boots stirring up clouds of white dust. He sauntered around the van. Where were the antennae hidden? The van was riding high; it either was empty or it had extra-stiff springs. He looked up at the sky. It was blistering hot and not a zephyr of a breeze stirred; must be slack water. Nick did not relish sitting inside the van.

"You got a key?" he asked Kimberly.

At that moment there was a click, and the cavernous door on the right side of the van opened. A cloud of gray smoke poured out. Dickman and Joe Willy sat there grinning like a couple of kids. Dickman, as usual, was puffing on a cigarette.

"You don't need a key," Joe Willy said.

Nick looked at him. "You heard me?"

Dickman smiled, reached to his side, and punched

a bottom. A whirring noise was heard, a few clicks, then came Nick's voice: "Okay, McBride, show me what you spent a hundred thousand dollars of taxpayers' money on."

A split second later: "You left it parked out here?" Then: "You got a key?"

Before Nick could speak, Joe Willy handed him a stack of color photographs; a sequence of Polaroid shots that began as McBride's car rolled into the park.

"This son of a bitch is fantastic," Dickman said. "We got hidden mikes on all four corners. We can put this thing in a mode where they are activated by movement or sound. Movement also. Anything in the camera's field of view moves, the cameras start rolling and the Polaroid automatically kicks out a print. Plus we get an alarm in here that something's moving. Mouse couldn't sneak up on us."

Nick leaned forward. "It's cool in there," he said in amazement.

Dickman grinned. "Air-conditioned. Ultrasilent. You could stand beside the van and not hear it. You could lean against the van and not feel it. Everything here can run off batteries for twelve, maybe sixteen hours."

"If it's air-conditioned, I want inside." Nick motioned for Dickman to step down. "You and your cigarettes, get outta there. Let Joe Willy show me how this thing works."

Dickman jumped down. The van didn't move. "The batteries, a big bank of ni cads, are underneath," he said. He motioned for Nick to follow him to the rear of the van. "Let me show you this before you go inside."

He opened the rear doors. A partition painted in flat black blocked the interior. The partition was divided into segments and cubbyholes. A small black cloth was against the rear side of one cubbyhole.

"Looks like one of those cable-TV trucks," Nick said.

"Supposed to," Dickman said. "We got signs for two or three companies we can slap on the side." He flicked his cigarette aside and reached toward the top of the partition. He pulled on two pieces of pipe. Nick was astonished when eight feet of pipe slid out.

"Little tunnel up there under the roof to hold this. Makes it all that much more believable," Dickman said. "If you're more than twenty yards from this open door, you don't see the partition. You think you're looking into the back end of a working van." Dickman reached into his shirt pocket and pulled out a pack of cigarettes.

Nick nodded. He walked to the open door. "Why is the thing so high off the ground?"

"It's not high; you're just short," Dickman said. He laughed and took a deep puff from his cigarette.

"You're gonna be short on payday," Nick said. He climbed into the van, then turned toward Dickman and McBride. "Not enough room in here for all of us," he said. Then he smiled. "I'm shutting this door so the air conditioning won't get out." The door slid forward and locked.

"Tell me about it," Nick said, moving to one of the two swivel chairs. He looked up at a small sign over the tape recorders: "In God We Trust. All Others We Monitor."

Nick nodded toward the sign. "Dickman's work?"

Joe Willy grinned.

"I thought so."

Dickman's humor ran in the same vein as that of Lance. When Dickman had been a city cop in Fort Myers, he worked narcotics and sold imitation crack out of his car in reverse stings. As soon as there was a buy, he would slap a set of handcuffs over the wrist of the buyer. The first click usually sent the buyer scampering, and Dickman, who was beginning to gain a little weight, grew tired of the long footraces. So he got thirty feet of nylon parachute rigging and tied one end to his handcuffs and the other end to the car's emergency brake. The next time a crack buyer bolted, the kid almost dislocated his arm when he reached the end of his rope. Dickman laughed, reeled him in, and astonished the kid by asking his weight. Dickman imagined himself some sort of dope fisherman and used to tally up his arrests not by how many people he brought in, but by their weight.

Joe Willy sat in the chair across from Nick. "First, the cameras," he said, pointing to three video cameras; one mounted on a track near the rear window; two by the side window. "This is stuff out of the space program we adapted to our use," he said. "We got three cameras; lenses go from nine-point-five-millimeter to a hundred-and-fifty. We can put a doubler in the lens and push it to three-hundred-millimeter. And we can put a tele-adapter, sort of a little snoot, on that, and double it again; up to six-hundred-millimeter. That will pick out the pimples on a gnat's ass from two miles away."

Nick nodded.

Joe Willy continued. "The cameras slide back and forth on the tracks. We can use them all at the same time if we want. VCR's hooked up to each one. They can also be operated by remote control. We can park this sucker and operate the equipment from a half-mile away." Joe Willy paused, then added, "Cameras have infrared lenses. We can tape at night."

He pointed to a bank of electronic equipment against the left side of the van. "Tape recorder for the externally mounted mikes." He patted an intimidating-looking piece of equipment, an ICOM-7000. "This baby scans from thirty megs up to nine hundred ninety nine megs. That's everything from the low end of the VHF spectrum up through UHF."

He pointed to a square box. "Crapper." His finger moved toward a door mounted low on the floor. "A refrigerator for film and sandwiches."

"Glad it's small," Nick said. "You guys would fill it up with beer."

Joe Willy laughed. "Keeping beer cold is more important than keeping film cold." His hand waved along the bank of electronic equipment. "VHF transceiver. Ground-to-air radio. Cellular telephone. We can hook the lap-top to the cellular and tie into the law-enforcement computers; same ones we have access to in the office. Our own system, NCIC, and—depending on personal contacts—Customs and DEA computers.''

Nick looked at Joe Willy in astonishment. ''One person can operate all of this?''

Joe Willy shook his head. ''Dickman or I can do it. We haven't checked out anyone else. But the normal crew will be two people.'' He pulled a stack of plastic signs from a container on the side of the van. ''We got names of cable-TV companies plus land surveyors plus every construction company licensed in south Florida. We put one of these on the exterior, and nobody pays any attention to us.''

He ran his hand over the side of the van. ''Steel-lined. Deflect anything but heavy artillery.'' He pointed to a rack of weapons. ''Mini-14 and a twelve-gauge.''

''An electronic war wagon,'' Nick said.

''One other thing,'' Joe Willy said. ''We got so much stuff on here, sometimes I forget it all.'' He opened a drawer and gently pulled out a small box. Inside were devices ranging from four to ten inches long, each about the thickness of a straw.

Nick looked at Joe Willy.

''Lenses,'' Joe Willy explained. ''Fiber optics. This is our secret squirrel stuff. We can put one of these babies in a wall, a window, curtains, keyhole; anywhere it will fit. By itself, it's inert. But we can use a data link from here''—he patted a panel of instruments—''to power it up. We can tie it to one of the VCR's and record whatever the camera sees.''

''From how far away?''

Joe Willy cocked his head and thought. ''Good clear line of sight; I'd say at least a mile. In town, where there are buildings to interfere with the signal, two, maybe three blocks.''

''Sound?''

Joe Willy shook his head. ''That has to be separate. We can do it and then match up the audio and video. Works pretty good.''

''Can you monitor bugs?''

Joe Willy nodded and pointed. ''The equipment behind you does that. We can monitor up to three bugs operating on three different freqs and record all three."

"Anybody else got one of these?"

Joe Willy shook his head. "Nobody. We had to have some help installing some of this stuff and tweaking it for max performance. Blew the minds of the factory guys. They said various law-enforcement agencies, mostly the FBI and DEA, have some of this stuff. But nobody's put it all together like this."

"No chance the bad guys will know of it?"

Joe Willy's eyes hardened. He shook his head. "Security is good."

"How did you do all this for a hundred grand?"

"McBride. She knew a lot of the suppliers from her days with DEA intelligence. She held their feet to the fire on the prices. Dickman and I did most of the installation. My father-in-law knows the dealer where we got the van; he cut us a rock-bottom price. He knows what I do, so he has some idea of what we wanted it for; said he'd repaint anytime we wanted to. Free."

"So if we're blown on a deal, we can repaint it?"

"Be like starting over," Joe Willy said. He looked around the van. "We're gonna hurt some people with this baby."

"Good." Nick slid open the front door of the van. Dickman and McBride stood there, both waiting for his opinion.

Nick eased to the ground. He suddenly had a sense of great professional satisfaction; not just with his investigative staff and the van, but with his job. His boss, State Attorney Joe D'Alessandro, was the finest man he had worked for in twenty years as a cop. D'Alessandro had done everything he said he would do when he hired Nick away from Broward County. He was tough, nobody on the staff tangled with him, but he was fair. His main concern was getting the job done. He had no sacred cows. If someone broke the law in the Twentieth Judicial Circuit, it didn't matter who they were, D'Alessandro's standing order to Nick was quite simple: "Go get 'em."

Nick walked forward to peer into the front of the van. It looked just like any other van. A partition separated the front seats from the electronics gear in the back. He leaned against the big rearview mirror on the right side. "You never did tell me where you hide the antennae," he said.

Dickman blew out a cloud of cigarette smoke. "You leaning on one of 'em."

Nick straightened up and turned. "Where?"

"Inside the frame of the mirror. Another one on the other mirror. The regular radio antenna is a dummy; we use it for one of the VHF radios. Another antenna is inside the grille."

Nick nodded. He pulled at his mustache, looked at the dust on his cowboy boots, and did not speak for a long moment. Then, thoughts obviously far away, he began. "You know, those people down at Everglades City say they're just a bunch of hardworking fishermen. They've had their fishing grounds taken over by the government; the government changed the rules on them about what they could fish for and how much they could catch. The government made it difficult for them to make a living. The government forced them to become smugglers."

McBride looked at Dickman and Joe Willy. No one spoke.

"Everybody's got problems," Nick said. "You got problems. I got problems. South Florida is filled with hemorrhoids. We all got problems."

Nick looked across the park, out over the river, where a slight breeze was beginning to ruffle the surface. Perhaps the tide had turned.

"Fact is, those people entered into a criminal enterprise with Cubans; with people who are in bed with the Russians. Communists." Nick shook his head. "Castro says he doesn't know about any of this. He executes a couple of generals and says Cuba is out of the dope business. But the next day a doper hid in

Cuban waters while a MiG chased a Customs sensor bird away.''

Nick looked at McBride. ''You got all the records. Have the Cubans stopped bringing loads of dope into Everglades City?''

Kimberly caressed her necklace. ''The amount seems to be increasing.''

''Castro has stopped about as much dope as we have,'' Nick said. ''And that's not much. We're not doing our job.''

He looked across the water and sighed. He had relatives in Everglades City. He hadn't seen them for years, but they were there. He had no doubt some of them were working with Cubans.

Nick looked at Dickman, then at Joe Willy. ''When I was with Broward County, we did a big case in the Bahamas and another down in the Turks and Caicos Islands. Those are islands that geography made ideal for being in the narcotics pipeline. In a way, I can understand that. But Everglades City is part of America. It's our jurisdiction. What I can never understand is how a town in America, an entire town, can cooperate with Communists in bringing in drugs. I don't care how poor you are, how much you need the money, that's just not right.''

Dickman and Joe Willy shuffled their feet. They looked at McBride. She looked at Nick and waited.

Nick rolled his head toward the van. ''You know how the courts have ruled on the use of this sort of equipment.''

Dickman and Joe Willy nodded.

''Those people down in Everglades City are worse than most dopers. They're not just smugglers. They're traitors. They allowed a corner of America to become a playground for Cuban dopers. No need in blaming it all on the julios, because they couldn't have done it without the locals. The locals are the key to the whole thing.''

Nick paused. He obviously had made up his mind about something.

"McBride, you did a helluva good job with this van," he said.

Kimberly nodded, bent her head, and blinked back the sudden rush of scalding tears. Her father and her husband had taught her to accept abuse and criticism as her due; she had never learned to accept the praise she so badly needed and wanted.

Nick turned to Dickman and Joe Willy. "All of you did a good job. When does it go to work?"

Dickman smiled his lazy smile and took a deep puff from his cigarette. "There's gonna be a lot of cable-TV installations in Everglades City starting next week."

Nick nodded. "DEA is down there. I don't want them or anyone else on the task force to know about this van."

Dickman nodded. "No problem."

"That includes the sheriff's office, FDLE, and the Park Service rangers."

"We don't talk to yogurt suckers," Dickman said. He didn't think much of Park Service rangers.

"This thing might get McBride the snitch she needs. It's our eyes and nose and ears."

Kimberly, anxious to please, said, "We could make a dozen or so arrests now if you want. We wouldn't get the big guys, but we could make some arrests."

Nick shook his head. "No, we'll wait."

He looked at Dickman and Joe Willy. "Don't let some blue-haired old person run over you."

Dickman laughed. "And we'll watch out for hemorrhoids."

"Work with Cunningham. He's in charge while I'm on this homicide. Get the job done."

Dickman and Joe Willy nodded. They were anxious to take the van to Everglades City; to play with the new toy.

"Let's go, McBride. I need to get back to the office." He looked at his dusty boots. "Next time we do something like this, you people pick someplace with a paved parking lot." Nick was fastidious about his boots. Many men wore expensive suits, fancy ties, and custom shirts. But their shoes were run-down at the heels, scuffed, and unshined. If a man's shoes were not shined and in good repair, that was a sure indication of grave character flaws.

As McBride's convertible pulled from the park, Joe Willy and Dickman looked at each other.

"What was that all about?" Joe Willy said. "Communist julios. The bubbas are traitors. What the hell was he talking about?"

Dickman puffed on his cigarette and stared after the Mustang. "Stuff about the court rulings was what I heard. I understood him to say we should use the van to do whatever we have to do to arrest that bunch of redneck dopers."

"But don't get caught?"

Dickman nodded. "But don't get caught."

Joe Willy looked at the cloud of dust left by McBride's convertible. "A lot of pressure on Nick. Seems to be loosening up a lot." He paused. "Think he's parked his Bible?"

Dickman flicked his cigarette aside. "Hope so. Bibles and cops don't mix."

20

"Hey, dude, what kinda boat is this?"

Lance, who was rearranging the lines, baling bucket, and collection of gear in the Boston Whaler, looked up. Melvin and Ben, both wearing camouflage fatigues and black jungle boots, stood on the dock. Both men carried automatic rifles and each wore a nine-millimeter sidearm. They weren't exactly inconspicuous. Each carried a green canvas bag that Lance knew was filled with everything from extra ammunition to clean clothes. Lance wore boat shoes, cut-off

jeans, and a T-shirt that said "I SWEAR TO GOD I
DIDN'T DO IT."

"What kinda boat is this?" Melvin repeated.

"Whaler. A Boston Whaler."

"Ain't very big. We got big boats at DEA."

"We make do with what we got."

"How many propellers it got on it?"

Lance looked at the two engines on the rear of the
boat, then back at Melvin. Didn't this guy know anything about boats? Lance turned thoughtful. He held
up his left hand and with a look of intense concentration began counting his fingers. "Well, if you count
the one on my beanie, it got three," he said.

"You drive it?"

Lance scratched his head. "I think so." He grinned.
"I'm a nineties kinda guy."

Melvin looked away and said with great feeling.
"Sheeeeeit."

Lance turned to coil a piece of line. Over his shoulder he said, "If you're ready, get aboard and we'll—"

He spun around. The Whaler had received such a
powerful blow that he thought another boat had drifted
down on it, pinning it to the dock. He was face-to-
face with Melvin. The DEA agent had jumped from
the dock, a distance of about four feet, into the Whaler.
It was a wonder he hadn't punched through the bottom. Ben was crouched, preparing to follow.

"Hold it," Lance said loudly. "You guys ever been
on a boat before? Use the ladder. Go light on my
boat."

Ben passed down the two canvas bags to Melvin.
Then he carefully maneuvered down the ladder. Melvin tossed the bags in the stern, stepped to the side of
the boat, and sat down heavily, causing the boat to list
sharply. Lance looked down at the two skid marks of
black rubber where Melvin had landed. It would take
hours to scrub them away.

"Hey, when you move about the boat, stay on the
centerline. Move slowly. Don't jump around," Lance
said.

Ben nodded as he sat down. Melvin swung his feet

forward and lurched to the forward seat. The boat rocked and the agent's automatic rifle almost slid off his shoulder into the water. He left dark skid marks from his boots.

"I'm sitting up here," he declared. "I ride in the front of the bus."

Lance shrugged. If the guy wanted to sit in the bow and be soaked with spray, it was okay by him.

"You guys have any tennis shoes? Any boat shoes?"

Melvin shook his head. Local cops didn't know jack shit. He turned, held up both hands, and dragged his fingertips down the front of his cammy shirt. "Man, this is the DEA uniform for field ops. We don't wear no tennis shoes."

Ben, who was sitting on the middle seat, smiled a different smile and shrugged.

"I understand you want to look around the Ten Thousand Islands, go up one of the creeks and see an off-loading site, look at Everglades City from the water and get a general overview of the territory. That right?"

Melvin, boots propped on the small cuddy cabin, did not turn around. He nodded. Over his shoulder he said, "I'll tell you where we want to go. Just show us the shit, man."

Lance smiled. He knew a few DEA agents who were nice guys; knew their jobs and were okay to work with. But all too many of them were like Melvin—assholes who thought because they were feds they had a monopoly on smarts. He checked the gas in the two tanks. His emergency kit was under the seat. A backup hand-held radio was in his small ditty bag, along with some other items he carried just for DEA assholes. He grinned when he thought of his special snake and bug repellent. He had a dozen Coca-Colas, two sandwiches, and a Snickers candy bar in a small cooler. He looked about the boat. All secure. Everything in its place. He was ready.

Lance turned the ignition switch, looking over his shoulder at the black housing on the port side Mercury outboard. It trembled twice and then surged into a low rumble of power before settling into a smooth, almost high-pitched song. He checked the gauges. Oil pressure in the green. Constant pressure. The other engine caught, noise audible over the first, raced, then settled down. Lance untied the stern line from the cleat at his left and tossed it atop the dock. He looked up.

"Melvin, you mind untying the bowline?"

The DEA agent untied the line and let it fall into the water. Lance sighed. "Pull in the line, please," he said.

Melvin pulled in the sopping line and dropped it on the sole.

Lance knew he was going to have to be alert today; these guys would be no help on the boat. He put the right engine in reverse, the left in forward, turned the wheel hard over, and waited as the boat slowly "walked" sideways away from the dock. Then he moved the right engine into forward, added a wee bit of power on the left until the bow slowly swung right, then slowly, leaving no wake, exited from the marina.

Melvin looked at his watch. "Man, why we fucking around? Let's get this show on the road."

"We have to go slow in the marina or the wake will bang other boats against the dock."

"Sheeeeit."

Two hours later the Whaler nosed into a small creek that emptied into the Barron River. As they slowed, giant mosquitoes swarmed about their heads.

Lance had taken the DEA agents offshore and showed them the difficult approaches to the few passes leading through the Ten Thousand Islands. He had gone no more than a half-mile offshore, but that was enough to make Melvin extremely nervous. Melvin also was extremely wet. He insisted on keeping his front seat even though his weight pulled the bow down and caused him to be drenched with salt water.

When he was offshore, Lance pulled power and let the Whaler drift to a stop. "Man, this boat is too small to be this far from land," Melvin said. He wiped water from his face. "Get in there close to some concrete. I want to see some paved roads and streetlights."

Melvin and Ben turned in curiosity as the boat stopped. "Look at this," Lance said. He put his right foot between the two engines and jumped overboard, the cries of alarm from Melvin and Ben ringing out even before he hit the water. They thought he had lost his mind; that he was abandoning them in mid-ocean. Both men were amazed that the water was not quite waist-deep.

"One of the problems we have is the waters are so shallow," Lance said. "It's only this deep a half-mile offshore. We could go out another mile and a half before the water was six feet deep."

The significance of what this meant to law-enforcement officers in pursuit of smugglers escaped Melvin. All he could think about was being offshore—it seemed he was in the middle of the Gulf of Mexico—and the crazy local cop had jumped out of the boat.

"Man, get your ass back in here. A shark or octopus is gonna get you, and I can't drive this fucker."

Lance laughed and swung aboard. He took the two agents through the mangrove clumps and islands and creeks and mud flats of the Ten Thousand Islands.

"Fucking place is like Mars. Man, this is like outer space," Melvin said. "Where are the paved streets?"

Now, as the Whaler nudged into the narrow creek, Melvin's eyes grew wide. He swung at the mosquitoes. It was like flinging his hand through a hail of BB's. He turned around. "Where we going?"

"The dopers load mullet skiffs and creek boats with dope and come up this creek to an off-loading site up on Highway Forty-one. I want to show you where they put it on the hill and then transport it into Miami."

"They come up here at night" Ben asked. His eyes were drawn almost shut against the mosquitoes.

Lance noticed that Ben did not talk much. A quiet guy. And Lance knew he was fully as apprehensive about being on the water and coming into the constricted creek as was Melvin. But he said nothing.

Lance nodded. "Dopers come day and night. But they like nights. Particularly when there's no moon."

"How they see?" Melvin asked.

"I think they see in the dark," Lance said. "We've been out here on surveillance and heard them go by. They usually don't show any lights. Musta memorized all these creeks."

Melvin snorted in disbelief. He pointed toward the trees that overhung the small creek. Giant bromeliads hung like great green spiders from the trees; dozens, perhaps hundreds of them.

"What's that?" Melvin asked.

"Locals call them air plants. Women around Everglades City like to put them in their homes."

A giant bullfrog bellowed from nearby.

Both Melvin and Ben spun about and looked with questioning eyes at Lance.

"Gator, I think," he said.

"Gator! You got fucking alligators in here?" Melvin asked. He looked about. Sagging trees leaned across the creek. Bushes occasionally reached out, forcing him to duck to avoid the branches. Overhead the sun was almost blotted out by thick trees. The humidity seemed to be a hundred percent. The clothes of the two DEA agents stuck to their bodies like clammy blankets.

"By the hundreds. By the thousands. Some of the biggest in the world. I've seem 'em twelve, fourteen feet."

"Sheeeeit." Melvin thought for a moment. "You said you think it's an alligator. What else could it be?"

"Could be snakes. The big ones make a noise like that. Could be a pit bull with AIDS. Had a big outbreak of that. They come back here and hide; breed with anything that walks. I'm not afraid of gators, but I'm afraid of pit bulls with AIDS."

"Pit bulls are mean dogs anyway," Ben said. "How does AIDS affect them?"

"Makes 'em meaner. A regular pit bull will chew down a tree; bite everything in sight. Gets AIDS, and he really gets hostile."

The boat slowly rounded a curve, and ahead was a small hill surrounded by grass. The sun filtered through the needles of a grove of casuarina trees and dappled the creek and the ground.

"I ain't getting on the ground unless its paved," Melvin said.

"I got some snake repellent," Lance said. "Snake and bug repellent. You need to get out so you can see the trail leading up to the road. This is a typical off-loading site. If you're going to mount an operation over here, you have to understand how the dopers do their thing."

Melvin drew his boots away from the bow as Lance nudged the boat into the soft mud. He picked up his automatic rifle and patted his hip. "This all the snake repellent I need," he said. "I see a gator or one of those pit bulls or a snake, I'll blow his shit away just like I killed the guinea dopers back in Jersey." He paused and looked at Lance. "They were wearing three-piece suits. I tell you about that?"

Lance nodded and said, "We're in a national park. The discharge of firearms is unlawful in here."

Melvin looked skeptical.

"We're not arresting someone," Lance said. "This is an intelligence-gathering mission. You discharge a weapon back here and you're no different from anybody else. The rangers will ticket you and call the newspapers. I don't think Dumnik wants that sort of publicity for DEA."

Melvin thought for a moment. "What kinda snake repellent you got?"

Lance reached into his bag and pulled out a small plastic bottle filled with a viscous green substance. He shook it, watching beads form and rise to the top. It was a mixture of after-shave lotion and olive oil with a small amount of dishwater. "This stuff works great," he said. "Old doper told me about it. The locals swear by it. Say it will keep snakes and mosquitoes away."

"Pass that shit up here," Melvin said.

Lance looked at Melvin in a questioning fashion. "I don't know. This is strong stuff. You don't have to use it. I don't use anything," Lance said.

"Pass it up here."

"I don't recommend it if you're not used to it."

"Just give it to me."

Lance passed the container to Ben, who passed it to Melvin. "Do you drink it or spread it on you?" Melvin asked.

"Both. You take a good swallow. Then you splash it on your hands and rub it on your face and clothes."

Melvin unscrewed the cap, turned the bottle back, and took a great gulp. He grimaced and made a sound of distaste. Then he splashed a healthy dollop on his hands, rubbed them together, then spread the oily substance on his face. He turned up the bottle and drained the remainder on his hands. He spread it over his clothes. He flicked the bottle top overboard and passed the empty bottle to Ben. "Wasn't enough for you," he said.

Ben held the empty bottle for a moment. He looked disappointed.

"Be careful when you step ashore," Lance said. "There's some pretty big snakes back here."

Melvin stopped. "What kinda snakes?"

"Cottonmouth moccasins, anacondas, boa constrictors. The moccasins are poisonous, the anacondas and the boas squeeze you to death." He paused. "But it's the hoop snake that's the worst. Watch out for the hoop snake."

"What the fuck is a hoop snake?"

"That one puts his tail into his mouth, stiffens his body until it forms a big circle; a hoop. Then he rolls through the woods after his victims. He can move faster than a man can run."

"Sheeeeit," Melvin said. He slowly stepped ashore. He was followed by Ben and then by Lance. The three men stood under the casuarina trees as Lance explained how mullet skiffs could quickly be off-loaded by a crew of skilled humpers. Trucks parked under the casuarina trees could not be seen from the air; even by low-hovering helicopters. And after the trucks were loaded they could be Miami-bound on U.S. 41 in minutes.

Melvin walked a few paces down the road. He

burped loudly and put a hand to his chest. Small spiked cones that had dropped from the trees crunched under his boots. He looked down. The ground was covered with the cones. "What's this?"

Lance came forward and kicked one of the cones. His eyes widened and he looked around. "Looks like alligator turds to me. We must be near a den. Keep your eyes open. Gators can be on top of you before you know they're anywhere around. They're faster than greased lightning."

"Fuck this shit," Melvin exploded. He slammed an open palm onto his chest. "I can see all I need to see from the boat. Or from a car." He waved toward the boat. "Let's get outta here."

"But you haven't seen the old hotel up near Forty-one that the dopers sometimes use for a stash house," Lance said.

"Fuck the stash house. Fuck the dopers. Fuck a bunch of alligators." He rubbed his stomach, made a wry face, belched, and said, "I feel like I ate at the wrong exit on the turnpike."

"You don't like turnpikes either?" Lance exclaimed. "I hate expressways. Bathrooms are horrible."

Melvin ignored Lance and led the way to the boat. He motioned for the others to get in. "You guys get in. I'm sitting up front." He waved again as Lance and then Ben stepped aboard. Melvin pushed the boat away from the ground and jumped aboard. Mud was caked on his boots. He stamped them on the bottom several times. Great clumps of black mud covered the bottom of the boat.

"Pit bulls with AIDS. Fucking hoop snakes. Alligators. Goddamn dopers ain't worth all this. I ain't walking through alligator shit to catch some honky smuggling a little weed. We need a goddamn air strike back here. That's what we need. Call in the United States Air Force and napalm this place off the map."

Melvin slapped his chest. He waved his hands in the air. "Your snake and bug repellent doesn't work. Mosquitoes are eating me alive. Only thing that stuff did was make me feel like I'm about to puke.''

Lance shrugged. ''Told you I didn't recommend it. You have to use that stuff for years before it really works.''

As the boat slowly motored down the narrow creek, Lance talked of techniques used by the fishermen-turned-smugglers in Everglades City. Just before the boat entered the Barron River, Lance said, ''It was a good trip. Hope you guys can make use of whatever you picked up today.'' He paused. ''I'm just sorry we didn't hear a mile-o-more bird. They're real special. Not many people ever heard of them. Woods back here are full of 'em.''

Melvin looked over his shoulder. ''What is a mile-o-more bird?''

''The thing stands about four or five feet tall. Biggest bird in the park,'' Lance said. ''Pink.''

''Why is it so special?'' Ben asked.

''The bird can't bend its legs. When it feeds, it leans way over to eat. Then it straightens up. After a few minutes, something about this process causes enormous gas buildups. Then every time the bird straightens up, it farts. Can't help it. Unbelievably loud. You can hear it all across the Everglades and sometimes out on the water in the Ten Thousand Islands. Locals say you can hear it for a mile or more. That's where it got its name.''

Ben turned and looked at Lance in disbelief.

Melvin shook his head and uttered a sincere, ''Sheeeeit.''

Lance looked away and grinned. Sometimes his devil brain took over and he was helpless.

21

The heart of Operation Everglades II, as conceived by Raymond Dumnik, was a fish house. The small fish house sat on the dock in Goodland, a fishing village between Marco Island and Royal Palm Hammock. Goodland, though it is only three miles from the million-dollar high-rise condominiums of Marco Island, is much like Everglades City in that its waterways open onto the Ten Thousand Islands, many of its longtime inhabitants are fishermen, and hard times have turned many fishermen to drug smuggling.

Dumnik's idea, and basically it was a sound one, was to lease a small fish house, then insinuate DEA agents—who would work at the fish house—into local drug-smuggling organizations. The smugglers of Goodland were closely aligned with the smugglers of Everglades City. The only flaw in Dumnik's plan was the people he picked to be the on-scene undercover operatives: Melvin, the black agent from New Jersey who felt, and rightly so, that he was surrounded by rednecks; and Ben, the corn-fed kid from Kansas. Neither man liked humping hundred-pound boxes of fish from before dawn until after dark, neither man was comfortable dealing with the taciturn hard-bitten local fishermen, neither man knew anything about the water or boats or weather, and—perhaps worst of all—neither man could distinguish a pompano from a squid. They were, as Nick said, strangers in a strange land. And by the third week of the operation, Lance, who worked on the dock with them, and the other agents in the task force were fed up.

There was no way they could ingratiate themselves into a bunch of smugglers when Melvin, probably the only black guy in Goodland, wore cordovan wing tips while working on the dock, complained about the smell of fish, and seemed limited to loud explosions of "muthafucker" or "sheeeeit" every time a boatload of fish arrived at the dock. He wore wraparound sunglasses day and night. And he constantly issued orders to other members of the task force working around the fish house. "Hey, boy, put that box of stinking fish in the cooler," he would say, causing local fishermen-smugglers to narrow their eyes in bewilderment. And Ben, who thought he was living in a comic strip, could not refrain from endlessly asking naive questions of the fishermen; questions that revealed again and again he knew nothing about fishing. He told the fishermen he was a college student who was taking off a year to earn money.

In the beginning Lance was amused by the whole thing. It was another DEA cluster fuck. But, hey, he was working outside, hanging out with fishermen, learning names, learning which boats and crews were most likely to be dopers, and—on the nights he was not drinking with the fishermen—filing voluminous intelligence reports with Kimberly. The two of them had feared that DEA's incompetence would cause the U/C operation to be blown. After all, Dumnik and Pete McBride, who were supervising this goat-roping, had rented a three-level town house in Pelican Bay replete with indoor pool, tennis court, audiovisual room, and a five-car garage. And DEA, through a dummy corporation, was paying $3,800 a month to rent the fish house, a business that usually rented for $1,500. Everything was so garish, so ostentatious, that it cried out in the quiet little fishing village.

Kimberly and Lance became almost hysterical when Lance came in late one evening and told her what a shrimper had said. The grizzled old shrimper put his hand on Lance's shoulder and said, "Son, be careful. You mixed up with Big Brother."

"With who?"

The shrimper nodded knowingly and leaned closer. "Organized crime," he whispered.

"What are you talking about?"

"Ain't you noticed the accents of them people you working with?"

Lance nodded.

"They ain't from around here."

"You got that right."

"They're organized crime," the fisherman said with a knowing nod. "Here to do one deal. A big one, we figure, and then they're gone."

Lance smiled. "Scared me there for a minute. You said 'Big Brother' and I thought you meant the government."

The shrimper laughed. "Naw, they too damn stupid even for the government." He leaned close again. "They from up north. Like I said, they gonna do one deal, we don't know how big but we figure real big, then they'll split. Be careful around that crowd. They seem dumb. But they got money. Big money. They'll kill you in a heartbeat."

Lance had nodded and assured the shrimper he would, indeed, be careful.

He and Kimberly later had a good laugh over how the DEA was so incompetent no one believed they were DEA; that the operation was so flawed the locals considered them a ring of organized-crime figures.

Lance had not expected Melvin and Ben to contribute much toward creative law enforcement. But neither had he expected them to be such incompetents. The situation was compounded by Melvin's overweening arrogance and Ben's bottomless naiveté. Then one morning, a sultry overcast day with lowering clouds scudding in from the west, Melvin announced he was no longer going to hump baskets of fish from boat to cooler to truck. "I be a fucking GS-thirteen," he said. "Step nine. Soon as this little dipshit operation is over, I'm gonna be a fourteen; a fast-tracking supervisor. And DEA supervisors don't fuck with baskets of fish."

"What the hell these local fishermen going to think?" Lance asked. He wore white gum boots, grimy jeans, and a T-shirt from a local oyster house that read "SHUCK ME, SUCK ME, EAT ME RAW."

"Who gives a fuck what they think? They can't think."

"Maybe not. But if they come to the dock and see a bunch of white guys moving fish, and they see your black ass sitting around like you own the place, they will know this ain't a legitimate fishing operation."

Melvin wiped the perspiration from his face, looked up at the overcast sky almost in anger, then looked at Lance. "You mean black people can't be managers?"

"Not at a fish house where all the customers are local fishermen. How many other blacks you even seen on the dock? You're the only one. This is Goodland, Florida, not some shit hole in New Jersey."

Melvin had not heard a word. "You mean you just can't find good help around here, that there are no black people qualified to supervise a bunch of white people even if those white people are too dumb to do anything but sling fish?"

Lance looked around the dock. "Melvin, for God's sake."

"It's time you white people learned to take orders from a black person; time you learned to work for a black supervisor. That's the way things are going to be. Get used to it."

Lance shook his head. "Hey, I can get along with anybody. If you want to make this racial, then you're saying blacks have a monopoly on dumb. I'm saying you can be dumb no matter what color you are. It's possible for you to do something stupid without it having anything to do with what color you are. Good God, Melvin, the local dopers think you and Ben are too stupid to be DEA; they think you're organized crime. It was dumb to send you here; just as it would be dumb to send me into some New York ghetto to sell crack. It's dumb. Dumb. Terminal dumb. Mega dumb. Not black dumb. Just dumb. Dumb with a capital D. Dumb."

Melvin crouched and cocked his fists in a boxer's pose. "That's it. Me and you. Right here. Right now. Come on. Show me what you got."

Lance held up his hands, palms toward Melvin, and

backed up a step. "I'm not gonna fight you. Not here."

Melvin moved forward, first circling and weaving. "Chickenshit white-assed muthafucker. I'm gonna clean your clock."

Lance backed up. "Goddammit, Melvin, people on the boats can see us."

"So they gonna see me wipe up the dock with your ass."

"Melvin, these fishermen don't fight blacks; they kill them. You been bitching about rednecks for weeks. You've seen these people. You've heard them call you nigger. Get with the fucking program. They see us fighting, one of 'em will shoot you. Think of the operation, if nothing else. You want to blow the last few weeks? If you want to fight, I'll meet you somewhere and you can have a shot. But not now."

Melvin paused, fist still circling.

"You fuck up Dumnik's operation over some imagined racial shit, and you'll be busted to GS-nothing. Your DEA career will be over. He'll have you shuffling papers at the embassy in Kingston."

Melvin slowed. He shook his head. "Ain't sending me down there to work with a bunch of tree niggers."

"Hell he won't. The attorney general and the President are involved in the Everglades City operation. You know that. Stats on this one go to the top. You think screaming discrimination will hold water against that kind of power?"

Melvin thought for a moment. He stood erect and lowered his fists. "You lucky. We do our business later. I won't forget."

"Me either."

Melvin motioned toward the fishing boat approaching the dock. "Unload that fucker. I got to go call Dumnik."

Lance sighed. He turned and waved at the crew of the fishing boat. His tanned face was split with a dazzling smile. "Hey, guys. Any luck?"

The skipper, who was leaning out the wheelhouse

door, did not answer for a moment. He had seen Lance and Melvin squared off. Then he pointed to the darkening sky. "Weather's coming in. We called it a day."

Lance worked until midafternoon unloading the fishing boat. When he finished, he wearily pulled off his gloves and went inside. Melvin stood up from the small desk in the corner.

"Go see your boss," he said.

Lance was too tired to respond. He looked at Melvin.

"Go see your boss," Melvin repeated. "You going to be working tonight."

22

"Hey, boss," Lance said with a wide grin. "I think we saw a window of opportunity and jumped through it." He waited a moment and added, "Should have had your Jesus brain at work. It never would have happened."

Nick did not respond. He sat on the middle seat of the small Whaler, slumped over, his body rhythmically flowing forward, then back, as large waves rolled in from the northwest, lifted the boat, then dropped it down the backside of the sloping wall of water. He was like a cowboy riding a bucking bronco, as the boat sunfished toward the gray overcast and the low-scudding sea fog. The thirteen-foot Whaler was eight miles south-southwest of Big Marco Pass, out in the open Gulf and fully exposed to rollers pushed high by a fetch that included the full north-south axis of the Gulf of Mexico. The wind had been rising for the past six hours, until it was a steady keening wail. Most people exposed to this sort of wind for several hours would find themselves irritable, restless, angry; it was the sort of wind that some fishermen said would steal a person's soul. But Lance, who had shut down one engine and had the other running at just enough speed to maintain steerage into the waves, sat there grinning and chewing on a salt-spray-soaked Snickers bar. He wore jeans and a T-shirt that said "GOD GUNS AND GUTS MADE AMERICA GREAT," one of the few T-shirts he owned that Nick liked. Nick was quiet; he had hunkered down to ride it out. He was phlegmatic, philosophical; a rock being pounded by the elements. He was thinking of the homicide case and the lack of clues. More than three dozen people had been interviewed and a dozen investigators were working the case full-time. So far, nothing. But Nick was patient. He knew he would prevail.

Lance tried again. He raised his head and shouted toward Nick's rounded back. "hey, jefe máximo. This is shit with a capital S and we're in it up to our necks." He laughed. " 'Course, on a little short guy like you, that's not very deep."

No response.

"What's a party animal like me doing out in this storm? I was born to party. Here I am caught in a storm from hell." He looked with respect on the giant rollers bearing down on them. "Waves must be from there too."

No response.

"Hey, you really think the bad guys will come out in this stuff?"

Nick's lowered head turned toward his right shoulder. "We're out here and we don't make any money."

Lance nodded. "Yeah, and the humpers will make five or ten grand tonight."

Humpers, the guys who schlepped marijuana from the Cuban shrimp boats to the local crab boats, and from the crab boats to the hill, or from the hill to trucks, were the lowest-paid people in an off-loading. And they would be out tonight. The dopers who worked boats, like smugglers who used aircraft, preferred bad weather to good. It helped hide them. And dopers believed that cops were reluctant to work in stormy weather. Nick was right; the dopers would be coming through. That was, if the intelligence information was correct.

"You think Melvin had good information?" Lance asked. He rolled up the paper from the Snickers bar and stuffed it into his pocket.

Nick's head, covered by the hood of a slicker, turned from side to side. "Don't know. But we had to come out."

Lance nodded in agreement. If the DEA, which was running the task force, advised a local agency that four loads of marijuana were coming through its jurisdiction, the locals could not afford to ignore the information. Not even if they didn't know the source of the information. Not even if they thought the DEA agent running the operation was, as Lance said, "mega stupid."

"So what time do you think the shrimp boat will show up?"

Nick lifted his head and looked around. Darkness was fast approaching. The wind continued to rise. In addition to the spray from the bow, the wind was blowing spume from the wave tops back over Nick and Lance. A light rain was beginning to fall. Lance pulled a yellow slicker over his shoulders.

"Soon, I hope."

Lance held on to the seat as he stood up and looked around. Visibility had been good until the rain began falling. But now he could see no more than a hundred yards. Soon it would be a hundred feet. Neither the Cuban shrimp boat nor the crab boats from Everglades City would be using lights. The off-loading could go down almost within shouting distance and he might never see it. He looked at Nick's back.

"Hey, jefe. We got to get a new boat. One with some electronics on it. We got to trade in this toy."

No response.

Lance looked down at the book about crystals he had been reading before the storm. It was sodden. He nudged it with his foot and mumbled, "Just like I thought. That crystal business is all wet."

Lance looked at Nick. "Wind gets much higher,

we're going to have to shut down the engine and just ride out the storm." He grinned as he remembered Nick's tendency to become seasick. "Hey, how about something to eat?"

Nick shook his head.

Lance's smile widened and his eyes danced. "Don't you want some nice greasy, slimy, stinky anchovies? How 'bout an anchovy-and-butter sandwich? Maybe dipped in olive oil? With lard for dessert?"

No response.

"Hey, you not gonna throw up, are you? Don't drop a plaid belch in my boat."

Nick sighed. It was going to be a long night.

About ten miles east of where Nick and Lance were battening down for a long stormy night, two Cubans stood on the docks that ran continually along the south bank of the Barron River. Both were in their late twenties. One was dressed simply in gum boots, jeans, and a blue shirt. The other, obviously the leader, wore tight black pants, black pointed shoes, and a sleeveless black undershirt. He was slender but with well-defined muscles. Around his waist was a brightly colored scarf that had been rolled into a ropelike belt that was tied in a square knot over his right hip. In the small of his back, under the tight black pants, was the handle of a nickel-plated forty-five-caliber automatic. His curly black hair reached to his shoulders. In the lobe of his left ear was a heavy gold ring studded with a large diamond.

The darkly handsome Cuban turned and paced down the dock, hands clenched as the high heels of his shoes knocked out a fast pace. He ignored his companion and the three Everglades City fishermen standing a few feet away. He glanced upward. The wind, which had been rising all day, was now blowing about thirty-five knots. A hard, almost horizontal rain pelted the men.

"Gringos. Pendejos," said the Cuban. "No cojones. Like dogs, they must be whipped."

The first Cuban, obviously a fisherman, as were the men from Everglades City, was impassive. Like most watermen, he knew tonight was not a night to be on the Gulf of Mexico; not even to meet a shrimp boat loaded with marijuana; the off-loading of which would net each person involved at least ten thousand dollars, double the usual price for humpers. But to the narco-trafficantes, especially the ambitious hard young lieutenants, nothing mattered except getting the job done.

The young Cuban, ignoring the rain streaming down his face and soaking his clothes, held his hands out toward the three Everglades City fishermen. They stood closely together in an unconscious symbol of their unity against the wild-eyed young Cuban; the man who was in charge of the load going down tonight.

"We must know what happened to the boat," the Cuban said, voice loud over the wind. "Why is there no radio contact? What has happened?"

For a moment the three fishermen were silent. Then one stepped forward. "Probably lost. He was not that experienced." The fishermen looked up. "It's bad out there."

The Cuban grimaced in anger. "You are fishermen. You know the waters. What does a little wind matter? What am I paying you for? You must send out another boat."

The fisherman shook his head. "You won't get anybody to go out in this weather. There's fourteen-foot seas offshore. Unless there's one hell of a skipper at the wheel, a crab boat will turn turtle before it's a half-mile out of the pass."

The Cuban had paced until he was face-to-face with the fisherman. He put his hands on his hips and moved even closer. The noses of the two men almost touched. "I'm paying good money to have you meet my boat and bring the shit inside. Are you old women? If my boat brings the shit up from the south, why can you not go out and meet him? He is out in the little storm. Why can't you go out?"

Suddenly the fisherman from Everglades City was pushed aside and the Cuban found himself staring up into the face of a giant. An angry giant. It was Big Knocker.

"I'll go meet your fucking boat. But you're gonna have to pay triple."

The Cuban smiled and shook his head.

"Triple," Big Knocker said. "Pay triple. If you don't, you lose it. If the storm doesn't get it, tomorrow morning you'll have a loaded shrimp boat a few miles offshore and the cops will get it." He leaned closer to the Cuban, poked him in the chest with a giant forefinger, and added, "In fact, somebody might call the cops. A lot of people know the boat is coming in."

The Cuban, angered that the big man had poked him hard enough to force him to back up a step, for a moment almost reached for his pistol. To threaten one's business partner with the cops was sufficient cause to kill a man. But something in the big man's eyes warned the Cuban that even if he were as fast as he thought he was, the big man might be faster. Then again, he must not forget the reason he was here—to make sure the load arrived safely. He had to get the load in. Everything else was secondary. He could always settle his debt with the big man. Besides, he knew who the big man was. Every Cuban who worked Everglades City knew him. Two Cubans sent to kill him had disappeared. The man also was known as one of the most daring and courageous skippers in Everglades City. If anyone could get a crab boat through the storm, it would be this man.

The Cuban stared. "Two and a half."

Big Knocker looked down on the Cuban with utter disdain. "You shit. Triple. Or somebody might call the Coast Guard and tell them a loaded Cuban shrimp boat is offshore."

"That is too much money. We will make no profit if we pay you triple."

"I was hauling this stuff when you were still shitting green. I brought in more loads than you got hairs on your ass. I know how much it cost to get a boat up here; how much it cost to off-load; how much it cost to move it to Miami. So don't try that with me. Last chance. I leave, and your load is lost. Triple."

The Cuban stared in defiance; trying to force Big

Knocker to avert his eyes, to show even a moment's indecision. But the big man's eyes never blinked, never shifted, never wavered.

The Cuban nodded once. "I will pay you one-half the usual amount in advance; the remainder when the load has been delivered."

"No. I don't want half the usual amount; I want half the triple rate."

The Cuban started to protest.

"Storm rules," Big Knocker said.

"My friend, you push hard."

Big Knocker poked the Cuban in the chest again, causing a flash of anger in the smaller man's eyes. "I am not your friend, asshole. Don't forget that. And don't forget you are in America. This ain't Cuba. You play by your rules in Cuba. You play by my rules here. Do it my way or lose the load. Now, stop mealymouthing and either pay up or start looking for a hole to hide in. 'Cause the shit's about to come down, one way or the other. You decide."

For a long moment the men on the dock were frozen in a tableau of tension and anger. The Everglades City fishermen usually were wary in dealing with the volatile Cubans. The relationship was formal and distant. They lived in an isolated community and all they heard of or knew about Cubans was bad. They dealt with Cubans because of the money. Now Big Knocker was backing this guy into a corner. They did not know how he would react. Nor did the second Cuban. He had never seen his boss lose control of a business deal before. He always dictated terms and people always jumped to do his bidding. Those who did not, often were killed. But the load tonight was particularly important. The amount of cocaine hidden inside the bales of marijuana made this load many times more valuable than usual.

Then the Cuban smiled up at Big Knocker. "It will be done. You have a crew?"

Big Knocker turned to the fishermen behind him. "Triple wages if you go out with me tonight."

The fishermen looked at each other, nodded in

agreement, and one said, "We'll go with you, Knocker."

Big Knocker talked earnestly with the Cuban for about five minutes; finding out the location of the shrimp boat; how much marijuana was aboard; and determining recognition and communication codes. Then he looked at the fisherman who earlier had been talking to the Cuban. "Call around. Line up a half-dozen mullet skiffs. Have them wait for me inside Indian Key Pass at marker twelve. Call December and tell her to get out there on the water with the park ranger." He turned toward the other fishermen and pointed toward his crab boat tied up at the dock. "Get aboard," he said. "I'll be there in a minute."

The fishermen paused a moment. They thought the storm would force Big Knocker to come inside the islands much sooner; that he would meet the mullet skiffs behind Panther Key, somewhere around marker twelve, and come up the Faka Union River to Port of the Islands, where the load easily could be loaded aboard trucks at Highway 41. To bring the loaded crab boat on down the coast to Indian Key Pass would expose the boat to the storm for a longer period.

Then the fishermen turned away. Big Knocker was the skipper. This was his deal. They trusted his ability to handle a boat.

As the fishermen moved to their duties, Big Knocker turned back toward the Cuban. He smiled. "Okay, Cube. Let's see what color your money is."

No sign of the first crab boat was ever found. It disappeared in the storm. Lost with all hands. Newspaper stories said the crab boat had been lost in a violent storm. Readers not familiar with crab fishing thought only passingly of the dangers of going to sea in small boats. Readers who knew it was not yet the season for stone crabs wondered why a crab boat was out at all. A few readers, those who knew the boat and the crew, knew it was a dope deal gone sour; that the men had been going out to meet a shrimper and that the skipper had been overpowered by the waves.

* * *

At eleven A.M. the next day, a bone-weary Nick and Lance limped slowly into a marina south of Naples. Water sloshed ankle-deep in the bottom. Nick and Lance had bailed all night. They had not found the Cuban shrimp boat that was to have arrived last night. Again, the radios aboard the Whaler had been drenched with salt water, soaked until the circuits were fried. None of the other electronics aboard the little boat worked.

As the boat approached the dock, Lance pushed his shoulders back, stretched, and said, "Boss, we got to get us another boat; a boat big enough to go offshore. I'm tired of going outside in this little toy."

"What we got to do right now is find a phone," Nick said wearily. He tied the bowline to the dock. "Get the sternline," he said. "I've got to call the office and see what went down last night."

Lance was wearily stretched out on the dock, half-asleep and enjoying the hot sun, when Nick returned. Nick nudged Lance with his toe.

"What's going on?" Lance asked.

Nick looked across the water and didn't answer for a minute. "We didn't get the job done. The load got through," he said.

"You sure?"

"Yeah, the wire taps and McBride's new van with all the electronics picked up enough stuff early this morning to know the load got in."

"She know the players?"

"Some of them."

Lance shrugged and grinned. "Let her put it all in the computer. Maybe she'll come up with something." He closed his eyes.

"That's not all."

"Oh?"

Nick sighed. "Couple of hours ago Dumnik called a press conference."

Lance opened his eyes. "For what?"

"The DEA went out this morning and arrested eighteen people from Everglades City. None of them had anything to do with the load last night. None had anything to do with the U/C deal in Goodland. These were cases McBride was working up. Every one was our case. They weren't ready. When they go to trial, the bad guys will probably walk.''

Lance jumped to his feet. He spun in a circle and laughed.

"What's so funny?'' Nick growled.

"Working with DEA is like working in a whorehouse. The better you do, the more you get screwed.''

Nick sighed and pulled at his mustache. "Dumnik set back this investigation at least six months. Maybe longer. The six-o'clock news in Miami and all the newspaper stories will say DEA came in and cleaned up the few remaining dopers in Everglades City; that you could hold Sunday-school picnics over there. The President will get excited. The attorney general will get an atta-boy. Dumnik will get another medal. Melvin will get his promotion.''

Lance nodded. "All we get is seasick.''

Nick nodded.

"We get something else,'' Lance added. "We get to deal with a town full of dopers. Nothing's changed in Everglades City. We still have to clean up that cesspool.''

Nick pulled at his mustache. "So let's go do it,'' he said.

Nick was not the only person unhappy about the DEA arrests and the closing down of Operation Everglades II. Andrea Dolan, Dumnik's secretary, was also upset. For weeks she had worked every Friday evening. She had told her husband that a top-secret investigation, one backed by the attorney general and the President, was under way. Her husband, Coast Guard dweeb that he was, was duly impressed. But now the operation was over and Andrea had to resume her Friday-night car payments.

23

The Baptist church in Everglades City is located across the street from the school and about a block from the Barron River. Nick waited in front of the church for the mourners to come out. It was almost noon and the palm tree under which he was standing offered virtually no shade. He wore a black suit, black hat, and a starched white shirt. The sun, white hot in its intensity, beamed down on him like the open door of a blast furnace. Not even the hint of a breeze stirred. The air was filled with multiple squadrons of voracious attack mosquitoes. Nevertheless, Nick stood patiently, hands clasped in the palms-together pose so favored by undertakers, and waited.

"It's hotter than the hinges on the back gates of hell," he muttered, lips not moving.

Inside a white van parked about thirty yards away, a van with placards on the side identifying it as the vehicle of a Naples florist, three men heard Nick. Joe Willy and Dickman were operating the video cameras, tape recorders, and radios of the new intelligence van while Lance—who was Nick's backup—waited nervously, eyes locked on his boss.

"We got good voice quality," Joe Willy said.

"On both bugs," Dickman added. He took a deep puff off his cigarette and nodded in satisfaction. Nick was wearing two bugs, one in his hat and one in his lapel. Each operated on its own frequency, and each was tied into a separate tape recorder in the van. Every sigh, every word uttered by Nick, every word anyone spoke to him, would be recorded. He had a small, almost invisible flesh-colored receiver in his ear. Anyone who noticed would think it was a hearing aid. One video camera was locked on Nick. Two others, backed up by a still camera, would be used to photograph everyone coming out of the church.

Three days after the crab boat went down in the storm, a funeral was being held for the one crew member whose body had been found. The bodies of the skipper and the other crew member were lost. The funeral was also a memorial service for those three men. Nothing binds the people of a small town closer together than the collective experience of burying or remembering their dead; especially in a fishing village where men often are lost at sea. It did not matter that they were going out to meet a shrimp boat loaded with drugs; or that they had gone out in a vicious storm that drove much larger ships into port. The important thing was that they were fishermen who lost their lives in a storm at sea. Nick knew that. And he knew that every fisherman in Everglades City, many of whom also were drug smugglers, would be there. It would be a rare chance to see and to photograph those men at a time when, he hoped, their natural reticence and wariness around outsiders would be diminished.

Some civilians, upon learning that cops consider funerals a prime source of intelligence gathering, might be a bit uneasy. But, just as young soldiers know that a pious manner and a uniform are—at church—the ultimate aphrodisiac for many young women, so cops know that, at a funeral, even the most hardened criminal has a brief sense of his own mortality. And in those few moments when the bad guy senses, however faint and however far away, his own death, he is vulnerable. In those few moments, the minds of the bad guys and the minds of the cops are locked on common thoughts of paradise; the bad guy is hoping his departed friend made it to paradise. And the cop is hoping, in a more practical fashion, that his investigation might reach the promised land; that he will identify a new bad guy, or overhear a snippet of conversation, or see two people talking, and suddenly it will all come together. The investigation will reach a new plateau; the end will be in sight.

Nick needed that. Once again he had been used by

DEA. Many of Kimberly McBride's cases had ended precipitately. People had been arrested too soon. Investigations that, months down the road, might have borne much fruit, were closed for the sake of arresting a few minor figures. On paper it looked good. DEA had seized a few loads, arrested a few people. It made the front pages of newspapers from Fort Myers to Miami. DEA said their follow-up investigation had truly cleaned up Everglades City; that drug smuggling was no longer a problem there.

Once again it was up to the locals, to Nick and his troops, to press on with the day-to-day grind of a lengthy and seemingly impossible investigation; an investigation in which the bad guys were twice burned and extremely gun-shy. Today was the first step in rebuilding the case against the smugglers of Everglades City.

Nick was not worried about being recognized by local dopers. His black suit, hat, and sunglasses were something of a disguise. But even if there were one or two dopers who might recognize him, they would not expect to see him at a funeral. Nick, like many cops, had discovered a psychological truth about people: even if someone had known a friend for years, he might, upon seeing that friend in a strange or unexpected place, fail to recognize him. This is particularly true if the friend is dressed in a different fashion or with unknown associates. To the people coming out of the church, Nick would be one of the group from the Naples funeral home. The owner of the funeral home, who was present today, knew who Nick was; two other workers were told that Nick was a potential new employee.

Nick's concern was the heat. He took a handkerchief from his pocket and slowly wiped his forehead, face, and neck. He looked up at the dozens of buzzards in the air over Everglades City, and a small grin tugged at the corners of his mustache. He ducked his head and mumbled, "Buzzards must know who the funeral's for. They're circling by the hundreds."

Inside the van, Dickman chuckled.

"Okay, I think everyone's inside. The music has started. So let's go to work," Nick said. With hands clasped behind his back and head bent forward as if in respectful remembrance, he began walking down the line of cars parked in front of the church. He walked slowly, and as he walked he called aloud the tag number of each vehicle parked by the church. Then he returned and walked down the side street to get more tag numbers. Inside the van, Joe Willy wrote down each number. Once he laughed. Lance and Dickman looked at him. "Nick just called out the tag number of the van."

"Wants to see if you guys are awake," Lance said, watching Nick as his boss rounded the van and continued down the street, still calling out tag numbers.

"Go ahead and run the van's number," Lance said. "Confirm that the return is good."

Ten minutes later, when Nick was reasonably certain he had located every vehicle whose occupants might be attending the memorial service, he returned to stand in front of the church.

Inside the van, Joe Willy took the list of tag numbers and turned to a Zenith lap-top computer that was tied by cable to a cellular telephone. He poked in the numbers that would connect him with the Florida Department of Motor Vehicles, then rapidly keyed in the tag numbers. He finished and punched another key. Immediately a small printer to his left began emitting a sound like that of paper being ripped. He had a printout showing the owner of record for each vehicle whose tag number had been keyed in. He smiled when he saw the van's owner listed in the innocuous corporate name of a Fort Myers leasing company.

After the funeral, as people began leaving the church, Joe Willy and Dickman would have a busy few minutes photographing people as they entered their cars and trucks. Then Nick would have photographs of dopers, their names, the types of vehicles they drove, and—simply by tying the computer into another data base—the criminal records, if any, of all those people. Plus, of course, whatever audio Nick managed to pick up from the dopers as they left church.

Dickman radioed Nick the identity of vehicles belonging to Heart Attack and Big Knocker, two people near the top of the ladder in the Everglades City smuggling hierarchy. Dickman had a problem because only one surveillance car was available. It was parked on a side street with a well-dressed couple inside; a couple dressed as if they had been to a funeral.

"You want to follow Heart Attack?" Nick asked.

"Yeah. Since he's supposed to be the honcho."

"Stand by." Nick sauntered past Big Knocker's four-wheel-drive vehicle, turned around to make sure no one was in sight, quickly reached inside the grille, then raised the hood a few feet. Three seconds later the hood was down and Nick was sauntering on down the street.

"Big Knocker's gonna need a ride. My guess is he will ask Heart Attack," he said.

Joe Willy laughed. Dickman turned to Lance. "How'd he get around the hood release?"

Lance shook his head in respect. "Old Nick can do anything." He reached for the microphone. "Hey, jefe, I'm surprised at you."

"We all have our Peniel, sooner or later," Nick mumbled.

The three me in the van looked at each other. "Peniel?" Joe Willy asked.

"Some of his Bible stuff," Lance said. "Don't worry about it."

At that moment, over the van's interior speakers came the sound of a piano playing the slow and mournful strains of "Nearer My God to Thee," The funeral was ending.

Lance turned to Joe Willy and Dickman. "Hey, guys. Showtime."

The two sorcerers began fine-tuning their electronic toys, reading dials, checking signal lights, keying up equipment that had been on standby. Dickman, to the great relief of Lance and Joe Willy, put out his cigarette and did not light another.

A moment later the doors of the church opened.

Dickman quickly punched a series of buttons. "Cameras rolling," he said. Joe Willy quickly checked the monitors. He punched another button and, two seconds later, a machine whirred and ejected a color photograph of the open doors of the church.

"We're in business," he said.

"Hey, boss, do your stuff," Lance said softly, eyes never leaving Nick as he stared through the one-way windows in the side of the van. He patted the left side of his chest, verifying for the tenth time that his big silver hogleg Magnum was in the shoulder holster. He didn't expect anything to happen at the funeral. It was a simple intelligence-gathering mission. But if someone recognized Nick and tried to move on him, Lance would be out of the door in a flash. Anybody tried to hurt Nick, and there would be another funeral in Everglades City.

As Lance stared through the window, right hand on the handle that opened the door, the eyes of Dickman and Joe Willy were fixed on the monitors and on the bewildering banks of electronic equipment.

Nick stood at the foot of the church steps, nodding solicitously as the first mourners, a man and a woman, exited. They looked at him. The woman returned his nod, smiled briefly, and the two continued down the walkway. A few feet later they stopped, and as is the fashion at rural southern funerals, waited for others in the church to exit. All the friends and relatives would stand around talking for a few moments; then they would go to the cemetery for the burial and afterward to the home of the deceased's nearest relatives. There they would sit down to a meal consisting of the special dishes prepared by almost every female member of the church. People who enjoy the traditional food of various regions in the South know that funeral food is the best to be found.

A big man, a man standing about six-feet-six, came out of the church, stood on the top step, and looked around. His eyes lingered briefly on the van, but passed on when he saw the florist sign. It was Big Knocker.

He ignored Nick's nod and walked down the steps, followed by Heart Attack and his four daughters.

Inside the van, the three men sighed and groaned. Lance immediately picked out the dark-haired one as December. The other three were blonds and all beautiful. But one of them had a soft innocence, while the other two frowned. Lance had eyes only for December. He looked out the window, then at the monitor.

"Zoom number one in on the one with black hair," he said.

Joe Willy didn't have to ask whom he was talking about. "How tight you want it?" he asked.

"Face. Full frame."

"No boobs? She's got great boobs."

"Okay, make a hard copy of one with boobs and one full face."

Lance reached for the microphone connected to the receiver in Nick's ear. "Hey, jefe," he said. "See the good-looking one off to your left?"

Nick grunted.

"I'm getting a stiffy."

Nick turned, rapidly walked away a half-dozen steps, and put his hand to his mouth. He leaned over as if he were suppressing a cough. "Don't talk that way in front of the church," he said angrily.

Lance laughed.

"How 'bout an ass shot?" Joe Willy asked.

"Okay, do an ass shot."

"Legs? God, she's got legs that reach all the way up to her ass. You want some leg shots?"

"Legs too."

"How about another boob shot? Side view."

"Do it."

Lance stared, almost as if hypnotized, toward December. Her legs were tanned and firm. The light cotton dress, draped so casually, revealed more than it hid. Her hips were wide, her bust full. She had the willowy, languid walk of an athlete. Or a tigress. As the camera zoomed even tighter on her face, Lance could see a fine sheen of perspiration on her upper lip. Do women perspire only on their upper lips? If not, why is it that men notice only the perspiration of their lips? But it was her eyes, the dark fathomless eyes, that made Lance sigh. December had young-old eyes, eyes that had seen decades ahead and decades behind; eyes filled with knowledge, wisdom, and challenge.

"If only she wasn't a doper," Lance said, "I'd marry her."

"I like the young one standing off by herself," Joe Willy said.

"Those other two ain't bad," Dickman said. "What do we know about them?"

"Very little now," Lance said. "But we'll know soon."

"You mean when we get our ears in place?" Dickman said.

Lance nodded, eyes darting from the window to the monitor to the printer, which was spewing out numerous color pictures of December. "Yeah," he said absently. The three men had almost forgotten the funeral.

"That's where McBride is today," Dickman said. "Leasing a building downtown and working out the final details of where to install some video cameras. We got something special in store for Everglades City."

"You're not afraid they'll snap to it?" Joe Willy asked, eyes on the youngest daughter of Heart Attack.

"Naw. They might worry about home phones. But they never think pay phones or motel phones are bugged."

December and her sisters stopped and turned to talk with their father. Lance stared for a moment at December's back, then shook his head. He returned to the window. "Almost forget why I was here," he said. He began taking pictures with a thirty-five-millimeter camera while Joe Willy and Dickman, like two medieval sorcerers stirring mysterious smoking caldrons, operated video cameras and tape recorders.

Almost two dozen people had exited from the church before the first person drifted toward Nick. It was a middle-aged man, face darkened and wrinkled by years in the sun. Nick knew the man was a fisherman. "Hidy," the man said, "You with the funeral home?"

Nick nodded, smiled sympathetically, and stuck out his hand. "Sorry about your friends," he said.

The man nodded—a lot of nodding goes on at funerals—and said, "Don't guess you knew any of them?"

Nick shook his head. "I hear they were good people."

The fisherman heard Nick's voice and unconsciously knew he was a neighbor from somewhere in southwest Florida. He saw that the stocky little guy had an open, trusting face. What he did not notice were Nick's eyes; the guarded wary eyes of a longtime cop. The fisherman pulled a pack of cigarettes from his shirt pocket and looked up, eyes unconsciously checking the sky and the clouds, anticipating the weather. He lit the cigarette, then said, "They were. They were. I knew them all. Especially Scott Wilson."

"The skipper?" Nick asked.

The fisherman nodded. "Knew him best."

Nick looked at the people coming from the church. "He had lots of friends."

The fisherman smiled and did not speak for a moment. He puffed on the cigarette. Then he said, "He was a good man." He paused, "He did a little smuggling. But he was a good man."

"Smuggling? You mean . . . ?"

The fisherman smiled. He looked around at the people coming from the church, nodded to several, and said, "Yeah. Most folk here are smugglers."

Nick stepped closer, as if he and the fisherman were sharing a secret. His low voice was filled with amazement. "Really? Uh, you're kidding?"

Inside the van Joe Willy and Dickman were chuckling. "Nick's trying to win an Oscar," Joe Willy said.

"It's working. It's working," Dickman said. He watched the monitor closely. "Wish I had that guy's cigarette."

The three men laughed, then sighed in mock sympathy as Big Knocker, an expression of anger on his face, returned to the church, looked around, and settled on Heart Attack. Big Knocker leaned over and whispered. Heart Attack spoke softly to his daughters, then walked away with Big Knocker.

"They're going for a ride," Lance said. "You notify the surveillance car?"

"I want to wait until I see which way they're going," Joe Willy said. "They might be tail-conscious and double back."

Nick and the fisherman were still talking. The fisherman puffed on his cigarette and smiled down at Nick. "Nope. About everybody I know in this church, except for the preacher, has hauled a little weed one time or another."

Nick shook his head as if in astonishment. "Including you?"

The fisherman shrugged. "Well, I might have done some in the past."

Joe Willy turned to Dickman. "He means yesterday."

"Isn't that against the law?" Nick asked in amazement.

Dickman turned to Joe Willy. "You're right. He's going for the Oscar."

"Best actor or comedy?"

"Probably comedy. Wait until I show this tape at the office."

The fisherman nodded. "Well, it might be. But we've all done it." He waved toward two men coming down the steps. "Come on. I want you to meet two of Scott Wilson's best friends." He puffed on his cigarette, grinned, and said, "They've hauled as much weed as anybody I know."

The fisherman stuck out his hand toward Nick. "I didn't catch your name. I know you work for the funeral home, but tell me your name."

"Bubba. Bubba Jones."

The three men in the van laughed aloud. "Bubba Jones," Lance said in derision. "Where the hell did he get that?"

"You a local man, ain't you?" the fisherman asked Nick.

"Raised right here in Collier County."

The fisherman nodded. "Thought so. Come on and let me introduce you to some of my friends."

Joe Willy and Dickman raised clenched fists in triumph. The intelligence van was proving its worth.

But Lance was curious about something. He bit his lip in concentration and stared through the heavily tinted window. Why had Nick said he was "raised in Collier County"? Natives always said they were "born and raised in Collier County." Lance made a mental note to check some records at the office.

24

Nick sat in the large dining room of his home, which was built in a pine thicket east of Naples. The door to the wooden deck was open and a gentle breeze blew through the house. Nick was three hours late coming home, so his wife, Susie, and his two children had eaten long ago. Susie was putting the two kids—a boy and a girl—to bed. Nick leaned over his plate of venison, cornbread, and vegetables. Like most cops, he ate fast; knowing the telephone could ring at any minute. As he ate he watched Elmer, his pit bull, sitting on the carpet in the living room.

Nick stared at the dog as he thought of the unsolved homicides and the Everglades City case. He wondered idly if they were connected. That theory had been considered and then discarded because the Everglades City crowd was supposed to be pretty laid-back. Then again, they were supposed to smuggle only marijuana. Nick needed a break in the two cases. There still was no clue on the double homicide. And the Everglades City case was more than a year old. The funeral had provided good intelligence on the smugglers. Lots of names. This time the investigation would be kept quiet; DEA would not know of it.

Every time his troops began building cases, DEA, through the task force, came in and took over. They grabbed a few headlines and ran.

Nick wanted to solve the case and he wanted his boss, State Attorney Joe D'Alessandro, to get the credit. Nick felt as if he owed Joe D'Alessandro a great deal. Joe had rescued him from the hell of working for Broward County Sheriff Hiram Turnipseed. Nick believed in loyalty up and loyalty down. It was easy to be loyal to Joe. The guy's integrity was a beacon for everyone in his office. His fairness and evenhandedness were legendary. He was the first one in the office every morning and was the last to leave that evening. Having him for a boss, after working in Broward County, was like dying and going to heaven. Joe D'Alessandro was a good man, and Nick wanted him to get the glory for cleaning up Everglades City.

Nick pushed his plate aside, then took a long drink of iced tea. He sat back in the chair, pulled at his mustache, and stared at Elmer. Elmer was getting old. His hip, broken years ago when he attacked a tractor tire, was becoming arthritic. Because of his hip, every time Elmer threw up his leg to urinate, he pitched forward on his chest. Elmer was the only dog in Florida who stood on his head to pee. And years of practice had enabled him to do it with a certain amount of panache. Lance still enjoyed giving Elmer copious amounts of water so he could watch the dog pee. Every time Elmer lifted a leg and lurched forward onto his chest, Lance went into gales of laughter.

Elmer was grizzled about the muzzle and his eyes had lost some of their sparkle. When he walked in the woods with Nick, no longer did he simply plow through bushes and shrubs; he walked around them. But Elmer's vital forces had not abated. He remained a stud dog of considerable renown. In fact, Nick already had picked two pups as the stud fee from Elmer's latest litter. Two muscular solid white pups that, when Nick stuck his baseball hat into their pen, would snarl and growl and bite down on it with such force that he could lift them high in the air. How long they would hold on, he didn't know. His arm grew tired before they released the cap. He told Susie he was going to name them Goodness and Mercy because "they'll follow me all the days of my life."

Elmer, tongue lolling, gazed expectantly at Nick. He sat on the rug in a hip-shot pose, waiting. Staring. Nick stared back, hardly seeing the dog as he drank his iced tea and thought about the Everglades City case. McBride was right. What the case needed was a snitch. Not a low-level humper or even the driver of a mullet skiff, but someone at the top; someone who could bring Lance in undercover. Then big-time cases could be made. A lot of people would go to jail for a long time.

Nick wearily rubbed his eyes. He needed to go fishing. A half-day on the water would clear his head and enable him to see things more clearly. But the trouble with fishing was that hemorrhoids were out on the water thundering around in big boats, almost swamping fishermen every time they passed.

Nick stared at Elmer. Elmer stared back, the stump of his tail wagging furiously, his eyes bright in adulation.

Nick knew that Heart Attack, who was dumb enough to go on national television, was a heavy breather among the dopers of Everglades City. So was Big Knocker. There were others, but these guys were the bigfeet. By now it was clear that Heart Attack controlled much of the smuggling and Big Knocker the security. Plus, Big Knocker did a lot of doping on his own. Flip one of them, and cases could be made against almost every smuggler in Everglades City.

Elmer shifted. The change in position brought a new light to his eyes. His head tilted back until his muzzle was pointed almost straight up. His tongue lolled farther. Keeping his eyes warily on Nick, he began pivoting, turning on the carpet; slowly at first, then faster and faster. His tongue began to dart in and out. His moans suddenly caught Nick's attention. Nick leaned forward, slapped a hand on the table, and whispered urgently, "Elmer. Stop it." He looked over his shoulder to make sure Susie had not seen. She hadn't. He turned back toward the dog. Elmer's head was tucked low; his ears hung limply, and his eyes looked up, imploring. Nick looked at the carpet and shook his head in disgust.

"Elmer, stop doing butt twirls on the carpet. It makes brown spots. Susie's gonna put you outside."

Elmer whined anxiously, almost as if he understood.

Nick pointed his finger at the dog. "Stay. Don't move."

Nick picked up the portable telephone on the table near his right hand. He punched in a series of numbers, put the phone to his ear. He spoke even before the person on the other end could say hello.

"Everything ready?"

"The U/C facility is ready," Kimberly answered without a pause. She had grown used to how Nick sometimes avoided social amenities. At those times she didn't engage in idle conversation; she simply reeled off the information Nick wanted. "Lance is about to leave. The van is there. It's operational. Audio and video are excellent. And within the next day or so, Joe Willy and Dickman will have the new computer program ready."

"The telephone thing?"

"Yes. It should have a tremendous impact."

"Okay, let's take these people down. It's going to take a while, but we can do it."

"I think you're right. It's only a matter of time."

"Let me know what's going on."

"I will."

"Put Cunningham on."

After a pause Lance came to the phone and mumbled something that sounded vaguely like, "Sí, jefe."

Nick looked at the telephone. "What's the matter with you?" he asked.

Another pause. Then Lance laughed. "I had a mouthful of Snickers."

"Well, quit eating candy and listen to me."

"Hey, I'm a trained investigator. I can do both at the same time."

"Cunningham, I got a job for you."

After a brief conversation, Lance's perpetual smile widened. "Hey, that's a mega idea," he said. He shook his head in respect for Nick's plan. "They're gonna be pissed with a capital P."

"Use that pickup truck we seized the other day. It's got a trailer hitch."

"You want me to use a truck registered to a doper? Jefe, I thought you had a Jesus brain."

"Can you do it?"

Lance was offended. "Does a hobby horse have a hickory—?"

Nick interrupted. "Let me know when you get back."

Nick hung up. He looked at Elmer, who sat, tongue lolling, staring up at Nick. The dog's eyes were bright. He wanted to continue his butt twirls, but not while Nick was watching.

Nick whistled. The dog arose and ran toward the table.

"Elmer, what would you rather be? A smuggler or a dead dog?"

Elmer performed his only trick. He collapsed, rolled over on his back, folded his front paws, and closed his eyes.

Nick nodded in approval. "Damn right."

25

Lance drove east across the arrow-straight unbending length of State Road 84 that stretched from Naples to

Fort Lauderdale. In six months, a year, whenever the environmental problems were solved and all the construction finished, this road would become the southernmost extension of I-75. That meant service stations and bathrooms would be built along the road, and there was nothing in the world Lance disliked more than a bathroom on an interstate highway. For all his flaky ways, Lance liked a solitary, quiet, and above all else, clean bathroom. His idea of hell was spending eternity using every bathroom on every interstate highway.

Almost as bad as the bathrooms were the teenage boys who worked in service stations along the interstates, and the people from whom one had to get a key in order to use the bathroom. Like a pointy-headed Cerberus, each of these slack-jawed kids guarded the bathrooms. These kids had mastered every grimace of impatience. They were doing patrons a big favor by bestowing upon them the blessing of the key. They flicked their heads toward a key hanging on a distant wall or tossed it across the counter with an expression of distaste. Their rudeness was palpable. It was clear that being key master was beneath them; they were all rocket scientists waiting for a phone call from the Cape. Not one of them had learned that a person must master menial jobs before he can strive for big jobs.

Lance wheeled off State Road 84 and turned south on the Palmetto Expressway. Not far from the DEA building, in an office park on northwest Fifty-third Street, he found the small street he was looking for and then drove slowly down a long double row of warehouses until he saw the building number he wanted. He looked until he saw where the telephone lines came to the roof, then led down the side of the building. He pulled to the curb, opened the door, but did not switch off the ignition. As he walked, he held a knife hidden in his hand. When he reached the telephone line's junction box, he reached out with his left hand, held the wires tightly, then slid the knife underneath and pulled. The wires parted. Lance turned and walked to the truck, drove to the corner, turned left, then pulled up before a closed door and blew the horn. A few seconds later he blew it again, this time longer.

A door opened and a uniformed security guard strolled toward the truck. The guard was miffed that Lance had blown the horn. Before the guard could speak, Lance leaned out the window, flashed his creds, and said, "Hey, I'm current occupant and I'm in a hell of a hurry."

"What can I do for you?" the guard said. The current-occupant bit went right past him, as it did everyone else. Lance was convinced that when people were introduced, they never listened for the other person's name.

"You can open the door and let me in. Got a big one going down."

"Show me that ID again."

"Ray Dumnik called you. Told you what I needed." He flashed his tin.

"Who?"

"Hey, pal, you don't have to play that game. You know who Dumnik is. If I don't get the boat he sent me for, a big-time dope deal is going sour." Lance looked at his watch. "Now, how about opening the door and letting me get the boat and get the hell out of here?"

The security guard was nervous. No one from DEA had called to say this guy was coming to the secret warehouse.

"Mr. Dumnik hasn't called me. I don't know anything about this."

Lance looked at the security guard and shrugged. "You know how it is. Dumnik is up there where the elephants mate. Sometimes decisions don't roll downhill as fast as they should."

Lance looked at his watch. "Tell you what," he said. "Open the door and let me in. While I'm hooking up the trailer, you call Dumnik's office. Fair enough?" He again looked at his watch. Then he picked up his hand-held police radio. "Hell, I'll call him. 'Victor two-six. Victor five-one,' " he said. He waited. He knew no one in Naples could hear him on the frequency he was using. But it looked good. He tried again. Then, as if suddenly remembering the security guard, he looked up. "Fair enough?"

The security guard paused.

"Victor two-six. Victor five-one." Lance paused. "No answer. They must all be over at Ma Grundy's getting drunk."

The security guard smiled knowingly. He had heard about the DEA drinking parties at Ma Grundy's.

Lance looked at his watch again. "Hey, guy. One of the biggest coke deals in history is about to go down and I'm the U/C guy. We gotta have that boat to make it work. You're gonna let a little paperwork botch it up? I showed you my creds. I tried to raise DEA on the radio. Don't let me lost a thousand keys just because the bureaucracy is in a wad."

The security guard was wavering.

"Just open the door and call DEA while I'm hooking up the boat," Lance said.

The guard nodded, turned, and walked inside. A moment later the large overheard door opened, and Lance, tires squealing, roared inside the warehouse. Even as the guard reached for the phone, he realized this deal was okay. Like most narcs, the guy in the truck acted as if he owned the world. But, just to cover his ass, he would call DEA.

Lance looked around in awe as he drove down the wide middle aisle in the warehouse. Dozens of motor homes, cars, trucks, and boats were lined up—all seized during drug deals. It was a gigantic candy store.

Lance was a connoisseur of boats. During his time in Fort Lauderdale he had driven Scarabs, Cigarettes, Magnums, and—during the Turks and Caicos investigation—an Executioner, the fastest production boat in the world.

"Eeny, meeny, miney, moe," he mumbled as he drove. Then he made a quick decision. The blue-and-white Scarab on the right looked good. A thirty-two-footer with two big outboards, looked like two-hundred-horse Mercs, slung on the transom. Over the cockpit, a handmade arch of pipes held an impressive collection of radio antennae. This baby was loaded. Dopers used nothing but the best.

He stopped, sauntered along the trailer, jumped atop the wheel, and looked over the gunwale into the cockpit. He whistled in approval. Depth gauge, loran, four radios, plus a plethora of buttons, dials, and gauges that Lance knew came only with a highly customized craft. Yep, this was the boat.

As he backed the truck toward the trailer, he saw the security guard bustling down the center aisle. "I need you to spot for me," Lance shouted. "Hurry up."

The guard was again caught off-balance. The telephone was dead. He was rushing to tell the young cop that he couldn't allow a boat to be removed from the warehouse. But the guy was yelling for him to hurry and help him back the truck up to the trailer hitch. Lance was following a basic dictum of tradecraft for U/C operatives: always control the situation. No matter what's going on, no matter who is with you, control the situation. The security guard was beginning to feel overwhelmed, as if he were caught in the grip of forces he could not control.

Even as he waved a cautionary finger at Lance, he moved toward the tongue of the trailer. There he stopped and held up his right hand, giving Lance a target as he backed up.

The security guard flashed both palms and shouted, "Stop."

Lance jumped out and walked toward the trailer. Before the guard could speak, Lance looked at the cup on the extreme end of the trailer tongue. It was directly over the ball of the trailer hitch on the truck.

"Perfect," he said. "You did a great job. We got it right the first time." He began unwinding the winch that lowered the boat trailer toward the hitch.

"Phone's not working," the guard began. "I couldn't get—"

"Don't worry about it," Lance interrupted. "I found the boat we need. Everything's okay. You can always call Dumnik."

"Yeah, but nothing is supposed to go out of here unless DEA tells me in advance."

Lance locked the trailer hitch, then crossed the safety chains and hooked them on the truck frame forward of the bumper. "It's okay," he said. He laughed. "Nobody knows about this place but cops. You think I'm a doper?"

"No, but . . ."

Lance stood up, dusted off his hands, then patted the guard on the shoulder. "Then what's the big deal? Hey, it's okay. But if it's not, blame it on me. Tell Dumnik I insisted. Have him call me."

The guard suddenly realized Lance had not signed in when he entered the warehouse. Everyone was supposed to sign in. He had a clipboard for that purpose.

Lance took a final look at the trailer. "Watch me when I pull out," he said. "I don't want to ding one of Dumnik's boats." He jumped into the cab and put the truck in gear.

"Am I clear?" he shouted as he slowly pulled forward.

The guard glanced at his clipboard and then toward the trailer. "Clear. But the phone is out of order. You didn't sign in. You never . . . You can't—"

"Thanks much," Lance said with a wave as he drove slowly through the large open door. "You're a big help."

The guard watched as the truck pulled the blue-and-white Scarab down the street. For a moment he was sure he heard the cop laughing and singing. Then the truck turned the corner and disappeared.

The guard picked up the phone, listened, and slammed it down in frustration. He pressed a button that closed the overhead door. He looked at his watch. There was a shift change in two hours. Then the telephone could be repaired and he could report to DEA.

As Lance reached State Road 84 and turned west for the long straight run across Alligator Alley toward Naples, he pounded on the steering wheel and shouted in glee. He loved it when his devil brain was working. Now he had a boat, a blue-water boat, that could go outside where the dopers roamed, handle heavy seas, and—by the time Nick's mechanics had finished—would outrun just about anything in the Gulf of Mexico.

"America's hero is on the move," he shouted. "I'm gonna kick some doper ass." He laughed and pounded the steering wheel. He looked in the mirror at the long clean lines of the Scarab. With a pleased grin he nodded and said to himself, "Yessir, I sure am glad DEA believes in cooperating with local law enforcement."

26

"What are you doing in here in the dark?" Nick asked. "You can't get the job done when you can't see."

"Close the door," Lance said, his eyes never leaving the small television monitor on his desk. He held up his right hand and, without taking his eyes from the screen, motioned for Nick to come closer. "Look at this. Will you look at this."

Nick shut the door of Lance's office. It was a small windowless room on the third floor of the courthouse in Fort Myers. The third floor was the state attorney's floor; lawyers in the larger offices to the front; Nick Brown's investigators in smaller, much smaller, offices to the rear. The cubicles, corridors, halls, offices, partitions, and numerous confusing turns made the offices a virtual maze of gray walls and gray ceilings and gray carpets. It was only inside the tiny closetlike offices of the investigators that one saw any sign of individuality; usually in the form of pictures or commendations. Lance's office, however, contained no pictures. He had circumvented the courthouse ban on painting the walls a color other than institutional gray by covering them with posters and maps. On the right was a large poster of Liberty in the guise of a bare-breasted Rubenesque woman carrying the flag as she led men into battle. On the left, over Lance's small desk, were two large charts—one marine, one aviation—of the Twentieth Judicial Circuit. A more detailed marine chart of the area around Everglades City was tacked over the larger chart. To the rear was a bookcase and a coatrack. Lance's Magnum with the six-inch barrel hung in its shoulder holster on the coatrack. A stalactitelike forest of strings hung from the ceiling; each containing some sort of memento of the cases Lance had worked on. A yellow plastic bucket, one of many he had filled with water and quick-frozen before dropping the resulting ice bombs from a helicopter onto fleeing smugglers in the Turks and Caicos Islands, hung from a string. So did a blackened piece of wood, about all that remained from a stash house on Bimini he had burned. Hanging from strings were models of all the aircraft in which he had flown; the predominant ones being the Cessna Citation and the Blackhawk helicopter used by U.S. Customs. Bones of whales and porpoises and various fish that had washed up on the beaches also hung from the ceiling.

"I feel like King Kong on the Empire State Building with all these little airplanes buzzing around my head," Nick said. He walked across the room, stood beside Lance, and looked at the television monitor.

"Surveillance tape from the funeral?" he said.

"You got it." Lance's eyes never left the screen.

"Why is it all of that woman? What's her name? December?"

"The one and only. Look at that. Boobs from hell. Ooooohh. Stiffy time."

"Where is the tape of me and the dopers—the important stuff?"

"Stand up and you can see it."

Nick cuffed Lance on the shoulder. "I am standing up."

"The heavy-duty, big-time U/C tape is separate. Good stuff. Names, faces, cars; McBride's got it all in her computer. Good info there."

Nick looked down at Lance. "Thanks," he said wryly. "I'm glad my work meets with your approval."

Lance nodded somberly. "For an old guy with white hair in his ears, you do okay." Lance looked up. "You heard what Dickman and Joe Willy got?"

"From the van?"

"Yep. Those boys picked up some stuff that might give you the hammer you been looking for with Big Knocker. Stuff with his little brother." Lance wiggled his shoulders and in a falsetto said, "Oooooooohhhh-oo-ooooohhh."

"So why am I looking at pictures of December? Show me the good stuff."

"Boss, I'm in love. I have never in my life seen a woman like that. She's my idea of heaven. I'd chase a laundry truck twenty-six miles barefooted over broken glass; I'd wade through ninety-two miles of alligator dooky just to—"

"You a sick person."

"I know. I know."

"Tell me about the good stuff."

"Jefe, you must be older than dirt if you'd rather look at pictures of dopers than of this little honey."

"What's the point in this? Why are you watching this woman? We know who she is."

Lance grinned. "Just looking."

Nick snorted. "If she had as many peckers sticking out of her as she's had stuck in, she'd look like a porcupine."

"Jefe," Lance said in pretended outrage, "you are talking about the woman I love."

"Why don't you grow up? Why don't you get married?"

Lance made a loud noise of pain and indignation. Then he stood, spun around in a circle, hands over his head, and in a simpering falsetto sang:

I don't go with the girls anymore.
I don't think I'll marry.
Gonna stay at home and play with myself.
Wheeee, I'm a fairy.

Then he sat down.

Nick shook his head and sighed. "For the fifteenth time, why are you sitting in here in the dark watching tape of this doper woman? Tell me about the hammer for Big Knocker. That's important."

"I'm taking the Scarab out tonight. Checking it out."

"Where you going?"

Lance shrugged. "I don't know," he said vaguely. "Might go offshore. Might go down around Everglades City. Not sure yet."

"You got any intel about something going down, or you just trolling?"

"Checking out the boat. Little trolling."

"Last time. Why you watching this tape?"

After a moment Lance said, "Boss, why are the really good-looking women, I mean the world-class knockouts, always screwed up? I mean big-time. I've known dozens. They're the most fucked-up people in the world. Crazy; twisted in some way, crooked, no morals, alcoholics, dopers; there's something bad wrong with every one of them. Hell, all I want to do is screw. But it's getting so I want to turn and run every time I see a really beautiful woman." He waved at the screen. "Good example. This is the sort of woman men die for. Look at that. Perfect. Men would give their left testicle and five years of their life to spend one night with her. And she's a doper. If McBride's intel on her is correct, she has co-opted God only knows how many law-enforcement people by screwing their eyes out. I bet most of those guys were good cops. If she told me she would screw me, I'd forget Everglades City. Hey, let 'em smuggle forever. Bring in all the dope they want. I'd help 'em hump bales. Who cares?"

"Sure you would," Nick said calmly.

"Why is a woman this pretty a doper? Why?"

"Pretty has got nothing to do with it."

"Humor me. Say it does. Now, tell me why."

"You really want to know?"

Lance paused. His voice changed. He was serious. "Yeah, I really want to know."

Nick paused. "In World War Two movies, you ever see an ugly Nazi?"

Lance looked up in astonishment. What was Nick talking about?

"Not only in the movies, but in real life, they were—generally speaking—good-looking people. Tall, blond, blue eyes, athletic. They were close to being the supermen they thought they were." Nick paused. "They also personified pure evil as much as any group of people ever did."

Nick looked down at Lance. "Ever see a picture of Gandhi?"

Lance nodded.

"Skinny little bug-eyed guy. Weighed maybe eighty pounds soaking wet. Arms and legs like toothpicks. Ugly as nine miles of dirt road."

Nick pulled at his mustache. "I have trouble with his passive-resistance stuff. I go to church and I know all about turning the other cheek. But I been a cop long enough to know that doesn't always work. Somebody comes after you to hurt you, you hurt them worse. And you do it first."

He paused. "Gandhi was a good man. One of the best. He brought about more change than the Nazis. And he is remembered as someone who made a difference. For good."

Lance arched his eyebrows, leaned toward Nick, and asked, "You saying I should screw only ugly skinny women who look like Gandhi?"

"I'm saying that evil is usually pretty; usually attractive. That's why people do it. Goodness sometimes has no appeal; at least not on the surface."

"Too profound for me," Lance said. He thought for a moment. "You mean like all the people who became dopers because of the money?"

Nick nodded. "Money is part of it. A big part. But I think most people get into smuggling because their lives are empty; they need something and don't now where to go to get it. They are—you might not understand this—spiritually desolate. The excitement of running dope makes them think they've found what they're looking for. That is, until we catch them.''

"I ain't screwing ugly skinny women.''

"Pretty gets old. If that's all there is, it gets old soon. And there's nothing left but ashes. Ashes and bile and shame.''

Lance almost laughed. Then he looked up at Nick's face. Nick was serious. "Boss, I ask you a personal question?''

"Ummmmm.''

"You ever been unfaithful?''

"No.''

"Ever wanted to?''

Nick pulled his mustache. He nodded. "A lot,'' he said softly.

"But you never did?''

"Nope.''

"Why not?''

Nick paused. "The pleasure is never as great as the pain.''

"Pain? Pain? Hell, I ain't talking about whips and chains. I'm talking about a little on the side.''

"The pain that comes with guilt.''

Lance shook his finger at Nick. "What if you knew there was no way, absolutely no way, you would get caught?''

Nick nodded in understanding. He didn't answer for a moment. Then he said, "That could be the worst punishment of all.''

Lance wrinkled his brow. "I don't understand that.''

"You can't jump from the lap of Delilah into the bosom of Abraham.''

Lance waved a hand is dismissal. "I'm talking big-time stiffy and you're giving me Bible stuff.'' He paused, then added, "And don't tell me I got to screw ugly women.''

"You asked me a question. I answered it.'' Nick looked at Lance. "Let me put it another way. Don't do things that make you feel guilty.''

"Only thing that makes me feel guilty is screwing ugly women."

"Why don't you go out with McBride? She too smart, too strong for you?"

Lance snorted. "Going to bed with McBride would be like a movie."

"Whatta you mean?"

"Romancing the stone."

"Forget bed. Just take her out to dinner or somewhere. She's a good person."

Lance shook his head and continued to stare at the screen of December. He didn't want to hear any more of what Nick had to say about women. Sometimes Nick was full of crap.

"You mentioned Joe Willy and Dickman," Nick said. He sensed Lance's change of mood. "Tell me what they got."

Lance stared at the screen for a moment without answering. "Okay, here's the big-time intel. Here's the hammer. Big Knocker has a brother, little faggot named Robert, and Robert has a boyfriend named Bobby. Joe Willy and Dickman got them on tape. The tape smokes. Boss, you see what those two guys are doing and it'll make you go to church every day for a month." He looked up. "Don't worry. The tape will be used only for intelligence purposes. We won't go to court with it."

"So what does this office want with a tape of two faggots? Is that all you guys got to do?"

"Wait a minute. I'm getting to the good part. Robert was on Big Knocker's boat and apparently witnessed him killing some guy. Cut out his gizzard and tossed him overboard to the sharks. We got Robert on tape talking to his friend about it."

"Big Knocker took his brother on a deal?"

"Yeah, and the kid witnessed a homicide."

"We can use the kid to get to Big Knocker?"

"Way this Robert talks, he and his big brother are close. Their parents are dead and they're the only two left in the family. Big Knocker apparently looks on

Robert as if he is handicapped. Robert thinks it's funny that Big Knocker is so protective.''

Nick thought for a moment. ''This deal went down while Big Knocker was on work-release?''

Lance was still watching the monitor. ''You got it.''

''So we can put Big Knocker aboard a boat bringing in a load, maybe find out who the other crew members were and squeeze them for more information about the homicide. What else can the kid give us?''

Lance looked up. ''Isn't that enough?''

Nick looked down at Lance. He didn't speak for a long moment. He and Lance had worked together for almost ten years; ever since he pulled Lance from the vice squad over in Broward County and put him into narcotics. He sometimes played too loose and sometimes he practiced what he called street-level law enforcement; but his investigations were taught in police academies; even DEA had copied some of his techniques.

''Do we have to do it this way?''

Lance knew what Nick was talking about. Sometimes Nick's religious nature got in the way of his being a cop. Nick wanted to get the job done, he wanted to clean up Everglades City, but he would prefer to do it without hammering a young gay man. Lance waited. He did not answer.

After a moment Nick sighed and slapped the back of Lance's chair. ''Okay, open up a file on young Robert. Squeeze him. Maybe you should arrest him; go for an indictment. The grand jury meets in a couple of weeks. Show Big Knocker we mean business. Then, when he thinks his little brother is going to the joint, we'll see what he has to tell us.''

Lance nodded. ''It's done.''

''You've already started?''

''Hey, I'm a trained investigator.''

''Sometimes I wonder who runs this office,'' Nick mumbled. He turned to leave. ''Before you go blind watching that women, tell me what you're calling the file about young Robert and his buddy. I want to read it.''

"How about Oral Roberts?" He waved his hands. "Just joking. I thought about some of the things these two boys were doing—boss, they use cocaine in a way you never heard of—so I called it Anal Roberts."

"You opened an investigative file that McBride and some of the women lawyers will be reading, and you called it 'Anal Roberts'?"

Lance spun around in the chair. "Yeah, you see, when these two guys do coke, they—"

Nick held up his hands. "I don't want to hear it." He walked away. At the door he turned and said, "Be careful on that boat tonight."

Lance turned back to the screen. He studied December's face for a long moment. Then he adjusted the controls and zoomed in until December's eyes took up the entire screen. He leaned closer, trying to look through her eyes into her very soul. After a while he pursed his lips, sighed, and shook his head. He turned off the monitor.

27

Lance was hurrying sundown as he stood at the wheel of the blue-and-white Scarab and thundered toward the southeast, keeping his heading on the one-five-zero and staying at least two miles offshore as he passed Marco Island and the ever-changing shoals in the mouth of Caxambas Pass. He veered more toward the south to clear the treacherous Cape Romano Shoals. He could have cut through Big Marco Pass, across Sanctuary Sound, out Big Marco River, then wound along the western edge of Goodland Bay and Coon Key Pass before reaching Gullivan Bay and the Ten Thousand Islands, but he was testing the Scarab, pushing it hard as he sought to learn exactly what the boat would do and for how long. Anyone could take a boat through the clearly marked channels; even the tourists whom Nick called hemorrhoids. But Lance had hung two more engines on the stern, and not many people could take the Scarab offshore, wind up the four big outboards, and go blasting through blue water at—he looked at the speedometer—seventy-six miles an hour. The dopers who had owned this boat had kept it in top condition. The engines were almost new; only about twenty hours on each of them. And she was built for high speeds, heavy seas, and big loads. Over the cockpit was a custom-made arch of two-inch stainless-steel pipes. Mounted atop the arch were four antennae. All but one were folded down toward the stern. Four aft-facing waterproof speakers also were mounted on the arch. Each was attached to a separate radio and each had enough power to blast out over the thunder of four screaming supercharged engines.

Joe Willy and Dickman, the two electronics geniuses, had spent two days with the boat and rigged up a few mods that Lance particularly liked. For instance, if Lance were working U/C and a doper was aboard the boat, Lance could wear a headset, ostensibly in order to hear the radios over the sound of the engines. And if the doper wanted to wear a headset, he would, in fact, listen to the agreed-upon frequencies. But Lance had access to a small series of switches that enabled him to listen to two separate frequencies—a different one in each ear—over the headset. He could receive instructions or monitor frequencies and the doper would never know what was going on.

As Lance rounded Cape Romano Shoals, he looked to his left. Coon Key light was blinking away. He passed Dismal Key Pass, Fakahatchee Pass, and West Pass. Then he slowed and looked to his right, searching the approaches to the Ten Thousand Islands, looking for crab boats or shrimp boats. Nothing. He angled more to his left. He passed the marker for Indian Key Pass and, keeping the marker on his left, slowed and turned northeast. He would take a quick look up around Chokoloskee Bay. Maybe the boys from Everglades City were on the move. It was dark enough that no one would recognize him; they didn't know the boat—at least not yet. He might get lucky.

The Scarab pushed through the dark waters, a wave of white water spreading from her bow, and a froth of foam steaming in her wake. Lance shut down two of the engines; no sense in needlessly burning gasoline at such low speeds.

He passed marker number six and, at the fork in the dark water, turned left into Russell Pass. He knew the navigable waters petered out somewhere before he reached the oyster reefs on the southwest side of Chokoloskee Bay; only a local fisherman in a mullet skiff could get through, and then only if he had a set of balls that wouldn't fit into a washtub. But the mangroves offered a good place to hide for a while. Lance turned off a third engine, pressed the buttons that raised the props of the three engines until they were clear of the water, and pressed on deeper into the heart of darkness, traveling slowly and quietly on one engine. At the edge of a mangrove thicket he slowed until only the rising tide was carrying him forward; then he eased into the bushes, used two lines to secure the boat, and turned off the engine. He checked the lines and watched for a moment as he made sure the lines were holding. Then he put on a dark nylon jacket, slathered his face and hands with high-powered insect repellent, turned up his collar, crossed his arms, and waited. He waited and he listened.

It was eleven P.M. when, eyes swollen almost shut from mosquito bites, he decided to call it a night. Nothing was going on in the Ten Thousand Islands. Like most surveillance, this one had turned out to be hours and hours of nothing. Zip. Now the tide was beginning to ebb and it was time to go home.

Lance fired up one engine and motored slowly through the mangroves. He lowered the other three into the water. Once he cleared the treacherous passes and mangrove islands, he was going to blast straight ahead into the Gulf, then turn and make a high-speed run up to Naples. Clear out the mosquitoes. Blow away the cobwebs. Enjoy a top-speed run knowing he was king of the night.

Lance motored slowly back down Russell Pass, passed marker six again and was closing on marker four when he saw a light and two small boats.

Instinctively, without stopping to consider, Lance quickly shut off the engine and turned his radios off. The people in the two boats would have heard him in another few seconds. He peered toward the light.

One of the boats, the one showing the light, was easily identified as a mullet skiff. The second boat, and there was something vaguely familiar about the tri-hull Whaler, was slowly approaching the skiff. A man was at the wheel. He was tossing a line to the skiff. A smaller figure in the skiff reached for the line. Neither person looked toward Lance. Apparently whoever it was had not heard him. Why were two boats meeting here at the entrance to Indian Key Pass in the middle of the night? He turned the wheel, using the four props for directional control as he drifted on the current at about two knots, maybe three. He angled the Scarab so he could come close to the other two boats, but not close enough to be seen.

Then Lance realized why one figure seemed familiar. The uniform was unmistakable—the guy was a ranger for the National Park Service. That's why the configuration of his boat seemed familiar. The rangers who worked law enforcement in the park drove Whalers. Then Lance recognized the woman. He would have recognized her sooner except his attention had been drawn to the ranger. It was December; the woman whom he had watched for hours on videotape.

Lance was about fifty yards away, drifting slowly with the tide, when he saw December shuck her cotton blouse and drop it to the deck. Her jeans followed. She was nude, legs braced against the slight roll of the boat, watching the ranger undress. Then the ranger was clumsily climbing across the broad open skiff toward December.

Lance moaned in what was almost physical pain. In his heart of hearts he had entertained the idyllic fancy of meeting December and convincing her to turn her back on smuggling. He would reclaim this goddess. And someday, who knew what might happen? But that idea suddenly disappeared.

He shook his head in sadness. She was even more beautiful than he remembered. He did not believe such perfection existed. From the top of her shining, gleaming black hair to her toes, she was perfection. Her face was sculptured; high cheekbones and a mouth that, even from yards away, had a smile that made Lance ache with desire. As she moved toward the rear of the boat, her large full breasts swayed slightly, but did not bounce. Her waist, a tiny tight muscular waist, flared into wide hips, a high rounded behind, and flowed into full thighs and rounded calves. If Lance could have designed the physically perfect woman, it would have been December. And there she was, pulling the clabber-assed ranger down into the bottom of the skiff.

Lance angled the boat closer. He was at the edge of the light from the skiff. He could see into the skiff. He saw December's legs thrust skyward, then wrap around the ranger's back, and he heard the animallike yelps that came from her throat.

Then there was another noise. A radio noise. Lance looked at his radio in panic. Had he turned the wrong switch when he thought he turned his radios off? Then he realized it was not his radio. The noise came from the mullet skiff.

December's yelps ceased. Her legs were still wrapped around the ranger, but she was—for a second—frozen. Then suddenly Lance heard her voice. It was filled with venom. She thrust the ranger aside and slid from under his body, causing him to yelp in pain as he poked the tarpaulin-covered load of mullet.

December picked up the microphone and suddenly began pivoting, looking into the darkness toward Lance. He knew what had happened. Someone was watching on radar and had seen his boat drifting down on the other two boats. It could only be a doper. December was out here fucking a ranger out of doing his job.

Lance reached for the ignition switches just as December reached for her shotgun. She began pumping rounds in his direction. He turned the ignition switch as she fired the first round.

Blam!

Four more came in rapid succession.

Blam! Blam! Blam! Blam!

One thing was sure. She didn't have a plug in her shotgun. Lance hunkered low. Her first shot had gone wide and the pellets had fallen in a sibilant whisper across the water. Part of the second load of shot hit the bow, dinging and whizzing off the fiberglass. The last three rounds were wide.

Lance pushed the throttles forward, trying quickly to crank up the engines even as he moved out of shotgun range. Somebody was out there; somebody bringing in a load. That's where he was going if he could get away from this madwoman with a shotgun. Holy shit, she'd never called out, never done anything but start shooting. Dopers had all the fun.

December rapidly shoved shells into the magazine, cursing under her breath, as the ranger, also cursing, tried frantically to put on his uniform. He wondered who was out there. Had he been identified? Should he go after the boat? Judging by the sound, he would never catch it. What would he do if he did catch it? The driver had committed no crime. But what if the guy was a cop? Who else would be drifting down the pass at midnight? Unless it was another doper. Not likely. A deal was going down tonight and the locals who were not involved would stay away; unless the deal went sour and Big Knocker started tossing bales overboard. Then word would go out on the radio and the bale chasers would come tearing through the pass like a bunch of berserk waterbugs. Who was in the boat? It sounded like a go-fast boat.

The ranger finished dressing. He jumped into his boat and slipped the shoulder holster containing the .357 Magnum over his shoulder.

"Where you going?" December shouted in anger and frustration. Her face was contorted.

"You're on your own. I'm outta here," the ranger said as he reached for the ignition. The sound of the disappearing high-powered boat deepened and he knew more engines had been fired up. The sound alone told him the guy was traveling, lights out, at extremely high speed through the pass toward the crab boat.

December swung the shotgun toward the ranger. "You son of a bitch. I oughta kill you. Go stop whoever that is. Get him."

The ranger backed away and swung his boat northeast into Indian Key Pass. He didn't answer. He was too worried about the identity of the person in the go-fast boat.

"Son of a bitch," December repeated after the disappearing ranger. She swung in frustration toward the mouth of the pass. She was unconscious of being nude. She picked up the microphone of the two-meter radio.

"Game warden has gone home," she radioed. "Whoever it was in the other boat, he's coming in your direction. Fast."

28

Lance pushed the four throttles against the stop and was still gaining speed when he roared past marker one at the mouth of Indian Key Pass. He maintained his heading of about two hundred and ten degrees as the screaming engines pushed him—now at sixty-five miles an hour—into the Gulf of Mexico. The doper had to be within line of sight for the radar to have picked up his boat as he drifted down on December and the ranger. If a sailor's eye is six feet above the water, the horizon is two-point-eight nautical miles away. The wheelhouse of a crab boat is about twenty-five feet above the water and the rider maybe another five feet. From a height of thirty feet, the horizon is roughly seven miles away. So the crab boat had to be within seven, maybe eight miles. And since the radar on the crab boat had picked up Lance's boat in the mouth of the pass, that meant he was within a narrow cone of coverage; otherwise the mangrove islands would have masked the crab boat's radar signal. Wherever the crab boat was, the skipper knew a strange boat was coming down on him at high speed. There was no need for stealth.

Lance removed the metal cover from one of the blue lights hanging from the stainless-steel arch. It appeared to be part of the bracing mechanism. He pushed the light upright until it clicked into place. He flipped a switch and the flashing blue light began rotating; visible for miles across the clear night.

Now the doper would know Big Foot was on the prowl; The Man was in town. Time for the doper to contemplate a career change; to think about riding the jailhouse express. They didn't know how many cops were in the boat. Other boats might be coming from out at sea to catch them in a pincer movement; aircraft could be moving in. The dopers probably had scanners; they almost certainly had scanners, so Lance would give them something to think about.

He picked up the microphone and pushed a button that activated channel sixteen—the marine frequency monitored by the Coast Guard.

"Naples Coast Guard. Victor Five Two, a unit from the state attorney's office, is in hot pursuit of vessel suspected of carrying controlled substances. About one mile off Indian Key Pass on heading of two-one-zero."

He pushed the button again, punching up the frequency of the Florida Marine Patrol, and delivered the same message. Then the Collier County sheriff's department. Just for the hell of it, he punched a frequency often used by DEA and broadcast the same message to whatever DEA undercover boats might be in the area. He hung up the microphone and squinted at the instruments. Seventy-eight miles an hour; respectable enough to catch whatever doper was out there.

He pushed the throttle harder, trying to coax an extra knot or so of speed. He leaned down, eyes half-closed as he squinted into the darkness beyond the flashing blue light.

Then he reached for the microphone again, flicked a switch that tied him into the two-meter band used by drug smugglers, and said, "Attention, marijuana and cocaine shoppers. This is the state attorney's office calling. We have a blue-light special this evening. For just a few minutes you can turn yourselves in. You can rat on a friend. Time is limited. Just direct your attention to the flashing blue light and ask the sales clerk for help. This blue-light special lasts only a few minutes."

Lance laughed and was about to broadcast his blue-light special again when a light suddenly appeared in front of him; then another, then another, then two more. He was in the middle of a small flotilla of mullet skiffs that had come to unload the crab boat. He swerved madly, throwing the Scarab in a tight turn and throwing up a four-foot wall of water that drenched the crew of one skiff, racked the wheel hard the other way to miss another, then suddenly he was through the flotilla. The Marine Patrol was on the way; these guys were history.

At that moment, no more than a half-mile to the south, Big Knocker was climbing aboard the go-fast boat he towed behind his crab boat. He already had tossed fifty kilos of cocaine into the boat. On the other side of the crab boat, two humpers were frantically tossing bales overboard. A string of bales, tons of marijuana, stretched out behind the boat.

Big Knocker cursed in anger. He had lost twenty thousand pounds of marijuana tonight. The Cubans who owned the load would raise hell. They believed every load should get through. But there were plenty of witnesses who had seen the cop, so that was covered. Now the battle would be between the Cubans and the bale hunters.

Big Knocker jumped into the go-fast boat. The real money—fifty keys of coke—was safe. He cast off and raced away toward Sandfly Pass in his shallow-draft go-fast boat. The cop could not follow.

Ten minutes later Lance was in earnest conversation with the young skipper of a mullet skiff. The kid was a sixteen-year-old high-school student on his first solo off-loading venture and, rather than making ten grand, he had a wild-eyed cop waving a Magnum in his face and threatening to kick his ass overboard. It took less than three minutes for the kid to tell Lance the position of the crab boat.

Joe Willy and Dickman, who kept scanners by their bedsides, had heard his earlier broadcasts and called the Florida Marine Patrol, Collier County, and the Coast Guard to make sure Lance would have backup. Not that it mattered to Lance. He would go up against every doper in Florida by himself. However, Collier County had a boat in the water that was racing to cut off the other mullet skiffs. The cavalry was in the water and on the way.

Lance cuffed the kid to a seat in the bow and racked the Scarab around toward the crab boat. The kid was terrified. Lance knew by the look on his face that he would tell him whatever he wanted. Trouble was, the kid probably didn't know much.

Lance turned on a high-powered searchlight and swept the surface, looking for the tall ungainly crab boat. But the first thing he saw was bales of marijuana, dozens of bales. He slowed, weaving in and out of the bales, following them. He tilted the searchlight higher and there was the boat; two men tossing bales off the port side. They froze in the glare of his searchlight.

Lance flicked one of the radio switches to the loud hailer. "This is the state attorney's office," he said, voice booming across the night. "You are under arrest. I want everyone on deck, hands where I can see them. Move to the center of the boat. If I see anyone with a gun, I start shooting. Now, move!"

When Collier County arrived, followed closely by Nick, who had heard the radio message and come out in his small open fishing boat, Lance was in the wheel-house listening to the radios and admiring the electronic equipment. Two Cubans were cuffed to the rail. Four bales of marijuana remained on deck.

Nick, obviously relieved that Lance was safe, looked about warily. "You checked down below? Anybody else aboard?"

"Hey, I'm a trained investigator. 'Course I checked. You think any doper would stay on board knowing America's hero was after his mangy ass?"

"So whatta you got?"

"We got bodies. We got dope." He held up several marked charts. "We got intel." He looked around. "What we ain't got is the daddy rabbit. He got away."

"Know who it was?"

Lance looked around to make sure the two men handcuffed to the railing could not hear him. "Big Knocker."

Nick kicked at the door of the wheelhouse. "We have almost caught him a dozen times. How does he do it?"

Lance smiled. "Boss, I got an idea. I know how we might put the big hurt on him."

"I thought you wanted to squeeze him through his kid brother."

"I do, but the indictment's not coming down for another week. We can put my idea in place tomorrow. If it works, and then is followed by the indictment, we'll have him between a rock and a hard place." Lance laughed. "Hey, like the man said. When you got 'em by the balls, their hearts and minds will follow."

"So what's your idea?"

A few minutes later Nick looked at Lance in astonishment.

"We are not taking any active role," Lance explained. "Whatever happens, happens. All we are doing is issuing a press release."

"Yeah, but you know what will happen."

Lance shrugged. "Fortunes of war. Nobody made

Big Knocker be a doper. If he wanted to be around nice people, he could spend his time in church.''

Nick thought for a moment. He smiled. ''I guess this is what you call your devil brain.''

Lance laughed. ''And it will make him see a thousand points of light.''

''See what?''

''That's what our leader in Washington is always talking about.''

''Don't be disrespectful of the President.''

''Hey, I'm just quoting the guy.''

Nick pulled at his mustache. Then he said, 'Okay. If it will get the job done, do it.''

The next day, WBBH-TV, the NBC affiliate in Fort Myers, broadcast a story about the seizure of ten thousand pounds of marijuana found floating in the wake of a crab boat after an investigator of the state attorney's office discovered a dope deal going down.

That same day, the Fort Myers *News-Press* and the Naples *Daily News* carried lengthy stories in which an anonymous police source talked about the ten thousand pounds of marijuana and how the skipper of the boat had escaped capture. It was speculated that he made his getaway aboard another boat, possibly from a few miles farther at sea.

That evening, a clipping of the story was shown to a slender Cuban who lived in Miami. The Cuban read the story and then, with a mirthless smile, turned to the man who had shown it to him.

''The hijo de puta split the load,'' he said softly. ''He off-loaded half of it before the cops got there.''

The two men stared at each other. The second man's face tightened in anger. But his voice remained soft when he said, ''And our friend told us he lost the load. You know what to do.'' He raised a finger. ''Be very careful. He is a dangerous man.''

The second Cuban smiled. ''So am I.''

Two days later, while Big Knocker was working at the county jail, his house in Everglades City burned to the ground. And in the front yard was a dead pig, its throat slit from ear to ear.

29

Nick was at the wheel of his green Ford pickup, the one seized from a convicted Everglades City smuggler, as he and Lance drove east from Naples on I-75. At nine A.M. on a Saturday, the temperature already was eighty-six degrees. The air conditioner was turned on high.

A few miles east of town, I-75 ended in a tangle of construction and became the two-lane State Road 84, commonly known as Alligator Alley, or, simply, the Alley, a road that stretches from Naples to Fort Lauderdale. It is a desolate one hundred miles of dark cypress swamp, pine trees, sawgrass, and shimmering heat. Fifty yards north of the Alley and running parallel to the old road, new bridges had been built and a raised roadbed constructed for the final leg of I-75. The earth-moving allowed easier access to property bordering the road where Nick and several friends had leased hunting rights. Nick looked to his left as he drove along, trying to see beyond the raised roadbed into the defilade where poachers often hid their trucks before making incursions into his leased property.

He slowed because of a car ahead. He peered through the windshied. "Look at that," he said, flinging his hand toward the car.

"Look at what?"

"That big-assed car with the hemorrhoid at the wheel."

Lance looked at the Lincoln with the New York plates. Nick was right. Visible through the rear window was the rounded top of a white head and a pair of hands locked on the steering wheel.

Nick tried to pass but a long row of cars was coming west on the Alley. He dropped back in impatience.

"Saw one of those die yesterday up in Fort Myers," Lance said.

"Who?"

Lance pointed to the car ahead. "Hemorrhoid on a bicycle," he said. "One of those three-wheel bicycles with the fluorescent flag on a tall antenna. Guy was wearing those flip-top sunglasses. He was bent over, pedaling down the road. All at once he died. Just fell over on the street."

"You serious?"

"It happened."

"What'd you do?"

"I called a uniform. Hey, the guy was blocking traffic."

Nick glanced at Lance, checked the traffic ahead, and glanced at Lance again. He didn't know if Lance were serious. Before he could further explore the case of the dying hemorrhoid, he was distracted by the traffic. The long line of westbound traffic seemed unabated. Impatient drivers occasionally darted into the eastbound lane, and, even more quickly, darted back. Nick sighed. Traveling on the Alley—even without Lance riding beside him—was a bizarre experience. Then Nick saw a sign: "Entering Panther Habitat."

"Damn panthers. Why don't they just finish the road?"

Lance laughed and clapped his hands. He was wearing faded jeans and a T-shirt replete with a picture of Lenin's stern face, a couple of red palm trees, and the caption "SURF RUSSIA." "What are you mumbling about?" he asked.

Nick stared ahead. "Look at that."

"Look at what?"

Nick pointed. Another sign alerted motorists that only twenty-nine panthers were known to exist. A hundred yards later a third sign cautioned motorists to drive slowly in order to avoid panthers.

"So?" Lance said. He had seen the signs a thousand times.

"So who cares about panthers? Some drunk starts hallucinating, reports seeing a panther, and the next day there are thirty-seven bow-tie-wearing faggots from Washington collecting panther piss in the palmettos and shutting down construction of an interstate highway for months. The world's gone crazy. Why can't they just finish the road and forget the panthers? It costs fifty thousand dollars to do an environmental-impact statement every time somebody finds a panther turd.''

''They're endangered.''

''Hell, people are endangered. We're not building a road because of a few overgrown house cats.'' Nick pointed down the long narrow length of the highway. ''You know how many people died on this road last month? Fifteen. Eight of them in a single wreck. The speed limit is forty-five miles an hour but this is one of the most dangerous roads in America. In the world. The Broward sheriff's helicopters spend more time hauling people out of car wrecks than they do chasing smugglers. Finishing the interstate highway would save lives. But we stop construction because somebody finds a panther turd.''

''Yeah, and when it's finished, there will be bathrooms along here. I hate bathrooms on interstate highways.''

''You don't have to use them just because they're here.'' Nick shook his head. ''Panthers.'' He made it a term of opprobrium and disgust.

Lance smiled. Twenty years as a cop and Nick still found unpalatable some of the fundamentals of law enforcement; such as using a smuggler's homosexual brother as a means of hammering the smuggler. Today Nick was having to do something he did not want to do. Even for a righteous doper like Big Knocker, Nick did not like using such a hammer. But he would do it. He would do his job. First, however, he would work himself into a lather.

''The double homicides and the Everglades City case make me feel like I'm in the state department,'' Nick mumbled. ''All I do is stand around pulling on my pecker, wondering what's going on.''

Lance laughed. ''Hey, don't worry. Be happy. We're

gonna win. And when it's over, they're gonna make a movie about how you solved this case.''

Nick looked at Lance. Waiting.

"Yep. Gonna make a movie. Name of it's *Walking Short*. A bow-legged dwarf is gonna play your part. They're looking around for a guy handsome enough to play me.''

"I got a new job for you," Nick said."Next weekend you put on a uniform and go over to north beach in Naples. Your job is being a traffic cop for julios out there on jet skis.''

Lance laughed.

Nick stretched, peering through the top of the window, trying to see over the raised roadbed to his left. "See any vehicles over there? Damn poachers.''

"I don't see anybody," Lance said, not moving from his half-slumped position.

"Somebody's been going in there. I found where they killed two deer last week. Field-dressed them and just took out part of the meat. Left the rest for the buzzards.''

"They won't be back. Might have been tourists.''

Nick looked at Lance in disbelief. "A hemorrhoid couldn't kill a deer if one walked up and sat on his lap. And whoever it was will be back; like a dog returning to his vomit, he'll be back.''

Lance's lip curled. "Like a dog returning to his vomit? Where do you get these expressions? That's disgusting.''

"In the Bible," Nick said, as if that explained everything. He stretched again. He pointed toward the raised earth bed. "When we come to that little low spot up ahead, look over here and see if you see a truck; a little white Datsun.''

"You know what kind of vehicle the poacher drives?''

"Yeah, if he comes back, I'll recognize him.''

"How do you know who it is?''

"Dummy invited people over to his house and fed them venison. Then he brags about poaching out here.'' Nick pulled at his mustache. ''He talked to the wrong person.''

''There it is,'' Lance said in surprise.

A white pickup, only partly visible through the cut, was parked adjacent to the deep canal on the north side of the roadbed. Nick glanced quickly into the rearview mirror, turned on his left turn signal, and swung the green pickup onto the graded marl. He stopped, picked up a pair of binoculars from the seat, and read the tag number. Then he picked up the microphone for his radio and within seconds had the name of the owner of record. The white Datsun pickup was registered to the owner of a landscaping service in Naples.

Nick nodded as he hung up the microphone. ''That's the guy. I knew he would be back.''

Nick slid on a pair of sunglasses, opened the door, swung his feet around, and slid to the ground. The heels of his highly polished cowboy boots sank into the white dirt. Waves of heat, shimmering and dancing in the bright sunlight, caused Nick to squint even behind his sunglasses. He unlocked the chrome storage compartment behind the cab of his pickup and pulled out a sheathed Rapalla, a fishing knife of legendary sharpness and strength.

Nick, arms splayed out from his body like the wings of an angry rooster, stalked across the bare ground toward the pickup. He walked around the truck, examining it, then stooped beside the canal and examined the mud. He pointed to skid marks going into the water.

''There's where he slid his boat into the canal,'' he said. He looked north. He's in there poaching my deer. I wish I could get back in there and find his boat. I'd tear the bottom out.''

Lance started to speak. He stopped when he saw Nick's face. The line on his forehead joined with the vein down the left side of his nose and joined with a line under his left eye. Nick's left eye seemed to protrude from his face in anger. He had on his bad eye.

Lance, who was from Fort Lauderdale, did not understand the rigid code of behavior among the rural people of southwest Florida. It was there; unwritten, but known to the natives and as inviolate as holy writ. The code covered rules of dress, behavior, talk, and even the home one lived in and the car one drove. It was ignorance of the code and unknowingly violating the code by the tourists, the hemorrhoids, that caused the local people of southwest Florida to dislike them with such intensity. Almost everything a tourist did— from wearing madras pants to talking too loud—grated on the sensibilities of the locals. The tourists were like missionaries among the savages; thinking that because they brought money and patronized local restaurants and golf courses and drove gas-guzzling boats, they were some exalted species. Lance knew there was a code, but not how to unravel the esoteric details. He knew that the rules governing land were sacrosanct; and he knew that among the people of southwest Florida, poachers were considered vermin. If caught, they sometimes were shot.

Lance looked at his watch. "Nick, we need to be moving on. They're expecting us at the prison."

"People in jail ain't going nowhere. They'll wait."

Nick turned back toward the white pickup. As he approached, he pulled the Rapalla from its sheath. He looked about. No one was in sight.

Lance started to speak but changed his mind. He'd burned down stash houses owned by drug smugglers, tossed hunks of ice from a helicopter onto cocaine-laden go-fast boats, and spent years, as he described it, "mind-fucking the dopers." He did so knowing that, if Nick caught him, he would be fired. The two men, even though only ten years separated them, were like father and son. Nevertheless, Nick went by the book. He would let a bad guy go free rather than take a shortcut in gathering evidence. He would not let the people who worked for him break the law in order to enforce the law. And it was a matter of great pride with Nick that, although sometimes his investigations were lengthy, once they went to court, the bad guy would be convicted. It was a given. Nick sewed him up so tightly, no jury would let him walk. In more than four hundred cases he had brought to court, not one person, not one, had ever walked. And now this same guy, the one who always insisted on going by the book, was about to commit an expensive act of vandalism; and all because some poacher had broken the code of conduct. For that, there was no trial; only retribution.

Lance smiled. His eyes danced. "Hey, jefe, nobody's around. Go ahead, do the guy."

Nick did not answer. He poked the Rapalla at the right-front tire. It went in effortlessly. There was a soft "whoosh" and the right-front end of the truck sagged. Nick pulled hard, pushing the knife with the strength of his wrist, and slashed a four-inch gash. He did the same to the right-rear tire. Then the two tires on the other side.

"Teach that sumbitch," Nick mumbled. He tossed the Rapalla into the big storage compartment, locked it, then climbed onto the seat of his pickup. Lance opened the other door and lightly slid onto the seat.

As the truck pulled onto State Road 84, Nick began humming and mumbling snatches of a song. Lance smiled when he recognized a few of the words: "This land is my land . . ."

Ten minutes later the green pickup slowed at a blinking yellow light and turned right onto Highway 29, the north-south road that begins at Palmdale, just west of Lake Okeechobee, angles southwest to La Belle, probes straight through the Okloacoochee Slough to Immokalee, jogs east, and then arrows through the Big Cypress Swamp and ends at Everglades City. It is a lonely, virtually uninhabited road. There are few houses. Drainage ditches filled with black water run parallel to the road. And either cypress trees or endless stretches of sawgrass stretch off to either side. There are also the frequent reminders that motorists are driving through the habitat of the endangered Florida panthers; signs that did not help Nick's foul humor.

North of Copeland, where a handful of homes crowd

the road as if fleeing the encircling swamp, is the Deep Lake Prison. Unlike the houses, the prison is shoved far off the road and into the swamp. This once was a maximum-security institution; a brutal place of sweat-boxes, solitary confinement, and backbreaking labor. Now the front of the prison has neatly trimmed broad lawns, oleander bushes, and brightly colored flowers. It is something of a country-club prison where those inside are no longer convicts but inmates; where there is no hard labor, only cutting grass and painting rocks in the driveway; a place where prisoners spend more time exercising than they do working; a place where prisoners on work-release are free to go home at night.

Nick slowed and turned down the sandy driveway that led into the prison. He pulled at his mustache. "Let's go flip the son of a bitch," he said.

30

It was not until the 1980's that Cuba, as the Bahamas, Jamaica, and the Turks and Caicos Islands had done earlier, began taking advantage of its geography and cashing in on its strategic location for drug smugglers. It was the Colombians, as usual, who were first to take advantage of the sanctuary Cuba offered to smugglers as well as that island nation's proximity to America. First, the Communist-dominated country became a sanctuary for dopers who were intercepted in the western Bahamas or along the east coast of Florida by U.S. Customs pilots. When airborne smugglers were intercepted, they turned and fled south, knowing that no U.S. government aircraft could penetrate the Cuban Air Defense Zone, an invisible line surrounding Cuba at a distance of about twenty-six miles. The dopers found that even if a Cuban MiG flew up for a look-see, once the Cuban pilot saw the small aircraft, no hostile action was taken. The doper orbited until the Customs aircraft ran low on gas and had to return to base, then brought his load into America. The Colombians, a world-class people either at killing or corrupting those who could affect their activities, later set up a network of senior Cuban military officers who allowed doper pilots to land, spend the day, refuel, and fly into America when Cuban radar revealed the risk was lowest. Dopers began looking upon Cuba as sort of a mini-vacation spot; a place to spend the day on the beach at Varadero, rest, and then bring the load to its final destination. An extra wrinkle was added when dopers began performing airdrops inside the Cuban ADIZ on the north coast. The drug-laden aircraft would fly up from Colombia, cross Cuba—sometimes with a MiG escort—drop the drugs to waiting boats, then turn and flee south to Colombia without ever entering American airspace. Drivers of waiting go-fast boats leisurely loaded the drugs and waited until Customs aircraft trolling north of the ADIZ turned for home. Then they spread out for the final run into the Bahamas or the Florida keys. Two things were at the heart of the Cuban cooperation with drug smugglers. First, as always, there were astonishing amounts of money to be had for providing services to people with limitless resources. And second, Cuban officials, including top officers in the Cuban secret service, not only were amused at the amount of marijuana and cocaine ingested by the Americans; they had no compunctions about doing what they could to make that usage even more convenient. So when Cubans became more and more of a presence in the smuggling world, it was natural they should take advantage of all the benefits offered by their mother country. Intelligence files of U.S. Customs bulged with hundreds of documented instances where smugglers found refuge in Cuba. In the summer of 1989 Castro publicly executed several senior military officials, ostensibly for their role in narcotics trafficking. The real reason they were executed was to serve as examples; they had become too ambitious. They sought to wrest power from Castro.

Even after Castro's public announcements about cleaning up his country, the drug smuggling continued unabated. The number of incidents inside Cuban waters and Cuban airspace, if anything, increased. DEA intelligence files revealed countless instances where, according to the debriefing of confidential informants, Cuban sanctuary was used to springboard a load of dope into America.

One way, though not a particularly effective way, to combat the use of Cuba is a hit-and-run operation. This is done by positioning a Customs boat or aircraft somewhere in the western Bahamas and then following the dope to its off-loading site. Most all of these exercise are futile; the pilot or boat captain spends hours, perhaps days, sitting in the hot sun waiting to launch, and then the aircraft or boat squirts past before Customs knows it is there. Many times the operations are nullified when the doper checks his 6, sees the Customs aircraft, and simply turns and flees to sanctuary in Cuba.

It was one of these hit-and-run exercises that Mike Love was participating in when there was an urgent radio message; a "Mayday" received from an aircraft that said it was west of Andros. The pilot of the aircraft, which was too low to be picked up even by the radar balloons in the Bahamas and the Florida keys, said he was making for Bimini, the closest airport. He gave position reports every few minutes as he struggled to keep the aircraft in the air. One engine was out and the second was overheating. The pilot was fighting to retain control.

Mike, who was sitting on Orange Cay in the Blackhawk helicopter, immediately launched in an effort to locate, track, and identify the crippled aircraft. He radioed the aircraft number, as given by the pilot in his distress call, to C3I. There a Customs technician entered the number into the TECS computer. Bingo.

"You have a hit. The aircraft is positive in the system," C3I radioed to Mike. Mike twisted the collective, trying to get a few more knots of speed out of the 'Hawk.

Behind him, in the cavernous interior of the 'Hawk, was an apprehension team consisting of two armed U.S. Customs officers and two Bahamian soldiers. It was necessary for U.S. Customs to carry Bahamian soldiers in order to work enforcement missions in the Bahamas. The team was under the leadership of Big Ed, the jovial giant whose black fatigues, red Rambo rag, CAR-15, and semiautomatic pistol had sent many smugglers to jail for many years. He was ecstatic. This looked like a good bust.

Bimini was the hottest locale for smugglers in all the Bahamas; even after years of unfavorable publicity and numerous raids, just last week a group of Cuban smugglers working with the Bahamians had fired on a U.S. Customs boat. It was entirely possible that Bahamian cops would try to free the dopers today. Big Ed would be ready. He pressed the intercom switch and ordered his men to have extra clips for their rifles when they landed.

And Mike called the Customs Air Branch at Homestead Air Force Base for backup. Two minutes later, a Blackhawk carrying eight heavily armed men had scrambled and was thumping its way toward Bimini at max speed. Four minutes later, Omaha 52, a blue-and-white Cessna jet loaded with five more heavily armed men, had scrambled and was racing at dash speed toward Bimini. That was enough firepower and grit and determination to declare war against the Bahamas.

The crippled smuggler aircraft—it was a Panther, a converted Navajo capable of speeds of almost three hundred miles an hour—made a straight-in approach to Bimini. The pilot was low, too low to fly at pattern altitude; he simply called on unicom, declared an emergency landing, and bored straight in, the left engine feathered and the right one smoking. He did not drop the gear until seconds before touchdown.

Mike came in hot; the 'Hawk was shaking and screaming as he lasered across the shallow banks. As he reached the runway, he pulled the nose of the Blackhawk high to bleed off airspeed, then plummeted like an elevator toward the ground. It's a maneuver

Customs terms an "enforcement stop." The military
calls the same maneuver an "assault landing." When
the tail wheel, built to withstand a landing force of
nine g's, touched, Mike leveled. He held the 'Hawk a
few feet over the ground and followed the Panther during its rollout. Near the end of the runway it turned
right onto the parking apron. Mike, hands light on the
controls, danced the chopper over the top of the Panther, then hovered a few feet over the ground. Mike
and the doper pilot, a Hispanic, were nose to nose.
Big Ed and his team jumped from the open door of
the chopper. One of the men raced across the parking
apron to where he could command the single road
leading into the airport. It was his job to watch for
traffic. Many times when a deal went down on Bimini,
friends of the dopers came to their assistance.

Big Ed, the team leader, trained his CAR-15 on the
doper as the two Bahamian soldiers, one off each wing,
ran to the rear of the doper aircraft.

Big Ed made a slashing motion across his throat;
the aviation signal to chop power. Instead the pilot
added power. The rudder of the Panther swung hard.
The pilot was going to try to rabbit. Instantly Mike
had the 'Hawk back in the air. In seconds he was atop
the Panther, which was trembling and shaking under
the rotor downwash. Mike came up on unicom, identified himself to the doper pilot, and ordered the doper
to pull power immediately. The Panther kept turning.

Mike grinned, the tight confident grin of a predator,
and slacked off on the collective. The 'Hawk, nineteen
thousand pounds of helicopter, dropped across the
back of the aircraft. The heavily reinforced landing
skids crunched the fuselage of the Panther. Incredibly,
the Panther continued to turn. Again Mike bounced
the 'Hawk across the back of the Panther; this time
harder.

The tires of the Panther exploded and the landing
gear collapsed, causing a shower of sparks as the props
chewed themselves to pieces against the asphalt.

Mike danced the chopper away, twirling so the nose
of the chopper always was toward the doper; keeping

himself eyeball to eyeball with the doper pilot. With the sun visor of his helmet dropped over his face, he was a fearsome anonymous apparition. He dropped the chopper a few feet and it was resting lightly on the tarmac. Big Ed and the Bahamians, rifles at the ready, rushed the Panther.

Mike quickly pulled the chopper up about fifty feet, just high enough to look down the long road toward the north end of the island. No auto traffic. No boats coming from North Bimini. Not yet. The backup Citation was less than ten minutes out; the 'Hawk probably a half-hour.

He settled to the ground, secured the controls, adjusted the power to idle, and jumped from the right door of the chopper just as Big Ed jerked the first of the dopers from the rear door of the Panther.

The man was tossed to the ground and cuffed. He rolled over and found that his shirt suddenly was ripped from collar to hem. His eyes were wide with panic and incredulity as his belt was jerked loose and his trousers snatched down around his ankles.

"No weapons," said the apprehension-team member. But he kept his rifle on the doper.

Another doper and the Hispanic pilot were pulled from the aircraft. Both went through the same routine. Mike looked inside the Panther. It was jammed to the ceiling with bales of marijuana. Two duffel bags stood in the corner. He opened one, pulled out a tightly wrapped package, and weighed it in his hand. He picked up one duffel bag, then the other. He walked to the door.

"What'd we get?" Big Ed asked.

"I'd guess eight hundred, maybe a thousand pounds of grass. Probably fifty keys of coke."

"We will take over now," said one of the Bahamian soldiers in his lilting English accent. He had to shout to be heard over the noise of the idling Blackhawk.

Big Ed and the second Customs officer stepped back a half-pace. They kept their CAR-15's trained on the bad guys.

Two uniformed men stepped out of the small building on the ramp; Immigration and Customs, by the uniforms; one white, one tan. Mike stepped in front of them. He wore a blue Customs flight suit. His helmet, visor down, still was atop his head. He towered over the two Bahamians.

"This is a joint operation of U.S. Customs and the Bahamian BAT team," he said, leaning close and speaking loudly so the two men could hear him over the noise of the helicopter.

The two uniformed officers scowled. Both had made small fortunes working with smugglers and did not like it when smugglers were rousted on the airport.

"This is Bahamian territory," one said indignantly.

"Bahamians are in charge," Mike said. He flicked a thumb over his shoulder toward the Bahamian soldiers.

"We are in charge. This is our jurisdiction," said the other, trying to peer around Mike.

"BAT teams have jurisdiction over local officers." Mike was scornful of these two officials; he knew they were bent; that they were trying to figure some way to get rid of the BAT team and get a piece of the action.

The two airport officers scowled, looked at each other, and turned to leave.

"Don't make any phone calls," Mike said in his level voice.

"Don't tell us what to do in our country," said the guy in the white uniform. His voice was filled with indignation.

That indignation turned to momentary fear when Mike said, "You make a phone call, I'll tear your head off and shit in the hole. You got that?" The two airport officials turned away. Mike knew they would call for help. Someone was going to crash this party in perhaps fifteen, maybe twenty minutes.

The three smugglers were sitting with their backs against the wing of the collapsed Panther. Their clothes were drenched with perspiration. It was perspiration engendered by fright; first the fright of knowing they were about to crash; second, the fright of being bounced by the wailing Blackhawk; third, the fright of having their faces pushed into the runway and their trousers jerked around their ankles. The latter was particularly humiliating to the Cuban. None of the three carried identification. They had anticipated being popped. Very well, it would not take long for the Bahamians to find out what they were made of.

The senior Bahamian soldier looked at the three men. His expression was stonelike. He, like the other members of the Customs team, was drenched in perspiration. The fear and tension of an assault landing on an airstrip where there is a load going down is perhaps more stressful to a law-enforcement officer than to the doper pilot bringing in the load.

Mike examined the three dopers. The Hispanic pilot was young, cocky to the point of insolence, and plainly thought it was an outrageous joke that he was being held by a Bahamian soldier; an enlisted man; a black man. The other two were middle-aged men. They wore jeans, old faded shirts, and had the sunburned faces and leathery skin of fishermen. These guys were rednecks who obviously represented the owner of the load.

"I shall ask you gentlemen several questions," the Bahamian sergeant said. "And you will answer quickly and truthfully."

He stopped before the Cuban. The Cuban eyed the Bahamian arrogantly.

"Who are you? Where did you come from?" he asked, rifle leveled at the Cuban's chest.

"Fuck you," the Cuban said.

The Bahamian smiled. Big Ed shifted his feet. He knew what was about to happen. The Bahamian sergeant nodded to his colleague. The younger Bahamian pulled the Cuban to his feet.

The sergeant approached closer. "Who are you? Where did you come from?"

"Fuc—"

The Cuban's curse was cut off in mid-word as the sergeant swung the butt of his rifle in a vicious blow that knocked his head to the side and sent half of his teeth and—it seemed—a pint of blood flying through the air. The other two dopers recoiled in fright when they found themselves suddenly covered with teeth and blood.

Mike stepped forward. "Excuse me for just a minute," he said to the cold-eyed Bahamian. "I'm not interfering with your job, but these are Americans. I'd like to say something before you continue the interrogation."

Mike was not speaking out of sympathy. The world, for him, was divided into smugglers and nonsmugglers. If a person was a doper, he deserved whatever befell him. Mike had forced a half-dozen smugglers to crash into the ocean. He had no sympathy for any of them. He simply wanted to let the dopers know what they were about to experience. If they didn't want to cooperate, fine.

The Bahamian clearly resented Mike's interruption. But he did not speak. He had flown with Mike many times. Mike was something of a legend among the Bahamian soldiers; his aggression at the controls of a Blackhawk had scared the hell out of most of them. Being abroad when Mike bounced the 'Hawk up and down atop a go-fast boat traveling at seventy miles an hour, or when he bounced up and down on an aircraft, was the high point of their professional lives. So while the Bahamian resented Mike's intrusion, he did not argue. He took a half-step backward.

"You fellows Americans?" Mike asked.

The two men looked at him, looked at the unconscious Cuban bleeding on the runway under the bright hot sunlight, then looked away. Neither spoke.

Mike sighed. "Look, this ain't America. This is the Bahamas." He nodded toward the two Bahamians. "They're in charge. U.S. Customs can do nothing. These guys never heard of Miranda or allowing you to call a lawyer. They do things differently. You need to know that."

Mike looked down at the unconscious Cuban and then back at the two Americans. "I would advise you to cooperate."

"We're Americans," one of the men said defiantly.

Even in those two words, Mike recognized the rural twang of southwest Florida. It was as clear as if the men wore signs.

"You're from Everglades City," he said. The men did not answer. But the quick look that passed between them answered his question.

The Bahamian sergeant had had enough. He politely but firmly elbowed Mike aside. "As you said, we are in charge of this interrogation," he said. "Stand him up," he ordered.

The younger Bahamian soldier slung his rifle over his shoulder. He seized one of the Americans under the arm and jerked him to his feet.

"Very well, let me ask you a different question. If you are from Everglades City, Florida, my first question is this. Who are the people you will meet?"

"I'm an American," said the smuggler. His eyes shifted nervously. "I got rights."

Wrong answer. Big Ed winced. Mike sighed and turned away.

The sergeant nodded. He and his colleagues had been through this many times. They had the routine down pat. The younger soldier seized the smuggler's handcuffed hands and forced them over the leading edge of the aircraft wing. He moved his grip to the thin chain of the cuffs and shifted his arm out of the way.

The smuggler looked at Mike in dismay. What was going on here? This was not the way arrests were conducted.

"The name of the people you are meeting?"

"I want my lawyer. I got rights. I'm an Amer—"

The smuggler's scream of pain was so loud and anguished that Mike flinched.

The sergeant had used both hands to swing the butt of the rifle against the smuggler's hands. The crunch of dozens of small bones was audible even over the screaming thunder of the Blackhawk. Blood splattered across the wing of the Panther. The smuggler looked at his crushed and mangled hands in shocked disbelief. Again he screamed.

But the sergeant had moved to the third smuggler. The eyes of the fisherman—he had to be a fisherman—darted about nervously. With a few exception, the fishermen of Everglades City are not violent people. The deliberate premeditated violence perpetrated by the Bahamian soldier was virtually unknown to the fishermen of Everglades City. The third smuggler was frightened. He looked at Mike. He looked at Big Ed. Then he looked in fear at the thin Bahamian sergeant who was standing over him. What would be next? The Cuban had lost half his teeth and had his face rearranged. His friend probably would never regain full usage of his mangled hands. What would they do to him?

He had his answer when the sergeant hoisted the rifle, nodded at his colleague, and said, "Spread his legs."

The smuggler suddenly had visions of his testicles being turned to jelly by the rifle butt. He decided to talk. He would tell all he knew. He would tell all he ever suspected. He would invent crimes perpetrated by his mother and sister. He would do whatever he had to do, say whatever he had to say, anything to appease the stone-faced Bahamian.

The smuggler was in deep conversation with the Bahamian, who was taking copious notes, when the backup Citation from Homestead landed, taxied up, and twirled around. The side door was open and armed men were running down the steps before the aircraft stopped. The pilot stayed in the seat and left the engines running.

"We need to get outta here," one of the men shouted to Mike. "Boats are headed this way from North Bimini. Unless we want a shoot-out, we need to go. Now."

Mike nodded. He put the notes of the interrogation into his pocket. He would call Nick with the details as soon as he returned to Home Plate. Big Ed quickly, and none too gently, shoved the uninjured smuggler aboard the Blackhawk. The two who had been hurt were aboard the Citation so they could be rushed to a hospital. The Customs officer guarding the road rushed back to the chopper.

Mike lifted off and looked to the north. Boats were landing at the dock, and armed men were rushing toward three trucks parked by the old motel. Mike pushed the nose of the chopper over, ducking lower to hide behind the trees, and picked up a southwest heading.

He pressed the transmit button on the intercom and spoke to Big Ed. "Dopers don't know how good they have it in America."

Big Ed chuckled. "Bahamian soldiers get information the old-fashioned way; they beat it out of people."

31

Convincing a tough and survival-hardened lawbreaker to become a snitch is one of the more arcane and sophisticated arts of the police world. It does not matter that cops have changed the meaning of the term "C.I." from "confidential informant" to "cooperating individual"; the person is still a snitch, a squealer, someone who gives up his friends, someone who is the very antithesis of what crooks perceive themselves to be—stand-up guys. While there are many ways to convince a person to become an informant, the traditional way is by threats. It is a process that leaves the bad guys feeling violated and the cops feeling soiled. Older cops, guys who have been on The Job for years, still refer to informants as "stools," which may or may not be an unconscious recognition of the lack of esteem enjoyed by informants, even by the people who depend on them.

It is the nature of drug smuggling that most cases—in fact, almost all cases—are made through informants. Occasionally an undercover agent will come up with good information; but the U/C guy's main job is to find people who will roll over, people who will flip, dopers who will tell all.

Flipping a doper is more art than science. It is true that some people can simply be muscled; threatened with the consequences of what will happen to them if they don't cooperate. But such snitches are ruled by fear and are bitter toward their handlers. They are the most unstable and unmanageable of all snitches.

With some crooks, the hammer—whatever it is that is used to convince them to become snitches—is the fact that a friend or associate stole money from them. A man who would go to the wall for his friends becomes outraged when one of those friends steals money.

A relatively young crook, especially one with a wife and children, sometimes can be flipped by reminding him how old he will be when he gets out of jail; by telling him his kids will be grown, his wife will have married another man, and that he will be a stooped, gray-haired old fart whom nobody remembers.

The old "do-yourself-a-favor" gambit also is surprisingly effective. Play to the doper's unenlightened self-interest. Hey, you think those guys would zip their lips if we had them? Hell no. They would spill their guts; they would send you up the river without a second thought. Go ahead and tell us what we want to know; then get out of this business. Go straight. Settle down. Put all this behind you. Do yourself a favor.

The essence of flipping a bad guy is the art of finding the right hammer; knowing his weak point; finding out what he treasures most in all the world; identifying his deepest fears, his greatest anxiety, his most hidden concern. It helps if the bad guy is in a trading mood; if he wants something; if there is a strong incentive for him to do business with the cops.

Young guys, particularly sheltered white-collar sort of guys who drift into the macho world of dope smugglers, are extremely vulnerable to graphic stories about homosexual rape in prison; particularly if, as with many young men, their own sexuality is not yet locked firmly in place. For a wizened old cop to look a young scammer in the eye, nod knowingly, and say, "You're an attractive fellow; the guys in the slammer are gonna love you. I give you two days, maybe three, before you get butt-fucked."

Inevitably, the young guy will shrug and say he can take care of himself. But the fear is in his eyes. Then the cop might say, "It will happen one of two ways. Most common way is for two or three guys to wait, catch you in the shower or the laundry, throw a towel over your head, flip you over a railing, then take turns packing the old dirt chute."

The young doper snorts derisively. But more fear is in his eyes.

"Or it can happen this way. One guy—a big rough, tough guy—picks you to be his wife. He's big enough and mean enough to keep all the others away from you. He's your protector. But you're gonna have to suck his dick every day. You're gonna have to like it when he fucks you in the ass. You gotta groan and respond. You don't, he sticks lighted cigarettes to you while he's fucking you. Some of those guys like to fuck their little wives out in the open so everybody can see them. You argue about it and he pulls out a shiv and he says, 'What's it gonna be? Blood on my knife or shit on my dick?' "

The young scammer knows the truth when he hears it. And he talks.

Some people simply cannot be threatened. There is no hammer big enough to hold over them. The toughest, most hard-core cases, the people to whom threats and violence are part of life, the people whom a cop can slam around and no one will care, often are the ones least susceptible to pressure. It is the same with country people or uneducated people. Their pride is so great they simply will not bend. The more they are threatened or pressured, the more silent they become. The people of Everglades City are that way. If threatened, they simply bow up and clam up. They will go to jail for the rest of their lives before they will allow themselves to be intimidated.

Flipping someone is an art form that at times approaches the metaphysical. If the cop uses his hammer with skill rather than force, he achieves extraordinary insight into the mind of the doper; he knows the doper better than the doper's mother knows him; he knows what the doper will do under virtually any set of circumstances. The bond between the two can be stronger than that between husband and wife; it can be the closest and strongest relationship either will ever know; and it is all in the mind, all between two adversaries, between two polar opposites who, for an intensive time in their lives, find a common ground.

Nick knew before he sat down with Big Knocker that morning at the county work farm that he was walking a tightrope. Big Knocker would laugh and walk away if threatened. None of his associates had, to Nick's knowledge, stolen any dope or any money from him; if so, he had probably taken care of that himself. He had no wife or children, so was not susceptible there. He would never roll out of self-interest. And since he was the meanest son of a bitch in southwest Florida, it was highly unlikely he would be the victim of a homosexual rape in prison.

No, none of the old standbys would work with Big Knocker. The only thing that would work, the only hammer big enough to use, was Robert, Big Knocker's homosexual baby brother, who had been on Big Knocker's boat when a deal went down and who, because he had fallen apart and babbled everything he knew when confronted with what he had said and done on the secret videotape, was now under indictment. Nick was in the position of being able to bestow something Big Knocker wanted very badly, and that was to keep his little brother out of jail. Big Knocker's pain was aggravated by the fact that he felt responsible for his brother's plight. If he had never taken his brother on a deal, the boy would not be in trouble.

Big Knocker's only weak point was his baby brother.

Nick was betting that Big Knocker would do anything to prevent Robert from going to jail.

The three men sat in the small bare white-walled room at the work camp. Big Knocker looked from Lance to Nick and back to Lance. He smirked. "I saw you in court," he said. "You and that smart-ass college-boy lawyer."

Nick and Lance did not respond. The reminder of Derek Tutwiler was still very painful; and, as the perp had not been identified, very frustrating.

"So where's the college boy? Why didn't you bring him with you?" Big Knocker's smirk took up half his face.

Lance squinted and looked across the broad expanse of sawgrass behind the prison. He'd like to stake this son of a bitch down out there and let the gators have him.

Nick pulled at his mustache and stared up at Big Knocker. There was something in the big man's eyes when he talked about Derek. Something that . . .

Nick ignored the gibe, pointed to a chair, and said, "Sit."

It was six hours later when the two cops drove slowly down the winding sandy road of the country work farm. The pink and white oleanders along the driveway stood as still as if carved from stone. Not a breath of air was stirring in the hot humid confines of the Big Cypress Swamp, in that water world where the swamp met and fought with the saltwater tides that pushed up from Everglades City. The air conditioner was whirring away at full blast. But even so, the dark green truck had absorbed the sun right into the frame. Even on the inside of the cab, the metal was hot to the touch.

Nick turned left on Highway 29 and slowly accelerated. A few miles north, when he saw the signs about the panther habitat, he mumbled under his breath, but other than that, neither man spoke. Each was lost in his own thoughts.

It was not until Nick turned left on State Road 84 that Lance spoke. "Think it'll work?"

"You're in charge. You make it work."

After a moment Lance laughed. "Boss, you did one hell of a job with that guy. I didn't think it could be done. But you put the bad eye on him; you made him believe."

"We'll see. I gave him a week to think about it. We'll go back then and see if he's had some sort of Pauline conversion."

"Pauline conversion?"

"Yeah. Pauline conversion."

Lance shrugged.

Nick pulled at his mustache. "I think he killed Derek and Grace."

Lance's head snapped around. His eyes were wide. "What?"

Nick shook his head as if trying to clear out the cobwebs and make clear whatever it was, deep inside, that had given him the idea. It was something in Big Knocker's voice; something in his eyes when he asked about the "college boy."

"I don't know. I'm not sure. Nothing solid to go on. I just think he did it. Gut feeling."

Lance sighed. "We can't deal with him if he killed two prosecutors. What will you do?"

Lance was right. Any homicide, but particularly if it were two law-enforcement people, took precedence over a dope case, even if the dope case involved half the population of Everglades City. No one but the FBI or DEA would use a homicide suspect as a snitch in a dope case. But Nick could not yet prove what he suspected to be true. So he would have to continue with the drug investigation and hope that it opened up the homicide cases. At the same time, he could focus the homicide investigation on Big Knocker.

"Nothing," Nick said. "We'll press on with what we're doing. But you be alert. And you listen. Because that son of a bitch is not going to skate."

32

Nick's legs were crossed and his cowboy-boot-shod feet were atop his desk when Lance waltzed into his office. Lance stopped, looked at the ceiling, rolled his head around, then nodded as if he had come to a conclusion.

Nick looked over the top of his reading glasses, eyebrows bunched together, and waited. After a moment he growled, "What are you looking at?"

Lance wore a T-shirt that said "I WORK FOR EXXON. I DON'T HAVE TO CARE." He smiled and said, "Thought you'd never ask. Boss, this office is too tall for you. What you need to do is build a ceiling right about here." Lance held his right hand about breast-high and drew an imaginary line along the wall. "I can put in a couple of steps and have the upstairs part as my office. The downstairs part will be yours."

Nick glared.

Lance laughed. "White hair in your ears keep you from hearing me?"

"See if you can hear this. Dumnik's been made head of the President's South Florida Task Force on Narcotics. He's coming over tonight with a bunch of agents. Says he has intel about a load coming in. It's tied to Everglades City. I want you to take him out in the Scarab."

"Dumnik's head of the Bush League? Well, cream is not all that floats."

"We have to cooperate with DEA and with the presidential task force, so take him out in the boat."

"Why don't they use their own boat?"

"Why do I have to explain everything to you? I run this office. Just do it."

"Hey, you want your ace U/C guy to be happy? I'm America's hero."

Nick mumbled something.

Lance cleared his throat. "Jefe, you remember I liberated the Scarab from the DEA warehouse? You want me to take them out in a boat I stole from them?"

Nick waved a hand in dismissal. "Forget it. He didn't mention it. They've got so much stuff in seizure over there, they don't know what to do with it."

"He doesn't know I got his boat?" Lance was disappointed.

Nick shrugged and said, "He's DEA." That explained everything.

"Not any fun this way," Lance said. "Guy's a flamer even when he doesn't try to be."

"Dumnik's making this a big deal. The Coast Guard will be offshore; Marine Patrol and Collier County will be out there." He grinned. "And you're driving the big cheese around in the lead boat."

"What kinda deal's going down? Does McBride know about it?"

Nick shrugged again. "No. It's some kind of DEA deal. Some snitch told them a shrimper with twenty-five tons of marijuana and a couple hundred kilos of coke is coming in. He thinks it's the Everglades City crowd and is trying to wedge his way back into that case."

Lance shook his head. "Still trying to grab our stats, huh?"

Nick did not answer.

"Hey, boss, I ever tell you my story about the three dogs?"

Nick shook his head and tuned Lance out.

"Well, there were these three dogs. One dog belonged to the state attorney in the Twentieth Judicial Circuit, one to the Coast Guard, one to the DEA. All of these were dope dogs; best in the world at finding hidden dope. Their agencies decided to have a sniff-off; find out which was best. Our dog sniffed around the room, found the dope hidden in a wall panel, wagged his tail, and sat down. Customs dog comes in, sniffs around, finds dope hidden in a man's coat, wags his tail, and sets down. Then the DEA dog comes in, rapes the other two dogs, and issues a press release taking credit for the dope they found.''

Lance waited. After a moment Nick, who was thinking of other things, looked up and nodded.

Lance shrugged. ''Jefe, if you don't mind DEA getting credit for our cases, then I don't mind. What I mind is Dumnik's lying. He can't be up-front about it. He thinks we're a stupid bunch of locals; a bunch of Joe Shit the Ragman types who luck onto every arrest we make, and that he can waltz in, take the credit, and so what.''

Nick pulled on his mustache. ''You haven't heard the latest DEA story.''

''What?''

Nick grinned. ''DEA went into court and testified on behalf of the sheriff's son; said he was helping them and that he should have immunity from any charges any local agency might make against him. They were afraid we might pop him. Thing is, according to one of McBride's informants, the sheriff's son has brought in ten loads since he started helping DEA. I told Dumnik and they gave the kid a polygraph. He flunked it. I'd put a snitch in jail if he flunked a polygraph, but Dumnik ignored it. His snitch is out there doping and we got a court order preventing us from popping him.''

Lance laughed. ''Hey, if you gonna be a doper, be a doper for DEA.''

For a moment the two men were lost in their thoughts about the bizarre world of narcotics enforcement. Then Nick waved his hand. ''Just take Dumnik out on the Scarab. DEA gave McBride a van loaded with records and files. We might have to go to them again. So make Dumnik happy. Do what he says.''

Lance stiffened, thunked the heels of his boat shoes together, threw up a quivering British-style salute, and said, ''For the glory of the empire.''

''The empire will get more glory, because tomorrow night you gotta do the same thing. Except it will be in a DEA boat and you'll be going up some creek near Everglades City. Dumnik says he has information about a big stash of dope back in there somewhere.''

Lance's eyebrows danced. ''Is the sheriff's son giving them all this hot information?''

''I didn't ask because I knew he wouldn't tell me.''

''You think he's sending DEA on a wild-goose chase?''

Nick grinned. Then his polished cowboy boots hit the floor. One scraped the corner or a drawer on the way down. Nick leaned over, licked his finger, then tried to wipe away the abraded spot. ''Dumnik couldn't find his backside with a search warrant. But go with him anyway.''

Dumnik snorted in disgust when Lance walked into the briefing room wearing high-topped red tennis shoes, fatigue pants, a red Rambo rag around his head, and a T-shirt that said, ''MY PENIS IS THICKER THAN YOUR LEG.'' His nickel-plated hogleg Magnum was in a shoulder holster.

Lance ignored Dumnik. He looked around the room at the half-dozen stern-faced DEA agents, all wearing camouflage fatigues, black combat boots, with side-arms, and carrying automatic rifles. They were wiping cammy paint across their faces. Lance recognized Ben Blumen and Melvin Foster and walked over to say hello. He saw Ben dip into the cammy paint and pass it to Melvin. When Melvin did not accept it, Ben looked up. Melvin was staring at him. ''Sorry,'' Ben mumbled, and passed the cammy paint to another agent.

''Hi, guys,'' Lance said.

Ben smiled and nodded. ''I would shake hands, but I got this stuff all over me.''

Melvin scowled. ''I remember you. We still got something to settle.''

Lance grinned, pointed at Melvin, and said, ''New Jersey. Exit six.''

Melvin's anger vanished. ''How'd you remember that?''

"Hey, can't forget something like that. You killed some guinea bastards wearing three-piece suits."

"You got that right." Melvin was pleased. Then he frowned. "I checked on that mile-o-more-bird shit. Ain't no such bird. You was blowing smoke up my ass. I shoulda kicked your ass off the dock that day."

"Awww, come on, Melvin. We gotta fight dopers instead of each other. And I've seen the mile-o-more. Whoever you talked to didn't know what they were talking about."

Melvin glared. He was not convinced.

Lance looked at Ben. "You got any exits in Kansas?"

Ben laughed. "One or two."

"Agent Cunningham, come up here, please," came Dumnik's strident voice. It was his command voice. Dumnik stood alone in the front of the room; cammies unbuttoned almost to his waist, gold chains around his tanned neck, and rivers of perspiration cascading down the rolls of fat on his chest and stomach. His nose was beaming through the heavy makeup. Lance knew he had been on the sauce. On the Listerine too, if the odor was any indication.

Lance sauntered toward Dumnik, got a whiff of the mouthwash, and backed up a step. He held his stomach, grimaced, and whispered confidentially, "I'm a little irregular today. Know what I mean? I think it was brought on by travel. I'm trying to avoid harsh chemical laxatives. All the fiber I've been eating works very slowly."

Dumnik's eyes widened. What was this whacker talking about?

Lance went øn, "Besides, I had to get the boat ready. I'm the chauffeur tonight. Didn't think you would want me to hear all the confidential DEA stuff."

Dumnik was mollified by Lance's realization of how the cosmos worked. He nodded in a patronizing fashion. "Well, you might be able to help us a little. This could be a big one."

"Just say the word. You tell me what to do."

"When I give an order, do it quickly. There won't be any time to explain."

"Got it."

Dumnik reached into his pocket and handed Lance a small piece of paper on which was scrawled a series of numbers. "Think you can find it?"

Lance studied the numbers; lat-long coordinates that he would plug into the loran aboard the Scarab. He did some quick mental arithmetic. "I think so. This looks like it's about twenty miles west of Naples."

Dumnik looked at him in surprise. "Eighteen."

"Close enough for government work."

"Close don't count. This is an operation of the President's South Florida Task Force, of which I am commander. Everything has to be on the button and by the numbers."

Lance backed up a half-step. Dumnik was blasting out wave after wave of Listerine. It was like being in the middle of a mouthwash typhoon.

Thirty minutes later the strike force was aboard the Scarab. Lance, knowing the DEA agents would be wearing boots, had placed rubber mats on the deck of the Scarab to protect it from scuff marks. He plugged in the loran coordinates Dumnik had given him and motored easily through light swells. The night was warm and clear, and the salty tang of the ocean was full in his nostrils. He looked over his shoulder. The props of the four outboards strung across the transom were leaving a creamy wake. He slowly advanced the throttles and adjusted the trim. The stern settled; then the heavily loaded boat slowly rose until it was on the plane. The speed gradually increased.

As he moved into the deeper offshore waters, Lance cast a quick eye around the boat. Dumnik sat on a small seat in front of the control console. He held the edges of the seat. His feet were braced on the deck, and from the rigidity of his body, Lance knew he was a little apprehensive. Melvin was all the way forward in the bow, standing up, legs spread, holding on to the bowline. The other agents stood along the sides of the Scarab; all looking very serious; all, that is, except

Ben Blumen, who had a wide grin pasted on his face. Farm boys from Kansas don't often experience the thrill of going offshore at night in a go-fast boat, and Ben was enjoying it to the fullest. Lance decided he liked the young DEA agent.

Dumnik saw Ben Blumen's smile. "Blumen, what the fuck you grinning at?" he snapped. "You think this job is funny?"

"No, sir." The smile disappeared.

Lance held the speed down to about forty miles an hour. No sense in blasting along at top speed. He arrived at the lat-long coordinates provided by Dumnik and looked around. Nothing. He slowed and leaned forward.

"You want me to set up a search pattern, cruise around, or just drift?" he asked Dumnik.

"Drift. We'll wait for the off-loading. Make sure your lights are off. And stand by to move out in a hurry."

"Okay."

"Oh," Dumnik said, almost as an afterthought. "Keep your radios tuned to the appropriate frequencies. I'll need to be in touch with all the agencies represented out here tonight."

"Got it." Lance held the steering wheel and did a quick soft-shoe routine. Then he slumped to the deck with his back against the console. It could be a long night. He leaned around the console and looked at Dumnik. "How you like our new boat?" he asked.

Dumnik shrugged. "It'll do." He looked around with little interest. "County buy this?"

"No. Sort of a cooperative thing between us and the federal government. New program. We might take advantage of it again."

"Sounds good. You locals can use the help."

For the next three hours Dumnik was on the radio almost constantly; checking in with the Coast Guard, the Florida Marine Patrol, Collier County, and with a Customs boat and two Customs aircraft. Then the Customs aircraft ran low on fuel and returned to Homestead. An hour later, Dumnik was plainly exasperated.

Lance figured that either the boat was late or Dumnik had bad information; it was no big deal; happened all the time. But Dumnik wanted to make something happen. He was too anxious; too determined to come up with some stats for the Bush League. He began pacing; one step to the right, one step to the left; back again, over and over.

Lance was looking out to sea, enjoying the calmness of the sea, the warm breeze, and the clear night, when suddenly, far to the north, he saw a brilliant slice of light. He was about to comment on the shooting star when Dumnik froze, pointed, and said, "There it is; the flare. That's the signal. Get outta here. Now."

He picked up the microphone and alerted the task-force units to stand by, that he had a visual on the suspect.

The stern-faced agents began checking their weapons and clearing space around their feet so they could move quickly.

Lance looked at Dumnik in amazement. "That was a shooting star," he said.

"That was a flare. I saw it," Dumnik snapped. "You just drive the boat. Now, move it."

Lance looked around as if expecting one of the agents to agree with him. But they all were busy.

He leaned toward Dumnik. "That was a shooting star."

"Are you telling me I don't know a flare when I see it? It was a flare. Goddammit, don't argue with me. Let's go."

Lance waved a hand in surrender. He looked off toward the north. "How long you figure it will take us to get there?"

Dumnik did not hesitate. "Ten minutes. Maybe less."

"Hold on, guys," Lance said. In seconds he had the boat on the plane and rocketing north. Ten minutes later he poked Dumnik, then pointed to his watch.

Dumnik sliced his flattened hand toward the north. "Two more minutes," he shouted. "We'll be on top of them."

The blacked-out boat was racing at more than seventy miles an hour; the powerful song of the engines echoing across the sea. Occasionally a cross-wave or a wave slightly larger than the others was encountered and spray splashed back over the strike team. Even in the dark, Lance could see Ben Blumen's smile.

Two minutes later, Lance retarded the throttles. "I don't see anything," he said.

Dumnik's head was on a swivel. He snapped back and forth in every direction, looking for the boat that had fired the signal flare.

"There," Dumnik said triumphantly.

Bearing down on them from the north was a boat, its uppermost white signal light barely visible over the horizon.

Lance's eyes widened in surprise and bewilderment. He could have sworn that what he had seen was a shooting star.

"What are our coordinates?" Dumnik snapped.

Lance reeled them off.

Dumnik was on the radio, ordering all task-force vessels to his position. Again his flattened hand, held so the palm was perpendicular to the deck, sliced toward the north. "Let's go get 'em.

As he drew closer, the distinctive signal lights of a tug pulling barges became clear; the single white light high over the tug, with three closely grouped white lights up forward, and then, high over the bow of each barge in the chain, another white light. The white lights stretched, it seemed, to the horizon. Must be eight or ten of them. Lance had seen these monsters in the daytime; an enormous three-deck tug with hundreds of yards of log-size cable—maybe a quarter-mile of cable—stretched out astern, pulling a train of barges. Everyone on the sea gave these juggernauts plenty of sea room. Without thinking, Lance veered a few degrees to the right. Those tugs threw up a bow wave that would sink even a Scarab. In addition to the bow wave, the incredibly powerful props of the tug created a roiling turbulent vortex that could suck the Scarab underwater. If the tug's skipper slowed, or if a rogue wave slowed the tug and caused a bit of slack to appear in the cable, it could snap and lash out like a mighty reaper. If the cable hit the Scarab, it would slice it apart and probably kill every person aboard. Few vessels plying the sea were more dangerous to themselves and to others than a giant tug pulling a train of barges.

"Closer. Get closer," Dumnik shouted. "We're going to board him."

Lance looked at Dumnik in utter astonishment.

"That's an oceangoing tug; not a shrimp boat filled with dope. This guy won't stop."

"We're going to board him," Dumnik repeated.

Lance picked up the microphone, punched in channel sixteen on the marine radio, and said, "Tug about twenty miles west of Marco Island, this is the motor vessel a hundred yards off your port bow. Skipper, switch over to channel seventy-eight and tell me how fast you going."

"Eight knots," came the reply. Then, "I have you on radar. You're a little close."

"Skipper, this is a law-enforcement vessel on a tactical mission. Tell us where you going, please."

"Key West, then South America."

"What's your cargo?"

"Don't know. It's a classified U.S. military cargo."

"How long does it take you to stop that freight train you're driving?"

A slight pause. "Twenty-two miles."

"Skipper, my boss here wants to board you."

"Fine. But I'm not stopping."

Dumnik grabbed the microphone away from Lance. "Skipper, this is Raymond Dumnik, commander of the President's South Florida Task Force on narcotics interdiction. You're in American waters. I demand that you allow us to board."

"Didn't say you couldn't board. Said I wasn't stopping. You're welcome to board."

As Lance swung around to track alongside the tug, Dumnik and the DEA agents saw for the first time the size of the tug, the enormous bow wave it created, and the boiling maelstrom it pulled along.

"Sheeeeit," Melvin said. He climbed down from the bow and moved toward the middle of the Scarab.

The skipper was back on the radio. "I got a dozen Special Forces soldiers on board. They're guarding the cargo and they're all armed. When I saw you on radar, their CO got on the radio to the Navy in Key West. In about, let's see, eight minutes, you're going to be looking at a Navy hydrofoil full of armed sailors. They're going to be boarding you."

Lance nodded. It was about seventy miles from his position across Florida Bay to Key West—no more than a twenty-minute run for the Navy's hydrofoil.

Dumnik squeezed the microphone in anger. "The U.S. Navy. Why is the U.S. Navy coming?"

"Told you I had a classified military cargo aboard." The skipper paused. "Got the hydrofoil on radar now. Wouldn't advise running. They've got some pretty heavy guns on board. You guys who you say you are, this won't take ten minutes to clear up."

Dumnik threw the microphone to the deck. "I'm the head of the President's South Florida Task Force. And I'm getting rousted by the fucking U.S. Navy? The U.S. fucking Navy. I don't believe this."

Lance picked up the microphone, squeezed the transmission button to make sure it still worked, then called the tug.

"Skipper, please advise Navy we're heaving to. Will await their boarding party. Sorry to trouble you. You have a good trip."

"I will."

Lance backed away to gain distance from the bow wave that would sweep under him when the tug passed. Then he retarded the throttles until the Scarab was barely making headway. He flicked on the navigation and clearance lights so the crew of the hydrofoil could get a visual on him. Then he grinned and looked around. Maybe it wasn't very productive working with the Bush League, but it sure was fun.

33

"I'm driving this muthafucker. You just tell me how to get where I want to go," Melvin said.

Lance looked at him and scratched his head. Lance was wearing a Mickey Mouse hat and a T-shirt that said, "DRAIN BRAMAGED." He wondered if there were no end to the arrogance of DEA. Even after last night's debacle, when Dumnik's crowd had been rousted by the U.S. Navy, Melvin was acting as if he were king of the universe. Today he was lead agent on what, from the get-go, was a true goat-roping; he wanted to go up some little creek and find what a snitch had told him was a ten-ton marijuana stash.

Lance knew it would be a repeat of last night. Dopers might have a stash; but it would be on one of the bigger keys out near the Gulf of Mexico; a place where there was plenty of water and plenty of hidey holes. To stash dope up a dead-end creek was absurd; too easy for a fellow doper to rip off the stash or for a cop to see it and seize the load. No one would stash a load of dope in the middle of a national park that was frequently patrolled by park rangers.

But Melvin was convinced he had the inside skinny on a big stash. He and three other agents, Ben Blumen among them, had driven across from Miami towing a twenty-foot Mako, a beautiful new boat with a flared bow and shiny chrome pulpit. The control console was in the center of the boat. A pair of fifty-horsepower Mercs was strapped on the stern, and a crisp white new Bimini top sheltered occupants from the burning sun. The Mako was launched from the marina on the southwest side of Chokoloskee Island. The DEA agents had very little experience with boats and were afraid to back the trailer into the water deep enough so the

boat could float off. They stood in the dark tepid water
and pushed and heaved and grunted and shoved as
they tried to get the boat off the trailer. Melvin spurned
Lance's offer to help. But finally—it was almost noon—
Melvin realized the boat could not be pushed or pulled
off the trailer.

"Take off that silly hat and tell me what we doing
wrong," he said to Lance.

"Hat keeps the sun off my head," Lance said. He
handed the bowline to Ben. "Hold this." He turned
to the other agents. "You guys get in the boat."

Melvin looked at him in disbelief. "While it's still
on the trailer?"

"While it's still on the trailer. Just do it, and we'll
be out of here."

The DEA agents climbed aboard the trailer, then
stepped into the boat, dripping mud and water. Lance
cringed. But it was their boat. Lance stepped into the
truck, released the brake, and pressed the clutch. The
truck rolled backward until Lance, who was leaning
out the door looking astern, saw water bubbling around
the exhaust pipe. He set the brake and stepped out just
as the Mako floated clear of the trailer.

Ben held tight to the bowline.

"Pull it in closer so we can get aboard," Lance
said.

Lance drove the truck under a gnarled oak tree,
locked it, and was bouncing the keys in his hand as
he approached Melvin.

Melvin had the engines revved up too fast; they were
churning the dark water to a froth. The cooling system
of the engines bubbled and gurgled frantically as a
mini-maelstrom boiled around the stern. "Okay, show
me how to get up the creek," Melvin said.

"I think we already there."

"We ain't even started."

Lance rolled the bottoms of his jeans up to his
knees, then stepped out of his boat shoes. He held the
boat while Ben swung aboard. Lance followed him,
slipped on his shoes, pointed east, and said, "Go slow.
The channel is small."

Melvin threw the Mercs into gear, causing a gigantic lurch as the overrevved engines jerked the boat forward.

"Slow down. You hit an oyster bar and you'll rip the bottom out," Lance said.

"I'll drive the goddamn boat. You just tell me how to get where we going," Melvin said. But he retarded the throttles.

A few moments later Lance told Melvin to turn hard left to enter the main channel. Then, northeast of the island, another hard right took them into the mouth of the Turner River.

"Move way over to the left," Lance said. "Shoals come way out into the mouth. Stay just to the right of the marker and you'll have good water."

"Don't look too good to me," Melvin said. "Looks like what we got in the sewers up in Jersey."

"This is some of the richest, most nutrient-filled water in the world," Lance said. "People come from all over the world to fish here."

"Ain't catching me eating shit what comes outta that water."

"Keep it slow," Lance said as they entered the Turner River. "I'd hug the left bank until the first turn. Then move across the river to avoid the shoals."

"Ain't much of a river if it's that shallow. I could damn near walk across it."

"That's right. That's why we have to go slow and be careful. The channel shifts back and forth and there are mud banks and oyster bars everywhere."

"Only bar I care about is a bar that serves yac and Coke," Melvin said. He reached down into his equipment bag and pulled out a small radio. "We need some sounds if we going to the jungle."

He fiddled with the dials and suddenly Marvin Gaye was singing "I Heard It Through the Grapevine." Melvin grinned in approval. He looked at Lance. "Listen to the brother, man." He rocked his head. "Wish I had my big box. Better sounds."

A half-hour later the boat passed the Left Hand Turner River and swung around a bend into Hurddles

Creek. Now the waterway was squeezing in on the boat; narrowing rapidly. The boat passed a small creek with no name, and then Lance pointed to the left, up an impossibly small little creek that led into a place called Hells Half Acre.

"That's where you want to go," he said.

Ben and the other agents instinctively moved to the center of the boat. Limbs closed overhead. The mangroves on each side seemed close enough to touch.

"You might want to take down the Bimini top," Lance said.

"What's that?"

Lance reached up and touched the overhead cover on the folding frame.

"Oh, the Bimini top," Melvin said. "That stays up."

Melvin pointed to one of the DEA agents in the bow. "Yo, there. Stand up and catch the tree limbs. Move 'em out of the way so we can get through."

The agent ducked and moved and twisted in order to avoid the overhead branches. Then there was one he could not duck under or move away from. He held it, pushing on it, bending it as the boat slowly moved ahead. Then the limb won; it bounced back with a force that knocked the agent to the deck and ripped off the Bimini cover as cleanly as if it had been sliced away. Lance, who had ducked when he saw what was happening, stood up and fingered one of the holes left where the frame had been pulled from the white fiberglass gunwale.

"Nice neat hole," he said seriously. He looked at the other jagged openings. "Shouldn't take more than a day or so to fix them. With new fiberglass, gelcoat, paint, and labor, cost maybe six hundred dollars. Plus a new top. That's about eight hundred."

Melvin stood up. The edge of the limb had caught him a glancing blow on the shoulder and it hurt like hell. Without looking to see where the boat was going, he turned to Lance in anger. Before he could speak, the boat came to an abrupt and jarring halt, bounced to the left, and slowly forged ahead to the sound of a horrendous scraping noise down the starboard side.

In the resulting silence, Lance sang along with Keith Sweat on the radio; oozing out the words to "Make It Last Forever."

Lance looked over the side at the oyster bar the boat had struck. The edge of the boat looked as if it had been ravaged by a dozen buzz saws.

"Now, that one's going to cost some real bucks," Lance said.

"We going too slow," Melvin said. "That's the trouble."

Melvin had made it clear he wanted only advice on the route and possible underwater obstacles from Lance; nothing else. So Lance squatted down and held on. He looked up once and saw a solid wall of greenery. He lay down in the bottom of the Mako. The DEA agents followed his example. Melvin was the only person standing.

As the Mako rounded the next corner, a broken tree stump protruding from the muddy bank caught the bow pulpit and caved it in. Again the boat came to an abrupt stop. The engines died.

In the silence, Lance looked up at the canopy of bushes and trees. On each side of the creek, which now seemed no wider than the boat, were cypress trees covered with giant bromeliads. They were big sprawling bromeliads, lush and green.

"Toto, I don't think we're in Kansas anymore," Lance said.

"Wish we were," Ben said.

Lance was astounded at the fullness and the color and the profusion of the bromeliads. "Incredible air plants," he said.

"Yeah, and next you'll be telling us about the mile-o-more bird and bull dogs with AIDS," Melvin said.

"Not bull dogs. Pit bulls."

Melvin angrily turned off the radio. He adjusted the throttles, opened the choke, and tried to restart the engines. The only sound was a repetitive whirring noise from the starter.

"I sort of like the one over there," Ben said.

Lance looked where Ben was pointing. A giant emerald-green bromeliad, feathered leaves drooping, clung to the limb of a cypress tree. In the middle was a moist carmine heart gleaming in the afternoon sun.

"Good eye, Ben. That might be the prettiest one I've ever seen."

Melvin looked around in disgust. A boat full of narcotics agents, all lying on their backs looking up at the trees, admiring silly little plants.

" 'Fucks the matter with you people?" he growled. "Just a bunch of houseplants. You sound like you about to wet your pants."

Lance folded his hands beneath his head. "No, they're more than that. Those plants are magic. That's why people around here like them so much."

One of the other DEA agents looked at Lance. "Magic? What do you mean?"

"Those things drive women absolutely crazy. Nothing in the world makes a woman more excited than some exotic plant like that. Your wife or girlfriend gets one of those, and there's no telling what she will do for you."

"Yeah, just like alligator turds and mile-o-more birds," Melvin said. "You always fucking with people. And why are you wearing that silly-assed Mickey Mouse hat?" He turned back to the control panel.

The starter ground away: waaaooo, waaaooo, waaaooo, waaaooo.

Melvin turned to Lance. "You supposed to be some kinda boat expert. What's wrong with this thing? Why won't it go?"

Lance looked at the panel. "Your sleeve must have snagged the keys. Turn on the ignition."

"Muthafucker."

Melvin turned the keys, then pressed the ignition switch. The first engine caught. Then the second. Melvin revved them, jockeying the throttles back and forth.

"What make those things—what did you call them

. . . air plants?—so special to women?'' ventured one of the DEA agents.

"That's right. Air plants. Real name is bromeliad. You've heard of bromeliads. Nowhere else in the world do they grow the way they grow here in the Everglades.'' He pointed to the plant Ben had seen. ''That thing should be in a museum.''

"Yeah, but what makes them so special to women?'' said the other DEA agent.

"The size. The species. There's air plants back in here that you can't find anywhere else in the world. Plant experts consider them some of the most exotic species on earth. Think about it: you guys are back here chasing a multiton load of dope. Lot of danger. Lot of risk. Fighting some of the smartest and meanest bunch of smugglers that law enforcement has ever gone up against. And in the middle of risking your life to protect America from dangerous drugs, you take time out to get one of these rare, expensive, exotic, beautiful plants.''

The DEA agents were silent. Even Melvin was listening. He turned off the engines.

"I don't know,'' Ben said. ''Seems wrong to take them out of their natural habitat.''

"Shut the fuck up, Blumen,'' Melvin said. ''What the hell some corn-fed Kansas farmer know about pussy?'' He turned to Lance.

"You some kinda Boy Scout?''

"Usta be. They kicked me out for eating a Brownie.''

"How you know about these—what you call them?— air plants?''

"The local guys told me about it. I tried it. Took one to my girlfriend just to test it. I didn't believe what they told me. But it's amazing what a stupid little plant will do to a woman. It's not like buying one in a store. There's something about bringing it out of the wild while you're chasing dopers that gets 'em. I couldn't walk for a week after I gave one to my girlfriend. She did things to me I never heard of. Damn near ruined me.''

The agents were staring at Lance. "Believe me, an air plant is the greatest aphrodisiac in the world," he said. "A woman gets one of these, and her gratitude has no limits. If she's average in bed, she turns cosmic. She will move around so much that you better not take your clothes off, because you might not come back that way. And even if she doesn't like blow-jobs, she gets one of these air plants and she will take you to the promised land."

Lance shook his head in wonderment as he looked up at the profusion of bromeliads.

One of the DEA agents stood up and looked around. "There's no dope back here," he said. He waited a moment, then put one foot atop the gunwale and stepped onto the dark slick mud of the bank. "Think I'll get a couple of these air plants," he said. "They'll look good around the house."

"Yeah," said the other agent. "I ain't buying that stuff about how they affect women. But I'll put a couple in my apartment. I like them."

"Not me," Ben said. "They look better growing back here than they could ever look in my apartment."

Melvin looked at Ben in disgust. "Well, that helps me make up my mind. Blumen, you too lame to pour piss out of a boot. If you don't want any, I do."

He looked ahead. It was impossible for the boat to go any further. The bow was wedged into the bank on either side. They would have to back downstream several hundred yards before there was enough room to turn around.

"Dumnik's gonna chew my ass about this boat. But this is rough country."

He looked at Lance. "Besides, home boy here was our guide. I'm gonna blame you."

Lance tilted the Mickey Mouse hat forward over his eyes and grinned. "Hey, I'll tell him we took the wrong exit."

Three hours later the battered Mako slid into the marina at Chokoloskee Island. It looked as if it had barely survived a rocket attack. The Bimini top was sheared off. Gaping holes marred the fiberglass. A horrendous gash ran the length of the right side. The bow pulpit was crushed and folded. The interior of the boat was streaked with mud and filled with bromeliads, dozens of them. On the radio, Bobby Brown was singing "Every Little Step." And five men, four of them in camouflage fatigues, all sunburned and weary, were slumped in the boat.

A park ranger at the Chokoloskee marina stared in astonishment as the Mako slowly motored across the shallow channel. The ranger waited, unsmiling behind his mirrored sunglasses.

"We got a Smokey the Bear waiting on us," Melvin said. "Maybe he'll put the boat on the trailer while I go take a leak."

Lance jumped from the boat as soon as it touched the edge of the dock. He took a close look at the ranger. It was not the one he had seen with December. As far as he knew, this guy was straight. Lance held out his hands and said, "None of that stuff is mine."

"Who are those guys?" the ranger said, eyeing the sidearms and automatic rifles.

"DEA."

"You a fed?"

"No, just along for the ride."

The ranger turned toward the Mako. "They never notified us they were in the park."

Melvin's voice rang across the marina. "Blumen, drive the trailer down here and load this piece of shit."

Ben jumped to the dock and walked wearily toward the truck, parked under the oak tree.

The ranger intercepted Ben. "Where you fellows been?" he asked casually.

"Up the . . . I think it was called the Turner River, and into some little creek."

"How far?"

"I don't know. Miles. As far as we could go. It was the end of the creek."

"Any of those plants belong to you?"

Ben looked over his shoulder. "No. I didn't want any."

The ranger turned and walked toward the Mako. "Who's in charge here?" he asked.

Melvin looked up in annoyance. "I am, Smokey. I'm Special Agent Melvin Foster, U.S. Drug Enforcement Administration. We're on official business. Why?"

The ranger pulled out his ticket book. "I'm a ranger with the National Park Service, and I, also, am on official business." He pointed toward the boat filled with bromeliads. "It violates federal statutes to remove plant life from within the boundaries of a national park. Show me some ID."

Melvin bowed up and tried to muscle the park ranger. "What the fuck you talking about, man? I'm looking for ten tons of dope and you raising hell about some goddamned weeds. Get outta my face."

The ranger was not intimidated. "They are not weeds. They are rare and endangered species. I asked you to show me some ID. You want to do this the easy way, or you want me to get on the radio and have a half-dozen rangers here in about three minutes?"

Melvin looked at the battered boat. That was going to take a lot of explaining. There was no dope. That was going to take even more explaining. Dumnik already was in a fire-eating mood because of the business the previous night with the Navy. Melvin had visions of this Smokey the Bear confiscating his boat and calling the press and telling them about DEA agents being arrested for stealing flowers. Dumnik would go into orbit. And Melvin, who was up for a promotion to GS-14, would wind up with a clerical job in whatever dead-end job Dumnik could find. Melvin gritted his teeth. He'd like to shove this goddamned Smokey aside and drive out of here. But there were several fishermen across the marina watching. He let out his breath.

Melvin looked at the ranger. "Sheeeiit, man, we're both cops. You're not gonna confiscate my boat, are you?"

The ranger glanced at the Mako. His eyebrows rose

in disbelief. "No, sir. But you'll have to leave the bromeliads here. You can't take those."

"Okay, man. Write me the goddamned ticket and I'll be outta here." He pulled out his identification and handed the ranger his driver's license.

Melvin whirled toward the Mako and sliced his arm across in front of his body. "Unload the goddamned weeds," he said. "Get 'em outta the boat."

"Hey, Melvin," came Lance's voice.

Melvin looked up. Lance had stopped his car, rolled down the window, and was smiling.

"What do you want?" Melvin shouted. "You knew about these air plants."

Lance laughed. He picked up his Snickers bar, took a bite, chewed a moment, and studied Melvin through the open window. "You got one consolation, Melvin."

"What?"

"You're not the biggest asshole in the world."

Melvin stared.

Lance took another bite of his Snickers bar. "Dumnik is a bigger asshole than you are," he said. He raised a finger. "But it's very close."

34

It was Saturday morning; Nick had grown exasperated trying to keep Elmer from doing butt twirls on the living-room carpet, and Susie was upset because she had lost a thousand-dollar commission the previous day. It happened when a tourist wanted to rent one of the condos she managed in Naples. The tourist, making idle conversation, asked Susie what her husband did. When she said Nick was a cop who was in charge of investigating a local drug ring, the tourist decided he would rent a condo from someone else.

Nick decided his weekend was getting off to a bad start. The best way to put the cosmos back in order was to go fishing. He towed his small open fishing boat down to Goodland, launched it from a public ramp, and then motored slowly south through Coon Key Pass. He anchored off the end of Tripod Key, pushed his tackle box aside, and picked up his eight-foot laminated rod with the Penn 750 spinning reel. He was fishing for grouper today, so he was using only the one pole.

It was not ten minutes later that the first boat, a forty-foot sport fisherman, rumbled down the channel toward Gullivan Bay.

Nick looked up, eyebrows pulled together, and shouted, ''Slow down,'' but the skipper never heard him, and the people on the deck didn't even bother to wave. He was some dirt-bag local fisherman out there in a funny little boat. It was amusing when the four-foot bow wave from the sport fisherman lifted his boat high, rocked it, then dropped it to be assaulted by the smaller waves radiating from the sport fisherman.

''Hemorrhoid,'' Nick mumbled.

He rearranged his seat, meticulously adjusted the anchor line, cleaned up the boat, opened a beer, and leaned back to do some serious thinking about the two homicides and the Everglades City case. He was now convinced the homicides were tied to Everglades City smuggling, but he still had no proof. He and Lance were to return to see Big Knocker Monday morning. Nick was sure he would cooperate, but, at the same time, he knew Big Knocker would be hard to control. Lance was going undercover with the doper and it was going to be extremely dangerous. But Nick had to force something to happen. The cases simply could not drag on forever. DEA had announced twice that Everglades City was cleaned up. They got the headlines and Nick got the headaches.

Another boat came churning down the channel; another big sport fisherman throwing out a bow wave that looked like the Banzai pipeline. Twenty people could surf on that wave. Nick grabbed the pole and held on as the boiling, foaming wave pushed his boat high in the air.

Again the fishermen on the deck looked but did not wave. They were no more than twenty yards away. Nick could see their faces; their expressions of unconcern. Why didn't they slow down in the channel? Hadn't they ever heard of common courtesy toward other boats?

He hadn't finished rearranging the equipment in the bottom of his boat when the next sport fisherman, even faster than the first two, came boiling down the channel.

The vein in Nick's forehead, the one that ran down along his nose and then under his eye, began throbbing. It stood out, leaping and pulsating. His eye appeared to protrude an inch from his face.

"Dammit, enough is enough," Nick exploded. He reached into his equipment bag, pulled out his nine-millimeter pistol, and stuck it in his belt.

"Okay, you water-going hemorrhoids. Come on," he said. By now he was too angry to fish. He sat there fuming, eyes up the channel, waiting. It was not five minutes before the skipper of the next boat cleared Coon Key and opened the throttles wide as he approached Tripod Key and the open water of Gullivan Bay.

The boat, its brightwork sparkling in the morning sun, was about a hundred yards away when Nick stood up. The eyes of the people aboard the sport fisherman swung his way. Nick pulled the nine-mil from his belt, held it up in the air, and jacked a round into the chamber. He aimed across the channel. Then his head swung toward the sport fisherman as if he had just realized it was there. He lowered the pistol but kept his eyes on the boat.

Almost immediately the skipper of the big fishing boat pulled the throttles back until the boat was barely making headway. The big bow wave settled until it was only a sibilant little hiss of foam an inch tall. Nick's eyes followed the boat. And the eyes of the people on deck were locked on Nick. The sport fish-

erman was fifty yards beyond Nick before the skipper
looked over his shoulder and slowly opened the throttles.

Nick gave a grunt of satisfaction, sat down, popped
the clip out of the nine-mil, pulled the round from the
chamber and inserted it in the top of the clip, then
shoved the clip back into the pistol.

Nick sighed in disgust. His fishing was ruined. He
slowly pulled up the anchor. He was tired of hemorrhoids. He sloshed the anchor up and down in the water, washing off the slick black mud, then placed it
gently in the anchor well in the bow. A drive across
the edge of Gullivan Bay would be a nice diversion. If
the winds remained light and the waters calm, he might
even go out to the edge of the Gulf. There, away from
the hemorrhoids, away from everyone, he could drift
with the tides and think about how to work Big
Knocker and how to investigate his possible link to
the two homicides.

Nick rounded White Horse Key. The surface of the
water was as flat and calm as a millpond. He decided
to turn more southwesterly into the Gulf, but then,
ahead and slightly to the east, he saw the sailboat. He
knew from the cant of the mast that the boat was
aground; either caught by a falling tide or run onto the
shoals. It was at the mouth of the channel off Gomez
Point; the channel that led across the islands into Faka
Union Bay. As with most cops, Nick's thought pro-
cesses always began with the assumption that whatever
was out of the ordinary had the possibility of being
some sort of scam. He didn't think first of rescuing
the crew of the sailboat, but rather he wondered why
a sailboat was in such relatively shallow waters. Boat-
men, if they knew nothing else, know how treacherous
these waters were. They knew the draft of their boat,
the depth of the channels, and the rise and fall of the
tides. But what if this boat were so heavily loaded that
it rode a foot or so deeper in the water than usual?
Where was this guy going? Let's see, Faka Union Bay
led into the Faka Union Canal. The canal was dredged
and relatively deep and ended at the Port of the Islands

Marina. And the marina was on the Tamiami Trail out in the middle of nowhere. It was the perfect place for an off-loading. Bingo. These guys probably were stone scammers.

Civilians find such thinking either deplorable or laughable. But cops know from experience it's one way to bag the crooks. No matter how smart a scammer might be, there is always the unexpected. No matter how meticulously he plans his operation, no matter the infinite attention to detail, something occasionally rises up and bites him in the ass. Clausewitz called it the "fog of war." Bad guys call it bad luck. Nick thought it was divine intervention. Whatever it was, it happened. Nick took his nine-mil from the equipment bag and stuck it under his shirt. He checked to make sure his portable radio was in the bag. Without increasing his speed, he motored toward the stranded boat off Gomez Point.

As he approached, Nick saw that the boat was between thirty and forty feet in length; a Swan, one of the most beautiful production sailboats in the world. Its lines and its seaworthiness and its appointments were functional, dependable, and beautiful. The three men on the deck stared but did not wave. They wore battered and stained baseball hats, jeans, short-sleeved sport shirts, and new tennis shoes. Not exactly the sort of owners, or crew, one imagined aboard a Swan.

Nick pulled closer. He was about ten feet from the boat. "Need any help?" he asked.

One of the men shook his head. "Naaa. We ran aground. Just waiting for the tide."

Nick nodded. Local guy, by his accent. What were these three yahoos doing aboard such an expensive boat?

Nick took another look at the boat. It was hard aground. And there was coral, not mud, here at Gomez Point. Antennae aboard the vessel revealed a plethora of sophisticated communications equipment. Nick had seen enough sailboats go aground to realize that when it happened, owners pulled out all the stops. They used anchors to kedge off. They tossed lines to other boats

in an effort to be pulled into deeper water. Simply to
sit there as these guys were doing, not sending out an
assistance or emergency call to the Coast Guard, just
waiting while they took a chance on the coral ripping
out the sides of their vessel, was not the way it was
done. At the very least, the Swan would be scarred
and deeply scratched along her port side. These guys
sat there as if it were of no concern.

"Anybody else on board?" Nick asked.

"Nope," said one, at the same time another said,
"Why?" They both spoke too soon, and they both
gave the wrong answer.

"Where you fellows going?"

The three looked at each other, more careful this
time. "We just sailing around," one finally said.

"Where'd you come from?"

One jabbed his finger toward the Gulf of Mexico.
The other two stared at Nick.

He was beginning to wonder if these guys were sailors. Asking a guy on the sailboat his point of origin
was an expected question. Both crew and owners liked
for people to know how far and how long they had
sailed. It was a matter of pride. These guys were too
defensive.

There was one way to make sure. These three guys
had not stood up and walked to the rail, and sailors
usually did when another boat approached. He turned
the throttle slightly and pointed the bow toward the
edge of the Swan. The three guys still didn't move.
Ordinarily a crew member would be tossing out fenders, leaning over to fend off his bow, and cautioning
him not to allow his boat to scratch the paint. These
guys were not sailboat people.

Nick drifted closer, easing along the side of the
Swan, always keeping his eye on the three bozos on
the stern. Then he smelled it. Whether it was from a
soft puff of wind or simply from the overpowering
odor, he did not know. But the odor of marijuana was
strong in the air.

Nick reached into his equipment bag, flashed his tin
and said, "State attorney's office. I'm coming

aboard.'' He jammed the portable radio into his rear pocket.

As one, the three men leaned forward and started to stand. "You can't come on our boat," one said.

"Sit down and stay down," Nick ordered harshly. He pulled the nine-mil from under his shirt. The three men sat down and stayed.

"Any of you assholes move and I'll blow a fucking hole in you big enough to park this boat in," he said.

He tied his boat to the railing of the Swan and swung aboard, eyes on the three mutts. "I asked you before, anybody else aboard?"

The men did not answer.

"You're hauling dope. Don't give me any crap. I asked you if somebody else is on board."

A slight creak betrayed the fourth man. As he opened a hatch in the bow and tried to ease on deck behind Nick, his knee scraped the edge of the hatch and caused it to emit a slight sound.

Nick ducked and swung around, holding the pistol with both hands and leveling it at the man emerging from a hatch. The angry determined look of the Hispanic guy—he was slender and looked to be in his mid-thirties—changed in a flash to a wide ingratiating smile.

"Close the hatch and move over here. Hands where I can see them," Nick ordered. He had heard a loud distinctive "click" when the hatch closed. His eyes narrowed. The boat was wired as a precaution against ripoffs; if anyone tried to open the hatch, and probably the companionway and every other opening on the boat, he would be greeted by an explosion; maybe not enough to wreck the boat, but certainly enough to kill the intruder.

Nick glanced over his shoulder. The three mutts were down and staying down. Nick knew immediately what was going on. The Hispanic represented the owners of the load. The other three were humpers chosen for their knowledge of local waters. Fishermen from Everglades City. Damn bubbas and julios were at it again.

He sliced his eyes back to the Hispanic. "Okay, José. Get your ass back to the stern with your three scumbag buddies. Do it now."

The lithe figure of the fourth man stood upright and looked down at Nick. He held his hands wide. "Do not get excited, my friend. This is a little misunderstanding that can very easily be cleared up."

Nick knew he was in trouble if he didn't get the four guys together where he could more easily control them. Even then it would be doubtful. Four against one. They probably had guns hidden all over the boat. They knew how to open the hatches without tripping the explosive charges. He had to keep them topside in plain sight until the cavalry arrived.

He jacked a round into the chamber. He had done that so much today it was an old comforting sound; rather like the closing of a refrigerator door.

His voice tightened as he pointed the pistol between the eyes of the Hispanic. "Listen to me, you dirtbag dope-smuggling Puerto Rican son of a bitch. I'm looking for an excuse to shoot your greasy ass. And if you don't move back there right now, you're shark bait. 'Cause I will flat kill you."

"I am *cubano*," the man angrily said. His eyes hardened and glinted and never broke contact with Nick as the man, arms outspread, slowly edged toward the stern.

"Cuban, Puerto Rican. All the same. Move."

"You are making a big mistake, my friend."

"I'm not your friend. Don't ever call me your friend. I'm gonna put your ass in jail." The vein on Nick's face was throbbing.

The Cuban smiled. "How will you do that? We are aground. There are four of us and one of you. It is more likely that we will take your gun and your boat. You cannot handcuff all of us." The smile widened. "You have no handcuffs, do you?"

Nick's silence was all the answer the Cuban needed. Nick had his creds, his gun, and a radio. But no cuffs. He had left the house to go fishing, not to arrest four dopers.

"I don't need cuffs. I got this gun. And if one of you so much as sneezes, I'll use it. Now, sit. And stay."

None of the four men would give Nick their names. One by one he read them their rights. When he came to the Cuban, the Cuban made a grimace and shook his head. "Read it to me in Spanish," he said.

Nick looked at him in astonishment. Nick's left eye seemed to leap from his face. All over South Florida were people from throughout Central and South America. Most of them learned, to one degree or another, the language of their adopted country. But Cubans were unwilling to do this. When stopped by state troopers on the highway, they insisted that everything be explained in Spanish.

"If I got arrested in Havana, would you talk to me in English?" Nick said.

"Fuck you, lavaperro. Read it in Spanish."

"This is America. If you want to smuggle dope here, you got to speak English."

The Cuban was adamant. "You have to read me the rights in Spanish. You have to explain everything to me in Spanish."

Nick shook his head. This was one of the guys Lance sometimes talked about; another doper who thought he was a Latin lover when he was nothing but a fucking Cuban.

"Up yours, Jack. You understand English. You got all you're gonna get."

The Cuban smiled. "It will be a long time before anyone can come to your assistance, my friend," he said. The smile, the smile of a Havana pimp, was flashing at full power. "Be reasonable. We can work something out here that will be to everyone's advantage."

"If you call me your friend one more time, my finger is gonna slip and I'm going to put a hollow-point bullet right between your beady eyes. You got that?"

The Cuban smiled.

"You got that?" Nick repeated. He was almost shouting.

The Cuban nodded.

Nick pulled the radio from his back pocket and held it in one hand while he kept the pistol pointing at the four men on the stern. He sat down, back against a stanchion, and rested the pistol on his right knee. He wiped perspiration from his face and neck. Then he keyed the radio with his left hand.

Although he showed no sign of it, the conversation did not please him. It would take two, maybe three hours, to launch a boat and get it to him. And he had forgotten to turn down the volume on the radio, so the dopers heard the conversation. And the Cuban was smiling again. Nick had developed a strong anger toward the Cuban. He didn't know the guy. But he was a doper. He had threatened Nick. He had hinted at bribery. He was the sort of smart-ass little Cuban who fulfilled every sleazy stereotype. He would not shut up and he would not give up. Now he was whispering to his three friends. They were frightened of the Cuban.

"You got anything to say, say it so I can hear it. Else, shut up," Nick said. The nine-mil was beginning to feel as if it weighed a ton. But if he swung the barrel away from the Cuban, the guy would make a move; or convince the others to make a move. He tightened his fingers on the grip. It was damp with perspiration.

"I was telling my compadres that we should rush you. You can't kill all of us. Not in such a short distance. We would get you. We would kill you. And then we would be free."

Nick looked at the three men to the right of the Cuban. "Where you boys from?"

They stared at him and did not speak.

"Everglades City?"

The three looked at each other. One nodded.

"You boys got walking-around sense. You gonna let this foreign son of a bitch talk you into getting killed over a load of marijuana?"

The men glanced at each other again.

Nick nodded. "So there's more than marijuana down

below, huh? Thought so. Maybe a little white powder.''

The shifting eyes of the three men along with the
hard unwavering stare of the Cuban gave Nick his answer. He propped up the pistol.

"So you gonna let the julio talk you into getting
killed over an importation charge? Why don't you three
do yourselves a favor, give up the son of a bitch? You
think he would stick by you? He'd burn your asses in
a New York minute. Do the same for him. You're
caught. But you tell me what was going down here,
the names of everyone involved, and I'll pass it along
to the judge. I'll recommend a lenient sentence.''

The Cuban laughed. "You're wasting your time, my
fr . . . you're wasting your time. What you must concern yourself with is how long it takes before we rush
you and take away your little pistol and kill you.''

Nick propped the pistol up again. It now weighed
slightly less than a Buick. His arm was beginning to
tremble. Cramps would be coming soon. He shifted
the pistol to his left hand. He wiped perspiration from
his face.

"Who's gonna lead the charge?'' Nick asked the
three guys from Everglades City. "Think José here
will do it? No way. He's gonna let you guys do the
dirty work. If you make it, fine. If you don't, he's still
alive.''

The Cuban shook his head. "We will charge you
together. All four of us. You cannot kill all of us.''

Nick propped up the pistol. Now his left hand was
tiring. He had never known a pistol weighed so much.
"Tell you what, José. Anybody charges, I'm gonna
take you out first. You're gonna take one in the belly.
So go ahead and blow the bugle. Go ahead and charge.
Anybody moves one muscle toward me, you die.''

The Cuban shrugged. "We could all dive overboard
and swim.'' He pointed toward Panther Key a hundred
yards northeast.

"A guy in the water is an easy target. I wing just
one of you, and it's shark city in about five minutes.

You wanna be shark bait, go ahead, jump. Save the taxpayers the expense of trying you."

Nick braced his left hand on his knee. It did no good. He shifted the pistol back to his right hand.

"You will make a mistake. We will rush you and you will die. It is that simple." The Cuban's voice was flat and hard. Nick knew he couldn't afford to drop his guard for a single second. If he did, the Cuban would make his play. The guys from Everglades City, like most American crooks, knew when they had been had. If they were arrested, the game was up. Almost never did they shoot. But three cops could be holding automatic rifles on a Cuban, and if the Cuban had a gun, he would go for it. He would try to shoot his way out. It was a given; an absolute. Cubans would, just for the sheer hell of it, start shooting even if outnumbered ten to one. Anytime there was a bust involving a Cuban, a cop could plan on gunplay. All this guy needed was a split second and he would go for Nick.

Nick's eyes swept the deck. No winch handles or equipment lying around. No lines. No boat hooks. No knives. It didn't matter. The guy would find something. Nick shifted the pistol back to his left hand. He squinted against the bright sun and ignored the perspiration streaming down his face.

An hour later, even though he had switched hands frequently, both arms occasionally trembled from fatigue at holding the loaded pistol. Nick had no choice. He couldn't get far enough away from the four men to put the gun at his feet and relax. He had to keep them looking down the barrel.

Two hours later he was seeing dancing sunspots and his arms trembled constantly. Twice he'd had to thumb back the hammer of his pistol to stop the humpers from sliding along the deck toward him. Nick was growing sunburned. His face was bright red. His eyes squinted from the glare on the water. Perspiration streamed down his back. His throat was parched.

Three hours later the men from Everglades City, proded by the burning anger of the Cuban, were openly looking about the decks, searching for anything they could use to attack Nick. They were slowly spreading apart; knowing from his face that he was fading fast. Soon the pistol would fall and they would rush him.

It was almost four hours later before two boats from the Florida Marine Patrol arrived. After the officers cuffed the four men, one turned to Nick to congratulate him. His eyes widened. The pistol had fallen from Nick's hand to the deck and Nick was unable to pick it up. His hand was trembling uncontrollably; trembling to such a degree that he could not wrap his fingers about the pistol.

35

In Everglades City, the buzzards had moved from their perches atop the pilings that lined the river and from the garbage dump to their evening roosts in the trees and along the cross-arms of tall electrical poles. In the gathering dusk they sat with ruffled wings and tucked heads; black-suited deacons of doom dozing over a congregation of malefactors.

Heart Attack didn't notice the buzzards as he walked across the parking lot and into the Captain's Table. The Captain's Table Hotel is an odd place that moves to a peculiar rhythm; perhaps the reason that the idiosyncratic people of Everglades City come there. When you enter the hotel from the parking lot, the first sight is of a long unrelieved hall. The dining room is to the left and the bar to the right. Straight ahead, in sort of a nook between the bar and dining room, is a cluster of several booths where waitresses wait and watch. It is clear that the presence of a guest is something of an annoyance; something that interrupts their smoking and gossiping. Somewhere it has been impressed upon them that when a man enters the door,

he is searching for neither food nor drink, but rather
for the rest room. When a man enters, one of the waitresses points down the hall and says, "Straight ahead
to the end of the hall and turn right."

The dining room has a lovely view of the Barron
River. Chairs are equipped with rollers; an appurte-
nance that makes it somewhat difficult for diners, as—
once you sit down—it is hard labor merely to move
the chairs across the dark red carpet. If you give the
chair a hard pull, chances are the chair's arm will remain in your hand.

Waitresses encourage diners to go for the buffet
rather than ordering from the menu; a decision made
easier when a waitress comes from the kitchen and in
a stage whisper tells a couple of other waitresses to
"eighty-six the meat loaf." The menu carries no item
that might intimidate the locals. Cheese sandwiches
and soup are staples.

But Heart Attack was not interested in food. As he
approached the little nook where several waitresses sat
smoking, he nodded.

One of the waitresses, from force of habit, pointed
down the hall and said, "Straight ahead to—"

"I know," Heart Attack interrupted. "But I'm going in here." He turned right into the lounge. The bar,
a long curved wooden affair, was to the left immediately upon entering. A few small Formica-topped tables were scattered about the room. It is a plain room
made for people who enjoy their beer cold, their whiskey straight, and their waitresses sassy.

Michelle, the cocktail waitress, is young, busty, has
a towering haystack of blonde hair, and—an anoma-
lous touch that, to the locals, gives her an extraordinary appeal—horn-rimmed glasses.

Heart Attack pulled off his battered and stained cap
as he entered the bar, nodded at Michelle, and walked
to a table against the far wall.

Michelle popped the top on a bottle of Bud, followed him, and, as he pulled out a chair, slid the bottle across the table and said, "Heart Attack, you know

you don't have to take off your hat in here. You just be comfortable.''

"I got an agreement with God," Heart Attack said without smiling. "He don't wear a hat in my house and I don't wear one in his house. I always take off my hat in church and in bars.'' He reached for the cold beer, held it up in salute, then drained half the bottle. He smacked his lips, loosed a long sigh, and said, "Bring me another one. Time you get it here, this one'll be gone.''

"On the way," Michelle said with a smile.

Heart Attack turned up the bottle, drained the remainder, crossed his arms on the table, and stared into space as he waited for Michelle to return.

"There it is," Michelle said. She thunked the bottle of Bud down on the table. "Heart Attack, guess you heard about the new ride up at Disney World?''

"Naw, I ain't heard about that. What they doing?''

"It's a ride for the disabled.''

"That right?''

"They call it 'Kangaroo Rides for the Blind.' ''

Heart Attack and Michelle laughed together.

"That beats all," Heart Attack said. "You a cutter, Michelle. That's what you are.''

"Better believe it.''

"I got to sit here and do some thinking, Michelle.''

"You call me if you need anything. You hear?''

Heart Attack nodded, picked up the cold beer, and took a long deep drink.

His appearance alone would cause many people to underestimate Heart Attack. He was lean, but his face was broad and jowly. His ears protruded, and there was about him the rustic simple look of a man who, by becoming a fisherman, had reached the limit of his potential. But then, if one looked closely, his eyes were bright, wary, searching, and filled with a feral survivalist sort of intelligence not gleaned from schools. The young Heart Attack—he was then known by his real name of Thorn Wells—had dropped out of school when he reached sixteen; he was in the ninth grade at the time, and his teachers considered him dull and slow-witted, a boy incapable of learning. But the reason he dropped out of school had nothing to do with his ability to learn; it had to do with an incident that caused him extraordinary embarrassment. It then was the practice among the boys in Everglades City to take the edge off their rampant libidos by gathering together in a dilapidated old chickee hut far back in the woods and fucking hollowed-out baked sweet potatoes. Young Thorn was too anxious one day, and thrust his penis into a baked potato that was still hot from the oven. He sustained such a serious burn that he was in the hospital in Naples for more than a week, and received so many humiliating and embarrassing nicknames—everything from "Barbecue" to "Brick Dick"—that he dropped out of school and began fishing.

Like many rural southerners who lack formal education, Heart Attack had a cunning business sense; in fact, he was—when it came to drug smuggling—something of a genius. He had developed techniques and methodology that would have caused a Harvard MBA to shake his head in disbelief and admiration.

It was Heart Attack who was first among the fishermen of Everglades City to realize that he and his colleagues could do at least one thing better than anyone else in the world—bring in vessels through the narrow, treacherous, and ever-changing channels of the Ten Thousand Islands; channels that connected the Gulf of Mexico to the remote landing sites around Everglades City, Plantation Key, and the hundreds of small creeks that pierced the Everglades along Highway 41.

After a couple of crab boats were unable to find the Cuban shrimp boats carrying multiton loads of marijuana, Heart Attack came up with the idea of having chase boats—electronic-laden go-fast boats—that roamed far afield at speeds up to seventy miles an hour as they searched for the shrimpers. Once a shrimper's load was being transferred to the crab boats, the chase boats also formed something of an early-warning line to detect cops.

It was Heart Attack's idea for his daughter December to have her mullet skiff in the mouth of a pass when he was inbound with a load. When she added the wrinkle of trading sex with a park ranger in return for protection, she proved she was her father's daughter.

Two of his other daughters, April and May, were performing brilliantly another gambit he had devised; one that continued to avoid detection. July, the youngest daughter, was a senior in high school. She was talking of going off to college, but Heart Attack still had hopes she would join the family business. After he built a new home, bought a swamp buggy, a swimming pool, a four-wheel-drive vehicle for each daughter, and a half-dozen pairs of lizardskin cowboy boots, there wasn't a hell of a lot he wanted to buy. He truly did not know how many hundreds of thousands of dollars he had jammed into three-foot lengths of PVC pipe and buried in his backyard.

Heart Attack was almost prescient in knowing what cops might do in order to bust a load; he could anticipate virtually every move. Although, in fairness, because the fishermen of Everglades City were so close, and because they were the only people who knew the waterways of the Ten Thousand Islands, the options available to the cops were limited.

But now, for the first time in the decade he had been smuggling, there was trouble. The cops were more persistent than he could ever have believed. God knows, December had been able to convince about a dozen cops or prosecutors to go home empty-handed. And the DEA had come and gone. But there had been too many arrests of late. He knew the state attorney's office up in Fort Myers had some sort of investigation going, but in spite of numerous efforts, he could not determine what it was. Nevertheless, he had a deep sense of disquietude about continuing to smuggle. That line of endeavor had just about run its course. His highly developed sense of survival told him that the way of doing business he had enjoyed for the past few years was about to undergo a sea change. And he was not going to simply step aside and let it happen. He

would have one last hurrah; one final load. It would
be the biggest dope deal ever to take place in Everglades City; one that people would still be talking
about twenty years from now. He had talked with the
Cubans. As usual, they wanted to shoot anybody who
might try to stop them from bringing in a load. They
wanted to continue with business as usual. He knew
that even if he stepped out, the Cubans would continue. They would run aground or become lost; the
cops would pop them every time—especially if the
people in Everglades City notified the cops that a load
was coming in.

Oh, well. The most important thing now was the
big load. He would need the help of his nephew Big
Knocker.

Heart Attack looked at his watch. It was nine P.M.
Big Knocker was through with his day's labor up at
the county work farm. He should be home. That is if
he wasn't running a load tonight.

36

It was one-thirty A.M. when Kimberly rubbed her eyes,
sighed, and stared wearily at the screen of her lap-top
computer atop the kitchen table. She slumped in the
straight-backed chair. Boswell, who had been sitting
atop the stove, uttered an interrogatory meow. How
could he punch the buttons on her alarm clock if she
would not go to bed? Bos stood up and wound his way
among the pots and pans atop the stove.

"Bos, it might work. It just might work," Kimberly said.

The large tabby cat rubbed the edge of his chin
against one of the pots as he sought to nudge if off the
stove. But it was too heavy, so he meowed again and
stared with baleful eyes at Kimberly.

She idly caressed the pyramid-shaped piece of rose quartz on the table as she stared at the computer screen. Operation Everglades City III was almost ready to implement. Her original ops plan had been named Operation Deep Six, but Nick insisted on Operation Everglades City III; he liked the irony of finishing what DEA had begun, and said that three was a powerful number signifying completeness. For a moment she had looked at him and nearly asked if he were a student of numerology. Almost as if reading her thoughts, he shrugged and said, "Look at the Bible." Whatever that meant.

The U/C work for what Lance called "Son of Everglades City Two" was going well. It was all Nick's idea. Kimberly and Lance had thrown in a few things, but it was Nick's idea. The state attorney, ostensibly because of the crowded jail, would recommend that Big Knocker be granted an early release if he found an acceptable job and performed twenty hours of community service each week. So Lance, in partnership with Big Knocker, had set up a business repairing airboats. Considering Big Knocker's background, bringing him into the airboat repair shop was a stroke of genius. The community service was worked off by performing maintenance on airboats belonging to the National Park Service. And locals were flocking to the shop. Because Big Knocker, the king of the local smugglers, was there, Lance was considered almost one of the family. Big Knocker brought him inside. At last Nick had what he had wanted so long: a high-level snitch. It was just a matter of time until Nick brought down the entire town.

There was much Big Knocker did not know about the operation. He was like every other snitch in that he could not be trusted with everything. For instance, while he knew a pay phone had been installed on the front wall of the shop, he did not know it was bugged. Nor did he know that the only other pay phone in Everglades City had been disabled and—in agreement with the telephone company—would not be repaired until Nick said it was okay. Local smugglers knew enough about wiretaps not to talk business on their home phones. But for some reason they assumed it was safe to talk on a pay phone. It was as if they didn't know pay phones could be tapped. And Big Knocker didn't know that built into the transformer on the electrical pole across the street from the airboat repair shop was a video camera. It operated twenty-four hours a day. Everyone entering the shop or using the pay phone was immortalized on videotape.

Nick had worried that because Lance had been part of the DEA's Goodland U/C operation at the fish house, he might be suspect by the fishermen of Everglades City. But the arrests that had come out of that foul-up were all cases McBride had been working up. None of them were from Goodland. So there was nothing to tie the fish-house operation to Lance's being at the airboat repair shop. Besides, the fishermen over in Goodland still were shaking their heads in awe over how the heavy-breathing organized-crime guys had come in, done a shot, and got out without anyone ever knowing what had gone down. Yessir, these organized-crime guys were some kinda slick.

Now, for the first time, all the unwieldy and disparate elements of the long-running investigation were beginning to come together. At long last, the narcs now had the means to shut down Everglades City. An investigation that had run for more than a year was about to come to a climax. When Nick rolled Big Knocker, that was the key that opened the door to the inner sanctum of Everglades City smugglers. Things were beginning to happen. Payoff time was coming.

Heart Attack had shown up unexpectedly at Big Knocker's rented trailer over on Plantation Key two nights earlier; the brains of the Everglades City smugglers calling on the brawn; the two main men coming together. It was all on tape. That was another thing Big Knocker didn't know: that the trailer in which he was living until his new house was built was so filled with electronic devices—including a camera lens no larger than the tip of a pencil—that Dickman and Joe Willy, listening in the intel van, knew of every burp, every wheeze, every move. And Heart Attack's visit was all on tape; enough to indict him on conspiracy charges. But that would come after the deal went down. Heart Attack had come to enlist Big Knocker's help in what would be the biggest load ever to come into Everglades City; about a hundred tons of marijuana and a thousand kilos of cocaine.

The load would involve dozens of local fishermen; the largest number of people in any deal that had ever gone down in Everglades City. The four Cuban shrimp boats bringing in the dope would not transfer the load at the "coke machine" as they often did, but instead would come to a position fourteen miles off the Ten Thousand Islands, where the loads would be transferred to crab boats. It was smart, keeping the loads to about twenty-five tons each; that way the shrimp boats would maintain good maneuverability.

The crab boats, after taking on the dope, would bring the loads into Sandfly Pass, where it would be stashed on a deserted island. Mullet skiffs and creek boats would move the cocaine and about twenty tons of marijuana to the hill that night. The dope then would be loaded into Winnebagos, trucks, and cars for the final run into Miami. Heart Attack, in a curious comment, had told Big Knocker that two of his daughters would be there in garbage trucks. Joe Willy and Dickman were checking that out. Over the next week, the remainder of the load would be transferred to the hill.

Nick had ordered Kimberly to analyze the dopers' operation and decide when and where and how to bust it. Of paramount importance was seizing the load. The entire law-enforcement operation would be geared to keeping the dope off the street. Had the Coast Guard been involved, they would have wanted to pop the shrimp boats far at sea. But that was too dicey. The Coasties might not be able to find the boats.

Kimberly, who looked at her job through discerning eyes and an analytical mind, continued to be baffled by the various agencies in the U.S. government's war on drugs. First, the war was a joke; a charade; a farce—it was not working.

Part of the reason was the inexperience, the unsuitability, and the internecine squabbling of various federal agencies involved in the war. For instance, the United States Coast Guard is without equal when it comes to performing daring and innovative search-and-rescue missions. They are quite simply the best in the world. They also are good at patrolling America's waters, protecting American fisheries, promoting boating safety, and enforcing rules regarding oil spills. But the Coasties know slightly less about narcotics interdiction than Hitler knew about compassion. Their involvement in narcotics interdiction is one of the most massive and expensive frauds ever perpetrated on the American taxpayer. Back in the mid-seventies the Coasties, for the first time, were called upon to help in a narcotics case; to assist in the apprehension of a Venezuelan freighter named the *Ecopesca* one of the first motherships loaded with marijuana. The Coasties botched their part of the apprehension but proved outstanding in taking credit for seizing some twelve tons of dope. The Coasties were unique in government agencies in understanding that the perception was more important than the reality; that public relations could make up for a startling lack of substance. When the war on drugs heated up in the mid-eighties and Coast Guard Commandant Paul Yost saw the hundreds of millions of dollars buying boats and aircraft for interdiction, he decided he wanted a piece of the action. The aircraft he wanted to use for interdiction—a sweptwing Falcon—was woefully inadequate for the job. Pilots had midair collisions practicing intercepts. The jet was down more than half the time for maintenance. The Coasties spent sixteen million dollars on each of five Falcons in Miami that were assigned to the intercept mission. They had to have five jets available in order to have eighty-eight-percent availability for a single aircraft. The Coasties published stats saying that within a given time period they launched two hundred and thirty-four intercepts; what they did not say was that two hundred and ten of those were on legitimate air traffic.

Then there was U.S. Customs, the oldest agency in the U.S. government and the agency with the job of defending America's borders. Customs radar technician worked out of a small room at the FAA's Miami Air Route Traffic Control Center. From here, Customs coordinated airborne intercepts. But the Coasties wanted in on it and lobbied successfully for construction of the seventy-million-dollar cost of C3I; a facility that gave them a role in interdiction. The Coasties were incredible; they used public-affairs officers to convince the general public that they were the only people in the interdiction business. After the Customs Air Branch put together a collection of FLIR tapes from numerous busts, the Coasties took the tape—ostensibly to use as a training tool—and began showing the tape at public functions. "This is what we do," they said. While the Coasties were absolute geniuses at smoke and mirrors, at convincing the public they were adept at airborne narcotics interdiction, they were extraordinarily quiet at not notifying the public of more substantive things they were doing—such as abandoning their boating-safety training because they wanted to divert the money to drug interdiction. None of it made sense. There simply was no logic in having untrained troops, who were transferred every two or three years, thrown into a job already being performed by highly dedicated and skilled Customs experts who had been on the job for years. While the public image of the Coast Guard soared, the taxpayer suffered. And Customs officials, for reasons no one could fathom, simply sat around and let themselves be co-opted by the Coasties.

Then there is the DEA. Few agencies in the U.S. government have been reshuffled and reorganized as much as the Drug Enforcement Administration. Survival has become more important than doing the job. When Reagan placed the DEA under the FBI, it was the fruition of DEA's worst nightmares. Even though both the FBI and DEA are federal law-enforcement agencies, they are poles apart in technique and philosophy. The shotgun marriage of the DEA and the FBI is roughly analogous to a union of the Anti-Defamation League and the Ku Klux Klan. The FBI is concerned with its image; with its tradition. The basic training of agents at Quantico is something like a college campus. Trainees rarely flunk out. Classes are from eight to five. It's all very civilized. Training to become a DEA agent is like a gladiator school. There is nothing civilized about it. The failure rate of some classes is twenty or thirty percent. DEA agents are probably the greatest undercover experts of any U.S. government agency; even better than CIA. If investigating a narcotics case called for an undercover agent who was a left-handed Chinese cook who spoke four languages, including Farsi and Urdu, and who held Olympic gold medals in horseback riding and pole vaulting, DEA could come up with the agent. Trouble is, the agency is more concerned with survival than with drug investigations; more concerned with outwitting the FBI than with fighting the war on drugs. The middle and upper layers of DEA contain a large number of alcoholics, and the lower ranks are people with little or no street experience. The DEA is paranoid; and because the paranoia is bureaucratic rather than personal, it leads to bizzare incidents where the consequences are almost impossible to comprehend. One example is the questionable practice of controlled deliveries of drugs; using DEA informants flying DEA aircraft to pick up loads fronted with DEA money. Reduced to basics, this means the American taxpayer is financing the importation of narcotics for the purported reason of "trading up"; of arresting big-time smugglers. DEA agents swear that no dope ever gets through; that their controlled deliveries of cocaine never reach the street. The DEA, by some perverted logic, is smuggling cocaine and calling it an innovative technique in enforcing the law. By the end of 1989, almost half the loads of cocaine intercepted by the Miami Air Branch of U.S. Customs were controlled deliveries. DEA smuggles the dope, and, when it is seized, adds the poundage to its stats. Bizarre.

Another aberration is that, despite its extraordinary

successes in undercover cases, there are all too often cases such as Everglades City, where the DEA never understands what's going on. They try to do a quick in-and-out and to grab some stats; they come back with the most illogical collection of undercover agents one can imagine, arrest a few people, and move on. But the dope keeps coming.

All too often these agencies work against each other. For instance, in the summer and fall of 1989, U.S. Customs realized that suddenly they were facing an unusual number of cases involving the turbine Commander, the only aircraft in America that had the combination of speed, range, and payload to beat the Citation jet. At low altitudes, this aircraft can outrun the Citation. Several times the CHET and Citation intercepted turbine Commanders entering Maine or Canadian airspace. The only one they caught was loaded with a thousand keys of cocaine. The Medellin Cartel had discovered a new technique and a new route. Then Customs found that a particular Commander dealer in the Southeast was selling an unusual number of the two-million-dollar aircraft. The FBI began making discreet inquiries about a secret Customs operation in Maine. It turned out that the FBI was selling turbine Commanders to the Medellin Cartel with the hope of seizing money. The drugs the Commanders were bringing in were irrelevant; the FBI was after money. Money makes better stats. When Customs complained, the FBI went to the attorney general, who told Customs to back off; let the dope keep coming; the important thing was to seize money.

Customs Commissioner William von Raab resigned in July 1989 and said federal agencies were too involved in peripheral issues to be effective in the war on drugs. He was right; but, as is usually the case with federal agencies, officials at the Coast Guard and FBI and DEA questioned his motives rather than considering the substance of what he had to say.

The bottom line in the whole business is not simply that the war on drugs is a joke; but that because the feds are so inept, a great burden has fallen on local communities all across America. Dozens, hundreds, thousands of Nick Browns in jurisdictions across the land are fighting courageously, fighting with their backs to the wall, fighting for the survival of the rule of law and for the American system. The feds fight turf wars while local cops fight the real drug wars. And their battle is largely anonymous. They are simply doing their jobs.

McBride caressed one of her crystals. People like Nick Brown were the unknown American heroes; fighting to keep their integrity and their honor against overwhelming forces.

She returned to the dopers and what they planned for their last hurrah. In addition to the shrimp boats and their Cuban crews, Nick wanted to arrest the local people who were the key to the smuggling. So the raid had to be aimed at the deserted island in Sandfly Pass where the dope would be stashed. The dope would be seized and the crews of the crab boats, mullet skiffs, and creek boats arrested. Humpers and drivers would be arrested on conspiracy charges.

The bust would be an enormously complex operation; fully as convoluted as a small military operation. Heart Attack had told Big Knocker that for three days preceding the off-loading, he would have small boats patrolling Sandfly Pass and the adjacent creeks to look for cops. Radio frequencies of Collier County, FDLE, and the Marine Patrol, not to mention the federal agencies, would be monitored. Airports within a fifty-mile radius would be watched.

That meant the bust crew for the island in Sandfly Pass would have to be in position at least four days—five would be better—in advance of the time the load was expected. There was always a chance the load could be early. Kimberly's ops plan recommended the bust crew to be in place six days in advance.

She shook her head in dismay. Camping out in the Ten Thousand Islands for six days would be unrelieved misery; a pure hell of alligators and snakes. The heat and humidity and mosquitoes could drive men crazy. No fires could be built, so only cold food would be available. And to avoid detection by Heart Attack's roving patrols, the officers would have to stay in the middle of a palmetto thicket or copse of trees. They would be dirty, sweaty, and just plain mean by the time the deal went down.

It was the sort of bust Nick and Lance would thrive on; Nick because he, like an Old Testament prophet roaming through the desert, thought there was some kind of glory in being miserable; Lance because he looked upon it as a camping trip.

The one part of the operation she had not been able to get around was the need for additional cops. The state attorney's office did not have the manpower to conduct the bust; not without a lot of help. This would call for troops on the ground, for marine units, and for air assets. Everyone who could help—local, state or federal—was part of the DEA task force that, on paper, still existed. She felt a moment of reluctant admiration for Dumnik's sense of bureaucratic survival. Keeping the task force operational, even while publicly saying it was closed, was a safety net. If anything went down, DEA could again come in and take the credit. It also meant that when Nick started seeking help among a dozen or so agencies, someone would go to DEA and tell Dumnik what was about to go down. He would insist on becoming involved and there was no way to keep him out. DEA agents would take part in the raid. Dumnik would try to take over the entire bust.

Kimberly stroked the crystal pyramid. There had to be another way.

37

Lance's eyes popped open but he didn't move when he heard the noise. He sat slumped in the seat of Big

Knocker's go-fast boat, which was about fifteen miles west of Naples in the Gulf of Mexico; drifting in that soft, quiet time that comes just before sunrise at sea. Fog, the reason he and Big Knocker had shut down the engines about midnight, was heavy about the boat—wet and soft and gray in the half-light. It was as if the boat were lost in a ball of gray cotton candy; both the sea and sky were gray. Not a breath of air stirred.

What was the noise that had come through the fog and jarred him from a fatigue-induced nervous half-sleep? He slowly raised his head and looked around. There, stern toward him and not fifty yards away, drifted another boat—a shrimper, by the configuration. Lance stiffened. He crouched and made his way carefully across the boat, watchful that he did not kick something that would make a noise. He reached out, seized Big Knocker by the shoulder, and shook him.

"Shhhhhhh," he whispered as Big Knocker awakened and started to speak. On the water, particularly in the predawn silence, even the smallest sound travels a great distance.

Lance pointed. Big Knocker leaned over the gunwale and peered through the fog. He turned to Lance in utter disbelief.

Written across the stern of the shrimper was her name: *My Girls*. It was a boat owned by Heart Attack; the boat Lance and Big Knocker were to have met at eleven P.M. the previous evening and guided to a point three miles off the light that marked the entrance to Indian Key Pass.

Then Lance realized what had awakened him—the sound of another boat. Coming through the fog, bow-on to the shrimper, was another vessel; from the sound, it was a fast and powerful sport fisherman. Was it an off-load boat?

"We're in mega shit if we don't get outta here," Lance whispered.

Big Knocker smirked. "Cops are always running," he said.

Lance and Big Knocker were in the chase boat that

was to have brought in a load boat the previous evening. Lance had given the Coast Guard the loran coordinates of the meeting at sea. The Coasties were to pop the load boat before it arrived at the rendezvous. Lance and Big Knocker had motored to a point twenty miles north of the rendezvous point, where Big Knocker began calling *My Girls* on the two-meter radio. His broadcast indicated he was at "the intersection," the agreed-upon loran location.

Then, as happens in almost every dope deal, either to the cops or the bad guys, came the unexpected—in this case a fog thick enough to sip through a straw. The fog was a benefit to Lance and Big Knocker; an excuse for missing a load boat. But Big Knocker did not have radar on his chase boat and the fog was too thick to find the entrance to the pass that led to Chokoloskee Bay. So, believing the Coasties had popped the load long before it arrived at the meeting place, they cut the engines. Big Knocker slept, reveling in his power over Lance, knowing Lance would not sleep.

"Afraid I'll kill you?" he asked as he watched Lance move to the far side of the boat and slump down in an uncomfortable position.

"Hate to have you try it. Would set us back if I killed a snitch," Lance said with a smile. He pulled the hogleg Magnum in the shoulder holster around a bit and placed his hand near the grip.

Now it was almost dawn. Within the next fifteen minutes the sun would jump above the horizon and burn a path through the fog. Within minutes the fog would be gone and the morning would be clean and clear with visibility unlimited. Someone aboard *My Girls* would see them. Or someone aboard the approaching boat would see them.

"You recognize the other boat?" Lance asked.

Big Knocker shook his head. "It's not one of the off-load boats. I don't know who it is." He paused. "Looks like a fisherman. Probably looking for bait."

It is a common practice for fishermen at sea to approach shrimp boats and buy some of the small fish that have been caught in the shrimper's nets. But this shrimper had no bait fish to sell; only some eight or ten tons of marijuana. Not getting bait fish would annoy the fisherman. If he saw Lance and Big Knocker, he would certainly approach them.

"As soon as he gets a little bit closer, we'll crank up, keep it at idle, and boogie on out of here," Lance said.

Big Knocker shook his head. "They'll hear us."

"We're getting outta here. If they see us, we'll have to bring that load in. We are not doing that."

Big Knocker grinned. "That will blow your little operation, won't it?" The smuggler enjoyed taunting Nick and Lance. He knew the cops depended on him; that he was playing a vital role in the investigation. At the same time, he was angry and defiant that he had become a snitch; even though it was the only way to gain protection for his brother, he didn't like it. He fought against it as often as he cooperated.

Lance gritted his teeth. He understood anew why Nick no longer would deal with Big Knocker. Nick would not even come into a room when Big Knocker was there. More and more he was convinced that the arrogant smuggler had been involved in the death of the two prosecutors. There was nothing definite; that is, nothing except Big Knocker's occasional derisive comments about Nick's office being unable to solve the deaths of two prosecutors. Nick had no proof of Big Knocker's complicity in the killings, but virtually all other possibilities had been exhausted. Only two possibilities remained: one, that the killings had been pure chance and done by an itinerant druggie. That theory was made somewhat unlikely by the fact the hotel where Derek and Grace had been grabbed was in the heart of Fort Myers. It was extremely unlikely that someone passing through on I-75—miles to the east—would have wound up there. So the only other plausible theory was that someone from Everglades City was the perp. And the person in Everglades City most capable of killing was Big Knocker. According to the videotapes obtained by the intelligence van, his brother had talked of one killing. If there were one, there could

be more. As soon as the big load went down, all bets
were off. Nick no longer had any compunctions about
using Robert, Big Knocker's homosexual brother, as a
hammer. He had decided he would jail the kid; he
would allow him to be raped in prison, he would do
whatever it took to squeeze Big Knocker. No longer
were there any rules in dealing with Big Knocker. Nick
was counting the days until the Everglades City operation wound down.

Big Knocker and Lance had not become close
friends during the past few weeks. Their airboat-repair
business was thriving; in fact, it was the only undercover business Lance had ever heard of that was making money, lots of money. And, with information
reluctantly supplied by Big Knocker, he had passed
along information to the Coast Guard that resulted in
six loads of dope being seized during the past ten days.
But Big Knocker was not happy with his role; and
Lance had to lean on him constantly. The Everglades
City case could blow sky-high just as easily as it could
be worked to a successful conclusion.

"It might," Lance growled. "But one thing it will
do for certain; and that is put your kid brother in jail.
We both know he's a little light in the loafers and we
both know what will happen to him if he goes to jail.
So I suggest you stay with the program."

"You fucking cops. You're all sorry sons of
bitches." Big Knocker laughed. "And you can't even
solve the biggest case you got; you make it okay for
somebody to blow away a couple of your snotty-nosed
lawyers. You guys couldn't catch a cold."

Lance looked away. He let the reference to Derek
and Grace slide. Maybe Big Knocker would become
more explicit in his references to the two prosecutors
if Lance didn't seem to respond. But he had to respond; he had to let Big Knocker know who was boss.
Otherwise the big doper, as so many snitches have
done in the past, would take control of the case; he
would be running the cops instead of the cops running
him.

"We might be sorry," Lance said. "But we ain't

sorry enough to be slimy goddamn dopers. We're getting out of here now, or I can promise you that within a week, somebody's going to be plugging your baby brother."

"Hello, the shrimp boat." The voice, loud and clear, drifted across the water. Big Knocker had been right; the driver of the sport fisherman wanted bait. A figure appeared on the deck of the shrimper, held his arms overhead, and waved back and forth; the nautical signal to veer away; to stand off. Lance and Big Knocker saw the figure on the deck of the shrimper shaking his head.

Big Knocker made up his mind. In less than thirty seconds he had reached into a locker, retrieved what appeared to be a box atop a long shaft that, on the other end, had a propeller, and snapped it into place on the stern. He reached for the fishing knife on his right hip and used the blade to tighten a screw. Now an electric trolling motor, a type used by bass fishermen, was in place. He pressed a button. A soft hum was barely audible as the trolling motor pushed the go-fast boat into the fog. Only the slightest wake trailed behind. Lance realized this was how Big Knocker had escaped surveillance in the past. The noise of the electric engine could not be heard fifty feet away.

"We don't have any bait," they heard a voice say as they disappeared into a thinning fog bank. A moment later, the sound of the sport fisherman's engines was clearly audible as they were revved up to high cruise.

"Stow that thing. Use the sound of that other boat to mask our sound. Let's get the hell out of here," Lance said.

Big Knocker nodded. As he stowed the small electric engine, Lance turned several switches. Speed increased as the chase boat disappeared toward the rising sun. He turned another series of switches, adjusted several controls, then peered closely at the numbers that appeared on the loran.

Big Knocker pushed Lance aside. "This is my fucking boat; I'll drive it."

Lance turned to his ditty bag. He pulled out a small hand-held radio and, eyes on the loran coordinates, radioed a brief coded message. The message would be relayed to the Coast Guard, and then, if those dumb asses could find *My Girls*, the load would be taken down.

Lance and Big Knocker were sitting in the back of their airboat-repair shop eating hot dogs and glowering at each other when Heart Attack wandered in. His tight, drawn face was a clear indication of his displeasure.

"Coast Guard got the load," he said with no preamble.

Big Knocker threw the remainder of his hot dog at the wall. "Son of a bitch," he said.

"Damn," Lance said. What sounded like anger was in reality amazement that the Coast Guard could do something right; that they actually took down a load.

Heart Attack looked from Big Knocker to Lance. "Where were you two clowns last night?"

Big Knocker stood up. "You calling me a clown?"

Heart Attack waved for Big Knocker to sit down. "You couldn't find the load boat. Where were you?"

"Where were we?" Lance interrupted. "Where the hell was the load boat? We were dead on target; exactly at the coordinates where we were supposed to be. The load boat wasn't there. We waited for hours. Then the fog came in. We didn't get back until after sunup this morning."

Heart Attack rocked on his heels; staring from one of the men to the other. He had been monitoring the radio last night and had heard Big Knocker's repeated broadcasts as he called for the shrimper. He didn't know what had happened. But another load had been seized by the Coast Guard. For years, no one had worried about the Coast Guard. Twice in the past year his men had picked up the Coast Guard's radar emissions and, when it was impossible to escape, shut down their engines and pretended to be disabled. On both occasions the Coast Guard had towed them into Naples, and on both occasions the boats were loaded with dope. Now all at once the Coast Guard was popping his loads. Heart Attack didn't believe in coincidence. Somebody was talking. He meant to find out who it was.

That evening Lance and Big Knocker were having dinner at the Oyster House, where they were putting away several pounds of sweet and moist stone crabs. Neither particularly wanted the company of the other, but Lance knew—and Big Knocker agreed—that they had to present a solid front. It was important that they show no sign of weakness, no lack of confidence. Word that the load had been taken down by the Coast Guard was all over town; the smugglers would be talking. Sooner or later Lance and Big Knocker were going to be asked by other smugglers what had happened. They had to maintain the initiative; to keep their heads high and their innocence waving like a flag nailed to the mast. They sat, not across the table from each other, but elbow to elbow so they could talk without their voices being audible at nearby tables.

The confrontation came even before the two men finished their salads. They were sitting in the main dining room, far down toward the end of the room located to the left of the front door, and clearly visible to anyone who entered.

Three smugglers, men who had begun as humpers, graduated to bringing in loads aboard creek boats and mullet skiffs, then moved up to crab boats used as off-load vessels, and finally bought their own shrimp boat, came in the front door. One saw Lance and Big Knocker bent over their plates, nudged his companions, and whispered. The three men were suntanned and hardened. Their eyes revealed their shallowness and their mouths their meanness; they were exactly what Nick had had in mind when he described Everglades City smugglers as "gators that walk upright."

The three men, toothpicks in their mouths, sauntered toward the table. They wore greasy sweat-streaked baseball caps. Their faded sport shirts hung out of their jeans. Their jeans were stuffed into the tops of white gum boots.

When they reached the table, Lance and Big Knocker looked up, nodded a noncommittal greeting, and continued eating. Neither wanted the smugglers to join them. But the three men didn't have to be asked; two pulled out chairs, spun them around, and straddled them, leaning forward and resting their crossed arms atop the backs of the chairs. The third reached for a chair at an adjacent table and did the same, placing his chair between the two chairs of his friends. The three men had wide grins on their faces.

"What the fuck you grinning about?" Big Knocker snarled.

Ordinarily the smugglers might have been intimidated by Big Knocker. It was said around Everglades City that he would rather fight than eat. But tonight there were three of them. The guy with Big Knocker, the guy who worked at the airboat shop, didn't look too tough. Besides, the three guys had been drinking at the Captain's Table for an hour or so before they drove down to the Oyster House for dinner. They were feeling no pain.

One of the smugglers, the guy in the middle, shifted his tongue around his toothpick and looked at one of his companions, then the other, and then back at Big Knocker.

"I'm looking at a guy everybody in town is talking about," he said.

Big Knocker's eyes narrowed. He continued to eat. Lance slowly placed his knife and fork on the table and picked up the large glass of iced tea by his plate. He knew what was coming. These guys were like sharks that had smelled blood in the water. They were circling, sniffing their prey before they moved in.

"Yeah. What are they saying?" Big Knocker asked. His voice was low.

The smuggler pursed his lips, rocked his head up and down in amusement. "They're saying you lost a load last night."

"We didn't lose a load," Big Knocker growled. "We were there. The load boat got lost." He continued to eat. "Besides, what business is it of yours?"

Lance sipped his tea.

The smuggler who was doing all the talking rocked his head again. It was as if he had not heard Big Knocker. "They're saying that ain't the first load you lost lately."

Lance slowly moved his feet until he had one leg on each side of the chair. He shifted his weight to his toes and continued to sip his tea. People at the next table were slicing their eyes in his direction and whispering to each other.

Big Knocker placed his fork across his plate and reached toward his lap. One of the smugglers tensed, but then Big Knocker's hands slowly reappeared with a napkin. He smiled and raised his napkin to his face.

Lance smiled. It was a big disarming smile. He tapped one of the men on the arm and said, "Pardon me. Would you have any Grey Poupon?"

"Whuuut?"

"Grey Poupon. For my stone crabs."

The man glared and dismissed Lance.

The smuggler's voice hardened as he continued. "People are wondering why you two guys have lost more loads than everybody else put together; they're wondering if—"

The smuggler stopped in mid-word as Lance threw the glass of tea in his face. The smuggler involuntarily sucked in his breath as three things happened simultaneously. Lance's left hand came across the table and hit one smuggler squarely on the nose, crushing it, splattering blood, and knocking the man backward; Big Knocker's knife, the one he had pulled from his waist and hidden in his napkin, came down hard atop the hand of the man sitting to his left, pinning his hand to the table and causing him to scream in anguish; and Big Knocker swung with his right hand, connecting with the chin of the smuggler who had a face full of iced tea.

One woman at the adjacent table screamed as the

other three people at the table sat frozen in disbelief. Lance knew the woman at the cash register was on the telephone calling the police. The substation was only two blocks away; the cops would be here in seconds.

Big Knocker kicked his chair backward, stood on his feet, and turned his attention to the guy with the knife stuck in his hand. He swung again, connecting with the guy's nose and knocking him backward with such force that the man's hand, still impaled, pulled the table over atop him.

Lance suddenly found himself face-to-face with two men who had displayed an incredible tolerance for pain. The one he had hit and the mouthy one struck by Big Knocker had shaken their heads and, grins visible through their bloody faces, were about to come for him.

He kicked one in the groin, almost lifting him from the floor, then spun in a blurred circle with his right elbow raised shoulder-high. As he completed the circle, his elbow struck the mouth of the man on his right, knocking his head violently to the side and again throwing him to the floor.

The guy with the knife through his hand and the table atop him was out of the fight. Big Knocker turned his attention to the smuggler who had been sitting across the table, the one doing all the talking. The man's face was blanched and he was bent over, still in great pain from Lance's kick. But the instinct for survival was stronger than the pain. He remained in a crouch and withdrew his right hand maybe two inches as he prepared to swing. Big Knocker ducked and the man's momentum carried him a half-step forward; enough for Big Knocker to scoop him up by the waist and charge at full tilt toward the rear wall of the restaurant about ten feet away. The man hit the wall, froze for a second, then slid down, limp and unconscious.

Big Knocker turned just as Lance's heel connected with the chin of the other smuggler, knocking him back to the floor with such power that the sound of his head striking the floor was louder than the sound of Lance's foot on his chin. The man did not move.

Big Knocker reached under the table and pulled his knife from the hand of the unconscious man. He wiped his blade on the man's shirt and replaced the knife in the scabbard at his waist.

Without speaking, he and Lance walked toward the front door. They both dug into their pockets and placed the contents on the table by the cash register. The hostess saw two hundred, maybe three hundred dollars.

"They didn't leave us any room," Big Knocker said in explanation.

The hostess nodded. At that moment the door opened and a sheriff's deputy entered, hand on his pistol. Lance sighed. It was one of the bent deputies; this guy had escorted dozens of loads.

The deputy sheriff nodded when he recognized Big Knocker. Lance let Big Knocker handle it.

Big Knocker tilted his head once toward the wreckage in the rear of the restaurant. "We were eating. They jumped us," he said simply.

The deputy looked at the hostess. She nodded. "He's right. Those other men started it," she agreed. "And Big Knocker here has already paid for damages."

"You wanna press charges?" the deputy said as he looked at the three men on the floor.

The waitress shook her head. The deputy looked at Big Knocker.

"No. It's over," Big Knocker said.

"Looks like it is," the deputy agreed. He nodded. Big Knocker and Lance walked out the door.

"Getting tight. Getting tight. That's the way I like it," Lance said once they walked down the steps and were in the parking lot.

"Whatta you mean?"

"Your buddies are getting nervous. Their sphincters are closing. Otherwise they never would have done that."

"Yeah," Big Knocker said angrily. "It also means they'll stop the business for a while. They'll shut it down."

''No,'' Lance said as he opened the door of the car. ''We'll shut it down.''

Big Knocker slammed the door. ''They pull something like this, it means they're suspicious. They'll come after us again.''

''Let 'em come. Let 'em come.''

Big Knocker snorted. ''These people will kill you.''

Lance laughed. ''Not unless they got silver bullets. I'm the narc from hell.''

38

Heart Attack looked upon the teenage boys of Everglades City as Dixie Cups—disposable objects to be used once, maybe twice, then tossed aside. He used teenage schoolkids in his off-loading operations. A muscular, energetic, tireless kid was well worth the five thousand dollars he was paid to be a humper. And if a kid had his own, or could beg or borrow or steal his father's mullet skiff, he was easily worth thirty thousand dollars for a night's work. It was simple work. Any kid could hump bales for a few hours; and all the kids new the intricate waterways of the Ten Thousand Islands. Using different boys, shifting the wealth around, did several things for Heart Attack. It engendered extreme competition among the ones who were hired; they all worked twice as hard as they would have if he had used the same crews for every load. It also built up a loyal—and quiet—coterie of employees. He never hired any of the boys directly; it was done through several layers of intermediaries. But Everglades City was small enough and parochial enough that everyone in town knew when a load was coming in, and they knew who owned the load. For several days before a load arrived, the entire town was abuzz. Competition was keen among high-school boys to be chosen as part of Heart Attack's crew. The boys and their families needed the money too much to do any talking if they were arrested. However, if one were arrested, that was the end of his career with Heart Attack. He never hired any kid who had been popped; they were too vulnerable to pressure from the prosecutor, they could be flipped. They were thereafter in a sort of limbo; they knew what was going on but could not participate; at least not with Heart Attack.

There were several dozen kids in the small school on the north edge of town near the fish houses who never were considered by Heart Attack. These were the sons of local tradesmen; the son of a car salesman, the son of the man who owned a local restaurant, the son of a teacher, the son of a television repairman, and the son of the man who owned the local grocery store. These were not fishing families; they lacked the cohesiveness of the watermen; the sense of us-against-them; the antipathy toward the Park Service and the federal government. These boys did not have the feral sense of survival that is part of the very bone marrow of Everglades City fishermen; the situational morality that enabled them to do whatever they wanted and justify it out of a narrow and personal ethic.

In a more definable and pragmatic vein, these boys had not grown up on the water and did not know the secrets of the winds and tides and the shifting channels and the movable oyster bars and the shallow flats.

Also, there were a half-dozen boys whom Heart Attack would never consider simply because he knew their fathers to be honest men; or at least honest in the sense they abhorred drugs and drug smuggling.

As a result of Heart Attack's hiring philosophy, a major schism, and one that was very painful to those involved, developed among boys in Everglades City.

The acolytes of Heart Attack were very visible in their new four-wheel-drive trucks, new cars, jewelry, and designer clothes. These lads, many of them only sixteen or seventeen, were conspicuous consumers who usually owned some sort of shallow-draft pleasure boat; always very fast. They were confident, even cocky, far beyond their years. Almost all of them smoked marijuana on a daily basis; a few used cocaine more or less regularly. They all shared the common ambition of wanting to be like Heart Attack; to buy a crab boat, then a shrimp boat, and to bring in the big loads that, in turn, brought in the big money.

Then there were the boys spurned by Heart Attack. Because, even in the best of times, Everglades City is a poor little town, these boys had few material belongings. They walked to school. Their jeans were patched, their shirts faded, and their tennis shoes were holed. Some of them tried to break into the group favored by Heart Attack, but none successfully. That failure was to them a harbinger of what life would be like once they graduated. They owned little jewelry; many of them did not even wear a watch, and few of them had ever been beyond Naples. They were, like many poor kids in small towns all over America, somewhat diffident and insecure. At an age when they were most impressionable and most vulnerable, they saw that their not being part of the drug-smuggling milieu of their hometown made them virtual outcasts; that they were different, that crime did pay, that their honesty brought them nothing but long walks home in the hot sun while the other boys were dashing about in new air-conditioned cars, almost always with the prettiest girls in school beside them.

Both the young boys who worked for Heart Attack and those who did not saw another sharp difference between the two groups. They learned that money can manipulate the system; that money changes the rules.

Heart Attack's cousin was assistant principal at the Everglades City high school. On the day a load was to come in, she walked down the halls and into the classrooms, where she handed out approval slips to be absent from school that afternoon and the next day. That was how the boys always discovered they had been picked to work a load.

Heart Attack knew they had to gas up their cars, get their boats in shape, pack dry clothes, and pack coolers with ice and food and beer. He even encouraged them to take a nap, because most of them would be awake all night. But, being young, they laughed and none of them napped. With much laughing and joking and wry comments about what would happen on the high seas that night, they stood up, usually leaving their books behind, and waved their approval slips at their classmates. Then they marched down the halls to their cars and four-wheel-drive trucks.

In their wake were various emotions. A few teachers felt impotent anger and frustration. A few girls always giggled at the romance of it all. The boys who had worked for Heart Attack in the past but who were not chosen this time spoke knowingly of the thrills and the dangers their friends would face. The outcasts, the boys who would never be chosen, either were angry that they could never be part of the smugglers or tried to dig deep and find the truth of all their parents had told them about smuggling and its evils.

All of these groups—the teachers, the girls, the second string of humpers, the outcasts—looked with curiosity upon one girl who was silent: July, the youngest daughter of the man who was causing all the excitement. July was a senior, and probably the fairest of her father's daughters, with a thick mane of blonde—almost white—hair that framed a deeply tanned face and cascaded down her slender back. Her eyes, an unusual shade of brilliant blue, were all the more startling because of her suntan and because of the haunted pain that seemed to lurk somewhere behind the beauty.

July was one of the smartest students ever to go through the high school at Everglades City; one of the few ever to bring joy and excitement to her teachers. She also was one of the quietest; one of the most withdrawn. Both her extraordinary beauty and the fact she was Heart Attack's baby daughter made her unapproachable for the boys. And even though several girls tried, they were kept at arm's length. They thought she was, as they said, "stuck-up," but actually it was her shame at what her family did that kept them at bay.

On this particular day, after the noisy exodus of her father's crew and after the resulting silence, July stared down at her books, her thoughts far away from school. She knew her oldest sister, December, would be on the water tonight, and she knew what her sister would be doing. She knew April and May would be busy tomorrow and—considering the size of the load that was coming in—probably for several days to come. But most of all she knew that she was expected to join the family business. Her father had told her years ago she could quit school if she wanted; that she could go to work. But when she said she wanted to finish high school and go on to college, he nodded in puzzlement. He didn't understand why someone would want to stay in school. But July was his baby daughter, and if she wanted a high-school diploma, that was fine by him. There would be a place for her in the business when she was ready.

And that was what, more than anything else in the world, brought stark terror to July. She did not want to perform the sort of role played by December. And she knew she was not like April and May. And, finally, she did not want to join the family business. She was serious about wanting to go to college. But how would she tell that to her father?

Unlike her fellow students in the senior class, she did not look forward to graduating in a few months. She was terrified of graduation. Because then she would have to make a decision.

39

"We're not a dirty dozen," Lance said. "We're a funky dozen, a stinky dozen, a rotten dozen." He laughed. "I'm not sure I feel like America's hero." He swung his hand in front of his face in a futile effort to discourage several dozen mosquitoes buzzing about his head, squinted at the broiling sun, and in a flat

resigned tone said, "I love being a cop. Being a cop
is my life."

Nick, Lance, and Ben Blumen sat huddled together
under a small scrub oak on an unnamed island in
Sandfly Pass. Twenty feet away, lined up around the
edge of the clearing, were another nine men. The sunburned faces of the men were covered with stubble and
marked by angry red insect bites that seemed never to
stop itching. Their hair was matted and shiny from
being unwashed for the past five days. Their clothes
were dirty and wrinkled. Everyone wore fatigues and
boots except Lance, who wore high-topped red tennis
shoes, jeans, and a T-shirt that said, "IT'S NEVER TOO
LATE TO HAVE A HAPPY CHILDHOOD." The men reeked
of suntan oil, insect repellent, and stale perspiration.
Hidden in the mangroves a few hundred yards away
were a dozen flat-bottomed boats; their high-powered
outboards tilted into the air. When the first load of
dope hit the beach, the cops driving the hidden boats
would roar out of the mangroves in a pincer movement. A Navy hydrofoil was hidden south at Rabbit
Key. A high-speed Coast Guard boat had been moved
in a large unmarked truck to a marina on Marco Island. A Customs Blackhawk was on strip alert at
Homestead Air Force Base and, once it was time for
the deal to go down, would be positioned a few miles
north of Everglades City. Raymond Dumnik and Melvin Foster were directing the entire operation from a
command post in Naples.

Nick and Ben and Lance waited in the bushes. There
was nothing to do but wait. Suddenly the small radio
between them broke squelch.

"Got a pop," Nick said.

As the three men leaned forward and listened, Nick
felt a great deal of pride in Kimberly McBride. It was
she who had discovered that the two-meter radios were
ubiquitous equipment among the dopers of Everglades
City. And now, on the lengthy stakeout before the big
deal went down, her intelligence work was paying off.
The Kenwood two-meter they were monitoring had
grown more and more busy the last two days. With

each transmission, Ben seemed to grow more apprehensive. And now, the afternoon before the load was due, when a dozen or more dopers—in the guise of fishermen—were scooting around the waterways looking for cops, the radio was constantly blaring forth Heart Attack's cryptic messages to the dozens of men who were crewing the crab boats, mullet skiffs, and creek boats; and to the humpers on the hill. Ben was so fidgety he could not be still.

The two-meter again broke squelch and a voice said, "How 'bout you, Cracker? What's it look like? This is Red Dog. You seen any deer?"

Almost immediately came the response. "I'm at the bridge, Red Dog, and it's clean and green. What you hear about that load of mullet we was talking about?"

"Ah, Cracker, that load of mullet will be on time. You be ready to pick up your two hundred and fifty pounds."

"Got you, Red Dog. Cracker out."

Lance laughed. Ben Blumen wiggled his shoulders and wrinkled his brow in bewilderment. Nick snorted.

"Sons of bitches think they're so smart," he said. He noticed Ben's expression and smiled. "Ben, you're a federal agent. Don't you know what's going on?"

Ben smiled ruefully.

Nick patted the two-meter. "Basically, this is a ham radio. It operates between a hundred and forty-four and a hundred and forty-eight megahertz."

"That's just under the police band," Ben said.

Nick nodded. "Right. Generally we work between a hundred and fifty and a hundred and seventy-four megahertz. When ham operators use these things, they usually stay up near the top end of the frequency. Dopers stay down at the bottom. They think they're low enough in the band that nobody knows they're there."

"What's the range on a two-meter?" Ben asked. "They don't appear to be very powerful."

Ben's interest in the radio seemed to have dampened his nervousness for the moment.

"A forty-five-watt unit will bang out maybe twenty miles," Lance said. The distance depends on the height of the antenna and where you are. Over the water or in an airplane, this thing will knock out a strong signal. It's not too good in town. Buildings interrupt the signal.''

''But even at the optimum distance, that doesn't seem very practical for the smugglers,'' Ben said.

Nick nodded in appreciation. Ben was a quick study.

''Right,'' Nick said. ''But the dopers run them through a linear amplifier and they got a hundred-watt transmitter. Over the water, it will bang out more than a hundred miles.''

Ben pursed his lips in appreciation. ''Sounds rather sophisticated to me. Why do you say it's dumb?''

''Several reasons. First, they think they have this little secret compartment in the broadcast spectrum where no one knows they're working. Today, with the technology we have, there are no hiding places. Anything can be monitored. Second, they use CB terminology on ham freqs.''

''How do you distinguish between a legitimate ham operator and a drug trafficker?''

''Easy,'' Lance said. ''Ham operators have FCC licenses, use sign-on and sign-off procedures; they have registered call letters that they use to begin and end every conversation. They're pretty crisp.'' He laughed. ''Frankly, they're a lot more professional in their procedures than we are.''

''Than you are,'' Nick corrected. He looked at Ben. ''And they don't use all that CB garbage. Anytime you hear some local guy on a two-meter using CB handles and that phony code, you know it's a doper.''

Lance laughed. ''You don't expect a bunch of nuclear physicists to come out of Everglades City, but until I started working this bunch, I didn't realize the combined IQ of everyone in town didn't reach room temperature.'' He pointed to the radio. ''Even the handles they use are stupid: Red Ryder, Cracker, Budweiser, Rebel, Bear, Gator. And they mix regular conversation with their codes, like that guy saying he was on the bridge. When you say 'the bridge' around here, it means the Chokoloskee Bridge. They've talked about the trucks, the names of their boats, their home addresses; hell, we've put names with virtually every handle used on the radio.''

Ben nodded. ''What do you mean about their phony code?''

Lance pointed to Ben. ''That guy who was just on there, Cracker; the one sitting over on the Chokoloskee Bridge?''

''The one looking for deer while he waits on a load of mullet?''

Lance laughed. ''He doesn't give a rat's ass about deer. He was talking about cops. He's parked there watching for law enforcement. And that two hundred and fifty pounds of mullet is two thousand, five hundred pounds of dope. If they'd mentioned snook, that would have meant cocaine.''

Nick nodded and smiled. ''What he doesn't know is that he's parked next to our surveillance van.''

Ben looked at him in surprise. He knew nothing of a surveillance van.

Nick shrugged. ''We got this old van over there; got some monitoring equipment in it. Simple stuff, really. Anyway, we got that doper on TV. His ratings are gonna be the highest of any show around here. Make him famous. And we're taping every two-meter broadcast that you hear.''

Ben's eyes widened. ''DEA can't monitor and tape two-meter broadcasts.''

''DEA doesn't have the capability to pour piss out of a boot,'' Lance said.

''Don't let my boss hear that.'' Ben smiled. ''I'm glad he's in the command post and not out here.''

Lance laughed and swung at the mosquitoes. ''You think Dumnik would park his fat ass on this island to swat bugs and eat cold food for five days when he can order Ben to be here?'' He looked at Ben. ''Why are you the only DEA agent on the island?''

Ben shrugged. ''Mr. Dumnik thinks the shipment will go straight from the boats up to the highway, where it will be loaded for transshipment all over

America. He's got dozens of agents on every road out of here.''

"I told him what was going down," Nick said.

"He didn't believe you." Ben was embarrassed.

Lance laughed and shook his head. "I've said it before and I'll say it again: working with DEA is like working in a whorehouse. The better you do your job, the more you get screwed."

"I'm sure you will," Nick said.

"Will what?"

"Say it again," Nick said. He turned to look at Ben. "Dumnik didn't mention that during the briefing. How close are the agents?"

"Fifteen or twenty miles. Mr. Dumnik's plan is for them to seize the dope once it gets on the road." Ben stood up and peered through the bushes toward the dark waters of Sandfly Pass, then hunkered down and doodled in the sand with his finger.

"You nervous?"

Ben scratched his ear. He looked around the little clearing in the middle of the island. "Yes. I am. Not because of the bust. I've been on other busts." He shrugged. "Not many, but a few. What bothers me about this one is that we're stuck here on this little island; a dozen of us plus those guys back there with the boats. I know Customs is standing by with helicopters and their apprehension teams, but they won't get airborne until the load is moving. What if the load comes in early? What if we are outnumbered? They could throw thirty or forty guys in here."

Nick and Lance looked at each other. Lance shook his head. "Don't worry about it," he said to Ben. "The beach here is not wide enough for more than three or four mullet skiffs at a time. So even if the load comes in early, they'll have a logjam offshore if they try to send too many boats in. But that won't happen. These guys are pros. They'll come in by the numbers and we'll bust them by the numbers." He laughed. "Even if they all come ashore at once, they'll be outnumbered."

Ben's forehead wrinkled. "What do you mean?"

Lance thumped himself on the chest. "Hey, Nick and I are invincible. We'll take on the whole crowd. We're America's heroes."

Nick snorted. He pointed to an M-16 that had fallen from a small tree where it had been propped. "Ben, your rifle fell on the sand."

Ben quickly stood up and moved to pick up the rifle.

Nick looked at Lance. "We got to do something about Ben," he whispered. "He's wrapped too tight. He might get hurt when the deal goes down."

"What can we do?"

"I got a plan."

"Want to tell me about it, or is it a secret?" Nick whispered rapidly.

40

Raymond Dumnik looked at the telephone in bewilderment. He was wearing nothing but a pair of red bikini briefs. Above the waistband, which acted as sort of a levee, were rolls upon rolls of cascading fat that began, more or less, somewhere in the vicinity of his primary chin.

Dumnik continued to stare at the telephone. He had just ended a conversation with Andrea. Why had she called to tell him she was in the Miami office monitoring the telephones and standing by in case he wanted to dictate a letter? It was Friday afternoon, for God's sake, and he was in the middle of supervising a bust that would bring him, the DEA, and the presidential task force on drugs an enormous amount of publicity. Why didn't Andrea go home?

He turned around to look at the office he used. The office, in reality the chambers of a federal judge, was in a special wing of the sheriff's building in Naples. Federal judges almost always used the courthouse in

Fort Myers. But, being federal judges, they had insisted that a special courtroom be built for their convenience in Naples. It rarely was used, which was how Dumnik was able to take it over for his command post. In the courtroom outside the office were representatives from each of the local, state, and federal agencies involved in Operation Everglades City III. Three Coasties manned a bank of radios against the back wall.

Dumnik glanced around as if afraid someone were observing, then opened a small suitcase and pulled a mirror from it. He held the mirror up and leaned into it, the fingers of his left hand rubbing his nose and across his cheekbones. He needed more powder.

Again he looked at the door. He pulled a flat container from the suitcase, opened it, and pulled out a powder puff. After another quick glance over his shoulder, he rubbed powder across his nose. The mirror told him he needed more. He dipped and rubbed, dipped and rubbed, then stared into the mirror as he turned his head first to the right and then to the left. The annoying redness of his nose and the surrounding red and blue network of blood vessels across his nose and cheeks now appeared as a muted map. He nodded once and tossed the powder back into the suitcase.

Dumnik glanced at the door. He awkwardly climbed atop the desk, lurched and waved about, making sure his feet were steady, then reached overhead to a panel in the ceiling, pushed the panel up and to the right, then reached to the left. His eyes widened in satisfaction when he found his bottle of bourbon. But when he saw it was almost empty, his eyes narrowed in consternation.

He slid the panel back into its proper place and slowly knelt, then sat atop the desk, and finally slid to the floor. His mouth and the bottle of Wild Turkey opened at the same instant. Dumnik took a long drink, emitted a belch that reverberated from the walls, rubbed his bountiful stomach, then opened his suitcase and put the bottle inside. His supplies needed to be close at hand. He wrinkled his lips, sucked on his teeth, and idly scratched his behind.

Dumnik was drunk. It was eight-thirty P.M.—just hours before the bust was to go down—and Dumnik was drunk. President George Bush's representative on the strike force, the chief narc in south Florida, was drunk. Not commode-hugging, knee-walking, loud-mouthed, pissy-eyed drunk; just numbed into a pleasant bemused state where most of his synapses were not connecting.

Dumnik belched again, smiled in satisfaction, rubbed his stomach, and eyed the waste can under the judge's desk. With a bare foot he edged it out from under the desk. Then he pushed down the top of his red bikini briefs, pissed long and loud into the waste can, pushed the can back under the desk, rubbed his balls in pleasure, and again looked around the office. He yawned.

The boys in the field could take care of business. The people out in the command post could monitor the radios. He would rest, maybe take a nap, as he conserved his energy until the bust went down. Then he would arise and take charge.

Dumnik opened his mouth and ran his tongue around his teeth. He wrinkled his brow in displeasure. He reached into the suitcase, pulled out a bottle of Listerine, turned it up, and drank several large swallows. He did not simply rinse out his mouth; he swallowed the Listerine.

"Bleeaaaahhh," he bellowed to no one in particular as he capped the bottle and shoved it back into his suitcase.

He walked stiff-legged to the door of the judge's chambers, threw open the door, and shouted, "Melvin."

"Yo," said the DEA agent from New Jersey. Exit six off the turnpike.

"Keep me informed." Dumnik held on to the door to keep from falling.

"You got it. Anything starts shaking, I'll notify you."

Dumnik's bleary gaze lurched around the court-room. "I am in charge," he said.

Silence greeted his announcement. Even the uni-formed Coast Guard guys seemed embarrassed by the fat guy in the red drawers. Like a muted counterpoint to the red briefs, his red nose struggled valiantly, like a light under a coating of sand, to shine forth. An occasional glimmer could be seen under the powder. And the odor of Listerine, crisp and clean, billowed across the courtroom. Dumnik lowered his head, looked around the room, hustled his balls, and re-peated in a much louder voice, "I am in charge."

He closed the door and lurched unsteadily toward a leather couch against the wall. The air conditioning and the soft leather of the couch chilled him. Dumnik reached for the back of the couch, where the judge's wife, in an effort to add a bit of color to the office, had draped a patchwork quilt; an antique patchwork quilt that cost sixteen hundred dollars; a museum-quality patchwork quilt that was an outstanding ex-ample of the ancient Appalachian art of quilt-making. Dumnik snuggled the quilt around his shoulders, bur-rowed deeper into the leather sofa, exhaled a giant sigh, and passed out.

Three hours later, just before the first flotilla of crab boats loaded with marijuana and cocaine landed at the small island in Sandfly Pass, and while still in a drunken stupor, Dumnik defecated. The leader of the Bush League shit all over himself, his red bikini briefs, the expensive antique quilt, and the judge's leather sofa.

41

For hours the two-meter radio had crackled with coded commands. If one accepted literally the radio trans-

missions about the loads of mullet coming through the
Ten Thousand Islands that night, then one would have
had to accept that the Gulf of Mexico had been virtually stripped of that particular fish. Nick's men had
lain quietly and watched as perhaps the largest flotilla
of crab boats and mullet skiffs ever to put to sea from
Everglades City had putt-putted slowly down the channel to the edge of the Gulf and the rendezvous with
the Cuban shrimp boats. It was clear from radio transmissions regarding the "snook boat" that Big Knocker
was bringing in the cocaine.

Lance had wanted to be aboard, but Nick said being
at sea with Big Knocker and several Cubans was too
much of a risk. After all, Big Knocker was the number-
one suspect in a double homicide. No, let him bring
in the dope. Big Knocker didn't know it, but a beeper
was aboard his boat. It would be tracked. If he decided
to become an entrepreneur, someone would be waiting, no matter where he landed.

It had been several hours since the boats, like a silent armada, chugged slowly out the pass and into the
Gulf of Mexico. The task force was using military radios in an effort to avoid being monitored by Heart
Attack and the dopers. Melvin Foster had wanted to
be in the field supervising the bust, but Dumnik kept
him in the command post. The Navy hydrofoil was
poised to the south; the Coast Guard high-speed boat
was at Marco Island, and the pincers were ready to
squeeze. The Coasties also had cutters on station in
the Gulf to cut off the retreat of the Cuban shrimp
boats. Two Customs Blackhawks had been moved to
the Ford automotive test track up on Alligator Alley,
where they were on strip alert; they could be launched
in less than two minutes and would be on the bust site
in about eight minutes. Dozens of DEA agents, Florida state troopers, and deputies from the Collier
County sheriff's office were in position to close off the
road leading out of Everglades City. And if the dope
was brought to the hill at a remote off-loading site,
Alligator Alley—east and west of Everglades City—as
well as Highway 29 could be blocked in minutes. All

was ready; waiting only for Heart Attack and the dopers to spring the trap.

Nick and Lance, the point men in Operation Everglades III, waited. They perspired freely; their clothes were drenched. Mosquitoes, great hordes of voracious saltwater mosquitoes, circled them in thick clouds. Their bodies were great welts of angry red bites that they were afraid to scratch because boats loaded with smugglers cruised within ten feet of the islands looking for tracks on the beach and for any sign of life. They were tired of the cold food they had eaten for six days. They were tired of hiding under bushes.

Nick and Lance were hiding near the edge of the water just behind where the mangroves gave way to palmetto bushes. Nick raised a pair of night-vision goggles and, for the thousandth time, peered across the water as he looked for the flotilla of mullet skiffs and creek boats that soon would be landing.

Several hours earlier Lance had seen December and a park ranger drift down Sandfly Pass, their boats tied together. The night-vision goggles caused the tiny light on December's mullet skiff to light up her boat like a searchlight. Lance watched December take off her clothes and sink to the deck of the skiff with the ranger. In that moment, he realized—perhaps for the first time in his life—that there were attributes a woman could possess that were far more important than beauty. Seeing December in the act of destroying the career of a law-enforcement officer, and knowing she had done it before with a dozen or so other cops, suddenly showed Lance, better than a dozen lectures from Nick, the bottomless depths of her mendacity and amorality. If Lance could have been so wrong about December, perhaps he was wrong about Kimberly McBride; maybe she was the woman he should pursue. He pushed the thought from his mind as soon as it entered. No sense in going overboard here. December was only one woman. It was not yet time for him to look at skinny women who wore quartz necklaces.

Lance's pensive mood was, for him, a long one; it lasted perhaps two minutes. Now he was waiting for the flotilla of mullet skiffs and creek boats, and he was bored.

"So how will we know when they're coming?" he asked. "You arrange for a pillar of fire by night?"

Nick turned to look at Lance. There was enough light that each man could see a rough outline of the other. Nick stared for a moment and then returned to the night-vision goggles.

"You know, with all the julios involved in this case, I'm surprised we haven't found Central Cuban Dispatch. I think they work out of the Everglades."

Nick didn't answer.

"They're having a seafood festival in Everglades City in a few days. You going?"

Nick, without taking the glasses from his eyes, answered. "You think I'm hanging out with hemorrhoids, you outta your mind."

"Why don't we go over there? You can wear your flip-top sunglasses. Fit right in."

"Hemorrhoids wear flip-top sunglasses."

Lance laughed. He looked at the sky, hummed a tuneless ditty, and again turned to Nick. "Hey, you in close touch with God. You think he hates mobile homes?"

Nick, an expression of exasperation on his face, turned to peer through the darkness at Lance. "Why you asking me if God hates mobile homes? What's that got to do with anything?"

"Every time there's a tornado, it always blows over mobile homes. Mobile homes are like a plague. Isn't that like the Old Testament?"

Nick shook his head.

Lance continued. "Okay, so you agree God doesn't like mobile homes. You also think AIDS is like tornadoes?"

Nick stared.

Lance shrugged. Now he was beginning to roll. He finally had Nick's attention. "It makes sense. AIDS wipes out fags just like tornadoes wipe out trailer parks. Same thing. God doesn't like either one."

Cops are almost universally homophobic. Rarely do

they use the word "gay" to refer to a homosexual; the common term is "fag." Testifying on a witness stand softens this to "homosexual."

"Cunningham, I don't believe I ever thought of that," Nick said with exaggerated seriousness.

"Jefe, you need to think of these things. You're my leader. You gotta show me the way to go."

"You're like a kid," Nick said. "You're babbling just to hear yourself babble. You don't believe any of this stuff. Where do you get all these ideas?"

"Hey, I got ideas I haven't thought of yet."

Nick grunted.

"I thought we were doing some of that male-bonding stuff," Lance said in a wounded voice.

Nick didn't answer.

Lance waited a moment, then tried again: "Wanna hear me sing a Croatian love song?"

"I'd like to hear silence from you."

"What if we need to go to Defcon I?"

Nick turned to look at Lance. "How do you know about Defcon I?"

"Hey, I'm a trained investigator. I know everything. I just can't always remember it."

Nick sighed.

Lance smiled. He looked at Nick and waited, savoring the moment, then, in a confidential voice, said, "How does it feel to be a hemorrhoid in disguise?"

Nick lowered the glasses and looked at Lance.

"I checked your personnel file," Lance said.

"How'd you get in there?"

"Sunday I picked the lock to the file cabinet."

Nick pulled at his mustache. "Why?"

Lance shrugged. He shook a forefinger at Nick. "Because you gave it away."

"How?"

"When people around here talk about being natives, they always say they were born and raised in Collier County. I noticed that you just say you were raised in Collier County. Then it hit me that you were being truthful." He laughed. "Boss, if you'd ever learn to lie a little bit, I never would have suspected. Being a straight arrow blew your cover.''

Nick pulled on his mustache and, through lowered eyelids, studied Lance.

"So how does it feel to be a hemorrhoid?" Lance repeated.

"I ain't a hemorrhoid."

"Yeah, you are. You were born in Wisconsin. That's hemorrhoid country." Lance giggled and pounded the sand with his fist.

"My daddy was up there after the war to work at a defense plant and I just happened to be born there," Nick said defensively. "We came back to Florida as soon as his contract was up."

"Doesn't matter. You were born in Wisconsin. Makes you a 'roid."

"If my daddy hadn't gone up there for the government, I'd have been born in Collier County. I was only a few months old when we moved back."

"Yeah, and if frogs had wings, they wouldn't bump their asses. You're a 'roid. No way around it." Lance laughed.

"Look, some things people don't talk about."

"Don't talk, hell. I'm gonna call a news conference."

"You haven't forgotten who signs your paycheck?"

Lance ignored him. "Just think; if you get lost in the Gulf of Mexico, the headline would read, 'ROID LOST IN VOID.' Whatta you think?"

"I think you tell anybody I was born in Wisconsin, you'll be in shit up to your ears," Nick peered through the glasses.

Lance laughed.

The conversation ended when Nick stiffened and said, "Here they come." He paused and then added almost in disbelief, "Must be fifty boats."

"I'll handle them. You take the rest of the day off."

Nick took down the night-vision goggles and looked at his partner. Even in the darkness he could see Lance's white teeth shining in a wide grin, and he could see Lance's eyes dancing with anticipation.

"Tonight the scumbags meet the mega narc," Lance said.

Nick looked over the dark waters of Sandfly Pass. "Getting closer," he said.

"I hear them," Lance said.

The deal was about to go down.

Now the low powerful chugging noise was clear. It sounded as if the boats were almost on the beach. But Nick and Lance could see nothing.

"Ben in position?" Lance asked.

Nick's idea to protect Ben was to bury him in the soft sand near the landing. He was buried on his back with his nose and eyes hidden under a yucca plant that had been stripped of leaves on one side and pushed over. In Ben's hands was a rope that stretched just under the surface of the sand to a tree across the path. At Nick's command, Ben was to pull the rope and trip the fleeing smugglers as they ran for their boats after the last load of marijuana had been stashed. The idea was to cause enough momentary confusion for Nick's team to charge from the bushes and take control before the smugglers could begin any gunplay.

"Yeah," Nick said. "He'll be okay. He knows what to do."

Then through the offshore darkness Lance saw the V-shaped ribbons of white that peeled back off the bow of each boat as it approached the beach. The ribbons stretched left and right as far as he could see. The boats, darker outlines against the night, were low-riding nautical mutants with marijuana stacked high on the decks. As the skippers retarded the throttles, the rumble of the engines died away and was overcome by the sibilant whisper of the bows sliding through the water toward the small beach.

The beach was no more than thirty yards wide. Dense mangroves surrounded it on three sides and funneled whoever came ashore through a narrow passage toward the south. The passage then opened up into a series of clearings surrounded by palmetto bushes and overhung with small oaks. It was in the dense palmettos and under the oaks that the dopers planned to stash their cargo until it could be taken to the mainland.

With his left hand, Lance pulled a flare from a pack in front of him. His right hand hoisted his big nickel-plated Magnum.

"Not yet," Nick said. "Wait until I tell you."

"Will Ben stay low until the signal?"

"He better," Nick growled.

"Dumnik is going to raise hell about burying one of his agents."

"We'll worry about that when it happens. Right now I want Ben to be safe."

Nick watched the first wave of shallow-draft mullet skiffs approach the beach line abreast, seven of them gunwale to gunwale. Before they touched the beach, crew members jumped into the water, bowlines in hand, and pulled hard. As the bows touched the beach, each skipper gave a final burst of power to edge the boat a bit more firmly onto the sand, then quickly turned off the engine, jumped into the water, and picked up a bale from the boat. Within seconds a dozen men were running back and forth down the narrow passage that led from the beach into the clearings. Through the night-vision goggles Nick noticed two things about the off-loaders. Several of them were young, high-school students by their appearance; and everyone was armed. He could see the automatic rifles they carried slung over their shoulders.

"Wait. Wait," Nick whispered from the bushes a few feet away. "Let them get it all ashore."

He watched closely as the dopers, a bale under each arm, pounded down the path. "Looks like thirty-pound bales," he whispered.

"They pretty close to Ben," Lance said.

"Close? They're on top of him."

Lance giggled.

Within a half-hour the highly organized crews had unloaded the first round of boats and stashed the pot under the trees.

"Flare is ready," Lance said. "Say the word."

Nick was staring down the long passage through the

trees to the south; waiting for the dopers to reappear. He knew they would be running at full tilt, anxious to get their boats back in the water, make room for the next off-load crew while they returned to the shrimp boats for another load.

Nick heard the dopers running; their breath coming hard and fast; their feet pounding the sand. Then they rounded the corner.

"Get ready."

Lance raised the flare.

A phalanx of dopers was charging down the lane toward the boats, elbows pumping, knees driving.

Nick moved to a crouch. He patted the nine-millimeter Browning automatic on his hip, dropped the night-vision goggles, picked up a powerful flashlight, and stuck it in his belt. Then he reached down, picked up the small military radio, pressed the transmit button, and said, "We're moving in." He picked up a battery-operated bullhorn and turned to Lance. "Flare," he ordered.

Lance pulled the trigger of the flare gun. There was a loud pop and a sputtering trail of fire as the flare arced high over the island in Sandfly Pass. Then the flare exploded, a brilliant white ball that turned the Stygian blackness of the Ten Thousand Islands into high noon.

Several things happened simultaneously.

In the command post, Melvin issued a command that caused the Navy and Coast Guard vessels to begin closing in. The Customs helicopters launched from the Ford test track. DEA and the other land forces moved roadblocks into position and began moving in on known off-loading sites on the hill. A dozen boats, crewed by DEA, the Florida Marine Patrol, and the Collier County sheriff's office, roared out of the mangrove thicket behind Nick and Lance to surround the crab boats and mullet skiffs that stretched up and down Sandfly Pass. Nick put the bullhorn to his lips and said, "Pull."

The strange command boomed across the quiet night, causing the charging dopers to stumble and pause for a half-second. Ben Blumen, who was buried in a shallow pit on the edge of the narrow passage used by the dopers, arose like a wraith from the darkness. He pulled hard on the half-buried rope just as six dopers were charging past. They tumbled to the sand.

"State attorney's office. Freeze," said Nick through the bullhorn. "You're all under arrest."

Nick and Lance, backed by nine other cops, all shining high-powered flashlights into the eyes of the dopers, crouched, waiting to see if there would be gunplay. The cops were as nervous as the dopers. Nick knew there were three kinds of cops when it came to firefights. The first kind, the macho posturing guys who consistently score in the top rank on the firing range; the guys who can shoot out a gnat's eye, more often than not are the cops who, in a real gun battle, when it's nose to nose and the pistols are popping like firecrackers, hide in the corner, crap in their pants, and cry like babies. Then there are the crazies; the guys who stand out in the open blazing away as if they're John Wayne. These guys either lead short lives or, somehow, get wiser and, in amazing numbers, evolve into the first sort; the cop who hides and cries. Finally, there is the cop who does his job; who doesn't go looking for gunplay, but when it comes, he blazes away. After it is all over, these are the cops who sweat and shake and become sick to their stomachs, sometimes for days on end.

Nick had so many cops from other agencies on this deal that he didn't know how they would react. If the bad guys cut loose with an automatic weapon, he might be out front with no one behind him. But there was no time to worry.

For a split second the dopers, sprawled across the sand or befuddled by the command "Pull" and their sprawling colleagues, froze, blinded by the light.

It is that split second of eternity when cops must make it absolutely clear to bad guys that they are outgunned, outmanned, and will be blown to hell if they go for their guns.

"You're surrounded. Throw down your guns," Nick ordered. "Now."

The high-school boys, who had demonstrated their great asset as off-loaders, limitless energy, now demonstrated what dopers would consider their weakness—a readiness to comply with orders from cops. One of the high-school boys quickly slid the strap of the automatic rifle off his shoulder and let it drop to the sand. He threw his hands high and said, "Don't shoot." Others quickly followed suit.

The older guys held on to their guns, indecisive, waiting. Lance jumped to his feet and strode into the bright glare cast by the flashlights. He was easily recognizable to other cops by the red Rambo rag and red high-topped tennis shoes. With his nickel-plated .357 Magnum at arm's length, he approached one of the armed smugglers. The smuggler eyed him warily. Who the hell was this grinning maniac with the eyes that danced as if he hoped somebody went for a gun?

Lance sauntered up to the grizzled fisherman and jammed the Magnum into his ear with enough force to cause him to curse.

"Pardon me, asshole," Lance said, twisting the pistol so the sight cut into his ear. "But would you believe this pistol will blow a hole between your ears big enough to park two cars, a motorcycle, and a jet ski?"

"Whuut?" the puzzled doper said.

Around them the other dopers milled about, eyes shifting nervously. About that time a sand-covered figure rose from their feet, stepping out of a hole in the sand like a ghostly apparition, pulled a Glock from somewhere in his shirt, and stuck it in the ear of another smuggler. It was Ben Blumen.

"I'll read them their rights," he said.

"They're dopers. They don't have rights," Lance said. He leaned closer to the smuggler. "I'm going to count to one. If you haven't dropped your weapon, I'm going to let in some daylight between your ears; more than already exists."

He paused. His lips pursed and he thumbed back the hammer on the Magnum.

"Don't shoot. I'll drop it," the smuggler said. His rifle slid to the sand. "Son of a bitch," he mumbled.

Lance shook his finger in the man's face. "Don't talk that way to America's hero." He seized the man's nose between his bent forefinger and middle finger, then twisted hard.

The old doper grunted.

Lance looked around as Nick and the other cops quickly searched and cuffed the smugglers. He let out a grunt of disgust. "Some of these dopers are babies. We got the damn kiddy patrol. All the other guys get to lock assholes with the bad guys."

"Important thing is we got them. This will put the big hurt on the Everglades City crowd," Nick said in satisfaction. "We're finally getting the job done."

"I haven't worked on this case for almost eighteen months just so I could arrest a couple of kids." Lance was not smiling.

"What the hell's the matter with you? Only one or two are kids. They're all dopers."

"Yeah, but, hey. I'm the narc from hell. I can't have somebody ask me what I did in the great drug war and not be able to say anything except"—Lance's voice changed to a simpering falsetto—" 'I arrested a kid who was barely weaned.' God damn. I need a big foot. I need some romping, stomping badasses."

Nick looked up at the sudden deafening thunder from the two Blackhawks roaring in from the hill, barely fifty feet over the water, the nine-million-candlepower night suns—searchlights under their bellies—turning the night into day.

"Let's tie up the loose ends," Nick said. He paused. "And watch Dumnik grab all the credit."

"Bullshit," Lance mumbled. He was watching the choppers.

It was time to activate Plan B.

42

Lance looked over his shoulder. Nick and Ben Blumen were doing the preliminary interviews with the busted dopers and would not notice his absence for a while. He nodded at the sheriff's deputy standing guard over the small fleet of mullet skiffs nosed up on the beach. With a gesture of impatience he pushed one of the boats free of the sand and into deeper water. The boat already had a seizure sticker pasted on the bow.

"Gotta check on something," he said vaguely to the deputy.

The sheriff's deputies in the five southwest Florida counties that comprise the Twentieth Judicial Circuit were wary of investigators from the state attorney's office. After all, state attorney's investigators, in addition to all their other criminal cases, were investigating the activities of two sheriffs in the district. Deputies figured those sheriffs would go to jail. Yessir, these guys from the state attorney's office, even if they were fellow cops, were people to be kept at arm's length. So when Lance took one of the seized doper boats, it was fine with the deputy.

As the water rose past his knees, Lance gave the mullet skiff a final push and swung aboard. He cranked up the outboard engine and continued backing into the darkness. When he was well offshore, he reduced power on the engine, pushed the gear lever into forward, then slowly added full power. The mullet skiff rose up on its hindquarters and tossed aside a full bow wave as it plowed up Sandfly Pass toward Chokoloskee Bay.

Lance picked up his small hand-held radio and keyed the transmit button. "Victor Five One to Avenger."

"Avenger. Go."

Lance smiled. Good old Mike; the most dependable man God ever made. He was sitting on the airport in Everglades City, undoubtedly being eaten alive by mosquitoes, but—judging by the alacrity with which he responded to the radio call—anxious and ready to go.

Lance looked up as he broke out of the mangroves into the broad expanse of Chokoloskee Bay. He pushed harder on the throttle. "Am about fifteen minutes from your position. Will be landing east end."

"I'll be ready."

Lance looked over his shoulder. The lights under the bellies of the Blackhawks still were scurrying about Sandfly Pass and the edge of the Gulf, rounding up stragglers, checking for floating bales. They would be easy to avoid.

Minutes later Lance ran the mullet skiff onto the slightly raised ground at the east end of the runway of the small airport in Everglades City. He jumped over the bow, then turned and shoved the mullet skiff hard. It would be found drifting and, because of the seizure sticker, would be turned over to the cops. Maybe. Lance scurried over the crest of the ridge. To his right, no more than fifty yards away, was the dark shape of the helicopter. The rotor was turning, hurling the oily burned odor of the exhaust into the warm still night.

"Approaching from your eleven o'clock," Lance radioed.

"Affirm. Careful of the rotor."

Lance crawled into the open left door. Mike's face, awash from the red and green and amber lights of the panel, had a surrealistic glow.

Lance strapped himself into the seat. He slipped the earphones over his head and adjusted the mike until it touched his lips. Before he could speak, he heard Mike's voice in the headset. "It'll take maybe thirty seconds to get the temp up. Then we gotta get outta here."

"What's going on?"

"They must be having some sort of festival over here soon. There's a lot of tents and portable out-

houses over near that open space in the middle of
town.''

"Yeah.''

"I came in too low when I was landing and the rotor
wash blew over one of the portable crappers. There
was a guy inside. All I saw was a Hawaiian shirt and
a bare ass being tumbled across the grass.''

Lance threw back his head and exploded in laughter.
"You blew a hemorrhoid out of a crapper. Wait until
I tell Nick.'' He slapped his hand on his knee. "You
ready to go out and do some street-level law enforcement?''

"Only way to get their attention.''

Lance rubbed his hands together in anticipation.
"We get to play by doper rules tonight.'' He looked
over his shoulder into the rear seat, where there were
stacked a dozen or so small valises. "All the stuff is
here?''

Mike nodded.

"Thank God for julios,'' Lance said.

Mike permitted himself a tight smile. Temp was up.
Time to boogie. He began the intricate, complicated
ballet of lifting a helicopter—in this case, an unmarked
JetRanger—from the ramp in a smooth coordinated
motion. His right hand was on the cyclic, his left on
the collective. He pulled collective and pushed in left
antitorque pedal until the turbine-powered JetRanger
was in the hover. Now the chopper was balanced atop
a column of air. He initiated a slow turn with the cyclic until the chopper was pointed in the direction of
flight. As he eased the cyclic forward, the chopper
emerged from the column of air and began to settle.
More collective. He pushed the nose over and the
chopper went into translational lift. The nose dipped
as speed across the ground increased. He was in a
shallow climb, seeking seventy knots as quickly as
possible. As forward speed increased, he lightened
pressure on the left antitorque pedal. As forward speed
increased even more, the weather-vaning effect on the
fuselage came to his assistance; helping keep the
chopper straight without pressure on the pedal. He was

halfway across Chokoloskee Bay with the dark reaches of the Ten Thousand Islands directly ahead. The noon-day brightness of the lights under the two Customs Blackhawks was easy to see. Mike swung further north to avoid the area where the bust had taken place.

Lance looked over his shoulder and again rubbed his hands. The helicopter had been seized a week ear-lier by Customs agents in Miami. It had been the spot-ter aircraft for a group of dopers. Mike had flown so many hours the past few days that he would be over his limit if he flew one of the 'Hawks during the bust in Sandfly Pass. He had signed out the JetRanger for an evaluation flight; to see if it would be suitable for use as an undercover aircraft by Customs. As soon as he was away from Homestead, he had disconnected the Hobbs meter so no one would know how much time he had flown.

He and Lance had made their contingency plans for tonight at the same time the raid was being planned. Lance had gone into the evidence room and taken a case of satchel charges; explosive devises used by groups of anti-Castro Cubans who constantly used the Big Cypress Swamp and the Everglades to practice for their long-dreamed overthrow of Cuba. The satchel charges were state-of-the-art equipment provided by the CIA. The devices were made with both ease of use and speed of use in mind; set a timer, pull a cord, and get the hell out of the way.

The lights of the two Blackhawks, still lazily going up and down Sandfly Pass, now were about five miles to the south. In the half-light from the moon, Mike recognized Jack Daniels Key. Then there was the end-less shimmering water of the Gulf of Mexico. He turned a radio-frequency dial, then pressed the trans-mit button with his foot.

"Danny Boy, Flint Six Niner."

Lance laughed. Flint was the radio prefix used by DEA.

"Flint Six Niner," responded the command post. "Danny Boy. Go."

"Danny Boy, can you give me a VHF freq to work

Shark One Five?'' Shark was the prefix used by Coast
Guard chase boats. Shark One Five was the boat whose
duty was to run down the Cuban shrimp boats that had
delivered the marijuana and cocaine to the crab boats.

After a brief pause the command post came back.

''Flint Six Niner, say your mission.''

''Intel flight. We have to get IR photos of the vessels
in question.''

Back at the command post, Melvin Foster pursed
his lips in confusion. It made sense to get infrared
photos of the Cuban shrimp boats, now fleeing at high
speed, but odd that he hadn't known a DEA chopper
would be working tonight. Either Dumnik had forgotten to tell him, which was possible, or the intel guys
had gotten with the Air Wing without notifying Dumnik. Also possible. But why would they be using an
easily monitored VHF freq when they could use DEA's
UHF freqs? He wondered briefly if he should awaken
Dumnik. Why do that? The operation had gone down
with textbook perfection. Dumnik would be more than
pleased. Melvin looked at the radio operator and nodded his approval. The operator radioed a VHF frequency being used by a Coast Guard vessel. The Navy
hydrofoil and the Coast Guard high-speed boats were
still roaring around Sandfly Pass and into the edge of
the Gulf; making sure no bales were floating and that
all the off-load boats involved in the deal had been
seized. It would be another half-hour before they could
be cut loose to pursue the shrimpers.

Mike pressed the transmit button by his foot. ''Shark
One Five. Flint Six Niner.''

''Go ahead, Flint Six Niner. This is Shark One
Five.''

''Shark One Five, we are en route to take IR photos
of the load boats. We need their last known coordinates.''

''Stand by one.''

A moment later the Coast Guard radio operator came
back. ''Flint Six Niner, say your position.''

Mike knew he was being painted by the Coast Guard
radar so there was no need to withhold his position.

He took a quick look at the VOR's on the panel, turned the knobs until the CDI's centered, did some quick mental arithmetic, and said, "Estimate two-six miles southeast of Marco Island, heading two-one-zero."

Pause.

"Flint Six Niner, we have you two-eight miles southeast of Marco."

Mike shook his head. "So I missed it two fucking miles, smart-ass," Mike mumbled. He pressed the transmit button. His voice was calm. "That's us."

A moment later the Coast Guard radio operator came back. "Flint Six Niner, Shark One Five will intercept those vessels."

Mike sighed and cursed under his breath. Of all times for the Coasties to get territorial. The Coasties were afraid the DEA would take credit for the seizure of the shrimpers.

Mike thought of the satchel charges in the rear seat. If he were going to put them to use, he would have to kiss some Coast Guard ass.

"Shark One Five, understand this is a Coast Guard intercept. No problem there. All we want are some photos. We'll courier copies over to Seventh District by daylight. It will be a quick in-and-out. It's your bust."

The Coast Guard skipper nodded in approval. All radio conversations aboard Coast Guard vessels were recorded; now he had the DEA on record as saying this was a Coast Guard bust. He could afford to display a little noblesse oblige. He looked at the coordinates on the chart before him.

"Flint Six Niner, several hours ago one of our aircraft was tracking the vessels on radar. Last known course was two-three-zero. Stand by for the projected position."

Mike thought rapidly. If the radar track was several hours old, that meant the Coast Guard aircraft no longer was on station. Probably had to go refuel, and left the seizure up to the cutter. Good. And the heading indicated the shrimper was plunging deep into the Gulf, seeking to become lost in the vastness of that trackless body of water before making the turn around the end of the Florida keys. Also good. Had the shrimper made a high-speed run across Florida Bay and through one of the cuts in the Florida keys, Mike's job would have been much more difficult.

The Coasties came back on the air and radioed the coordinates where the shrimpers, if they continued on their last known heading at their last known speed, could now be located. Mike repeated the numbers as he wrote them on a pad. He calculated rapidly, then turned left forty degrees. "Hope they're leaving big wakes," he mumbled. Unless the shrimpers were traveling at high speed and leaving broad wakes, easily seen from the air, he might not find them.

"And, Flint Six Niner, let us know what you find. We were painting five boats."

Mike's eyes widened. Lance grinned. Intel had said four boats. If there were five, that meant a bonus; an additional twenty tons or so of marijuana. Five Cuban shrimp boats in one night. Incredible. Now he knew why the Coasties had been so quick to assist him. The Coasties were not cops. Any situation where there might be gunplay made them scurry about like berserk water bugs. They wanted him to fly over and see how hostile the julios might be when bounced by the law. If the DEA bird took small-arms fire from the Cubes, the Coasties would unlimber their big guns, stand off a few miles, and make a big display of their muscle-flexing before they attempted to board.

"Affirm that, Shark One Five."

"Flint Six Niner, we estimate radar contact in about six minutes."

Mike and Lance looked at each other. They would have to work fast. "That's affirm, Shark One Five. Thanks for your help." Mike paused a moment. "You guys have any action tonight?"

The Coast Guard skipper paused. "Not much. We were detailed to bust the shrimpers once the operation began at Sandfly Pass. But we had one incident; stopped a crab boat named *Swamp Fox*."

Lance groaned and slapped his brow. "That's my

snitch's boat. Ask him what happened.'' *Swamp Fox* was a new crab boat owned by Big Knocker. He looked at the panel of the chopper in frustration. The helicopter had only VHF radio. Virtually every home in Everglades City had a VHF scanner. And tonight, when a bust was going down, they would all be listening. Hundreds of people would overhear Mike's conversation with the Coasties. But Lance had to know what had happened to Big Knocker, who was driving the boat carrying the cocaine.

''Skipper seemed angry that we stopped him,'' the Coast Guard skipper said in near-astonishment. ''He got out of earshot of his crew and told one of my officers he was working U/C with some local agency; state attorney, I believe. He told us his U/C name was 'Popeye.' We confirmed with Danny Boy.''

Lance looked at Mike. ''Oh, shit. The Coasties blew my snitch. That's the end of this case. We'll have to hide him somewhere.'' He slammed his fist into the palm of his hand. ''He didn't say anything about a seizure. Ask him if the boat was loaded.''

''Shark One Five, was the boat empty?''

''Affirmative. We think he was a load boat but there was nothing on board. At his request, we took his crew on board Shark One Five and have them in confinement.''

''The skipper was not arrested?''

''Negative. Not since he was an informant. These locals are out of control with their investigations.''

''That's affirm, Shark One Five. Flint Six Niner out.''

Lance and Nick looked at each other without speaking. Both were thinking the same thing: where is the load of cocaine the informant's boat was carrying?

Then Lance exploded in anger. ''Dammit, they were briefed about that boat, told to stay away from it. We had someone waiting on the hill. But it looks like he unloaded offshore. So they pop the boat after the load is gone, then get on the radio to confirm a snitch's ID.''

Mike instantly sensed the gravity of what had happened. "You have a contingency plan?"

Lance nodded. "The snitch will be okay. He knows where to go until I get there. But it ID's our snitch, it ID's me, it ID's the airboat business, and it damn sure brings the investigation to a screeching halt. Shit. We could have run it a few more weeks, arrested a few more people."

"Right now we got to worry about the boats."

Lance nodded in agreement. There was nothing he could do about Big Knocker until he returned.

Lance and Mike leaned forward, both scanning the darkness of the sea, looking for telltale wakes. Mike glanced at the fuel gauges. Dopers always installed long-range tanks on their aircraft, so he had plenty of fuel.

He and Lance had two problems. The first was finding the dopers. Then they had to evade radar detection on their return. Mike shrugged. One thing at a time. His right hand was light and sure on the cyclic. The chopper was pulling full power, throbbing and thumping, and it probed deeper into the vast darkness of the Gulf of Mexico.

"I didn't notice. Does this thing have the inflatable floats?" Lance asked.

Mike smiled and shook his head.

"What about survival equipment?"

Again Mike shook his head. "Dopers don't carry that stuff. I put in two vests."

"No raft?"

"No raft."

"Hmmmmm." Lance laughed. "What the hell? This thing goes in, we'll walk on the water."

It was Lance who first saw the fleeing shrimp boats. Mike was making an instrument scan when, from the corner of his eye, Lance saw a long slash of white in the darkness—the wake of a boat laboring at high speed—then another, and another. One more. Then, at the far edge of his vision, the fifth. They were in trail as they bored deep into the Gulf.

Lance reached out and poked Mike with a thumb.

"Hey, we haven't done this in more than a year," he said.

Mike grinned tightly as he remembered. During an investigation in the Turks and Caicos Islands, he had flown a Blackhawk while Lance tossed thirty-pound blocks of ice at fleeing go-fast boats loaded with cocaine.

"Tonight we get to use the good stuff," Lance said. He flicked his finger toward the boats.

Mike looked, stiffened, and nodded. "We'll make one pass over the stern of the last boat. They won't hear us until we pass. We'll ID the boat. If it's a Cuban shrimper, I'll swing in a tight circle, then come straight up the line. They won't see us in the dark. And they know the Coasties have DF equipment, so they might not get on the radio."

Lance nodded. He unplugged the radio cord and unclasped his seat belt, then stepped between the seats into the rear cabin. He plugged in the radio cord and strapped himself in the right seat, directly behind Mike. He pulled the satchel charges closer. Then he pulled a pin from each of the two hinges on the door, stuck one hand through the open window, and pulled sharply. The door suddenly was in his hand. He turned it on the side and pushed it to the left side of the cabin.

"I'm on the starboard side. Right behind you," he said over the intercom.

"We're on the Coasties' radar. So let's not play around. Do it fast. Then we'll drop down on the deck out of their radar coverage and run for home."

Now the chopper was no more than fifty feet above the dark surface. Flying at such a low altitude over the ocean at night, when there is no outside frame of reference, is like flying inside a black bag. It is flying of the most hazardous and dangerous sort. But Mike had done it before, many times. His instrument scan was rapid as he watched the altimeter and the situation indicator. He bent the chopper around slightly to the west, lining it up for a run straight up the wake of the last boat in line.

"Ten seconds," he said. His mouth was tight. A

shrimper could carry upwards of fifty thousand pounds of marijuana in the cavernous holds. There was quite literally no way to know how much marijuana and cocaine these boats had brought into southwest Florida in the last few years, but there was no doubt that they had contributed their share of pain and misery to those who used the goods they hauled.

Mike looked at the froth of white water boiling a few feet below the right side of the chopper. He looked ahead and turned the chopper a few degrees to the left. Then the deck flashed past, almost at eye level, and he rocked the chopper in a right bank to the left.

"Altas Modas," he read. Then he laughed. " 'High Times.' What a name for a load boat.''

"Varadero is the home port,'' Lance said. "Those are our boys. See anybody on deck?''

"Nope. You?''

"Naa. Must be in the wheelhouse. But they'll be there when we come back.'' He giggled. "Until they see these things hit the deck.'' He put four of the satchel charges at his feet and held one in his lap. "I'm setting the timers for ten seconds. That's enough for us to clear but not enough time for somebody on deck to toss it overboard.''

"Just make damn sure they get out the door,'' Mike said. Ten seconds seemed too short. If Lance dropped one inside the chopper and it got blown aside by the tornado of wind tearing through the cabin, they would become a fireball. Now the chopper was arcing back over the wake, lining up for the run up the chain of boats.

Lance adjusted the timer on each of the satchel charges. Now all he had to do was pull the cord to begin the countdown. He was singing "The Boys Are Back in Town'' and laughing to himself as he pulled the valises close.

Mike laughed. "About twenty seconds. Right under the door.''

Lance gathered the charges closer. "How close are the others?''

"No more than ten seconds apart. You won't have much time."

"Enough."

"Stand by."

"Ready to rock and roll."

"Two seconds."

The stern of the last shrimper came into view through the open door. The white deck made a good target. In one smooth continuous motion, Lance pulled the cord and flung the satchel charge through the open door onto the deck. He quickly reached down, picked up another, and seized the cord.

"Get it?"

"Does a fat dog fart? 'Course I got it. Do it again."

"Two seconds," Mike said.

The first explosion came just as Lance was preparing to toss the second charge overboard. The sudden flash of light and the dull boom, audible even over the sound of the chopper, jarred his aim enough that the charge missed and fell into the sea.

"Oh, nooooooo," Lance said. He sounded as disappointed as a small boy who has just been told he can't go to the movies.

"Next one's close. Two seconds," Mike said calmly.

"Bomb away," Lance radioed in exultation as the charge fell to the deck. "They oughta make a movie of our lives—*Thirty Seconds over the Gulf of Mexico.*"

"Stand by, three seconds."

Lance leaned out the open door, slipstream blowing his hair flat on his head, singing aloud the pulsating rhythmic theme from *Jaws*, the music that always presaged a shark attack.

He pulled the string and dropped the satchel charge. "Holy bombmobile. Pow!"

Just as Mike approached the next boat, a figure ran onto the deck, one hand in the air. Mike broke left, causing Lance to drop the charge prematurely.

"Sorry, guy. Thought he had a gun. We'll come back. One more. Stand by. Two seconds."

"Bomb away. Take that, scumbag doper."

As the chopper swung in a tight circle to the right,

the night was afire. Three burning boats had come to a halt in the water. Two boats were unmarked and clearly visible in the flames.

The radio broke squelch. "Flint, Six Niner, Shark One Five. How do you read?"

"Tell him to piss up a rope," Lance said.

"Okay, these guys will be ready and may fire at us," Mike said. "So we'll cross the deck at a ninety-degree angle. Can you hit them?"

Lance leaned forward and lightly punched Mike on the shoulder. "You ask a question like that to the guy who sank three Cubes in one pass?"

The chopper skimmed the surface, staying in the darkness and out of sight of the crew of the undamaged boat as it continued to the right. Then the chopper rocked to a level position and, within a few feet of the surface, rocketed on an intercept heading toward the fleeing shrimp boats.

Lance had two charges in his lap. He leaned out the door, eyes squinting into the night as the speed of the chopper caused tears to stream from his eyes. The shrimp boat was growing rapidly.

"Flint Six Niner, Shark One Five. Come in. Come in Flint Six Niner." The Coastie's voice was urgent.

Mike ignored him. "Stand by."

"The narc from hell," Lance intoned. He jerked the two cords simultaneously and flung them downward as Mike popped the chopper up a few feet to clear the deck. The first charge fell fifty yards short; the second bounced off the side of the shrimper and fell into the water. It exploded about two seconds after the boat passed.

Mike continued his climb and began turning to the right. The boat was slowing. The charge had exploded at the water line and crippled it.

"Flint Six Niner, this is Shark One Five. You will respond. Flint Six Niner, come in. This is Shark One Five."

"I winged him," Lance said. "Next time he's gone."

Mike shook his head. "He can't get away. Let him

pick up the survivors." He twisted around for a quick look at Lance. "Running out of time. Do this guy."

Lance nodded and pulled four satchels close. His demonic grin stretched from ear to ear. The chopper dropped low and roared astern the last boat. Two of the charges struck the shrimper; the first on the fantail, the second on the bow. The simultaneous explosions blew both ends off the boat and turned the remainder into a towering column of orange and red flame. A secondary explosion, the fuel tanks, left nothing but small pieces of broken and burned wood smoking on the surface.

"The crip will get the survivors," Mike said, bending the chopper around to the northeast. "We outta here."

"Survivors?" Lance looked at the blazing surface of the ocean; aflame with burning boats and burning fuel. He thought for a moment. "Yeah, even sharks won't eat those fuckers. They're just Cubans." He tapped Mike on the shoulder. "Let's do one more run. I want the crippled boat. Let's finish him."

Mike shook his head. "We did what we came to do. Besides, Coasties are getting antsy. They'll be here in a few minutes. We need to get out of Dodge." He looked at the scene of fiery desolation and then, with a satisfied nod, turned northeast and pushed the chopper toward the deck.

"Guess you're right," Lance said reluctantly. "We get caught out here and the EPA will charge us with polluting the Gulf of Mexico."

"Yeah, fuel will do that."

"I wasn't talking about fuel. I was talking about the Cubes."

Epilogue

Nick drove up the incline and around the curving driveway of the Marco Beach Marriott, the fanciest of all the fancy hotels on Marco Island, remembered Hurricane Donna, and shook his head in amazement at the folly of man.

He had been only eleven years old when Donna came through, but, like every other person who lived in southwest Florida at the time, he remembered as though it were yesterday. There have been many hurricanes in the thirty years since Donna, but none approached her power or malevolence. Most of south Florida's transient population has no frame of reference for storms such as Donna. Hurricanes are little more than an excuse to have a party. Today Marco Island is covered with multimillion-dollar homes and with glass-and-steel towers; a mecca for the snowbirds who, if they know of Donna at all, consider her something of an aberration and don't believe there can ever be another such storm. But she will come one day. Her name won't be Donna, but she will be just as big, just as vicious, just as strong. And when she moves on, every building will be destroyed. Glass-walled concrete buildings that the snowbirds thought would be as eternal as the pyramids will be broken and tossed and turned into jumbled heaps of rubble. The island will look like the old pictures of Hiroshima.

Nick pulled under the cantilevered awning of the Marriott. Two uniformed carhops materialized, one opening the door on the driver's side of his green pickup truck, the other opening the door for his wife and helping her to the driveway. Nick involuntarily looked at the sky and then out to sea as he stepped down. The storm would not come tonight.

Nick had had enough storms in his life since the night of the raid in Sandfly Pass two months ago; he was looking forward to tonight's celebration. After the raid it seemed that everything he had worked for had suddenly come to pass. Ninety-seven people were arrested; some of them, like Heart Attack, were repeat offenders. Cops had been arrested. One park ranger had discovered that sex with December was very expensive; his career was gone and so was he—to jail for many years. And it seemed as if everyone in Everglades City suddenly wanted to talk. Nick's office had more snitches than it could handle. His investigators had the luxury of picking and choosing. The result was that many of the fishermen had nothing to trade; they were going to jail.

The trials were starting next week, and two judges from another circuit were coming in to hear the cases. The visiting judges were coming ostensibly because of the heavy caseload, but in reality to keep the cases away from the Great Emancipator. The outside judges were expected to deal out some big-time jail sentences. And then the second round of indictments would begin. Nick could have arrested another fifty-four people, but the state attorney's legal staff was so overloaded by having ninety-seven dopers tossed at them, they asked Nick to hold off until the first cases were adjudicated. Joe D'Alessandro had come to Nick, laughed, and said, "I never thought I'd say say this to anyone on my staff. But slow down. At least until we can get some of these cases out of the way."

Nick was pleased. He was getting the job done. Arresting so many people that the courts couldn't handle them was good policework in anybody's book.

The back door to America had been slammed and locked. For the first time anyone could recall, Everglades City was shut down. No smuggling of anything was going on there. Nick guessed the dopers had moved west across the Gulf of Mexico to Texas.

Nick's greatest satisfaction was solving the deaths of Derek and Grace. As with many drug-related homicides, the resolution had come about in a peculiarly circuitous fashion. After the raid in Sandfly Pass, Big Knocker had been arrested. He tried to lie about the load of cocaine he had hidden, but two of his humpers talked. It was good the humpers talked, because DEA followed the load of cocaine, then lost it in an industrial park in Fort Myers. The cocaine would have hit the street had not the humpers told Nick not only where it was stashed but also where Big Knocker had hidden fifty kilos as a retirement policy.

By attempting a little smuggling venture when he was supposed to be an informant, he had negated his arrangement with Nick. All bets were off. Nick astonished Big Knocker by saying he was not going to be arrested; that he was going to be left in Everglades City that night; left in the middle of a town full of fishermen who knew they were going to jail largely because of what they had told Big Knocker at his phony airboat-repair shop. Even Big Knocker knew he couldn't deal with several dozen smugglers whose hearts were filled with vengeance.

He agreed to do what he had never done: to sit down with a tape recorder and reveal everything he knew about smuggling in Everglades City. Nick called a prosecutor, arranged for witnesses, and did it that night. Big Knocker, with all the proper legal caveats, pleaded guilty to numerous cocaine-trafficking charges. But he had to be protected. So Nick and several officers took Big Knocker to his trailer to pack a suitcase. He was going into protective custody up in north Florida. Nick, playing a hunch, had the surveillance van parked nearby. And he let Big Knocker go into his trailer alone. Sure enough, Big Knocker called Robert to say he was going away for a while. In his anger he couldn't resist a parting shot at Nick: "The dumb fucker is hiding me in connection with this dope business, and he doesn't know I killed two cops." When Robert oohed and aahed in amazement, Big Knocker gave him a few details. It was all on videotape.

Nick knew that Robert could be squeezed until he

Robert Coram

gave a deposition telling what his brother had said; that he would testify at the murder trial.

When Big Knocker came out of his trailer, Nick cuffed him and told him he was being arrested for the murder of two prosecutors.

"What about our deal?" Big Knocker asked.

"I lied," Nick said.

Big Knocker was in jail charged with murder. No bond was allowed. Big Knocker probably would get the electric chair for the double homicide. If by some quirk of the legal system he got life, Nick would ask the court to tie the drug-smuggling sentence onto the life sentence. Big Knocker would never again be a free man.

Derek and Grace could rest in peace.

As for Heart Attack, he lived up to his name. When Nick came to arrest him, the king of the Everglades City dopers had another heart attack. The doper was a virtual invalid; he would never fully recover. And his pain would be increased by knowing that December was facing a half-dozen felony charges; April and May, whom Nick referred to as "the carpet munchers," were looking at jail time; and July, his youngest daughter, had not only agreed to testify against her father and sisters, she had applied for a scholarship and been accepted at a girls' college up in Atlanta; a place called Agnes Scott. A real shame.

Ben Blumen, as Lance had predicted, got into serious trouble when Dumnik discovered he had been buried in the sand during the raid at Sandfly Pass. Dumnik suspended Ben and instituted proceedings to have him fired. Then Nick, who was a member of the Florida Sheriffs' Association, wrote a commendation for Ben and nominated him as Florida's Peace Officer of the Year. Ben's job had been saved. And tonight he was being given an award.

Dumnik might have been the busiest federal agent in America for several weeks after the raid. His most immediate problem was explaining to an irate federal judge how an angry doper had somehow sneaked into the judge's office and ruined an antique quilt.

Dumnik tried to take credit for the raid in Sandfly Pass. But this time it didn't work. Except for Ben Blumen, his agents were far out of position that night. It was Nick Brown's troops who testified at the preliminary hearings on the Everglades City cases. It was clear that DEA had had little to do with the raid. Dumnik also was having to do a lot of explaining about a DEA helicopter that, after the raid in Sandfly Pass, had been in radio contact with the command post and later had been picked up on radar by the Coast Guard. The Coast Guard cutter tracked the chopper performing low-level maneuvers around the fleeing shrimpers. When the cutter arrived on scene, the Coasties found one crippled boat and a lot of burning wreckage. A few Cubans plucked from the water said they had been attacked by a helicopter. The Coast Guard repeated to anyone who would listen that the chopper driver had used "Flint"—the DEA call sign. Dumnik said it was not his chopper; that DEA birds were on the ground in Miami that night. No one seemed to know who owned the chopper that bombed the Cuban shrimp boats. Newspapers in Naples and Fort Myers were filled with letters to the editors applauding the action and suggesting that the mystery pilot, whoever he was, should take to the air whenever there was another raid. The public, to Nick's surprise, liked the idea of bombing dopers.

Nick had his suspicions about the helicopter. But when he asked Lance, the young agent was indignant. "Would America's hero do such a thing?" he asked.

"Where did you disappear to that night?" Nick asked.

"I went to another island and went to sleep. I was exhausted."

Nick grunted.

"My devil brain was in control," Lance added. "I couldn't help it."

Nick knew what had happened, but he had no proof.

As he stood on the driveway under the awning of the Marriott, he suddenly became aware the carhop was talking to him.

"Your ticket, sir." The carhop gave Nick a white stub, which he, in turn, passed to Susie, his wife. She put it into her purse as they walked up the steps. Another uniformed functionary saw them coming. His smile was almost as wide as the glass door he opened.

The first thing Nick and Susie saw when they entered the posh and spacious lobby was Lance's smile. He had a maniacal smile that always was the focal point of whatever room he was in; no matter how large the room or how many people were there. Lance wore a tan poplin suit, a shirt so white it had to be new, and a striped blue-and-green silk tie. Nick laughed when he looked down and saw Lance was wearing his battered boat shoes and no socks.

Kimberly stood beside Lance. Her hands were clasped anxiously. She wore an emerald suit of nubby silk. Around her neck was a string of orange crystals. The necklace stood out sharply against her white silk blouse. Her blonde hair was turned under in a sleek pageboy, and she looked every inch the patrician.

"Hello, Susie," she said. Everyone in Nick's office loved Susie. Not because she was the boss's wife, but because she was a kind person with a generous heart.

"Kimberly, you look so pretty tonight," Susie said. "That suit is wonderful. Makes you look sixteen."

Kimberly blushed and her hands unconsciously moved to her necklace.

"Is that a new necklace?" Susie asked. She stepped closer to examine it. "Ummmmmmm," she said in appreciation. "What is it?"

Before Kimberly could answer, Lance leaned forward. His eyes danced and his smile increased. "Madeira citrine."

Susie looked at him, her eyes a question mark.

"I been reading about crystals," Lance said.

Kimberly almost blushed. Madeira citrines, or "mad cits," as Lance called them, were said to increase one's sexual energy. When Lance had given it to her, he said the necklace would be the ultimate test of whether or not crystals had any power.

"You gave this to Kimberly?" Susie asked in surprise.

Lance nodded. "Yeah. She did some great work on the Everglades City case. I just wanted to show her that not all us street cops are slugs." He shrugged. "Besides, it was cheap."

Nick grunted. "Sumbitch never gave me anything but a hard time."

Lance laughed. "Jefe, how does it feel to be among your people tonight?"

Nick looked at Lance with a wary eye. "Whatta you mean?"

Lance waved his arms expansively. "This is where all the 'roids hang out."

Susie and Kimberly looked at the two men in bewilderment.

Nick pulled at his mustache. He would deal with Lance later. He nodded toward the convention hall across the lobby and said, "Let's go see who's in charge of this goat roping."

"I am," said a loud voice. Nick turned to face Raymond Dumnik, who was lurching in his direction. Nick nodded. He did not smell Listerine tonight; only straight booze.

Dumnik nodded toward Susie, then looked at Lance and Kimberly. "Miss McBride and agent Cunningham, I believe."

Lance looked away. "No, it's Heidi and the Goat Boy," he mumbled.

Kimberly laughed.

"I'm the master of ceremonies tonight," Dumnik said. "The Sheriffs' Association people said since a DEA agent was the honoree, that I should run this thing."

"Good idea," Nick said noncommittally. He knew Dumnik had lobbied hard to be MC, and that he had had the DEA public-affairs officer call newspapers and television stations all across south Florida in an attempt to have them cover the banquet.

Dumnik laughed and leaned toward Susie. "Your husband is still a bit peeved at me."

Susie smiled and said nothing.

Dumnik patted Nick on the back. "We are all in the same business. We all work together. We are all brothers."

"Since when?" Lance interrupted.

Dumnik ignored Lance. He put his hand atop Nick's shoulder, nodded, and escorted Nick a few steps away. Dumnik leaned down, face close to Nick's, and said, "I gotta ask you something."

"What is it?" Nick mumbled. He pulled back. He had been wrong. Dumnik had been drinking Listerine. And at close range the blast of Listerine and Wild Turkey was overpowering.

Dumnik looked around. Then he whispered, "Tell me again. Why did you bury my agent?"

"Just like it says in the commendation," Nick answered. "Someone had to take the initiative. It was a very dangerous deal that was going down. We talked, agreed on what had to be done, and decided Ben was the best-trained and best-suited of all of us to perform that particular job."

Nick paused. Then he added, "Ben's a hero."

Dumnik pursed his lips, digested that bit of information, patted Nick on the shoulder, and nodded as if trying to convince himself Nick was right. Without another word, he turned and walked toward the bar.

Nick waited as Susie walked toward him. To Lance and Kimberly he said, "You two are sitting at the head table with us. If I have to make a speech, so do you." He paused. "Ben's sitting between us."

Lance laughed. "The hero of the hour. Good old Ben." Lance threw his hands wide. "Hey, jefe. I'm a mega speechmaker. I'm gonna give 'em words from hell."

"Don't you embarrass this office," Nick said.

Lance turned toward Kimberly, held an open palm toward Nick, and they walked side by side into the dining room.

An hour and a half later, the meal was over. Raymond Dumnik, his blinking beacon of a nose sending out signals that he was almost on the shoals, held on to the lectern and looked out over the annual meeting of the Florida Sheriffs' Association, a group whose membership included state attorneys' and investigators. The high point of tonight's annual banquet was recognizing the Florida Peace Officer of the Year. As is the usual case at top conventions, a great deal of liquor had been consumed. Even Nick had been in the booze. He was not quite in the bag; but he was on the way. He sat at the head table smiling beatifically over his glasses at cops from all over Florida. Some four hundred officers and their wives were present.

Dumnik belched into the microphone, straightened his shoulders, and said, "Turn on the lights."

"They're on," Lance said. He turned aside and added, "Dumbass."

"Dumnik," Kimberly said.

"What?"

"His name is Dumnik," Kimberly said. She giggled. And Lance realized that Kimberly, for the first time since he had known her, was high. Get her away from her computer and she turned into a real human.

Kimberly pointed at Dumnik and in the exaggerated solemnity of someone trying not to show how much alcohol she has consumed, said, "Sperm donor's boss."

Lance scratched his head and grinned.

"Okay, I'm told the lights have been switched on. So let us continue," Dumnik said.

Kimberly pulled on Lance's sleeve. He leaned toward her.

She pointed toward Dumnik. "If you believe this man is a professional law-enforcement officer, you would believe a pig can repair a watch."

Lance threw back his head and laughed. Kimberly might even have a devil brain. Nick sliced his eyes toward Lance in warning.

Dumnik turned toward Lance. Then he looked at the crowd and said, "This guy is laughing and I haven't told my joke yet. He must have seen my speech."

A courteous ripple of laughter sounded through the hall. Dumnik was well known and little liked by Florida's local cops. They were presenting their highest award to a DEA agent tonight only because Nick Brown had nominated him and then sent out the word that it was important the young agent be honored.

Dumnik told a few flat jokes and introduced several DEA supervisors scattered throughout the room. He made a rambling speech about the need for cooperation among local, state, and federal law-enforcement agencies, during which many in the audience took time to replenish their drinks; then he introduced Lance as the local agent who had been on the operation that led to a DEA agent's manifestation of bravery and his subsequent nomination for Florida's Officer of the Year.

Lance, eyes dancing and smile wide, stood before the lectern and, for a long moment, simply looked over the crowd. In his expression was a silent message understood by every local cop in the giant hall: Dumnik is a fed who doesn't know what went down the night of the raid and who doesn't know what's going down tonight. Ben Blumen is a good guy and we're rallying around him; around one of our own. This is to save his job. So we'll do this thing tonight. We'll do it without embarrassing Ben, and, at the same time, we'll give Dumnik a tube steak.

That message, combined with Lance's expression, a lot of liquor, and the frustration local cops feel after most dealings with DEA, caused a low chuckle to begin throughout the room. It grew louder. Dumnik looked around in bewilderment. The guy was just standing there at the mike not saying a word, and everyone in the room was laughing. The laughter grew. It became a roar that changed into loud and sustained applause.

Dumnik looked at Lance in bewilderment. He turned to Nick, who was sitting beside him. Only one thing came to his booze-befuddled mind. In a voice heard up and down the table, he asked the question he had asked a dozen times: "Tell me one more time. Why did you bury my agent in the sand?"

Lance spread his arms wide and turned up the voltage on his maniacal smile.

"Listen to Lance," Nick told Dumnik. The DEA supervisor took a long drink.

"I'm going to be brief," Lance said.

Loud applause. Ben Blumen, who was sitting next to Dumnik at the head table, smiled in relief.

"I'm proud to say that I was with DEA Special Agent Ben Blumen the night of the raid in Sandfly Pass; the night we seized more than a hundred tons of marijuana, a thousand keys of cocaine, and arrested almost a hundred suspects. Agent Blumen's courage that night is an example for all of us. He is the sort of man . . ." Lance paused and then looked at Kimberly and corrected himself. "He is the sort of person . . ."

Kimberly nodded in approval.

"He is the sort of person," Lance continued, "all of us want as a backup when we have to kick down a door."

He paused. "After obtaining a proper search warrant, of course."

Applause and laughter.

"One measure of the effectiveness of the raid that night in which Agent Blumen was such a standout is that the annual seafood festival in Everglades City was canceled this year. So many smugglers from over there are in jail, there aren't enough men in town to have the festival."

Applause. Cheers.

Lance shrugged. "I'll leave this thought with you. We in law enforcement know and experience . . ." He paused, then added with emphasis, ". . . and appreciate . . . much that is buried to the general public."

A roar of laughter.

Lance turned toward Ben. "Ben, I'm proud to have been with you that night."

Ben knew that the ceremony and the award had saved his career. DEA was in too much trouble with local cops to ignore the award as Peace Officer of the Year. But Ben Blumen was an honest man who knew he was too young and too green to be Peace Officer of the Year. He was grateful to Nick, but he was uncomfortable at receiving an award he knew was being presented solely so Dumnik would not fire him.

Lance looked out over the audience. "I want to introduce my boss, Nick Brown, who will make the award."

Applause. Whistles.

Nick moved behind the lectern, mumbled a few words of thanks toward Lance and Dumnik, and took his speech—typed on five-by-seven cards—from his pocket. He pulled the microphone down toward his mouth.

"Hey, Nick, stand up," came a voice from the audience.

Almost four hundred people roared with laughter.

Nick was uncomfortable speaking to so many people. He pulled at his mustache and glowered. "Who said that?"

Again laughter filled the hall. Nick had a friendly audience.

Nick kept his eyes locked on his notes. He began by saying, "Not long ago, Lance Cunningham, who sometimes runs my office . . ."

Laughter.

Nick continued. "Cunningham came to me and asked a question. He wanted to know, when the Everglades City case was completed, when it was all over, how many people would have been arrested. What would be the number of people we put in jail?"

Nick looked over the crowd. "I told him, 'Every male in town over the age of puberty.' "

Applause.

Then Nick told in a serious and straightforward fashion the official version of what had happened that night in Sandfly Pass. He ended by saying, "And the main reason we were able to do that is because of Agent Ben Blumen and all the other officers who took part in the raid."

Cheers.

Lance looked over the audience and smiled in satisfaction. The investigation had taken eighteen months and was the toughest case he had ever been involved in. But now it was over. As Nick liked to say, "We got the job done." Lance looked at Kimberly. Then, under the edge of the tablecloth, he reached for her hand. She smiled. After a moment she leaned closer and nudged him with her shoulder. He turned.

"Tell me again," she whispered earnestly. "Why did you bury my agent in the sand?"

Lance laughed. He looked out over the crowd and realized anew how much he loved being a cop.

ABOUT THE AUTHOR

ROBERT CORAM has written about drug smuggling for more than a decade. He was twice nominated for the Pulitzer Prize while a reporter for *The Atlanta Constitution*. His articles have appeared in many national magazines, including *The New Yorker*. For eight years, Coram was a part-time journalism instructor at Emory University. He lives in Atlanta.

27 million Americans can't read a bedtime story to a child.

It's because 27 million adults in this country simply can't read.

Functional illiteracy has reached one out of five Americans. It robs them of even the simplest of human pleasures, like reading a fairy tale to a child.

You can change all this by joining the fight against illiteracy.

Call the Coalition for Literacy at toll-free **1-800-228-8813** and volunteer.

Volunteer Against Illiteracy.
The only degree you need is a degree of caring.